CHASE ME IF YOU CAN

CHASE ME IF YOU CAN

Heather Frances

BERKLEY ROMANCE
NEW YORK

BERKLEY ROMANCE
Published by Berkley
An imprint of Penguin Random House LLC
1745 Broadway, New York, NY 10019
penguinrandomhouse.com

Book design by Ashley Tucker

Library of Congress Cataloging-in-Publication Data

Names: Frances, Heather author
Title: Chase me if you can / Heather Frances.
Description: First edition. | New York: Berkley Romance, 2026.
Identifiers: LCCN 2025039780 (print) | LCCN 2025039781 (ebook) |
ISBN 9780593956434 trade paperback | ISBN 9780593956441 ebook
Subjects: LCGFT: Romance fiction | Novels | Fiction
Classification: LCC PS3606.R36428 C47 2026 (print) | LCC PS3606.R36428 (ebook)
LC record available at https://lccn.loc.gov/2025039780
LC ebook record available at https://lccn.loc.gov/2025039781

First Edition: June 2026

Printed in the United States of America
1st Printing

The authorized representative in the EU for product safety and compliance is Penguin Random House Ireland, Morrison Chambers, 32 Nassau Street, Dublin D02 YH68, Ireland, https://eu-contact.penguin.ie.

for the ones with lightning in their
veins and storms in their hearts

AUTHOR'S NOTE

I was the kid who'd sit on the porch or plaster myself against the side of the house to watch the summer storms until thunder rattled my teeth—or someone made me go inside. It was usually the latter, if I'm honest. When I got the opportunity to learn to chase storms on the plains for the first time in 2019, I was instantly hooked.

Being able to write a romance set in the world of storm chasing has meant so much to me, and I'm so excited to share that with all of you! I want to note that this is a work of fiction, and though my own experiences at times provided inspiration, liberties have been taken and embellishments made in service of the story. Storm chasing can be relatively safe with the right knowledge and preparation, but incredibly dangerous without. If you ever decide you want to try it out, don't be like Wes. Learn from someone with the experience to keep you safe. Girls Who Chase, an organization founded with a mission of getting more women involved in storm chasing and meteorology, is a great place to start!

For a full list of content warnings, please visit heatherfrances.com.

CHASE ME IF YOU CAN

CHAPTER ONE

I CHASE LIGHTNING.

A fact, but also a phrase that used to be inscribed on church bells. A couple hundred years ago, someone got it in their head that ringing said bell could prevent lightning strikes. No one seemed to consider that a tall tower with a giant hunk of metal is a terrible place to be during a storm.

Then again, maybe an open field—my preference—isn't much better than a church steeple.

Today's church bells have nothing to do with the weather. I sneak a quick peek into the nave on my way back to the bridal suite and hope no one notices. White roses and pale pink peonies decorate the aisle, lush and fragrant, as their delicate scents mingle with the pillar candles set at the end of each pew. The aisle itself has been covered with a thick cream carpet shot through with gold thread that I can't wait to see in the ceremony photos. My excitement only grows when I glance up to find soft light streaming through the church's enormous stained glass windows. With a final sigh of relief that most of the guests are already settled—no last-minute wrangling of relatives required—I hurry back to finish the last of the pre-ceremony preparations.

Twenty minutes later, when the music swells into the bridal march and two hundred people get to their feet, a particular set of amused gray eyes grabs my attention over all the others. He winks while I'm still trying to digest the perfectly tailored suit in place of his usual baseball hat, T-shirt, and shorts, his dark hair carefully styled instead of windblown and dusty, tattoos tidily hidden by formalwear, and face cleanly shaven. My mind blanks, no longer ruminating on church bells or lightning or much of anything except the sight of him.

At least until he has the nerve to jerk his chin up the aisle and mouth *That way* with a pointed finger and an unfortunately familiar know-it-all grin.

"Sloane!" Amy, my assistant photographer for the ceremony, hisses into my earpiece. "You're going to miss the bride!"

I jerk out of my stupor and quickly lift my camera until a froth of white fills the viewfinder, the bride's smile radiant with her arm looped through her father's. Shoving aside my own personal drama that I will *not* let unfold in front of my client, I focus on capturing the bride's joy.

This is my favorite part of photographing weddings. It's why I keep doing it, despite the bridezillas and the neurotic family members and all the other insanity that comes with a couple's big day. The reception and the staged photos are always a little awkward, sure, but the bride walking down the aisle, the groom's expression when he sees her? This is the stuff of fairy tales.

At least it would be if perpetual pain in my ass Wes Talbot—Wild Wes to those who have the misfortune of knowing him—wasn't smirking at me from his pew. His height ensures he doesn't disappear into the crowd. Lucky me.

I'd love to demand an explanation for what he's doing here, disturbing my peace a full week ahead of our annual battle of wills, but it's a wedding and he's in a suit. Judging by the side of the aisle he's on, he's a friend of the groom. We're in Houston. I vaguely remember that Wes lives here, when he's not tormenting me in gas station parking lots or providing less-than-helpful tips on a dusty road in the middle of nowhere every spring.

Despite being only a couple years older than me at thirty-three, he's something of a legend among storm chasers. One of the first out at the start of the season in April, he usually stays on the road through summer monsoon season in the Southwest, transitioning seamlessly from tornadoes and supercells to lightning and dust storms. Unlike the rest of us who have to squeak our chase season in around jobs that pay the bills.

Wes is impossible to avoid during storm season—even without him being close to my best friend's fiancé, we share too many of the same friends to not end up on the same roads all too often. Not that I would exactly call us *friends.* There's no denying all six foot four of him is nice to look at, and he's always flirty bordering on friendly. But Wes has a reckless streak a mile wide that's racked up more close calls than I want to think about. When everyone else backs off, he's the first to charge directly into the bear's cage if he thinks it will get him a shot.

At least he has the decency to leave me be while I'm shooting the wedding ceremony and portraits, but when everyone sits down to eat, he can't help himself.

"You know, if you swapped that hot garbage lens out like I've been telling you to for years, you wouldn't have to worry about cropping out fuzzy corners," he says as he leans over my shoulder to peer at the image I'm hastily editing.

"Only you would call something that cost a couple grand *hot garbage*," I say without looking up, one hand on my mouse and one attempting to fill a fork with pasta. The only thing wrong with the lens is that Wes prefers a competitor—and never shuts up about it. Especially after shooting a campaign for the brand last year.

"A couple grand can still be a was—"

"Nope." I don't bother to turn around. "We're not doing this. I'm working. Your reign of terror doesn't start for another week. Shoo."

Of course that doesn't get rid of him. Unfazed by my dismissal, Wes slides into the chair across from me. He's already ditched his jacket, pale-blue dress shirt sleeves rolled to his elbows and exposing ink on his muscled forearms I've never gotten a close look at. His hair has reverted to its more natural state of artful chaos, though for all I know that's courtesy of a quickie with the bridesmaid who's been eye-fucking him all evening.

She's welcome to him. Wes might be beautiful, but he's beautiful the way tornadoes are beautiful—something to be admired from afar or risk getting caught in the storm. I have no interest in becoming collateral damage.

"You're far from home," he drawls, his slight Texas accent

creeping in. Probably thanks to the glass of amber liquid dangling from his fingertips.

I look up momentarily from my screen to squint at him in the semidarkness of my tucked-away corner. Every time I take in his appearance tonight, there's a jarring moment where it doesn't fit. Like running into an old elementary school teacher at the grocery store, Wes doesn't belong in this part of my life.

Storm season is a bit like adult summer camp. Week after week seeing the same faces over and over again, that time on the road exists in a liminal space outside of our real lives. The version of Wes I know best is the one pushing my buttons on the side of the road with raindrops splattering his tanned skin, not this walking and talking spread from a men's luxury magazine.

I've stayed quiet too long. His eyes catch mine and hold, expression too intense for my liking. "I'm a wedding photographer. This is a wedding. Cora was the maid of honor for a wedding I shot in Estes Park a few years ago," I say, getting us back on familiar footing.

The fact that the bride is a friend of a prior client is the only reason I agreed to squeeze this in. I'm going to be editing around the clock for the next week to finish all my client work waiting at home before I put up my proverbial *gone fishing* sign—fishing for tornadoes.

"Oh, Aidan's wedding." Wes takes a sip of his drink and relaxes more into his chair. "I was chasing in Argentina."

"Of course you were," I mutter under my breath. Argentina can produce incredible storms, but chasing there is an expensive and logistical nightmare. Of course, money solves a lot of problems, and Wes comes from an old Texas oil family.

It's why he's here in the first place as a guest at a six-figure wedding while I'm the hired help. If I ever get married, it definitely won't be at a place like this. My budget is more backyard and barefoot than champagne and caviar.

"Chasing definitely has more comfortable clothes." Tugging at the collar of his shirt, his hand slides down to unknot his tie, silk sliding against silk. "At least for me. You ever deviate from that all-black wardrobe? I don't think I've ever even seen you in a dress."

I'm wearing the same thing I always wear to photograph weddings: black dress pants with enough stretch to maneuver and a long-sleeved black T-shirt. The look is completed with a pair of black sneakers and my dark hair in a once-tidy French braid falling halfway down my back. It's not the most flattering outfit—I may be just shy of six feet tall, but my hourglass shape makes it a challenge to find pants without an elastic waist that fit well. With my concealer wearing off and dark circles on display, it's not like I'm winning any fashion awards, anyway.

Exasperated, I don't bother to look up. "Yeah, okay, let me just go throw on a dress so when I bend over to get a close-up, I can give grandma a close-up of my ass at the same time."

Wes's laughter turns choked. He sets his glass down with a *thunk* and coughs a few more times. When I glance up, his face has gone red. With one finger pointing accusingly at his unfinished drink, he rasps, "That really burns going down the wrong way."

"Sounds like a you problem." I wave my hand vaguely toward the rest of the guests. "Go terrorize a bridesmaid." I narrow my eyes and smile sweetly. "Those stilettos look . . . pointy."

Wes doesn't move. He stares long enough that I have to fight the urge to fidget before he asks, "You hear about the *Nature Shots* contest?"

"Yep." I curse under my breath when my hand slips, slashing a line across the bride's face. Nothing a little *undo* won't fix, but I need to get rid of Wes if I'm going to have the preview gallery ready tonight. I have no idea why he's decided to chat me up, but then again, this is the same man who regularly attends the Sweetwater rattlesnake roundup each spring. I stopped trying to figure out why he does half the crazy stuff he does years ago.

"Are you entering? They must have invited you."

Leaving the bride momentarily disfigured, I level a glare across the table. There's no *must have* about it. In the twenty years that *Nature Shots* has been in publication, not once has a female photographer been featured on the cover.

"Yes, I'm going to enter." I don't bother asking if he was invited. Of course he was. He may not have graced the cover, but his work has appeared in the pages of the magazine a half dozen times. Despite knowing he's likely to win, I'll be damned if I don't do everything I can to beat him.

"That mean you're not bailing early this year? I told you if you left last year, you'd regret it. That High Plains magic gets better every season."

Shoving a sharp breath out of my nose, I try not to otherwise react. The worst part is that he isn't wrong—I *did* regret leaving, but I also didn't have a choice. It's bad enough that as a wedding photographer I close my books for the month of May. In June, when the storms tend to shift north into the High Plains, with their lush rolling hills, I have weddings booked every Friday, Saturday, and Sunday night. There are even a few Thursday ceremonies, not to mention several dozen engagement shoots crammed in around everything else. I work practically nonstop, and the cover contest isn't going to change the fact that weddings pay my bills.

"Just because you need three months doesn't mean I can't make it work in six weeks," I tell Wes with a syrupy smile.

The muscles in his throat flex as he swallows more alcohol, but to my surprise, he ignores the barb. "You think it's going to be an active season? Last year was kind of quiet." He flashes me a goading grin. "Except that June system."

There it is.

Momentarily forgetting that my clients paying me many thousands of dollars may walk up at any second, I finally give Wes what he wants: my full attention in the form of a murderous glare.

"I'm trying to work," I manage through gritted teeth. "I know it's very hard for you to comprehend that there are things in life that don't revolve around you, but someone else's wedding day is *their* day. I'm here to capture *their* memories to the very best of my ability. You might think weddings are beneath you, but I'm good at what I do."

Wes's usual smile full of practiced charm slips a notch. "I never said that."

"Right. I totally made up your *I'd get so bored shooting nothing but flowers and cakes and people pretending they like each other in fancy clothes all year* comment? Or maybe it was the time you told me that the nice thing about tornadoes is they don't argue about discounts?"

"Well, they don't," Wes says with a chuckle, polishing off

the rest of his drink. He shrugs, the movement pulling his shirt snug against his broad chest. "I guess I'll see you on the road next week. Try to remember weddings are supposed to be fun, yeah?"

"For guests. Weddings are fun for *guests.*" I give him a long look over the top of my laptop. "You're the one who's supposed to be having fun, not hanging out with the help."

Wes shakes his head as he pours himself onto his feet in a motion that shouldn't be so smooth for a man of his size. "Sloane, you are a great many things, but you are *not* the help. I'll see you next week."

The fact that I can't tell if he's being sincere or screwing with me like usual is absolutely the reason I watch him walk away. It definitely has nothing to do with the snug fit of his tailored pants or the weirdly warm sensation in my chest—one that quickly cools when he looks back over his shoulder, catches me watching, and throws back a smug wink.

ϟ

WHILE I CAN'T think of a way to make **I will be traveling on personal business April 16th through May 30th. Email responses may take several weeks during this time. I am fully booked through the end of the year** any clearer, I'm sure someone is still going to miss the bright pink, bold lettering splashed across the top of my website. That's future Sloane's problem.

With the website updated, the last thing that stands between me and six weeks of storm chasing is to finish the edits from the Houston wedding and send the final photos off to the newlyweds.

Yawning and reaching for my long-cold coffee, I rub my tired eyes and bring up the next image, only to blink at the screen. Wes is in the background of a photo of the couple dancing, his head thrown back in laughter as he twirls the mother of the bride. I stare at it for longer than I should.

And yeah, okay, maybe I'm a little jealous. I can't remember the last time I laughed like that. The last time there wasn't so much going on in my life that I could just be in the moment. Not worried about my family. Not worried about maintaining my business. Not worried that it's selfish of me—or career suicide—to take these six weeks every year to do the thing I love most.

But Wes isn't my client, and he's not the one I need to focus on.

I'm forced to take a break when the reminder goes off to dial into the *Nature Shots* pre-contest call. The last thing I feel like doing right now is sitting on a video call, but I could probably use the break before I overwork myself into a migraine. It's also mandatory that everyone invited to participate attend.

Wes included.

I quickly braid my hair, swipe some mascara over my lashes, and turn on my ring light before joining the call. Fifty photographers have been invited to take part in the contest, and as I skim over the names, it's impossible to miss there are only five women.

One of them is my closest friend. I grab my phone and shoot off a quick text to Tracy when I don't see her signed into the call. Not ten seconds later she pops up on the screen and winks at the camera, her wide grin definitely directed at me.

I had another minute! Can't wait to see you next week!!

Her text is followed by at least five tornado emojis.

The new *Nature Shots* editor in chief, Carter Walsh, kicks off the call right at five. I'm not the least bit surprised when Wes pops up on camera a few minutes later. Of course he's late. And of course he's in his car, obviously distracted. I don't know why he even has the camera on.

If Carter notices, it doesn't show. He continues with his introduction, full of sound bites that had to have been written by the magazine's marketing department. The contest is a first for them, and they're excited to partner with such talented photographers, as are the other sponsors, blah, blah, blah.

I tune out, texting with Tracy while we wait for them to get to the good part.

Weddings pay the bills, but there are only so many ways to shoot a bride walking down the aisle. Only so many ways to photograph dresses and cakes and flowers when a client's preferences come before artistic expression, especially when there's one particular Pinterest shot list I now recognize by the font alone. After almost a decade, there's still a lot about it I love, but it's hard to feel the same creative satisfaction I had at the start.

And as a bonus, being on the cover of a magazine with international reach might be the thing that finally shuts my mother up. According to her, I've wasted enough time chasing storms when I should be chasing a husband. Despite my many assurances that it's no longer the fifties—which even *she* wasn't alive for—it's her favorite refrain.

"Right, now on to the rules," Carter continues, drawing

my attention back to the call. "First and foremost, be safe out there. We don't want to lose anyone over a photo."

He pauses to let his words sink in. Storm chasing *is* dangerous, and though we all know it, it's easy to shove to the back of your mind when your adrenaline is up. Experienced chasers can get caught off guard too—and some have, with deadly consequences.

My attention drifts toward the little square on my screen full of Wes's face. He still isn't paying attention, his brow furrowed and his mouth moving like he's talking to someone offscreen. He's back in his normal clothes, dusty Texas Longhorns baseball hat jammed low on his brow, a snug black T-shirt showing off the definition in his arms and chest, and familiar dark stubble once again coating his jaw.

"Only images shot this season are eligible. Final entries are due by July 1. Unlike some of our previous contests, this is *one* entry per photographer. Any additional entries will be disqualified, so don't try to sneak anything by us. Let's respect everyone's time with the number of you participating." Carter levels a stern look at the camera. "Finally, *Nature Shots* prides itself on featuring true-to-life images without heavy edits, and it's our expectation that the winners of this contest share our position on this. Absolutely no AI will be tolerated."

I nod along as Carter covers the technical details of the contest requirements. I've been a fan of the magazine since high school, when I first picked up a camera and thought maybe it could be a fun way to escape my house. The requirement to submit the digital negatives to prove they haven't been heavily doctored is part of why I want to win this contest so badly—in the age of Photoshop, photography skills can be easily inflated.

It's much harder to snap the shot in camera without needing big adjustments in post. Winning would be irrefutable proof of my skill.

"All photos will be scored without the photographer's name attached. For the winners, the terms of the contest allow us a first look at any photos you choose to license for a two-year period. You remain free to turn us down if we offer to run any of your photos, though we hope you'll agree."

Usually a downside to these things is that your rights to the images aren't entirely your own. It's why I've largely stayed away—I don't want one of my shots to end up selling some product I've never heard of. But *Nature Shots* is different. The sort of people I'd like to work with in the future, the brands that I'd actually want to partner with, put a lot of stock in photographers with *Nature Shots* credits.

It's part of what makes this contest such a rare opportunity. There's a big enough market for wedding photographers that plenty of us can exist even in the same city without worrying too much about taking business from one another.

Landscapes are altogether different. Making a living off this type of work requires almost constant publication and licensing of images, and there are a lot more photographers interested in the field than there are paying jobs.

There are also a hell of a lot more men than women, which has led to rampant misogyny that often goes unchecked. Though no one has ever admitted as much, I've long suspected the last *Nature Shots* editor outright refused to feature female photographers. Not surprising from the guy who publicly called the #MeToo movement *overblown female hysteria* on a podcast.

Carter took over last year, so maybe things will be

different—and the blind judging means that any bias over gender shouldn't be a factor.

"Keep in mind that we're also looking for an image that tells a story. We want to feel something when we view your work."

My mind whirls. Part of the magic of photographing storms is the duality of it. The power of nature to both heal and destroy. I'm not certain yet how to tell that particular story in a single frame, but my first instinct is to find foregrounds where I can create a juxtaposition between the delicate and the destructive.

After a review of "the lawyer stuff" the call wraps up. One final glance at Wes leaves me certain he hasn't heard a word, his attention still on someone or something out of the frame and a hard set to his jaw.

I can't focus on Wes. The contest is too important and I have too much left to do.

CHAPTER TWO

IT DOESN'T TAKE LONG TO FINISH UP THE LAST COUple of photos and send the final images off to my remaining couples. My bags are mostly packed, with just about everything stacked next to the door for the morning. All that's left is one last thing I'd really rather just . . . not.

Reluctantly, I open the text thread with my two younger brothers and take a deep breath.

> Reminder that I leave tomorrow. Mom is your responsibility for the next six weeks. That means check on her. Repeatedly. The lawn NEEDS to get mowed so the HOA doesn't fine her again. No repeats of her losing her shit on Mrs. Campbell in the driveway like last year.

Sam sends back the saluting emoji within thirty seconds. Eric types for so long I'm expecting a novel, but in the end, he just says, You give us this lecture every year. Mom is almost fifty. House hasn't burned down yet.

Of course it hasn't. I've spent my whole life running around with fire extinguishers—the metaphorical *and* literal kind.

I scowl at the screen. Eric is the older of my brothers at twenty-five, with a very selective ability to adult. When it comes to his business—an auto body shop he's worked hard to turn into reliable income—he's nothing but responsible. On the other hand, there's not much difference between him and Sam, who's two years younger and finishing law school, when it comes to managing our mother.

And she definitely needs managing.

Mom had us young. I never knew my dad, who took off when I was still a baby, and though my brothers sometimes see their father, he wasn't much interested in having a stepdaughter for the short time he stuck around.

Eric and Sam only know the *after* version of our mom. The one with a bad case of learned helplessness and a firm belief that a man is the solution to all of life's problems, even if that man is ten red flags in a trench coat. *Especially* if he's ten red flags in a trench coat.

And my brothers only know the version of me who became responsible for picking up the pieces far too young—and never figured out how to stop twenty-something years later. Consequently, our relationship teeters between periods of closeness and times where I wonder if we're just trauma bonded from the same never-ending chaos surrounding our mother.

Not wanting to go to bed with lingering resentment toward my man-child brothers so fresh, I open my chaser group text thread to check in. I've been chasing long enough that there are dozens of names and numbers in my contacts I can always reach out to for intel or advice, but I spend the majority of my time with a smaller core group. Years ago, it was just me and Tracy. Once she started dating Matt, unfortunately for me, his best friend, Wes, got added to our merry band of misfits. Now that Tracy and Matt are engaged, there's no escaping Wes for the foreseeable future.

I must have pissed in the universe's Cheerios this morning, because Wes is the first thing I see when I open our text thread. Matt's Enjoy that paint job while it lasts is followed by a barrage of baseball, tennis ball, and tornado emojis, along with a series of screenshots taken off Wes's social media. In his usual snug T-shirt and a pair of dark jeans, he's leaned back with his elbows on the hood of a brand-new SUV, gazing off into the distance like he's posing for a fashion shoot. The fact that the custom CHASE vanity plate is visible confirms that the shiny new ride definitely belongs to him.

It's the sort of thing he's known for. One part adventure photographer, one part thirst trap. As talented as Wes is behind the camera, he doesn't have a million-plus followers who are just really into landscapes. Every time I glance at his page, there are plenty of women—and men—in his comments with everything from cheesy pickup lines—*I'll be a tornado if you'll chase me* might be the most eye-rolling yet—to explicit invitations.

Wes's reply in the group text is twenty minutes old. You can admit you're jealous. This is a safe space. He added a few more shots of himself in the same general pose, except this time he's drenched, and he's found a cowboy hat who knows where. His clothes cling like a second skin, jeans painted to his thighs and thumbs hooked into his belt while he smolders directly into the camera.

He *should* be staring at the storm looming like the end of

the world behind him—but that's Wes. Too busy feeding his ego to pay attention to anything else.

Annoyed, I swipe out of the group text and tap on Tracy's name instead. I see Wes is on his usual bullshit already.

Her reply comes back a few minutes later as I'm brushing my teeth. I was just about to text you! Matt and I had lunch with him today. He said he saw you last week. Are you out here early and didn't tell me?!

I'm surprised that he mentioned it, but then again, he's close with Matt, so maybe it's not that strange. Shaking my head, I quickly explain about the wedding. Thankfully the conversation turns to the forecast and our hopes that the models for the next couple of days showing higher dew points—the moisture-rich air needed to fuel storms—prove accurate.

With promises to bring Tracy some snacks from "civilization" when I see her tomorrow, I set my phone down, determined to focus on myself for the next six weeks. Not my mother, not my brothers, and definitely not Wes Talbot.

I can't help that I'll run into him at gas stations, hotels, coffee shops, and restaurants countless times over the next six weeks—likely as an involuntary witness to the *finding out* part of his fucking around. We'll do our usual snarky jokes-that-aren't-always-entirely-funny thing, probably piss each other off a few times, share a beer at an Applebee's at one in the morning in the middle of nowhere when I'm too exhausted to remember he's bad news, and do it all again next year.

Wes will be insufferable if he wins the contest, but if *I* win, I can't deny that rubbing it in his face is absolutely on the agenda. Maybe I'll have my cover printed on a coffee mug. Or postcards that I can leave under his windshield in hotel parking lots for the next couple of years. Not to mention that the next time he starts lecturing me about switching out my gear to his oh-so-superior pick, I can remind him that *my* choice landed me on the cover of *Nature Shots*.

The thought puts a smile on my face as I sink into a deep sleep.

ϟ

THANKFUL TO BE hitting the road and inaccessible to my mother—not being able to find her favorite handbag is not the emergency she thinks it is—I point myself east early the next morning.

In my rearview, pink paints the still snowcapped Front Range, while ahead of me, oranges and reds burn across the eastern sky. Buoyed by the high of witnessing some sky magic, I stop long enough to grab a cup of coffee and top off my gas tank. I've got about eight hours to get into West Texas ahead of today's storms. Which means it's me, my favorite road trip playlist—a chaotic combination of genres featuring my favorite songs to sing along to with an audience of none—and a couple hundred miles of highway for the rest of the morning.

Once I'm clear of Colorado Springs, I savor the open fields and fresh air—at least until I drive past one of the massive cattle operations hours later. I can't recommend taking a deep breath of *that* particular odor.

Trading voice notes with Tracy, we eventually agree to

meet in a small town just over the New Mexico border. There's a gas station right off the highway where we can relax before things fire up in the next hour or two.

It's plainly one of those places that stays in business due to truckers coming through on cross-country routes. Today, there are easily thirty-something storm chasers milling about. I instantly spot several familiar faces standing around in a loose circle, though Tracy's last message puts her and Matt another ten minutes out. For now, it appears I'm the only woman. Not unusual, but depending on who else is lurking, could be unpleasant.

After a quick fill up, I head inside. The cashiers have a shell-shocked looked about them, not exactly surprising when this place probably sees twenty customers a day, not fifty in an hour. Half the shelves are empty, and at least one of the trash cans is overflowing.

Welcome to storm season.

There are a couple of other unfamiliar chasers roaming the store, easily identifiable by the embroidered tour company tornado logo on their hats. I'd recognize them as chasers even without the hats. These two stick out like a sore thumb in their expensive tech fabrics and high-end watches in this part of the country.

I flash a tight smile, not in the mood to socialize with strangers, and gesture to the drink case they're blocking. "Mind if I get by you?"

"Sure, darling." The two men shuffle to the side but don't move entirely, leaving only a narrow gap to reach into the cooler. I bite my cheek so I don't react to the *darling.* Wes calls me that sometimes, but when he does it, he's always wearing a shit-eating grin. It's obnoxious, but childishly trying to push my buttons isn't what this guy is up to. His leering isn't a joke, his tone patronizing. "You out here with your boyfriend, sweetheart?" the other one adds while dragging his stare over my legs.

My temper flares. It doesn't matter that I switched out my colorful leggings years ago for plain black, or that I'm not the only one wearing flip-flops for the long drives and swapping into sturdier shoes before the chase gets serious. The baseline assumption that I'm only here because I'm some guy's arm candy persists.

"No. Excuse me," I say stiffly, holding my water bottles in a death grip so I don't throw them. I instantly regret admitting I'm alone and can't wait to get outside to friendlier faces.

They don't move. One elbows the other and says loudly, "Hear that? Fresh meat!"

Considering I've been chasing for a decade and don't recognize their faces, I'm tempted to ask if it's *their* first season. I swallow it. No matter how much I'd like to tell them to go fuck themselves, pissing off a bunch of strange men isn't smart.

Except when I turn away, I nearly crash into Wes. He reaches out to steady me, his touch light on my biceps. "You good?" His eyes race over me from beneath the brim of his well-worn baseball cap, mouth tightening into a frown.

"Wes Talbot!" Asshole One beams at Asshole Two, their entire demeanor changing. Now it's all friendly smiles. "Hey, man, we're huge fans. We were just joking with your girl."

I stiffen at the implication that I'm Wes's anything and duck around him. "Good luck with that," I mutter, beelining for the register on the other side of the building. It's hardly the first time, but I'm in no mood to watch the same jerks who treated me like nothing more than an accessory worship at Wes's altar.

I step back out into the hot afternoon sun after paying and take a deep breath, determined to recapture my excitement. It could be a big day, and there's nothing like catching a tornado at the start of the season to set the tone. Or in this case, correct the tone from those idiots inside.

"Hey, Sloane, wait a sec," Wes calls, jogging up behind me as I start across the parking lot. He flashes an obnoxious grin that he probably thinks is charming. "You look way more murderous than usual. Those guys say something to you?"

"I don't need a knight in not-so-shiny armor."

He scowls. "That's not—"

"Don't worry about it." I step around him without another word. The last thing I need is Wes using the excuse of playing hero to start shit.

He doesn't follow me. He just stands there, arms folded across his chest, river tattoo snaking around his forearm and bicep before disappearing beneath his T-shirt. I shove away the thought that I prefer him like this over the buttoned-up suit at the wedding.

Having any kind of preference when it comes to Wes is like preferring the wind to blow in a certain direction—pointless. Forces of nature will always follow their own whims.

Leaving Wes behind, I check my phone for an update from Tracy, but nothing yet, so I head for a group of chasers I'm friendly with. Not exactly friends, per se. More like a group of guys that can be trusted not to be outright sexist when we're all waiting around at random gas stations for storms to kick off. The overall chaser community out here isn't *that* big, so it's not unusual to end up chatting in parking lots with other photographers or researchers or thrill-seekers, even if they're not my preferred chase partners.

We fall into easy small talk, the sort of generic catching up I imagine is common among coworkers who see each other a handful of times a year. Jamie got married, Chris's wife had a baby, Tony moved to the opposite coast. The conversation quickly drifts back to chasing, phones whipped out to show off shots from earlier in the season. Even though I'm not particularly close to this group, it's good to belong to something. To effortlessly slide into a conversation and be accepted as one of them, unlike the chasers inside the gas station that see me as nothing but some guy's tagalong.

This sense of community is in short supply when I'm home acting as involuntary cruise director for my family. Yet as much as I want to wrap myself up in the feeling of belonging, it makes it a hell of a lot harder to ignore the loneliness that stalks my shadow the rest of the year.

Loud honking yanks me out of my thoughts. I glance up to the familiar sight of Matt's hail-dimpled SUV pulling into the parking lot, Tracy's bright smile visible through the dusty windshield. As soon as she slams her door shut, she makes a beeline for me and lets out a loud whoop before yanking me into a sweaty hug, nearly plowing us into Matt in the process. "Sloane! I've missed you!"

Tracy came crashing into my life as a fun-loving blonde with a dirty sense of humor that could give a sailor a run for their money at the start of my chasing days. I couldn't be happier for her that she found Matt, but I selfishly miss our long, rambling conversations in the car when we were chase partners more than I'll ever admit.

Every year after the season ends there's a slow fade from daily texts to weekly notes that eventually trickle off into the occasional trading of memes. Even Wes usually loses interest in cracking jokes at my expense in the group chat before the first aspens turn yellow in the fall.

Everyone gets busy, but the annual reminder that I'm no one's priority still stings.

It's not that I'm entirely alone in Colorado Springs. There are occasional drinks with the makeup artists and bakery owners and florists I've met along the way, but those are more impromptu vent sessions than meaningful friendships. They all think I'm nuts for running toward the kind of storms most people can't get away from fast enough. And as for my family, even when we manage to have a good time together, there's always another disaster looming over the horizon.

I wriggle out of Tracy's embrace with a laugh. "You're just saying that because you know I've got a bag from Whole Foods with your name on it."

Her lips curve into a sly smile as she playfully elbows me. "Chocolate-covered cherries aren't the *only* reason I'm happy to see you. You ready to show these boys how it's done? I can lose to you, but one of us *has* to win."

Darting a glance across the parking lot, I watch Matt laugh while he playfully shoves Wes's shoulder. Wes gestures toward the convenience store, then points to the back of the building. By the way Matt shakes his head, Wes is suggesting something so absurd even his chief enabler wants nothing to do with it.

Maybe it's Tracy's influence—or maybe Matt has just matured in a way that Wes never will.

We're too far away to hear whatever Matt says, still shaking his head, but then Wes points to the ground. The look on his face is full of challenge, but even if it wasn't, I've known him long enough to recognize what his widened stance means. Some sort of dick-measuring contest is about to begin, and while Matt might be the more mature one, Wes knows how to goad him.

Determined not to get involved in their drama, I turn to Tracy with a teasing smile. "Matt know you're plotting against him? He was invited too, right?" From the corner of my eye, I catch Wes whipping off his shirt and throwing it in Matt's face.

"Of course." She gives me a wide-eyed look of faux innocence and stage-whispers, "He loves it when I'm in charge."

"Too much information." I wrinkle my nose, but deep down, I can't quite ignore the flash of jealousy. Not over Matt—he's never appealed as anything more than a friend—but Tracy's confident happiness in her relationship, not to mention her fiancé's unwavering support, isn't something I've ever experienced.

The thought is forgotten when Matt and Wes both drop to the dusty asphalt and start counting off push-ups. I can't help rolling my eyes at them despite having seen this before—Matt admitted last year it's how they solve disagreements.

Men really will do anything but go to therapy.

"You better bathe Matt in hand sanitizer before you let

him back in the car," I mutter, eyeing the various stains, cigarette butts, and hardened wads of gum littering the pavement.

"Mmmhmm" is the only reply I get with Tracy's attention glued to the two men. Matt's shirt is sitting in a heap next to Wes's, back and arm muscles flexing in a steady rhythm under his olive skin. She licks her bottom lip and mutters under her breath, "Worth it."

When I glance back at the two men, Wes catches my eye and has the nerve to wink. "Twenty-seven," he shouts, staring directly at me. "Twenty-eight, twenty-nine . . . You want to count for me, Sloane? I can do this all day!"

"You sure you didn't just forget what comes after twenty-nine?" I call back, folding my arms over my chest like I'm above their childish game. No one has to know that I'm not exactly immune to the sight of Wes's bare skin, draped in tattoos and gleaming in the sunlight. It's a shame his personality isn't anywhere near as attractive.

"Thirty-two!" How Wes has the lung capacity to laugh is beyond me. "Thirty-three!"

"Fifty-five, forty-three, sixty-four . . ." I count loudly over him. Tracy giggles next to me when Matt shoots us a murderous glare. His face is red now, darker than the flush beginning to creep into Wes's cheeks, and sweat drips off his forehead.

"This," Tracy begins with a sigh, pretending to fan herself, "this is what they *should* mean when they say 'boys will be boys.' I don't even care what they're arguing about. In fact, if Matt wants to solve all our fights by taking his clothes off . . ."

I laugh, nodding toward her left hand where her engagement ring should be. "Should I take the missing ring as a sign wedding planning is going well?"

"One of the stones was a little loose so it's being fixed." She sighs and brushes her thumb over the faint tan line left behind. "Planning is . . . You're probably the last person I need to tell this, but I swear, weddings aren't even for the couple anymore. My parents, his parents, everyone thinks they deserve a piece of the day."

I nod sympathetically. I've seen the fights up close. It's one of the many reasons I'll be passing on a big wedding if it's ever my turn to go down the aisle.

Across the parking lot, Matt finally admits defeat. Wes gets to his feet with ease, bends to grab his discarded T-shirt, and uses it to mop sweat off his chest. "See something you like, Sloane?"

"Not even a little." Pointedly turning my attention back to Tracy and ignoring him, I ask if she's figured out her plan for the contest yet.

Instead of answering, she gives me a long, indecipherable look, a slight slant to her brows.

"What? Do I have something on my face?" I scrub my fingers over my mouth, hoping the chocolate I ate on the drive hasn't left evidence I've been walking around oblivious to.

Tracy shakes her head, glances at her fiancé once more, and then finally answers my question when the guys disappear around the side of the building. "I think I'm going for structure. Turquoise skies are always my favorite. Maybe a tornado and rainbow combo, if Mother Nature decides to cooperate, but you know how hard those shots are."

"What's so hard about having less than a second to line up a shot, make sure it's in focus, and hope like hell there isn't a raindrop on the lens?" I joke. "Cakewalk."

Tracy huffs out a laugh. "What've you got in mind?"

I shrug. "I haven't decided, exactly. More vibes than anything right now."

"Sloane Michaels doesn't have a plan? Is the sky falling?" Wes makes space for himself between us, thankfully with his shirt back on. He props his elbow on my shoulder, the scent of sweat and dust and hot asphalt pouring off him.

I shove him away with a muttered "Gross" not quite under my breath. He doesn't care, his expression lit up with mischief right before he exchanges a smug look with Matt. That's never a good sign. Especially when I glance behind them and notice the two assholes from earlier heading around the side of the building.

"Very funny. Sure you don't want to catch a ride with your new besties?"

Wes shakes his head, his expression settling into uncharacteristic seriousness when his eyes catch mine. "You couldn't pay me to get in a car with those guys."

"Then what were you . . ."

I trail off when a massive SUV emerges from the side of the building. On the back of the extremely dusty bumper, someone—my money is on tall, dark, and smug standing next to me wearing a frat boy grin—has scrawled *Honk for dick.*

Tracy and I explode into laughter while Matt lets out a quiet chuckle at what I can only presume is his part in Wes's handiwork.

"What was that look about?" Tracy asks in a voice too low to be overheard before nudging her shoulder into mine. "You have something to do with why Wes went after them?"

I'm not about to pretend he did this for me. He saw an

opening to start shit and took it. That's nothing new. "Of course not. He's a five-year-old in a grown man's body."

Tracy makes a noncommittal noise, but before I can question it, someone shouts that it's time to go. Phones whip out, radar apps are checked, and maps are consulted while we all hustle toward our cars. I quickly hand Tracy her snacks before she rushes away with a shouted, "Text me!"

Wes is parked next to me. Of course he is.

I make a point of walking a full circle around my car like it's a rental I'm inspecting for preexisting damage. "You write anything on my car and I'm slashing those," I threaten, pointing at his brand-new beefy tires with my entirely harmless keys.

"You wouldn't dare."

He's right—it's an empty threat, but empty threats are a key part of our interactions. "Fine. I'll go to every gas station and buy out the entire supply of those Nerds Gummy Clusters you're addicted to. Just the blue ones."

"You wouldn't." Aghast with exaggerated horror, he folds both hands over his heart. "Everyone knows the red ones are subpar."

"Try me." It comes out far more serious than I intend.

Wes steps closer, his chest nearly touching mine. I don't back down. Not even when he's so close I can see the flecks of color in his storm-cloud eyes as he leans in. There's a level of seriousness that can only be mockery in his voice when he says, "One of these days, I'm going to figure out who turned you into the fun police. We need to have a very long talk."

"Good luck having *that* conversation with my mother," I fire back. The second some emotion I don't want to examine too closely flickers across his expression, I know I've made a mistake. I quickly change the subject. "Let's just get out and chase, all right? We both have the contest to focus on. I don't have time to play games with you this year."

"You know what I think?" Wes closes the little remaining distance between us, leaning down so we're eye to eye. His glint with challenge. "I think you look forward to playing games with me. Admit it. I made your night better last week at that wedding in Houston."

"It's a miracle you fit that ego of yours in your shiny new car."

"Sounds an awful lot like a yes."

I roll my eyes and absolutely don't think about the fact that he's so close I can smell his soap. "Stay out of my way, Wes. I mean it. There are too many new people out here for you to be fucking around."

"But fucking around is what I do best." He hooks his thumbs into his belt loops and rocks back. "You should try it sometime. Might help you relax."

Typical Wes. When outright mockery doesn't work, he switches tactics and tries to get under my skin another way. And yet, for some stupid reason, the image of him dancing at that wedding flashes through my mind. I shove it away and take a wide step around him, determined not to waste any more time on pointless verbal ping-pong.

"If you need the number to an STD clinic, a couple of my old clients are nurses," I call over my shoulder before closing my car door. In the rearview, I watch him laugh the dig off before getting into his own car and pulling out behind me.

CHAPTER THREE

WHILE I CHASE ALONE THESE DAYS, I'M NEVER *REALLY* alone.

A dozen or so cars leave the gas station in a haphazard caravan. Of course when the road narrows into one lane, I end up stuck behind Wes and his ridiculous custom CHASE plates. I guess it's better than some of the elaborate glittering decals some of the tour groups use.

My mood climbs along with the updrafts as we clear the old grain elevators at the edge of town, and the sky opens up in an endless expanse of blue. The base of the storm is almost due east, a darkening oval bruise that stands out against the otherwise clear sky. Without taking my eyes off the road, I reach behind me to grab the ancient Rocky Mountain National Park ball cap that lives in my car, stuff my braid into it, and lower the windows to breathe in the hot, dusty air.

Spring on the plains smells like freedom.

Ahead of me, Wes has his arm resting outside his window as he drives. When a bolt of lightning drops in the distance, his arm is suddenly up in the air, fist raised toward the sky. I can practically hear his loud *whoop* to match the one I let out as adrenaline floods my system.

We're all just a bunch of weather and photography nerds racing down country roads in search of the kinds of storms that most people avoid. And sure, we might not be entirely sane, but it's good to remember that despite making a living by documenting the biggest moments of someone else's life, these six weeks are about *my* moments. That there *are* people who don't think I'm out of my mind for wanting to be here.

Cars start to peel off as we get closer to the storm. Everyone has a slightly different preference for how they line up their shots. Some go for the awe-inspiring wide angles that capture the towering height of the clouds punching into the upper atmosphere. Some choose the story in the details. Some are shooting time-lapse video, and some people just want to see something cool on the other side of their lens.

My heart lies with sweeping wide angles. I've grown up surrounded by towering Colorado mountains and golden oceans of wheat bending and swaying in the wind. I imagine it's a bit like the coastal dwellers with their love for the ocean *because* of its vastness. While I don't really need a reminder of my own insignificance, standing in front of a storm cloud punching sixty thousand feet into the atmosphere definitely makes me feel small. Like for once, I'm not taking up too much space.

Ahead of me, Wes flips on his turn signal. I glance down at the iPad mounted in between my seats to double check the map. It's the same left I was planning to take. Ugh.

The car behind me follows us, but everyone else keeps

heading east. I'm a little surprised Wes isn't trying to get closer to the storm, but he must have some other master plan. Obnoxious as he can be, he's got a sixth sense for getting himself to the right spot to get his shots.

The abandoned house I had in mind sits half collapsed a couple miles down the road. Radar confirms what I can already see through my windshield—the storm is starting to spin like a top.

Wes pulls off onto the shoulder, kicking up dust as I park behind him. There's no point in pretending we're not both thinking the same thing, as are the chasers behind us. When they hop out, I'm thrilled to see two women, though I don't recognize them from prior seasons.

After giving us a brief wave, they set up a respectful distance down the road, claiming a spot on the right side of the house. I'm debating introducing myself, but then I spy bright pink flowers crawling up the house's rotting siding. Delicate, small blooms cling to the ruins of what was once a vibrant family home centered against the backdrop of the deep purple-gray sky. The pinks will pop against the darkness of the storm, but more than that, it's exactly what I'm looking for. Growth versus decay. Beauty versus destruction.

Wes gives me a wide, goading smile. "If you're looking for tips for the contest, you can just ask. No need to follow me."

"Don't flatter yourself." I point at the side of the house, already lifting my camera to adjust my settings. I take a test shot, glance at the preview, and adjust the exposure before trying again. "I'm following the storm. And those flowers."

We fall into silence as we line up our shots. The storm is

gorgeous, a classic wedding cake structure that has me smirking to myself. It makes for stunning photos from a distance, the distinct layers of cloud banding giving it its name. They're also known for dumping torrents of rain, making it dangerous to get too close.

"Just can't escape those wedding cakes, can you?" Wes says as though he's in my head. He's taken off his sunglasses to shoot the storm, leaving them dangling from the neck of his shirt.

"This is the best kind of wedding cake." My mood is too good to let him get to me. "Too bad everything will be rain-wrapped if it kicks out a tornado."

Roads will flood quickly, especially out here where drainage isn't great. It can be impossible to know what you're driving into over the next rise. I'm content to stay right where I am with my flowers and abandoned farmhouse as the hot, moisture-rich inflow winds race toward the storm.

We work around each other in comfortable silence. I lower my camera eventually and breathe in the scent of rain, taking a moment to savor it without distraction. Tipping my head back, I close my eyes and let the wind tug on my hair and cool the sweat on the back of my neck. It's only when I open them again that I spot another storm off to the north, a towering cloud shooting up.

A quick jog back to my car and I've got my iPad in hand, rechecking the latest radar scan. The northern storm has less rain, which is more my speed, and the echo top scan shows the clouds are already pushing over thirty-five thousand feet. It's also not moving that quickly, giving me plenty of time to catch up.

I replace my iPad and shut the car door, wincing as the

wind slams it harder than I mean to. The sound attracts Wes's attention. "Heading out?" he calls, lowering his camera.

Feeling generous with some incredible shots already on my memory card, I point to the storm on the horizon. "That one's less soggy."

He nods, then glances back at the storm behind the farmhouse. "Mind texting me a shot of what it looks like when you get up there?"

"Sure, I'll put it in the group chat." When he drops the Wild Wes persona, Wes is a lot easier to be around. At some point, he'll return the favor. "Happy hunting."

I'm ten minutes into my drive when Tracy calls. "Where you at?"

"Heading for the northern storm. You?"

"Already there. Get your ass up here, Sloane. I think we're getting a tornado out of this one."

I grin wildly to myself as I peer through the windshield at the storm. "Got it. See you soon."

I fire off a quick voice note to Wes, check Tracy and Matt's location, and then lower my foot on the gas. I might break a few speed limits, but luckily the route I choose is fairly empty, at least at first. Once I get closer, I'm forced to slow down as chaser rush hour takes over the country highway.

About fifty yards down a dirt road, I find Tracy and Matt with their tripods already set up. "You made it!" Tracy yells over the wind as I quickly grab my gear before jogging across the road. There's a steep ditch for runoff, which requires a careful leap across before scrambling up the sandy soil to the fence line.

"We got a funnel for a few seconds." Matt points to the

telltale horseshoe section of the storm where the tornado will form if it's going to. "Fifty-fifty on whether it gets its act together."

I tilt my head, stare at the storm, and then check my phone again. A severe thunderstorm warning has been issued, but no tornado warning yet, which isn't a surprise. These types of storms are less likely to have the strong rotation needed to kick out a tornado than the one I left behind. Not impossible. Just less likely.

Then again, the ingredients are all there. The dew point is already oppressive, humid air clinging heavily to my skin while the temperature climbs and climbs. A hot breeze does little to combat the sticky air as the storm greedily sucks in even more fuel. And tornado or not, the towering structure is gorgeous.

As promised, I snap a quick shot with my phone and add it to the group text before concentrating on my camera and the storm, which is quickly getting stronger. Tracy spots the funnel first, whooping with delight and pointing like a madwoman at the same time our phones all howl with the incoming tornado warning.

My cheeks ache from smiling so wide. I couldn't have asked for a better start to the season. There will be down days, and long drives, and terrible meals cobbled together from gas station snacks, sure, but today is epic.

When the tornado finally drops, the sun is low enough to light the whole thing up. A loud cheer goes up, adrenaline igniting at the thrill of a tornado sighting, and with a practiced hand, I high-five Tracy while pressing the shutter release with the other. The infectious joy of the moment is almost as magical as the scene in front of us.

Then it's a mad dash for the cars, peeling out in a cloud of dust as we race along the road running parallel to the swirling vortex. It's not strong—a blessing for the locals—but the angle of the sun makes it incredibly photogenic, gleaming against the red-brown earth. In a time-honored, if questionably safe, chaser tradition, I hang one hand out the window as I drive, filming with a death grip on my phone while gleefully ping-ponging my attention between the road and the tornado.

It's a full twenty minutes before it finally ropes out, leaving us sweaty but exhilarated as mammatus clouds fill the sky.

"Are you going to be our good luck charm this season?" Matt jokes as we pack up our gear.

I laugh and shake my head. "Just a nice welcome back from the universe."

"We're going to keep with it," Tracy tells me as I slide my camera back into its protective bag. "I'm on the hunt for night shots this year. You in?"

I hesitate with my bag halfway shut and chew on my lip. Night chases can produce some spectacular images, but I've been going since dawn. Even if I load up on coffee, I'd rather not risk continuing in the dark when I'm not at my best. Too dangerous. The smart thing to do is check in on tomorrow's forecast, pick a hotel for the night, and sleep while I can.

"Not tonight," I say with an apologetic smile. "Send me a text when you stop for the night. I'll find you guys tomorrow. We can grab breakfast if nothing is going on until the afternoon."

With another round of sweaty hugs, they head off after the storm. There's a twinge of FOMO, but it's only the first day. As soon as the adrenaline high fades, I'm going to crash hard.

I don't notice the text from Wes until I pull into the hotel parking lot. Heard you caught a danger noodle.

I can't resist a little taunting when it's so rare I get to one-up him. You didn't?

Wes replies instantly. Nah. The text is accompanied by photos of two distinctly different tornadoes. I got two.

My grin turns to a scowl. "Of course you did," I mutter under my breath, then do the mature thing and send back a middle finger emoji.

MORNING COMES FAR too soon.

I reach for my phone with one hand while scrubbing a palm over my face with the other. A few taps on the screen and my exhaustion disappears as soon as I scan the latest Storm Prediction Center forecast.

Unsurprisingly, the group text is already active. Matt and Tracy ended up staying at this hotel last night too. For once I can't even be mad that Matt is one of those obnoxious morning people who's been up for two hours—he's already found a coffee shop. There's no mention of Wes joining, which hopefully means he ended up somewhere else.

Grinning to myself, I fly through getting ready in ten minutes. It's a small thing, but I make a point of getting my coffee from local businesses whenever possible. These communities deserve to get *something* back in exchange for hosting the small army of storm chasers rampaging through their towns every spring.

My good mood falters when I step into the lobby and find Wes holding court. He's surrounded by a group of guys, some of the faces familiar, but most not. It's nothing new. The combination of charm, money, good looks, and devil-may-care recklessness that surrounds him—and his social media presence—attracts attention anywhere he goes. The newer chasers idolize him and the risks he takes.

Wes has never been one to shy away from praise. Hopefully he's too busy being admired to come to the coffee shop.

As I do my best to slip by unnoticed, someone tosses him an energy drink. He grabs it out of the air with ease, jabs a hole in the can with his keys, and proceeds to shotgun the whole thing in a couple of seconds. Raucous cheers go up from the group instantly, and judging by the scowl of the receptionist, I'm not the only one who finds a man in his early thirties behaving like this obnoxious.

"Morning, Sloane," Wes calls across the lobby. He wipes his hand across his mouth and offers me a shit-eating grin. "Going to be a big day!"

"Sure is," I call back with exaggerated brightness. "Try not to end up in a ditch again!"

Wes learned the hard way two seasons ago that speeding in reverse, only to yank the wheel to spin around on wet pavement, isn't as easy as stunt drivers make it look. But rather than being insulted like a normal human, he laughs as I walk away.

I find the coffee shop easily enough. It's a small space, and so new that the smell of fresh paint still lingers beneath the rich scents of brewing coffee and pastries. Tracy and Matt have claimed two of the overstuffed chairs in the corner, their camera bags tossed on a third. I flash them a quick smile before heading to the counter and scanning the quirky drink menu.

One *chocolate on the beach* and a croissant later, I flop into a chair and take a giant bite of the enormous pastry. "You're my favorite person today," I tell Matt through a mouthful of flaky deliciousness.

He wrinkles his nose in mock disgust. "Swallow, then talk."

"Not what you said last night." Tracy lifts her coffee and takes a long sip as Matt flushes and I cackle.

"*Anyway.*" Matt lifts his iPad and turns it toward me. He points to a spot on the screen where the model playing on loop shows supercells popping up by two or three this afternoon. "We're thinking this is today's target. There's another cluster to the south, but the dew points down that way look too low to do anything exciting. Up here"—he zooms in on the area and then swipes into a different app—"dew points are already in the sixties and climbing."

I do a little shimmy in my seat. With highs forecasted in the upper eighties and clear skies in western Oklahoma, the heat of the day should set us up for a great afternoon.

We linger at the coffee shop for another couple of hours, catching up and occasionally double checking the forecast before hitting the road in high spirits. Wes, thankfully, texts to confirm he's on his own today, sparing me from having to deal with him.

With my hair tucked into a hat to keep it from snarling hopelessly, I follow Tracy and Matt north, windows down, music blaring, and breathe in the sweet scents of wheat, dirt, and sunshine.

By the time we stop for lunch, the brilliant blue sky is dotted with small, puffy clouds. Heat broils me right along with the asphalt when I get out of the car and tip my head back, squinting even with my sunglasses. The wind out of the south toys with the fine hairs escaping my hat, and the air has that telltale feel to it, a low ache in my sinuses forming as the barometric pressure destabilizes.

Northerners will tell you that they can smell snow on the air—in tornado alley, we know when a storm is coming.

"Oh, how I missed good barbecue," Matt moans as we step into the restaurant, woodsmoke and spices thick in the air. "I'm about to eat my weight in pulled pork."

"Colorado Springs has great barbecue," I remind him while eyeing the menu board. "You guys could move closer. Just saying."

"Or *you* could move." Tracy grins, all faux innocence when she adds, "I hear Houston is nice."

"Oil refineries and swamp-like humidity? No thanks."

She laughs. "Like you'd be seeing anything other than the inside of a certain high-rise condo."

"Not this again," I groan. "Wes isn't into me. What you two call flirting is just Wes being Wes. He thinks his inflated opinion of himself is shared by everyone and just wants to preen."

"That man looks at you the way I eye my nana's Thanksgiving pies," Tracy protests. "He's into you. He's *been* into you."

"No, he just hasn't met a woman who isn't instantly charmed by him." I roll my eyes, grateful we're next in line and this conversation is about to end. Especially since I never know how much Matt repeats back to the pain-in-my-ass topic of discussion. "If I turned into one of the *what big muscles you have* fangirls, he'd lose interest in a heartbeat."

Tracy and Matt exchange a look, but when Tracy opens her mouth, I hold up a hand to stop her. "And even if Wes *was* genuinely into me, it wouldn't matter. I'm not interested in getting tangled up in his circus. What I *am* interested in is just how much pulled pork I inhale in the next twenty minutes."

Tracy laughs and gives me an affectionate pat on the shoulder. "Sloane, I hate to break it to you, but if you're looking for help with your meat, Wes is far more—"

"If you finish that sentence, I'm going to . . ." I scramble for a decent threat while they both barely manage to contain their laughter. At least until I smile triumphantly and point at Tracy. "I'm going to call your nana and tell her you've been shit talking her pie!"

Tracy snickers and shakes her head. "Empty threats. You don't even know where she lives."

AFTER LUNCH, THE focus shifts toward exchanging information with other chasers and getting into position for the afternoon. We stop on the side of a dirt road between two massive wheat fields to evaluate our plan, a storm already starting to form in the distance. Billows of white rapidly build on each other as it grows, the cloud tops punching higher and higher into the atmosphere.

Matt rubs his hands together and grins widely before pulling his phone out. "Looks like we caught one! Even better, a lot of people went south. Shouldn't be too crowded."

I glance at my own screen and the cluster of blue dots that mark the locations of other chasers on the radar app. I leave it off most of the year, but when chase season gets underway, it doubles as a safety feature in addition to making my friends easier to find. There's a big group to the south, with another couple sprinkled across the interstate heading in our direction, and a dozen or so others spread out across our current area.

Including Wes, who's currently positioned miles to the northwest on the opposite side of the building storm. If he's hoping to catch another tornado today, he's in the wrong spot.

With a mental shrug, I put him out of my thoughts as we pile back into our cars and head into position just as thunder rolls across the plain, the grumble of a freshly woken dragon.

Storms can form quickly this time of year, especially under conditions like today's. Within twenty minutes, we're staring up at a beast of a supercell glowering above a long stretch of freshly plowed dirt.

I set up next to Tracy and fiddle with my camera settings while the wind drives against my back in a rush of hot, howling air. "Looks promising!" I yell over the noise, pointing toward the sky where the smaller wisps of cloud known as scud are rapidly being sucked into the storm.

Tracy lowers her camera long enough to shoot me a gleeful grin. It's so familiar that for a few seconds, everything falls away and it's like we're back to being chase partners. "We're a little nuts, aren't we?"

I nod my agreement before switching my attention to my

camera. Our phones all wail at the same moment when the storm goes tornado warned. We share a couple of high fives and whoops of joy—this storm is thirty miles from the closest town, thankfully—while Tracy reads aloud from the warning discussion.

"Thirty miles east of . . . moving northeast at fifteen miles an hour . . . golf ball hail . . . radar indicated." She scrunches her nose and glances back at the storm. No confirmation that anything is on the ground, but we can all see a couplet on the radar, a strong area of rotation that may or may not be a tornado.

At least for now.

Matt has his phone out too, eyes flicking between the radar app and the storm. A hook echo has started to form, the comma-shaped curve extending southeastward further confirmation of the rotation that prompted the warning. "Shit," he mutters, tapping on the little blue dot sitting just to the west of the hook. "What the hell is Wes doing?"

I watch as the screen refreshes and Wes enters the outer edge of the storm. "The idiot is going to try to punch it."

Matt scowls down at his phone, furiously taps into his recent calls, and jabs his thumb down on Wes's name. Seconds later, he's shouting over the wind, "Wes? Wes! This thing is tornado warned! What the hell are you doing? Don't you see that couplet?"

With the call on speakerphone, the static of rushing wind comes across the line along with Wes's garbled reply. "Can't let you guys have all the fun!"

"Bad idea, man!" Matt knows better than anyone how *Wild Wes* earned himself that nickname—he was there for a lot of the early days, taking the same stupid risks. But Matt grew up.

Wes didn't.

I snatch the phone, infuriated that he's being this reckless. "You're going to get yourself killed!" I yell. "What the hell is the matter with you?"

"Calm down, darlin'. I'll be fine. Done this a hundred times."

"You're playing chicken with a freight train! In the dark! You could drive right into it coming through the rain!" Shouting at him isn't working, but my temper is too firmly in the driver's seat to stop. "You really want to die over a goddamn photograph?"

The last thing I hear before the call drops is laughter.

Matt swears under his breath. The three of us exchange worried glances, Tracy chewing on her lip. Her attention stays glued to her phone while the little blue dot with Wes's name on it crosses from the lighter green that marks the start of the rain and moves into the darker yellows.

The road he's on will eventually bring him straight to us, assuming he makes it. I can't help holding my breath as the dot crosses from yellow to orange, and then into the red area that marks the worst part of the storm.

"Thank god," Tracy murmurs when the screen refreshes and the blue dot is still moving steadily east, nearing the outskirts of the deep reds. Another minute, another refresh, and he's cleared the worst of it. "Freaking Wild Wes, at it again."

I watch the road, waiting for him to emerge from the rain a mile or so off. A few minutes later, a speck of black eventually reveals itself as Wes's rain-soaked and mud-spattered SUV, music blaring so loudly it drowns out the storm when he lowers the window.

Wes holds up his camera, points it at me, and releases the shutter. "You should see your face!" He tries to mimic my scowl, but the idiot is laughing too hard to make it effective. "Live a little, Sloane!"

My temper flares white-hot. There was no reason for him to do what he just did. No one else is laughing. "That was beyond stupid."

Wes flings open his door and hops down to the pavement with a shrug. His T-shirt and jeans are soaked, his usual ball cap missing and his hair in wild disarray. There are a couple of blades of grass clinging to his left arm, yet another sign he was someplace he shouldn't have been. "As you can see, I'm perfectly fine."

"Sloane is right." Matt comes up behind me and folds his arms across his chest. He isn't laughing. "That was really stupid."

"And pointless," Tracy adds with her own scowl, gesturing toward where the storm is starting to weaken already. "It's falling apart."

Wes's smile dims as he takes in our small group. Behind me, Tracy and Matt are silent, their stances stiff with tension. Matt slides an arm around Tracy's waist, tugging her into his side as he lets out a long breath as though fighting for calm. I just shake my head and start toward my car, the awful churning sensation in my stomach not quite gone.

"You're fine this time," I say as I pass Wes, pausing long enough to meet his eyes. "But one of these times, you won't be."

"Oh, c'mon, it isn't that serious," he starts to protest. "We've all done it. Last year, you—"

"Last year, I made a miscalculation that left me no choice." I jab my finger into his chest, ignoring the flood of memories. Almost everyone who's been out here for any amount of time has had close calls. I don't like to dwell on mine. "You did that for *fun*, Wes. You took an enormous risk. You got lucky. One day, that luck is going to run out."

He only smirks and shoves a hand through his damp hair. "You worry too much."

It's an old argument I'm not in the mood to repeat. "Someone has to," I say wearily over my shoulder before getting into my car and heading for the next storm.

CHAPTER FOUR

THE STORMS TRACK EAST, DEEPER INTO OKLAHOMA, chasers trailing after them like a flock of starlings in formation along I-40. Somewhere east of Elk City, I watch a brilliant burner sunset next to Tracy, our cameras on tripods pointing toward an impressive lightning show.

"I love sunset lightning," she says with a happy sigh as another cloud explodes into pale lavender splinters and thunder rolls lazily across the open fields. I hum my agreement, captivated by the brilliant oranges and reds and pinks peeking out from the horizon while the storm grumbles in the distance.

"Kansas looks like the place to be tomorrow." I glance back over my shoulder to where Matt has his camera pointed at a different part of the storm. Wes is thankfully off doing his own thing. "I'm probably going to try to get north tonight so I have time to pop into Mae's in the morning. In the mood for donuts?"

"I'm *always* in the mood for donuts." Tracy pivots, then shouts across the field, "Matt! Sloane wants to stop at Mae's in the morning. You in?"

"I ever tell you I don't want a donut, that's how you know I've been kidnapped." Matt grins wide with the excitement of a kid left unsupervised with a cookie jar. "I'll text Wes."

My groan slips out before I can stuff it back down. "Do we have to?" I grumble to Tracy, too quietly to be overheard.

"Matt chewed him a new one about the hook punch earlier." Her eyes slide to mine, something curious peering back at me. "You know Wes. Stubborn as the day is long. Just like someone else I know . . ."

"My stubbornness doesn't extend to idiocy."

Tracy shrugs. "Maybe not, but I'm just saying, the two of you have an awful lot in common. He's not a bad guy, Sloane. He stayed with us for a week when he was in LA for a job and—"

"And he's reckless and arrogant and mocks me at every opportunity," I interrupt. It's not the first time she's tried to convince me that Wild Wes isn't exactly what he appears to be since she started dating Matt. After enduring her teasing earlier, I'm beyond not in the mood. "I get he's close with Matt and that you want us to be friends, but we're too different. It is what it is. I keep the peace for your sake."

I let out a long breath, my gaze straying to the horizon where the vibrant burn of the sunset is fading into twilight. "I think I'm going to call it a night and knock out a chunk of the drive before I crash. See you in the morning?"

Tracy stares at me, a slight crease between her brows, and then nods. "Ten work for you? We shouldn't have too far to go from Mae's to catch the storms if they pop off east of Dodge City like the models are saying."

I nod my agreement and head for my car, but I'm still

turning our conversation over in my head when I pull into the dusty parking lot of Mae's Donuts the next morning. I've known Tracy a long time, and she's always been a straight shooter. When we were chasing together, before she started to get closer to Matt, she agreed that Wes was an obnoxious adrenaline junkie with a death wish.

Nothing has changed as far as I can tell. Her relationship status aside, Wes is the same guy he's always been, all of his antics alive and well.

As if in answer, he pulls into the parking lot behind me in a cloud of dust and music that cuts out abruptly when he kills the engine. "Mornin', darlin'," he calls, exaggerating his drawl before emerging with a neon pink cowboy hat plopped on his head. It would look ridiculous no matter what, but the fact that he's in flip-flops, hiking shorts, and a T-shirt hardly helps.

"You and those cowboy hats this season," I mutter, squinting at him in the bright sunlight. "Do you even know how to ride a damn horse?"

"I do, actually." Wes tips his hat at me with exaggerated charm, like he's not a trust fund kid cosplaying a guy with a grueling job. "Been a while, though." Shadows flicker across his face, and when he speaks again, his accent is tidily tucked away once more. "Tracy and Matt are running a little late. Should be here in fifteen."

Of course they are. I make myself breathe out slowly before I say anything. "Great."

Wes chuckles, my obvious irritation yet another joke to him. "Still pissed about yesterday? I'm fine. I got this amazing video—"

"Good for you." Not wanting to rehash the argument, I

point at the monstrosity on his head before starting for the door. "Where did you even find that hideous thing?"

He grabs the handle and holds the door open for me with a dramatic sweep of his hand. "There's this magical place called the internet."

Rolling my eyes, I step past him into a blast of air-conditioning with a distinctly sugary scent. Mae is waiting for us with her usual brand of over-the-top friendliness. She's got to be in her sixties now, gray hair streaked with pink, and giant plastic tornado earrings dangling from her ears. A small mountain of her signature neon pink boxes sits stacked on the counter waiting for a stampede of hungry storm chasers.

"Well now, aren't you two a sight for sore eyes!" She comes around the counter to embrace each of us in a cloud of vanilla, her expression alight with excitement. "I saw the forecast this morning and hoped I'd be seeing y'all on your way west. You just tell those storms to stay away from my shop."

"We'll do our best." Wes grins, kissing her cheek before straightening from the hug. He reaches up, grabs the pink hat, and gently places it on her head. "Saw this and couldn't resist."

Heat crawls into my cheeks. The hat that I called hideous only a few minutes ago was a gift all along, one that Mae obviously appreciates by the way her expression softens.

She's one of the kindest souls I've met in all the years I've come to the plains to chase each spring. She started selling her donuts out of a food truck, and once she realized that storm chasers are a bunch of sugar fiends, made a habit out of turning up year after year where we were likely to be.

It was a great marketing tactic until it wasn't. A couple of years ago, a night tornado tore through the town that Mae was staying in. She was safe in a storm shelter, but her truck wasn't so lucky.

It was a gut punch when I heard what happened. In the weeks that followed, it quickly became clear just how many lives she had touched with her endless optimism and steady supply of baked goods. The community rallied around her and organized a fundraiser that, together with the insurance payout, enabled her to buy the shop we're now standing in. Most of us stop in every chance we get.

"I sure do miss being out on the road sometimes," Mae says now, slipping behind the counter and reaching for a paper coffee cup. "But it's awful nice to only have a ten-minute drive at five o'clock in the morning." She slides the first cup of coffee in front of me and then starts to pour another. "Weddings still treating you right, Sloane? I just can't thank you enough for sending that bride my way last summer. Never would have thought of that myself!"

I shrug off the compliment. "She mentioned she and her husband got donuts and coffee on their first date. It was an easy suggestion."

"Well, I still appreciate it!"

"Business is good?" Wes leans his elbows on the counter, his sunglasses dangling from his fingers while he waits for Mae to fix his coffee.

She laughs and wags her finger before setting down the paper cup. "As if you don't know! I still have no earthly idea how you did it, but I guess my granddaughter was right."

Wes shrugs. "Least I could do," he says with uncharacteristic bashfulness, the tips of his ears turning pink.

Mae must see the confusion on my face. She pulls her

phone out of her apron, taps the screen a few times with her long nails, and then turns it toward me. "Isn't he just the sweetest?"

On the screen, Wes's social media page is open to a video of him in one of Mae's signature bright pink aprons. The sound is off, not that I need to hear what he's saying to see that the clip went viral. Wes being topless beneath the apron probably violates some kind of health code, sure, but it's effective.

It was also awfully generous of him to put his thirst-trap tendencies to good use.

"I'm still getting people driving from all over creation just to try one of the pink-velvet donuts." Mae gestures to the pastry case with a happy sigh. Behind the sparkling glass, an assortment of treats sits tidily lined up, though most of the space is reserved for the donuts from the video. Like the rest of the shop, they're over-the-top, the dough itself a deep pink, with lighter-colored frosting and tiny high-heeled pink sprinkles. "Might even start shipping during the summer when my granddaughter and her friends are off school!"

"That's dangerous information." I grin over the rim of my coffee cup before taking a sip. "You taking preorders?"

Mae laughs while grabbing one of the boxes and a square of parchment paper. "You want the usual?"

"Yeah, that's great."

"Or you could live a little, Sloane," Wes taunts from my side. "All these concoctions to choose from and you're going with boring plain glazed?"

"I *like* plain glazed," I retort. "It's a classic for a reason."

"Lucky Charms are a classic. C'mon, taste the rainbow!"

"That's Skittles."

"I've got those this year too!" Mae sets the box with a half dozen plain glazed donuts on the counter and winks. "If you're feeling adventurous."

I pluck one of the donuts out of the box and take a giant bite, letting out a quiet groan at the perfection of sugar and light, airy dough. "Nah," I say with my eyes on Wes while he takes a big gulp of his coffee. "I know what I like. And what I don't." I turn my attention back to Mae and offer her a genuine smile. "These are fantastic. Even if *some people* think they're boring."

BY THE TIME Matt and Tracy show up and everyone heads back to their cars loaded up with donuts and coffee, the Storm Prediction Center has a wide swath of western Kansas marked with a high probability of strong storms. With the phrase *numerous tornadoes with very large/destructive hail* included in the discussion notes, just about every chaser in the area will be out. There's a trough coming in this afternoon, the atmospheric equivalent of dropping a mass of cold air into a seething cauldron of heat and humidity.

All the ingredients for a nice simmering pot of tornado soup.

When Tracy, Matt, and Wes opt for the core of the storm on the hunt for aqua skies and menacing clouds, I hang back, more in the mood for structure and scale today. If a tornado pops out, I can throw on my telephoto lens and still pick up detail at a distance.

While I miss the tornado—it's hidden behind rain and I'm too far away—I do get some of the shots I'm after, including a panorama of the whole storm looming high above freshly plowed fields. The distinct rows of tilled earth provide perfect leading lines, the warm brown of the dirt a great contrast to the whites and grays of the sky.

Wes texts the group chat while I'm piling my gear into the car to reposition. It's a selfie uncomfortably close to the tornado, his hair and shirt soaked with rain and a mile-wide grin on his face. I sigh, type out Try not to end up under a house in Oz, and stuff my phone into my pocket before getting back behind the wheel in search of sunset's cotton candy colors.

Twenty minutes later, I pop out on the backside of the storm just as the angle of the sun is starting to paint the towering mass pale pink. With any luck, that color will intensify shortly into the brilliant oranges and deep reds I'm hoping for.

What I'm not hoping for is the sight of Wes's SUV. I'm too far away to be certain, but there aren't many chasers out here in brand-new vehicles, and there definitely aren't that many with his towering height.

Sure enough, as I get closer, the guy standing on the edge of the road is definitely Wes. Not in the mood for his gloating, I'm about to blow by and find a spot farther down the road, but the red stains on his exposed forearm look a hell of a lot like blood.

Which is when I notice that his windows, including the rear windshield, are smashed out. Bits of broken glass crunch under my tires when I pull over just in front of him, the storm at our backs. I hop out and scowl at the wreckage with my camera in hand out of habit. Whatever happened, Wes is lucky it didn't end up much worse.

"She's going to light up like a damn firework," he calls

while I stand there gaping at the broken glass and blood spattered across his leather seats with my heart in my throat. There are only a few things that could have blown windows out like this. All of them are scary as hell.

Not that Wes gives a damn.

"Have you lost your mind?" I gesture wildly to his car when he glances back at my shout. Blood dribbles down his cheek from a gash uncomfortably close to his eye. "You did a hook punch again, didn't you? For fuck's sake, Wes, you need stitches!"

"I'm fine." He has the audacity to grin. "It was just a little impromptu shower."

"In glass!"

Wes shrugs and turns back to the storm, leaving me to stare incredulously, camera dangling at my side. I want to rip his camera out of his hands, but I've known him too long to bother. This is classic Wild Wes. Anything to get the shot. Consequences and collateral damage be damned.

"Well, fuck it," I mutter under my breath, moving around him to line up my own composition. We've got maybe ten to fifteen minutes to shoot this thing before the sun sinks under the horizon. His injuries will keep that long, and it's not like his windows are going to get any more broken.

Besides, I can work and give Wes *I told you so* face at the same time.

We move around each other in silence. Wes makes me nuts, but he's a talented photographer, and when it comes down to it, it's not because he has the cash for the best equipment or connections with big brands. When we're out here shooting, he's all business.

But when the colors fade and I lower my camera, there's still blood leaking from the cut on his face. "I really think you need stitches. At minimum, you need to clean that."

His hand starts to rise. I snatch his wrist and jerk his arm down. "You're covered in dirt and who the hell knows what else. Do not touch an open cut on your face. What's the matter with you? You should be on your way to urgent care." I glance back over my shoulder at his ruined windows. "And a repair shop."

Wes stares down at my hand on his wrist with an odd expression. I quickly let go and fight the urge to rub my hand on my leggings.

"It's Friday night in rural Kansas," he says dismissively. "Nothing is open for a hundred miles. I'll deal with it tomorrow."

"This could have been really bad. You get that, right? You get *this* is why we were all pissed the other day?"

Wes's god complex is even worse than I thought. He laughs, as though the very idea that he wouldn't simply walk away from everything in one piece is ridiculous. "With the steam practically coming out your ears it seems like you're building up to a good shout. Don't stop on my account."

"Goddammit, Wes! Do you have a death wish or something?"

It's not my finest moment, standing on the side of the road surrounded by nothing but endless stretches of tilled earth, yelling at a bleeding man. A bleeding man who finds this whole thing so amusing that my lingering trickle of guilt for shooting the sunset and not making him go to a doctor immediately fades away with the storm.

"You worry too much, Sloane. I'll be fine." He flashes that

trademark Wild Wes grin. "And if I'm not, at least I got the shot, right?"

"That's insane!"

"I'm not your responsibility." His attention slides toward the horizon and the empty stretch of road heading west. Far in the distance, the faint red lights of a wind farm throb. "I could use some dinner. You?"

"That's your plan? Just drive into town and leave your car in the parking lot of a hotel, asking to be stolen? Even without windows that thing is worth plenty." I jerk my chin toward his SUV. "I have a first aid kit. I can clean your face up at least and then . . ."

Exhaustion seeps into Wes's carefully applied mask of good cheer when he turns to face me again. "I am not your responsibility," he repeats with an edge to the words, as though this whole conversation is trying his patience. "It's not your job to fix me."

It sounds an awful lot like *I'm not worth fixing.* Wes has been a lot of things over the years, but his rare seriousness tells me he's not nearly as okay as he's pretending to be.

"We're three hours from my house, give or take," I blurt out, mentally cursing myself even as the words keep spilling out of my mouth. "My brother owns a garage. I'll call him in the morning, and you can sleep on my couch. No one will fuck with your car if it's in my driveway for the night."

All traces of Wild Wes are completely absent from the thousand-yard stare he levels at me. "Why?"

The bitten-off, one-word question makes his point for him. Inviting Wes to my home, doing him this kind of favor, it goes beyond the standard duty we all feel to help each other out of a bad situation. It's definitely outside the realm of our standard frenemies routine.

"I'm not going to force you," I say wearily with a glance down at the crumbles of safety glass littering the pavement.

Wes's expression doesn't so much as flicker. His inscrutable look leaves me clueless as to whether or not I managed the easy-breezy tone I was aiming for, or if some of the uncomfortably squishy feelings I'm desperately trying to ignore escaped. But then he nods, sweeping his hand out toward my car. "After you, Nurse Sloane."

WES BEGRUDGINGLY ALLOWS me to clean up the various cuts and scrapes caused by the glass. By the time I'm done, I still think he could use a few stitches in the largest cut by his eye, but he waves me off and dry swallows a couple of ibuprofen before he slides off my rear bumper.

"You going to tell me how this even happened?"

He only shrugs. "RFD got me."

The RFD—rear flank downdraft—is an atmospheric punch from the sky. Supercells are powered by hot surface-level air slamming into cold air in the upper atmosphere. Once the storm starts to rotate, cold air gets kicked out on the storm's backside—sometimes with enough force that it can knock over trees like matchsticks.

I rub my temples, where a headache is starting to form. "We *told* you something like this could happen."

"Yep," Wes says dismissively, opening the map app on his phone. "What's your address?"

Trying to get him to see how dangerous his decision was to chase this thing the way he did is a losing battle. If he doesn't care about his own safety, nothing I say is going to change that.

Shoving aside the realization that Wes is going to know where I live now—obviously, I'm the idiot who invited him—I rattle off my address before opening my car door. "You sure you're okay to do the drive? Windshield will make it?"

There's a long spider crack across it, but it's low enough that he should be able to see. And he's right that there's nowhere around here where he can get the glass fixed until morning, if that. Camping out on the side of a farmer's field isn't going to solve anything.

Wes brushes some loose bits of glass off his seat and leans on the doorframe. "Guess we're going to find out, aren't we?"

Gritting my teeth at his blasé attitude, I point at the windshield. "Call me if that gets worse."

"Anyone ever tell you that you worry far too much?"

"Just you," I grumble before slamming my door shut.

The uncomfortable twist in my belly at the sight of all that shattered glass and Wes's blood lingers. I'm not sure I've really managed to push it aside three hours later when we pull into my driveway in Colorado Springs just after midnight.

My house isn't anything special. The front steps are sagging in places, and the roof probably needs to be replaced sooner rather than later, but I was so happy when I found something I could afford that I figured I'd get to it eventually. Eventually has turned into five years. Oops.

"It may not be up to your standards," I tell Wes when he gets out of his car parked behind mine in the short driveway. I know from his social media that his condo is one of those gleaming, modern palaces in a high-rise that probably has a doorman. "But I'm tired and don't want to hear it."

He mutters something too low for me to catch, then reaches through a blown-out window into his back seat. Out comes a massive camera bag and a smaller black duffel he slings over one shoulder after brushing off more glass.

"Watch the second step," I call back, pointing to the half-rotten board I keep meaning to replace.

From my spot on the porch—I'm taller than Wes for once—I catch the full breadth of his annoyance when he stares up into my face, the porch light illuminating the hard line of his jaw. "You're going to end up with a broken leg if you don't get this fixed." He skips the step entirely, one long leg stretching up before he effortlessly joins me on the porch.

"That's rich coming from you. You could have died today."

Another one of those maddening shrugs. "I didn't."

"This time," I snap, shoving my key into the lock and twisting hard. The last thing I need is for the lock to stick and Wes to crawl up my ass about that too, but thankfully it decides to cooperate.

My place isn't huge. Living room, kitchen, bathroom, and what the real estate listing optimistically called two bedrooms. Only one of those rooms has space for an adult-size bed. The other is my office. At some point I'll finish off the basement to give myself more space, but for now it works just fine. It's not like I have even so much as a plant to share it with.

What I do have is a handful of my favorite storm images I've shot over the years printed on large metal canvases sprinkled around the house. Wes walks right up to the one closest to the door, an elephant trunk tornado half twisted over a road, and lightly traces the shape of it with his index finger. "I remember this one." He throws a sheepish grin over his shoulder. "My shots didn't come out this well." His attention drifts to the next image, mammatus clouds and a double rainbow over a brilliant green field. "Gorgeous colors."

The praise sits uncomfortably in my stomach. I know I'm good when it comes to weddings—I wouldn't be booked out more than a year in advance if I wasn't—but having Wes in my house is strange enough without him complimenting my storm work. "Yeah, that lab does a good job with color," I reply. "It's late. Maybe you can play art critic another time?"

He lets out a snort of laughter, but turns away from the prints on the wall and gestures to the couch. "This me?"

I eye my couch dubiously. "Maybe we should see if one of the hotels in town has a room. You're too tall for life."

"Nah." Wes drops his duffel on the floor. The camera bag he sets down more gently on the ottoman with a jaw-cracking yawn. "I sleep in my car all the time. This is fine. I'd rather get to the shop first thing so we can get back out there."

"I'll get ahold of my brother in the morning. I'm sure he can fit you in for the right price."

Wes leans back into the couch and folds his arms behind his head in a move that not only shows off the flex of his biceps but the wide expanse of his chest. He doesn't belong on my secondhand couch with its mismatched Costco throw blankets looking like that. At least he changed his shirt at some point so it's no longer covered in blood smears.

"Price gouging to help the family business, are we?" Wes

takes off his hat and lets it fall to the side. His dark hair is just long enough for him to shove his fingers through.

Despite my efforts to not notice *anything* about Wes tonight, I sure am noticing a whole lot. His easy manner isn't faked. It's more matter-of-fact, as though being taken advantage of financially is nothing new for him. And while the bitchy demon on my shoulder insists he can more than afford it, my more reasonable side winces at how often it must happen for him to react this way.

And what the hell has Wes been doing sleeping in his car?

"It's my brother's garage. I have nothing to do with it," I feel the need to explain. My cheeks inexplicably heat when Wes's attention once again settles firmly on me. "I'd text Eric now but he's been asleep for hours. The garage opens at nine on Saturdays. I'll set an alarm and try to get to him before he gets busy. There's not much in the house, but help yourself to anything in the pantry if you're up before me."

Wes nods. "You mind if I grab a shower?"

The last thing my misplaced attraction needs is for him to be naked in my house on the other side of a flimsy wall from my bedroom, but we're both covered in sweat and dust, never mind the flecks of dried blood along his hairline. "Of course." I gesture down the hall and hope he doesn't notice the squeak in my voice. "First door on the right."

Wes pushes to his feet, taking his time with a long stretch. He's so damn tall his fingertips graze the ceiling, not that my attention goes anywhere other than the sliver of tan skin exposed by his shirt riding up.

"You could always join me," he drawls, mischief sparking

to life as his lips curl. "I know how much you hate wasting time. Much more efficient to shower together."

I've never denied that Wes is attractive. He's built like he chops wood for a living instead of running around the wilderness with his camera, and the combo of dark hair and tattoos is a weakness of mine.

But he's also a swirling vortex of chaos. My life is chaotic enough.

I force myself to laugh in his face. It doesn't have the intended effect.

Wes's smirk only grows, but at least he doesn't press the issue. "I'll be quick."

After grabbing a toiletry bag and some clean clothes, he slides by me. I stand there, rooted to the spot far longer than I want to admit, before I march myself off to the tiny linen closet to grab clean sheets for the couch.

It's just one night. My brother will replace the windows tomorrow, and we'll start the drive southeast in separate cars. I can survive less than twenty-four hours of Wes in my house.

CHAPTER FIVE

TURNS OUT THAT SHOWERING AFTER WES, SURrounded by hot, humid air smelling distinctly like him, isn't a cure for insomnia. When my alarm goes off, I swear I've only just fallen asleep. My dreams were a hazy mix of images that fade before I even fully open my eyes, but the dampness between my thighs and the accompanying ache of unsatisfied desire linger.

Determined to ignore it, I grab the first thing my hand lands on in the closet—a dress—before the smell of fresh coffee lures me out of my bedroom, still finger-combing my tangled hair. I'm too tired to bother with anything else. The dress has a built-in bra that mostly keeps things contained, and I can get dressed properly after we drop Wes's car off. It's exactly the kind of dress my mother would label *sloppy*, but it's one of my favorites.

I'm texting my brother as I stumble into the kitchen, which means I hear the low noise Wes makes before I see him. It's not the sort of noise that belongs in my kitchen, scraping over my skin in a deliciously feral way, and when I jerk my head up from my phone, there's something wild in the way he's staring at me.

My sleep-fogged brain struggles to processes what I'm seeing. Wes stands at my stove, frying bacon that I know for a fact was not anywhere in my house last night. Shirtless and barefoot, his jeans ride dangerously low on his hips, the ends of his hair curling and damp from another shower—which is about when I remember him giving me a hard time at the wedding over wearing a dress.

When his eyes dip to my chest and then lower, where the dress clings to my hips before swirling around my legs, heat crawls into my cheeks. "I didn't put this on for you."

"Didn't say that you did."

"I wear dresses all the time at home."

"Your hair is longer than I thought," Wes says before abruptly turning back to the stove. But not before I catch the faintest hint of color washing into his cheeks and the bird tattoos that spread across his upper chest and onto his left bicep.

I can't think of a single time in all the years I've known him that I've seen Wes *flustered*.

Suddenly aware of the weight of the long waves of hair falling down my back, I fight the urge to twist it into a knot and instead study the vertical tattoo along his spine. My fingers itch to reach out and touch. The piece extends in a long column I've only caught glimpses of before disappearing into his waistband. I'm too far away to be sure, but they look like a random assortment of letters and numbers. "Just how many tattoos do you have?"

Wes turns his head slightly toward me, one eye still on the

stove. "You asking for a little show-and-tell?" he teases with his usual innuendo.

I scoff and roll my eyes, grateful to be back on more familiar footing. "Hard pass."

If he's offended, he hides it behind a good-natured laugh. "I got most of them when I was younger. Probably due for a new one but I can't decide what I want."

Curiosity gets the better of me. "Do they mean anything in particular?"

A flicker of emotion dashes across his face, the muscles in his arms flexing before he gives me another of those charming Wild Wes grins. "Whatever seemed like a good idea at the time."

It's a reminder of his impulsivity and recklessness I sorely need now that he's doing his best impression of a bad-boy-turned-good fantasy cooking breakfast. *Seemed like a good idea at the time* is what landed him in my kitchen in the first place.

My phone lights up with a text, excusing me from having to dwell on the strangeness of the conversation. Sparring with Wes in parking lots has never been as intimate as this early morning duel.

"Eric said he's already at the garage if we want to come by now before he opens." My stomach grumbles a protest as I cast a forlorn glance at the food on the stove. "We can reheat that. Assuming it's edible."

"It's more than edible." Wes points with a spatula to the counter, where he's laid out tortillas I hadn't noticed. "I just need another minute and then we'll have tacos we can eat while we drive."

I was somewhere around seven the last time anyone cooked

me breakfast. There have been guys who went out and picked something up, sure. But actually *cooked*? The fact that it's Wes is all the more surreal. I highly doubt his parents have ever cooked a day in their lives. They have staff for that. How did he even learn?

Texting my brother to let him know we'll be there soon is as good an excuse as any to push my curiosity aside. Wes and I aren't having a cozy morning chat by choice. He's only here because he took a needless risk that could have gotten him killed. "Maybe you should worry about finding a shirt. Seriously, who cooks bacon without a shirt?"

"If it's not a little dangerous, are you even living?"

There's the Wes I know and want to push in front of a tornado.

Except he came awfully close to doing that to himself last night, and the uncomfortable twist in my belly still hasn't entirely loosened. Thankfully, he doesn't notice, turning back to flip the bacon while humming under his breath.

"There's coffee." Wes points to the counter, where there are two take-out cups waiting, along with several packets of cream and sugar. "Wasn't sure how you liked it."

"How long have you been up?" I yawn while carefully stepping around him and his still very naked chest to grab one of the coffees. I dump some sugar into it and skip the cream. "I'm surprised I didn't hear you."

"I'm quiet when I want to be."

"You went out with all your windows smashed?" I can only imagine the looks he got.

"Not many people out at six thirty on a Saturday."

I wince, eyeing my far-too-small-for-him couch. It was close to two by the time we both settled in for the night. "Did you sleep at all?"

Wes shrugs and grabs one of the tortillas before adding a scoop of scrambled eggs. "Couple of hours."

"Sorry about the couch."

"Don't worry about it." He finishes adding cheese and bacon to the tortilla and expertly wraps it before handing it to me. "Eat your breakfast."

ERIC LETS OUT a low whistle when he steps out of the garage. "I thought you were exaggerating." I follow his gaze toward where Wes is parking his mangled SUV. "Uh, Sloane, when you said you had a friend who needed some work done fast, you left out that it was *him*."

I shrug, not for the first time wishing I'd kept my mouth shut and never ranted to my brothers about Wes after too many cocktails at Christmas. "Chaser code," I lie.

"But I thought you—"

"I do."

"So why is he—"

"Not now," I hiss as Wes drops to the pavement and starts toward us. He's put on a shirt, thankfully, but I'm having a hard time not picturing all the skin and ink hiding beneath the snug fabric.

My brother shakes his head. "I hope you know what you're doing," he mutters before he throws me a warning look and goes to inspect the hot mess Wes made of his vehicle.

I make introductions quickly. It's a little odd to see Eric and

Wes side by side. Growing up, my younger brothers rapidly outgrew me once they hit their teenage years. I'm used to Eric and Sam towering over me, but next to Wes, Eric is the short one.

"This is a good news, bad news situation." Eric gestures at the SUV with a grimace after poking around for a few minutes. "We can fix 'er up for you no problem, but I've got to order in the glass. That'll take a few days. You might have better luck at the dealer up in Denver or one of those glass replacement services. Once it's here, it's not going to take too long, as long as you didn't fuck up the mechanics of the door. If there's glass in there too, it'll take longer to take it apart and clean everything up."

Wes glances at me. "How far are we from Denver?"

"An hour, give or take. Maybe a little longer depending on where you need to go."

"I'll make some calls." He paces away, tapping on his phone, while next to me Eric shoves his hands in his pockets and gives me that classic, I'm-your-brother-I-see-your-bullshit stare.

"I thought he was, and I quote, *the biggest jackass on the plains*." Eric's brow goes up. "Or is it the *even if he's hot* part that's driving all this? Don't tell me you're pulling a Mom."

"Did you really just compare me to Mom?" I hiss, giving him a shove that he hardly seems to feel.

"You showed up with a guy you told me is a dick to you. What am I supposed to think?"

"It's not . . . He's . . . Sometimes he's not so bad." I fold my arms over my chest and jerk my chin toward the lack of windows. "The only reason he's here is to get his car fixed. You fix cars. He's willing to pay extra to have it done faster."

"That's nice, but what's he doing with you in the first place?"

"I told you, chaser code. He needed help and I was there." I shift uncomfortably, my attention drawn to Wes's tense form as he paces the garage's driveway. With one hand clutching his hair, his shirt is riding up again, exposing just enough of his bare abdomen to make me wonder about those other tattoos.

"Sloane? You in there or has the man's ass mesmerized you? I might not swing that way, but even I can admit that's gym goals."

Face flaming, I yank my attention away from Wes. "I don't want to win the magazine contest because of something stupid, all right? I want to beat him on my own merit so he can't blame circumstances."

It's not a lie—but it also didn't occur to me until this morning. After Wes was already in my house.

Shoving the thought aside, I continue, "I'm sick of hearing how my shots are never going to be as good as his because I'm not willing to dangle myself out of a helicopter or hike glaciers or any of the other insane shit he does."

Not like I could even if I wanted to. Those trips don't come cheap.

"Then you better hope your boy—"

"He is not *my* anything."

"—has better luck up north because the earliest the glass will come in is Monday, and that's not a sure thing with tomorrow being a holiday." My brother scowls. "You *do* remember tomorrow is Easter, right?"

"Sure," I lie. Holidays don't tend to stick out much in my head these days. We make an effort for Thanksgiving and Christmas with Mom, but the rest tend to go by unnoticed.

It *does* mean that Wes is going to be relying on me for

transportation longer than either of us thought unless he finds someone in Denver willing to work not only a Sunday, but a holiday at that.

My attention wavers back to him pacing by the road. Even with sunglasses jammed over his eyes, I can see the frustration climbing into his expression, his shoulders high and tight. He tips his head back and stands there for a long moment, motionless, as though he's hoping to find an answer in the distant mountain peaks.

Eric sighs, his focus on the car when he says, "You going to stop by Mom's while you're here?"

"Wasn't planning on it. I haven't even been gone a week." I don't want to interrupt the relative peace of my chase season—Wes and his blown-out windows and puzzlingly thoughtful breakfast aside. "I'll check on her if I have time. Have you or Sam been by?"

Eric only shakes his head. "Been busy with the garage. I called her yesterday. She said she's fine. You don't have to do all this shit for her, Sloane. She's an adult."

I love my brothers. I do. But as Eric stands there without having the decency to look the slightest bit guilty, the urge to get in my car and leave both him and Wes to solve their own problems is hard to resist.

This is the only break I ever get. Why the hell did I interrupt that for *Wes*? I might want to beat him fairly, but it's not even remotely my fault he got himself in this mess.

The man in question growls out a string of curses under his breath as he comes back to where Eric and I are waiting. "I forgot tomorrow is Easter," he says in a tight, controlled voice.

"No one can do anything today. You can get it done Monday when the glass comes in?"

"If I don't find any nasty surprises, sure," Eric says easily.

"I'll pay whatever it takes."

My brother nods toward the garage behind us. "Come inside and I'll run a quote. Just need the keys." His eyes slide toward me and narrow. "You staying at Sloane's?"

"Yeah."

"No," I answer at the same time. Wes lifts a brow at me in question, which I guess is fair with his stuff still spread across my living room. "We can find you a hotel. That couch is fine for one night but I doubt you want to stay there another two," I explain, already wondering if it would make me a total asshole to drop him off at a car rental place—if there are even rentals available with the holiday—and head south.

"I've slept in far worse places." Wes flashes another of his broad grins and heads toward the garage.

In search of a distraction, I pull out my phone to check the forecast again. There's a text from Tracy.

You went home?? AND WHY IS WES WITH YOU?!

"Shit." I squeeze my eyes shut with a long groan. I forgot about the radar app tracking our locations. Anyone who bothers to look for us can easily see that we're together. And nowhere near storms.

Before anyone else catches on, I snap a quick photo of the mangled SUV and send it to Tracy. Dumbass finally ran out of luck. We're at my brother's garage.

My phone rings immediately.

"Are you okay?" Tracy demands, worry coating every word. "Is *Wes* okay? What the hell happened?" Then, more muffled, "Did you know Wes wrecked?" and Matt's distant "What the fuck?"

"We're fine." I take a deep breath and quickly explain how we ended up here.

Tracy is quiet when I've finished, though I hear Matt's low curse in the background. "Please tell Wes I said he's a fucking idiot," she finally says, worry and fear and anger all wrapped up in one. "Matt agrees."

"Oh, I did. I'm sure I'll tell him again."

"Good." She sighs. "Does that mean you're stuck in town? Because Monday is looking *really* good."

Of course it is. "I didn't check the forecast this morning. Where?"

"Southeastern New Mexico into West Texas for Monday. Storms are going to wobble around for the next week before shifting north into Oklahoma and Kansas, possibly Nebraska. Monday's spot—that's what, six hours from you?"

"More like eight to ten." I grimace, glaring at Wes's SUV. "I should just leave him here and go on my own."

Of course, if I do that, and I get the cover shot while he's cooling his heels, he'll never shut up about it. I can practically hear him complaining that if I hadn't left him, he could have gotten an even better shot. That I only won because I ditched him.

"Or," Tracy says, drawing out the *r*. "You could both leave. In your car."

"We'll kill each other before we get out of Colorado," I

protest. But even as I say it, my mind wanders back to my kitchen. Wes didn't have to go out and get me coffee or make us breakfast. Just like he didn't have to do that promo for Mae. Maybe he's not *all* bad—but I'm still not sure I want to be trapped in close quarters with him.

"If we get a good weather pattern, backtracking to pick up his car would cost us days of chasing. We could be stuck together for a while."

"True." Tracy hesitates, her tone turning contemplative. "You could always tell him if he pulls any shit you'll drop him off at the closest airport." And then, softer, "I think he'd behave, though. He's really not a bad guy."

"So you keep saying." I blow out a breath and glance toward the garage. Signing off on a quote can't take much longer. If I'm going to do this, I need to make a decision pretty quickly.

It's not like Wes can just get any old rental, and I doubt the kind of SUV with good tires he'd need is going to be available last-minute right before a holiday. If we don't go together, neither of us is going—and I *really* don't want to sit around my house for the next couple of days.

"I'll talk to him about it," I finally relent. "Maybe. Probably."

"For what it's worth, I have a feeling it will go a lot better than you're thinking."

"I'm going to remind you of that when I dump him at an airport in two days." Movement catches my eye as the garage office door opens. "Looks like he's done with Eric."

"See you in a few days!"

Before I can question her singsong tone, Tracy hangs up, and Wes is crossing the parking lot in his long, ground-eating strides.

I'm surprised to see Eric coming too, now that the garage is about to open, but it turns out he hasn't come to say goodbye to his big sister so much as dump a problem at my feet.

"All good?"

Wes nods. Eric is the one wearing a scowl. "Mom might call you. She's looking for help with something."

Far too aware of the heavy weight of Wes's stare on me, I struggle to maintain a neutral expression while silently cursing. "Mom doesn't even know I'm in town," I remind my brother. "I'm not supposed to be here."

The guilty shuffle of Eric's feet tells me what he's about to say before the words come out of his mouth. "I accidentally told her. She heard his voice"—he gestures to Wes—"and wanted to know who was at the garage with me this early. It just came out."

"Eric!"

"No one says you have to go." He shoves his hands in his pockets and shrugs. "You can just ignore her drama, you know. Sam and I do it all the time."

"Yeah, I'm well aware." My eyes dart toward Wes before settling back on my brother. "Seriously, you and Sam can't just figure it out?"

As if on cue, my phone lights up with an incoming call. Mom. Great. I decline the call and start to shove my phone in my pocket, but it just starts ringing again.

"I hate you right now," I tell Eric, wishing I had never opened my big mouth and had just left Wes on the side of the road.

"Tell her you're busy."

"Like that will stop her from calling me for the next two

days nonstop." I take a deep breath and accept the third call, striving for a neutral voice. "Hi, Mom."

"Oh, so you do know how to answer your phone," she says by way of greeting. "The lengths I have to go to for my only daughter to speak to me."

"It's storm season."

"Well, Eric says you're in town. I'm sure you can spare your mother some of your precious time." She sniffs, the crocodile tears always waiting in the wings for another performance.

"Mom, I really don't—"

"If you're already at your brother's garage, you can drive ten minutes more to my house before you run off again."

She hangs up without another word, leaving me fuming and embarrassed.

"I'm sure it won't take long to help your mom out." Wes slides his hands into his pockets and shrugs like it's no big deal that he's getting such an unflattering glimpse into my shit show family life. "Moms like me."

Oh, my mom will definitely like Wes. That's the problem.

I resist the urge to scream and stamp my feet like the child I was never allowed to be. "Did she say what she needed when you did your Benedict Arnold routine?" I choke out, still glaring daggers at my brother.

Eric shrugs. "Something about a lamp."

"A lamp? You and Sam can't handle a *lamp*?"

"I'm busy with the garage," he says with a pointed look at Wes's SUV. "Sam went to the mountains with his girlfriend's family for the weekend."

"And you couldn't tell Mom you'd just come by after you close up?"

"You and I both know it's not even going to be about whatever lamp she claims she can't plug in herself. This is just her way of getting attention. If you would stop playing into it, she'd leave you alone. She never calls me or Sam with this crap other than when you're gone every spring."

Familiar irritation floods my veins. I don't ask much of my brothers. "She's our mother."

"That doesn't mean—"

I wave a hand to cut him off and avoid Wes's questioning look. "I'll just go. It's easier than fighting with her. But you owe me."

Not like that means anything. The favors my brothers owe me stack higher than any of the Colorado Fourteeners, not that they ever seem to try to make a dent in the pile. I'm sure Eric will claim that fixing Wes's windows *is* a favor to me, despite the fact that he's going to make a tidy little sum off the work. If anything, I'm the one doing *him* a favor.

Just like that, my decision is made. I'm not staying in town for another night, never mind until Monday. And if that means I have to chase with Wes, so be it.

"DOES YOUR MOM live close by?"

I use the excuse of pulling out onto the busy street to give myself a few more seconds to decide how to play this. Exposing the full extent of my family's dysfunction to Wes is not on today's bingo card.

"I'm going to bring you back to my place before I go over there," I explain, internally wincing at the waste of more than an hour driving in circles. "Trust me, you don't want to be part of this."

"I don't mind. I know something about difficult parents."

"It will be faster if I go by myself." No matter how curious I am about the story lurking in his words, taking a personal interest in Wes isn't part of the plan. Besides, I have a Band-Aid to rip off. "Have you seen the morning refresh?"

He hesitates like he's going to argue some more about my mom, but he must change his mind. "Yeah. Of course it's going off when we're stuck here."

"We don't have to be. Stuck here, I mean." I tighten my grip on the steering wheel and finally sneak a glance at his face. His eyes are concealed behind sunglasses, but the tense line of his jaw isn't. In his lap, he's toying with his phone, big hands flipping it over and over.

"*You* don't have to be." Wes turns back to the passenger window. "I can grab a hotel and wait for the glass to come in."

"Like you'd ever let me hear the end of it if I got the winning shot off this storm." I expect a reaction. Wes just shrugs. It's the nonchalance more than anything that pushes the words out of my mouth. "We could go together. I mean, my car, my rules, so none of your usual Wild Wes shit."

I swear he flinches at his nickname, but when Wes turns back toward me, he's grinning like he's just been handed the keys to the kingdom.

"You want to team up?"

"*Want* is a strong word," I grumble. I'm careful. He's reckless. Chasing together probably won't go well, and yet here I am, making the offer anyway. "What I *want* is to beat you fair and square."

It's the truth, but deep down, some part of me likes the idea of not chasing by myself this season. I spend so much of my life alone. It wouldn't be awful to have company—even if that company *is* Wes.

"I'll enjoy watching you try." His eyes dip to the neckline of my dress before darting back up. "You could bring that dress along."

I scowl, tugging on the bodice where it's slid down to reveal a little too much of my chest. "What is it with you and the dress nonsense?"

"It's a compliment, Sloane. Normal people say thank you." His overly casual tone does nothing to dim the devilish gleam in his eyes. "In fact, I was thinking—"

"That must have hurt."

"Oh, c'mon, you can do better than that."

Luckily my driveway is just ahead, sparing me from having to answer. "This shouldn't take more than an hour," I say, determined to avoid any further conversation about the damn dress. I pull my keys out of the ignition long enough to separate the front door key from the rest. "Do *not* go snooping through my things. You can tell me what you want to do after I deal with my mom."

Wes takes the key with an odd expression, his eyes darting between me and the house. "I don't need to think about it. I'll be ready to go when you get back."

"Great. I'll get this over with, and then we can head south."

He hesitates, and then asks, "Do you need to check with your brother about storing my ride?"

"I'll tell Eric to leave it in my driveway when he's done. He's got a key to my house, so he can leave your keys inside. If you come back to get it without me, I can have him or my other brother stop by."

"There's another one of you?"

"Yeah. Sam is a lawyer, or at least he will be. My brothers are very different people."

"A lawyer, a car mechanic, and a wedding photographer. You must have some interesting conversations at the holidays," Wes says with a chuckle.

I force a tight smile. "Oh yeah." I barely keep the sarcasm out of my voice. "Holidays are definitely interesting."

Interesting is one way to describe the scene that usually unfolds after my mom drinks too much and descends into a crying jag that can last for days, but there's a better chance that I'll get hit by lightning than tell Wes that.

"You're sure you don't want me to go with you?"

"Yep." I pointedly shove my keys back into the ignition and restart the engine. Mom is sure to be insufferable enough knowing I brought a guy to Eric's garage, thanks to my snitch of a brother. I don't want to find out what kind of stunt she might pull if she actually meets Wes. "I'll text you when I'm on my way back."

Wes takes the hint and gets out of the car, though he doesn't immediately go into the house. Instead he stands in the driveway with his hands jammed in his pockets and watches me leave.

Ignoring an inexplicable trickle of guilt at the sight of him alone in my driveway, I head for my mom's and brace myself for whatever emergency could possibly apply to a lamp.

CHAPTER SIX

IT ISN'T JUST A LAMP. IT'S NEVER JUST A LAMP.

After completing a laundry list of tasks that were far from urgent, I pull back into my driveway and blow out a long, aggravated breath. At least Wes didn't witness my mom's theatrics.

Needing a few more minutes to calm down before facing him, I rush through the living room. "Just need to change," I say quickly over my shoulder without making eye contact.

When I emerge from my bedroom in my normal chasing uniform of leggings and a tank top, dress firmly back in the closet, there's a brief moment when disappointment flashes across Wes's face. Refusing to think about what that might mean, I grab my bag and head out to the driveway.

He tosses his duffel haphazardly into the trunk, only to stare at me like I've lost my mind when I yank it right back out. "Unless you want to chase with a naked guy, I'm going to need that," he drawls, propping his hip against the side of my car and folding his arms across his chest. I absolutely don't notice the way the muscles in his forearms flex.

I *definitely* don't think about Wes naked.

"No one is taking their clothes off in my car," I say with a pointed look. "We're also not just chucking stuff in here. I've got a system."

"Of course you do."

My eyes snap to his. "You don't have to come with me. Just take your credit card to whatever dealership you want and buy yourself a new car. No one says you have to do this."

A muscle flexes in his jaw, but Wes doesn't say another word as I carefully stack our bags so that the camera gear is both accessible and not about to fall on the ground the first time we open the back hatch. If he wants to trash fifteen grand worth of gear, that's on him, but it's not so easy for me to replace.

After a quick stop to fuel our raging caffeine addictions, I merge onto I-25 and do my best to settle in for the long drive south. "I'm thinking we stay in Hobbs tonight. Any objections?"

"I'm good with that." Wes gives me a long look and then asks more quietly, "You sure you're okay?"

"I'm fine."

He leans back into his seat and folds his tanned arms across his chest. "*Fine* usually means anything but."

I tighten my grip on the steering wheel and focus on the long stretch of road ahead. "I don't want to talk about it."

"Fair enough." Wes yawns and tips the brim of his baseball hat down over his face. "Mind if I grab a nap?"

"Nope. The music going to bother you?"

"Nah. I can sleep through just about anything."

Wes doesn't say another word for the next two hours. Maybe he's asleep. Maybe he's just pretending to be because he has even less to say to me than I have to say to him. If I just ignore the bulk of him in the passenger seat, it's almost like I'm alone.

Almost.

His eyes crack open when I stop for gas just over the New Mexico border, the deep green of spring in the mountains giving way to a long expanse of dry desert scrub. We're too far west to run into other chasers yet, the parking lot full of truckers and a group of bikers having lunch in the afternoon sun.

"Gas is on me," Wes says, his voice rough with sleep. "Least I can do."

"We can just split it," I insist, the low rasp of his just-woke-up voice making me question if spending days in close quarters together is a good idea. "You don't have to do that."

"I know." The nap seems to have improved his mood. Wes grins before he grabs the door handle when I pull up to the pump. "But I'm going to do it, so let's not waste time arguing about it. As long as we're chasing together, I'll cover the gas. We both know you're doing me a huge favor."

One part irritated at the high-handedness and one part grateful that my budget will stretch further than I planned, I fumble out a "Thank you" just before the passenger door falls shut. I can't remember the last time someone pumped gas for me, never mind paid for it.

Banging my head back into the headrest, I stare out across the parking lot at the clouds. Off to the east, barely visible at the very edge of the horizon, the telltale profile of a building storm grabs my attention.

While Wes is pumping gas, I scan data on my iPad. A couple of hours ago, the models showed scattered storms that weren't going to amount to much forming in the area where Texas, New Mexico, and Oklahoma all meet. Now, roughly a hundred miles or so to our east, the picture has changed, the black ovals of supercells dotting the area over the next several hours.

"Look at this," I say without preamble when Wes gets back in the car. I hand him the iPad and move into a parking spot. "If we detour east now, we can probably catch it."

He looks up with a smirk. "Let me drive and we'll *definitely* catch it."

My hands tighten on the steering wheel reflexively. "You forget I just saw what happens when you're behind the wheel."

It's hard to believe that all went down only yesterday afternoon, but that's the thing about chase season. Time gets slippery. Yesterday I woke up in Kansas and went to bed in Colorado; tonight we'll be in New Mexico or Texas, depending on how far we chase this system to the east. By June, I'll be so sick of my car that I'll vow not to go any farther than the grocery store for weeks.

I'm still not letting Wes anywhere near the driver's seat.

"Don't worry, darlin'," he says in an exaggerated drawl. "I'm not about to steal your keys. East works for me. Just going to head inside for some snacks. You need anything?"

"I'll come with you."

Thanks to holiday travelers, the store is far busier than usual for a middle-of-nowhere truck stop. A pretty blonde in a pastel-yellow sundress clocks Wes the second we walk in, her focus locked on him as he heads for the energy drinks. I split off to the sad fruit display. She waits all of three seconds before sidling her way over to him.

Rolling my eyes, I dig through the apples in search of one that isn't bruised. When I look up again, Wes is grinning at the blonde and making no move to separate her hand from his arm.

"Seriously?" I mutter under my breath while she leans closer. Wes being a flirt is nothing new, but we've barely been on the road for a couple of hours. If he thinks I'm going to wait around while he has a conversation with her perky cleavage, he's going to be walking back to Colorado Springs.

Stomping over to the water case, I catch movement from the corner of my eye. Wes has his phone out, tapping on the screen while laughing at something the blonde said. I don't even want to consider how many phone numbers that man has accumulated.

My phone buzzes a second later, and eager for a distraction, I pull it out—only to find a text from Wes.

Little help??

Snorting under my breath, I quickly reply, I am NOT your wingwoman before shoving my phone back in my pocket. When it buzzes again, I ignore it and focus on grabbing the coldest bottle of water I can find.

"Sloane, there you are, darlin'," Wes says, suddenly at my side. His new friend scowls and takes a step closer to him. It's all I can do not to roll my eyes again.

I transform into a five-foot-eleven popsicle, frozen in the middle of the aisle, when Wes drapes his arm around my shoulders. He leans closer, his lips almost brushing the shell of my ear as he murmurs, "Play along and I'll owe you big time."

"You already owe me," I hiss under my breath, but I don't shake off his arm. Despite Easter Barbie glaring daggers at me, being tucked into his side feels pretty nice. At my height, it's not often I meet a guy that makes me feel anything close to dainty. Despite the shrieks from my inner feminist, some lizard-brain part of me likes it.

Or I'm so touch-starved that I'm starting to lose my mind.

"So what do you say, Wes?" The blonde bats her eyelashes and leans forward in an unnatural posture that puts her chest on full display. "I'd love to show you a good time while you're visiting New Mexico. My family's place has a private hot spring. It's *very* secluded."

"Sounds like an invite to get murdered." It should be too quiet for her to hear, but by his choked laugh, Wes catches my muttering just fine.

"Thanks, but we've got to get going," he says while sliding his hand low on my hip. I get a little thrill at the possessive move, which has nothing to do with Wes and everything to do with the novelty of someone claiming me so blatantly. Even if it is for show.

"Oh, you can bring your . . . friend." She smiles at me like a snake about to strike, the wrinkle of her nose unmistakable as she takes in my faded leggings and the remnants of chipped pink polish on my toenails. "My cousin has a thing for tomboys."

Pressed into his side, I feel Wes go rigid, though his charming smile doesn't so much as flicker. "Best of luck to him. This one is mine."

I must not do a great job of hiding my shock. The blonde rolls her eyes with a scoff.

Not in the mood for a second round of gas station insults in one week, I turn to tell Wes he can meet me in the car when he's done with whatever the hell this is. To my surprise, he only tightens his grip and steers us toward the cashier without another word.

I keep quiet when he plucks my water and snacks out of my hands and pays for everything, the weight of the blonde's stare heavy between my shoulder blades and a host of confusing feelings swirling in my head.

It doesn't help when Wes tucks me back into his side as soon as he's done paying—and keeps me there despite the heat.

I recover myself once we're at the car and lift a mocking brow like I can't still feel the weight of his touch when he lets go. "Not in the mood to be tied up in her basement?"

He laughs under his breath and shakes his head. "Definitely not. Thanks for that. I—"

The click of heels on pavement precedes a cloud of perfume marching toward us, determination pinching the blonde's mouth. She gives me another of those dismissive up-and-down glances before turning her attention firmly to Wes.

His eyes follow mine, narrowing as he lets out a sound somewhere between a growl and groan before snapping his attention back to me. I don't understand the intensity of his stare or the way his gaze drops to my mouth until he says in a low voice, "In about two seconds I'm going to kiss you."

I swallow hard, the sound of those damn heels louder than ever. He can't be serious. Except he's already leaning closer, and there's a tiny voice in the back of my mind insisting this is a perfect chance to satisfy my curiosity.

Fuck it.

I'm prepared for a light peck when I nod my permission. What I get is Wes plunging his hand into my hair, his lips as soft as they are demanding. It's the kind of kiss that arches my spine and nearly makes me drop my snacks, his mouth hot and insistent. He hasn't shaved in a few days, his persistent stubble now the start of a dark beard that lightly scratches my skin. He tastes like those candies he loves so much.

"Kiss me back," Wes breathes out, too low for our approaching audience to overhear. That rough voice does things to me it has no business doing coming out of his mouth. I melt into him, and he meets me with a soft moan that has to be fake but heats my blood as if it's as real as it sounds.

Then the madness starts all over again, my free hand clinging to his shirt. Because the thing is, as stunned as I am by this turn of events, Wes is really good at kissing. Confusingly good. This kiss should be awkward, but it's so natural it might as well be a puzzle piece falling into place.

Then again, he's probably had plenty of practice.

Wes keeps kissing me until the blonde walks off in a huff, and then he kisses me for a few seconds longer. When he finally lets go, he slides his hand down my spine to rest low on my back, his pinkie just grazing the swell of my ass, and offers a grin that's not remotely apologetic.

I want to hate it. I want to be outraged that he just used me rather than tell the blonde off—but I don't say a word. Not when my pulse is so loud it's drowning out just about everything else.

"Breathe, Sloane," Wes says softly. There's a slight furrow between his brows as if he's concerned, which is about as far as he can get from the smug satisfaction I expect. Surely he's going to start gloating any second.

I swallow hard. "You kissed me."

"Sorry. I shouldn't have grabbed you like that." He shifts his weight from foot to foot, pink climbing his cheeks. "But, uh, thanks for the assist."

"It's fine. You're welcome." I sidestep out of his hold and remind myself that I don't even *like* Wes. The pinch of rejection at his apology has everything to do with stress and a lack of sleep—and okay, the distinct lack of romantic affection that is my adult life—rather than any genuine attraction. "Let's go catch a storm."

And so begins an awkward drive east.

Wes checks in regularly with Matt and Tracy along with a bunch of other chasers I don't know well, narrating the stream of texts. He knows damn near everyone who's out here regularly. I'm more of a wave-across-the-parking-lot-at-familiar-faces-and-stick-to-my-small-circle person. At least the constant dings of his phone fill the stilted silence.

We've known each other for a decade, but my interactions with Wes have always been limited to semi-friendly ball busting while shooting the same location or killing time waiting on the weather. Occasionally drinks late at night in a bar with Tracy and Matt as a buffer. Spending six, eight, ten hours alone together—after that damn kiss, no less—is entirely new territory.

Wes keeps one eye on the radar and models while I drive, but we're not relying solely on the data. He's also cross-referencing with friends on the ground. By the time we get into position an hour and a half later, there's a massive, picture-perfect mothership of a supercell looming above us.

I pull off to the side of the road, leaving plenty of space between us and the other chasers—friends of Wes's—who are already standing along the fence line with their cameras pointed up at the sky. Tracy and Matt are here somewhere, but it's crowded enough I don't immediately spot them.

"Up for a friendly wager?" Wes waves his camera toward the storm and cocks a brow at me in challenge, an effortless return to his usual brand of teasing arrogance.

Clearly he isn't going to give that kiss a second thought, so why should I? Taking a deep breath, I grab my camera. "Just how friendly are we talking?"

"How friendly do you want to be?" He offers a devilish grin, and I swear there's innuendo there. But that's Wes. He flirts with everyone. It doesn't mean anything. Whether he kissed them only hours ago or not.

"Don't be gross."

"Dinner, Sloane," Wes says with a snort of laughter. "We compare shots at the end of the day and decide who got the best frame. Loser buys dinner."

I give him my best skeptical look. "Let me guess. You're going to be the one who decides which of us that is?"

Even if this is his way of sticking me with the tab, he's covering gas, so unless he plans on ordering half the menu wherever we go, it's probably a fair deal. Not that I want to sign up for him tearing apart my work at the end of the day.

"Nah. We'll decide together. Unless you're telling me you can't be objective about your own work?" Wes shrugs, utterly unbothered. "If we don't agree, you pay for you and I pay for me. Doesn't need to be complicated." It's only when I don't immediately respond that his expression tightens. "I *can* be objective. I'm not screwing with you."

Reading Wes is more difficult than it should be. Screwing with people is his specialty, as those guys at the gas station learned the hard way not even a week ago. Then again, they definitely deserved it.

"Fine. I'm in." I move toward the fence, glad I have my ultrawide lens already on. The monster of a storm looms above us like an apocalypse, dwarfing houses dotted across the fields. It's spooky, sure, but it also creates a fantastic sense of scale. The storm spinning almost lazily above the farmhouses renders them little more than tiny dark squares popping out from the green of the grass.

At the far end of the group, I finally find Tracy and Matt. She catches my eye and jerks her head toward Wes with raised eyebrows. I'm already shaking my head when she adds a goofy thumbs-up.

To my surprise, instead of heading for Matt on Tracy's other side, Wes waves and shouts a hello, then aims straight for me. Just like the other night, we move around each other easily as we squint at our cameras to make adjustments. Except this time, when he squeezes by me to adjust his angle and his fingertips graze my back, I'm hyperaware of his touch.

Inconvenient when I'm trying to forget how good it felt to be wrapped up in his arms—when I'm trying to remind myself that just because I get so little affection in my day-to-day life, it doesn't mean habitual-flirt Wes meant a damn thing.

The first splats of rain are refreshingly cool on my bare

shoulders as the warm inflow winds continue to rush past us to power the storm. We'll have to move before the hail catches up, but for now I get low to the ground and tilt my lens up. The angle leaves only a thin strip of the field in my shot, allowing the storm to overtake the frame.

As soon as I release the shutter, a lightning bolt smashes out of the storm, close enough that a boom of thunder follows seconds later. A whoop goes up from the line of photographers along the fence, quickly followed by a chorus of *Please tell me someone got that* and various curses. Holding my breath, I quickly scroll back to check my shot. I'm almost certain my shutter was open, but daytime lightning without a tripod can be borderline impossible. With so much ambient light for the camera sensor to pick up on, getting a clean shot that isn't washed out is a tricky balance of exposure and luck.

I feel the heat of Wes at my back just before he murmurs too close to my ear, "Looks like I'm buying you dinner." And then, louder so the others will hear, "Sloane got it! Perfect CG!"

His excitement is contagious, and for a few seconds, everyone crowds around me to see the shot of crisp cloud-to-ground lightning. There's a flurry of introductions to the new faces, though Tracy manages to slip in a murmured "Looks like you're getting along?" that I pointedly ignore.

I'm so used to flying under the radar that suddenly finding myself the center of attention is a little overwhelming, in the best way possible. It's also not something I'd ever expect of Wes, the way he thrusts me into the spotlight and steps back to let me enjoy it without saying another word.

There isn't much time to linger. With the storm powered by an outflow boundary—the atmospheric line in the sand between storm-cooled air and the typical heat of the region—we travel steadily east until twilight sets in. The storm is still producing so much lightning we don't need to be that close to it in the dark, so we decide to grab some night shots while it lasts.

The storm has faded to little more than flickering flashes of lightning on the horizon by the time we pull off I-40 somewhere east of Amarillo. Wes points at the diner attached to the truck stop we pass on the way to our hotel. "Might not be gourmet, but I'm a man of my word. That place has killer waffles."

It doesn't look like much, the parking lot flooded with bright lights and the neon DINER sign half burnt-out. Tired and hungry, I shrug and turn around. Even waffles won't be enough to lure me out of my hotel room once I'm within falling-down distance of a bed and strong air-conditioning.

"Yep," Wes declares fifteen minutes later when the server drops a massive pile of whipped cream and banana slices in front of him. "Just like I remember."

He gleefully pours syrup over the whole mess, the waffles themselves barely visible under a mountain of toppings. My own selection is probably boring by his standards, a little powdered sugar, butter, and sliced strawberries sprinkled across a singular waffle.

"Where on earth is that all going?" I ask with a laugh, too tired to remember to have a filter. "You can't possibly eat that whole plate."

Wes shoves his fork into the pile and emerges with a chunk of waffle dripping with syrup and whipped cream. "Challenge accepted." He laughs at my scowl, swallowing down a bite before sawing off another. "I've got my own waffle iron at home. I could eat these things every day."

With a skeptical lift of my brow, I jab my empty fork toward his plate. "You're telling me you know how to make waffles from scratch?"

He grins. "Invite me over again. I'll prove it."

"No thanks," I say quickly, hoping my face doesn't give away just how much a part of me would enjoy having a shirtless Wes back in my kitchen. "I don't need food poisoning."

"My mom would murder me on the spot if I gave anyone food poisoning." He shakes his head, though behind his good-natured laugh, there's a flash of something deeper. "She's the one who taught me to make them. Her mom was from Belgium. Old family recipe." He leans closer, mischief dancing in his gray eyes. "Ask me very nicely, and I might be willing to tell you the secret."

Scoffing, I dive back into my waffle and try not to think about how nice it must have been to have a mom like that—or how much I've laughed over the last couple of days.

Or that Wes might not be as spoiled as I've always thought.

Later, when I'm in my room and brushing my teeth, I nearly spit toothpaste all over the bathroom mirror when I open a text to find a photo of Wes with the caption Too tall for life again. He's in the shower, the showerhead hitting just below his collarbones. The look on his face of exaggerated dismay only has me laughing harder.

With the camera off to his side, I can't see anything but a faint sprinkling of dark hair on his chest, but the water is on. Which means Wes is naked.

Sounds like a you problem but thanks for the laugh, I quickly text back before locking my phone. I don't look at the photo again. And I definitely don't feel any kind of way about Wes quoting my own words back to me.

I SWEAR I'M halfway to a coma when the knock on my door jerks me out of sleep. Not awake enough to think too hard about who the hell would be knocking this early in the morning, I stumble out of bed and yank the door open.

Grinning like a madman, Wes is barely managing to balance two cups of coffee and two packages of violently pink Peeps. Where the hell did he find those in the middle of nowhere at whatever terrible time it is?

His expression falters slightly when I grunt incoherently, and that's before his eyes dip down to my thin tank top. My hair is long, but not quite long enough to cover up the fact that I'm not wearing a bra.

Wes jerks his attention up to my face, color crawling into his cheeks. "Uh, sorry. It's ten. I figured you were up by now."

"Ten?" I twist my wrist to stare at my watch, where the tiny numbers read 10:06 a.m. "Shit! I forgot to set an alarm."

He shuffles his feet, suddenly very intent on looking anywhere but at me. "I can leave this with you while you get dressed."

My sleep-fogged brain is determined to give Wes a show. I bend over to grab a sweatshirt out of my bag, only remembering at the sound of his sharp inhale just how short my shorts actually are. He just got an eyeful of my ass.

Face burning, I yank the sweatshirt over my head and tug on the hem as though embarrassment has magical powers to summon up a few extra inches of fabric.

At least I'm not the only one blushing like a teenager.

"You might as well come in," I mumble, taking the coffee gratefully as I give myself a firm internal lecture. "You already checked the models?"

Wes takes a few tentative steps into the room and hovers by the door as it slides shut behind him. "Yeah. I don't think it's going to do anything exciting. Nothing to make it worth driving three hours in the opposite direction of where we want to be tomorrow."

"So it's a down day?" I pull up a quick mental map of anything nearby we may want to check out, but there's not much besides ranch land between us and tomorrow's target.

"Looks like. Carlsbad isn't too far from Hobbs. If we get down there early enough we might be able to catch the bats. It's been so warm this year I wouldn't be surprised if they're out."

"You want to spend your Easter driving seven hours to photograph a swarm of bats?" I grin, thankful to be on more familiar footing, and take a small sip of coffee. It's gas station brew—local shops are likely closed for the holiday—but it's useful for prying my eyes fully open. I'll think about Wes paying attention to how I take my coffee, never mind presenting it to me without being asked, later. "Sounds fun. I'm just going to need pants," I add with a sheepish grin at my bare legs.

Wes is still staring at my legs when I look up. He takes a

hasty sip of his coffee, swallows in a gulp, and then tosses me a package of Peeps. "Breakfast," he says by way of explanation.

"Radioactive marshmallow is not breakfast!"

"You don't want any part of the sandwiches they've got next door, trust me." He shakes with an exaggerated shudder, though he still won't look directly at me. His free hand fiddles with the brim of another of his hats, this one from an outdoor brand he did some work for a few years ago. "I'll just . . . meet you downstairs in a little bit, yeah?"

"I only need ten minutes."

Wes leaves with another awkward wave. I can't help staring at the door after it's fallen shut, wondering how after so many years of seeing him nothing but cool, calm, and collected, I've now managed to fluster him twice in the span of a couple of days.

Yet when I flip the light on in the bathroom and grab my toothbrush, there's no denying the color in my cheeks, or that my unbrushed and rumpled hair makes me look like I did something far more exciting than wrestle insomnia all night. Even my brown eyes have a little bit of an extra sparkle to them.

"Hormones are stupid," I tell my reflection. Because that's all this is. Some sort of weird chemical leftover from that kiss yesterday. A kiss that Wes already told me was nothing more than a favor. It's not his fault that my hormones have hopped aboard an express train to Bad Ideas Land.

I quickly brush my teeth, twist my hair into a tight braid, and yank on clothes. With a firm vow to get it together, I grab my bags—and the Peeps I may or may not attempt to eat—and head for the lobby.

Begrudgingly, I let Wes take over driving about halfway to

Hobbs. It's weird to sit in my own passenger seat, but it turns out I don't need to hold on to the door with a death grip. Maybe he's just on his best behavior driving my car, but he doesn't do anything crazier than ignore the speed limit signs like everyone else going south.

CHAPTER SEVEN

MONDAY DAWNS BLISTERING, BAKING THE ROAD AND us along with it. Wes and I are both up early, buzzing with energy ahead of what looks to be a big day. Multiple storms. Likely multiple tornadoes.

The long hours in the car yesterday after our detour to Carlsbad—the bats *were* kind enough to put on a show for us—pay off. We're in a good position, maybe an hour or two away from our target area, once things get going in the afternoon.

To kill time, we find a tiny local coffee shop that makes the most incredible iced cherry mocha I've ever gotten my hands on. I pair it with one of the largest cinnamon buns I've ever seen.

Wes shakes his head as we settle in at one of the café tables. "If I knew all it took to make you stop scowling was some decent coffee, I'd have thrown a French press at you ages ago."

I laugh the comment off and shove a bite of cinnamon roll into my mouth. It's nothing different from what he's said to me before. I'm too serious. I need to relax. Try to have more fun.

Except Wes isn't actually poking at me this time, is he? I frown into my coffee, wondering when he started to care about my mood—or if I'm just sleep-deprived and reading more into it because of that stupid kiss I need to stop thinking about. Especially when Wes licks away a trace of chocolate from the corner of his mouth.

Thankfully, once we sink into our work, I mostly forget about him. I've been ignoring my business email since my break started, but I try to still go in every week or two to clear it out. I groan when I open my inbox and see one bride has sent no less than twenty messages over the last week. The latest one is an all-caps ANSWER ME!!!!! that makes me want to throw my laptop into traffic.

"Everything okay?"

Not realizing my groan was loud enough to get Wes's attention, I wave off his concern. I'm not unloading my tale of burnt-out wedding photographer woe on him. "Just a cranky client who can't read."

"You get a lot of those?"

I shrug. "Weddings stress people out. Most women are told from the time they're toddlers that it's *the* single most important day of their life. I get why they freak out the way they do sometimes. Comes with the territory."

"Maybe you need new territory."

"Some of us don't have a trust fund, and I'm fresh out of magic wands." I take a long sip of my coffee before I say something I'll regret. Wes and I are going to be spending too much time together for me to fire back at him full tilt. "It's fine. I'm used to it."

He scowls at me across the table. "You say that like I don't have clients of my own." I must do a poor job of hiding my surprise because his frown deepens. "You really think I just sit on my ass all year, don't you?"

I shift uncomfortably. I'm aware of Wes's commercial work, but I've always assumed he got those jobs trading on his daddy's connections, not the usual grind most professional photographers go through to work their way up to high-profile clients.

Wes laughs under his breath, a humorless puff of air. "That campaign I shot last year is getting national placement. A trust fund didn't do that. I earned it. I know how to work for the things I want, Sloane."

"I'm sure your family name helps."

A muscle twitches in his jaw, his expression turning cold. "My family had nothing to do with it. Trust me, if my father had his way, I wouldn't even own a camera."

There's a depth to the undercurrent of anger in Wes's voice that makes me want to comfort him, but getting personal about his feelings—especially if his relationship with his dad is anywhere near as complicated as mine with my mom—is a step in the wrong direction. It's better for everyone if Wes stays in the tidy little box I've labeled *reckless* and *shallow*.

"Fine, but weddings are very different from commercial work," I remind him, steering the conversation away from the family minefield.

"I know." Wes lets out a short breath that's not quite a sigh. "I'm just saying you seem more and more stressed out every year. Do you even *like* shooting weddings anymore?"

I stare at him and wonder why he's pressing the issue. First he wants me to be happy, and now he's concerned about my stress levels. I didn't know Wes even paid enough attention to notice if I'm stressed out or not.

"I'm good at what I do," I say slowly.

He yanks his hat off long enough to jerk his hand through his hair and jam it back on. "That wasn't . . . Never mind."

His visible frustration leaves me feeling like an asshole for not answering. We're not having one of our drive-by insult contests on the side of the road. His question wasn't unreasonable.

"There's nothing quite like the way a couple looks at each other in that first moment of the ceremony," I say quietly. "Even when everyone is stressed out, for the most part, it all falls away for them when they finally see each other. It's a beautiful thing to witness."

It also gives me hope that maybe one day I'll meet someone who looks at me like that—but that's far too personal to tell Wes.

He gives me a long, skeptical look. He must decide I'm not worth arguing with and goes back to his own work, leaving me to mine.

It's a relief to close out of my email and switch back to photo editing. I'd much rather spend twenty minutes cleaning up yesterday's freehand lightning shot, fussing with the tiniest adjustments to shadows and highlights to make the storm's structure really pop, than answer another email.

Wes's phone buzzes over and over as the morning wears on. He ignores it at first, his eyes glued to his laptop and his leg bouncing as he works. With his Longhorns hat flipped backward and short sleeves exposing the tattoos on his forearms, he looks more like Wild Wes than ever, even if we are plunked in the middle of a coffee shop.

My attention strays to the ink. Usually we're moving around too much for me to get a good look, but today I have the time to study the designs. There's a collection of what appear to be stamp marks on the inside of one forearm. I lean closer, trying to figure out what they are, when Wes chuckles under his breath and twists his arm so the designs are more visible.

There's no point in pretending he hasn't caught me. "Passport stamps?"

He nods, already stretching out his other arm for me to inspect the tattoo there. "Seemed like a good way to commemorate my more memorable travels. Paddling the Colorado was pretty special, though, so it got its own."

The detail work is incredible. What at first appears to be the meandering path of a river curling around his arm is shaded with tiny details suggesting canyon slots, the curl of campfire smoke, a tent, and a smattering of wildflowers growing along a riverbank. My hand is halfway extended to trace the images before I snatch it back.

Wes lifts a brow. "I'm not going to bite if you touch me, Sloane."

"I wasn't going to."

We both know I'm lying, but he doesn't push the issue. I go back to my laptop. He goes back to his. At least until his phone starts ringing a few minutes later. He snatches it up, glances at the screen, and shoves it in his pocket without responding. For how outgoing he is, the move piques my curiosity instantly. "Spam?"

Wes lets out a sharp noise, not quite a laugh, not quite a scoff. "Yeah," he says, shadows lurking in his voice. "That's a good way of putting it." He closes his laptop and yawns like a bear after winter hibernation. "We should head out soon. I'm going to grab another coffee for the road. Want another one of those cherry chocolate things?"

"Sure." I start to hand him cash, but he waves me off and goes back to the counter. I don't put up a fight. I'm not about to turn down a freebie coffee. Especially not when my phone lights up with yet another text from my mom, who's been sending me links to wallpaper designs I've ignored all morning. She claims she's going to redo her powder room. Translation? She's going to buy a bunch of stuff, moan about the cost of hiring a contractor for four months, and then guilt me into doing the majority of the work.

I'll take all the chocolate I can get.

Today is going to be the real test of whether or not Wes and I can chase together. Yesterday's storms had nothing on what conditions are due to spit out today, the heat and humidity setting up a tinderbox. I want to get my shot as much as anyone else, but I'll be damned if I let him put me in a bad situation because he doesn't know when to back off.

I accept my coffee with a smile of thanks, and when we stop to top off the tank and give the windshield a good scrub an hour later, I impulsively grab a bag of the candy he's obsessed with and tuck it under my cheese sticks.

We show up at the register a tale of two personalities. There's me with my somewhat healthy snacks, while Wes is clutching two different kinds of energy drinks, three different types of candy, and a family-size bag of Doritos.

At my dubious glance, he just grins. "You'll thank me later when you're tired and want something unhealthy," he says as we head back out into the heat.

"Did you not see that massive cinnamon bun I already ate?" I stop next to the car and toss him the blue bag of candy. "But since you clearly never have enough . . ."

Wes snatches the Nerds Gummy Clusters out of the air with a surprised laugh. "You bought these for me?"

I shrug. "You bought me a coffee."

"You sure it's not that you secretly like this stuff too?" He grins, a little too pleased.

I scrunch my nose with exaggerated distaste. "Pure sugar and violently orange fake cheese? No thanks."

"Yeah, okay, so when you ask for some in an hour, I should remind you that you don't actually want them."

"You should." I glance up at his amused expression, warmth that has nothing to do with the day's heat flooding into my cheeks. "But give me some anyway."

His lips curve, eyes doing that intense thing again. "All right," Wes drawls, his attention still focused a little too much on me. "I'll give you some, but only when you ask."

Are we still talking about junk food? I swear we are.

I ask for a handful of Doritos an hour later. The salty goodness and satisfying crunch is absolutely worth the smug look on Wes's face and the orange cheese dust on my leggings.

BY THE TIME we get into range, storms are popping up on the radar left and right. We stop to decide which way to go, both silently evaluating the data as we stare at our devices. I know my vote pretty quickly but brace myself for an argument. Wes is nothing if not opinionated.

"The northern cell here"—I point on the iPad to the map—"is probably going to cut off the energy, and this one to the south is going to die." I zoom out slightly and tap on the cells popping up farther to the east. "These look like they're just going to line out, and by the time they really get going, they're going to be in the canyon. I don't think we should mess with it."

"Agree. Too hard to get a good shot."

I roll my eyes. "Yeah, and also *the canyon*. You know. Almost no roads. Easy to get trapped."

"Sure, that too." Wes flashes me a grin. "Want me to drive for a bit? I don't expect you to chauffeur me around."

I hesitate, half expecting more of an argument. I'm also not sure I want to give up control behind the wheel during a chase, but we haven't heard from my brother. We could be together for longer than either of us thought, especially since it looks like everything is shifting farther east over the coming week. There's really no point in exhausting myself by insisting on driving the entire time.

As long as Wes behaves.

"No stupid risks," I finally say, my hand on the door. "I can't afford to replace all my windows as easily as you can."

The sound he makes is a little too short to be a laugh. "Sure, Sloane. Whatever you say."

It's what I want to hear, but for some reason my stomach twists as we quickly swap seats. Wes fiddles with the seat and mirrors, adjusting everything for his longer legs with finicky precision. I'm just starting to relax about him taking this seriously when he grins, throws the car into gear, and peels off the shoulder fast enough to send gravel flying.

All my glare gets me is a laugh.

"You good to navigate?" he asks. "If you want to grab a nap—"

"I am *not* going to sleep while you're driving my car."

"Oh, c'mon, nothing happened yesterday."

"Yesterday we were road-tripping. Today we're chasing. It's different."

"I haven't died yet," Wes says a little too cheerfully.

"Not for lack of trying."

"Don't worry, darlin'." He reaches over to pat my thigh, his long fingers settling on my bare skin a little too easily. I stare down at his hand, watching his fingers flex as he squeezes. "Nothing is going to happen to you under my watch."

The flicker of interest I thought I buried back at the coffee shop roars to life, a steady pulse throbbing between my legs. This is bad. Wes isn't relationship material, and I don't do casual. No matter how well he kisses.

"Hands on the wheel, please." My attempt at stern lands somewhere around uncertain.

It's a full thirty seconds before he removes his hand, his lips curving up in a faint smile. The rest of his expression is shadowed by his sunglasses, but his fingers flex before they slowly lower to the steering wheel. Neither of us says anything at first, the silence thick with all the things we're not saying.

And then Wes grabs his phone and opens a playlist labeled "Shhh We're Hunting Tornadoes." Seconds later, AC/DC's "Thunderstruck" pours out of my speakers. When he starts singing along and I discover there's something he's definitely *not* good at, my irritation melts away.

Just to come roaring back a couple of hours later.

"I don't like the look of this, Wes. Turn around."

He doesn't take his focus off the road, or at least the amount of road visible through the downpour. The cell we're on now is crawling along, which should be a good thing for a bunch of photographers, but it's dumping inches of rain on areas that can't absorb that kind of water. We've already gone down two roads only to find them flooded out, forcing us to turn back. Anything dirt is completely out of the question, putting a dangerous limit on our escape routes.

"The storm isn't moving fast. Plenty of room to maneuver."

I refresh the radar and stare down at my iPad in frustration. "There's rotation in the middle of the rain. We could drive straight into a tornado."

"But if we drop south, we're going to lose it entirely," Wes points out. "The sun is low enough we'll probably catch a rainbow on the backside and salvage something out of this one."

I grimace, just as irritated by how the day has gone. We've watched several storms collapse before they ever got going. Thicker cloud cover has made for a cooler day than forecasted. Less heat means less instability. And while I need all the mental stability I can get, storms fall apart without atmospheric chaos to fuel them.

"You see any paved roads heading west?" Wes asks.

With my phone in one hand and the iPad in the other, I bounce between radar scans and the map. "About a mile up, but I can't tell if it's paved. We're going to get into the hail if we keep going. Turn around. It's not worth it."

"We can make it." Wes accelerates, despite the fact that we're already hurtling along far too fast for the amount of water on the road. "You watch the radar. I'll watch the road."

No sooner do the words escape his mouth than hail starts

to ping against the roof in metallic *thunks*. I jump at an especially loud crack. Thankfully the windshield doesn't break. "Neither one of us is invincible!" I shout over the rain and hail. "The roads are flooded! No stupid risks, remember? This is the definition of stupid!"

With his Wild Wes grin in place, he lets out a loud whoop when a bigger chunk of hail slams into the roof. "That one sounds like it left a dent!"

I grab hold of the doorframe and dig my nails into the trim. I can't decide who I hate more in this moment—myself for letting a madman drive or Wes for being so reckless. I don't care about the hail dents—there are plenty of them already pockmarking the paint as something of a storm chaser badge of honor—but the flooded roads are something else.

We bounce over a teeth-rattling pothole, and before I know it, we're turning left, the back tires fishtailing wildly.

Thankfully the road is paved. The hail stops after another minute, rain already slowing. Wes drops his window and leans out, breathing in the familiar scent of rain and dust and grass that lingers on the air. "See? I told you we'd be fine. Done it a million times," he says, clapping one hand on my thigh again.

I'm about to tell him to keep his hands to himself when his grip tightens sharply at the same time he slams on the brakes. Our skid stops all of ten feet from a swiftly moving river of water where the road should be. It's at least fifty feet across and deep enough to touch the bottom of the speed limit sign. Another few seconds and we'd have been swept away.

"Fuck." Wes goes pale, his mouth a thin line. "You okay?" He doesn't take his eyes off the water—or his hand off my leg where his fingers dig into my thigh. "Couldn't see it until we came over the hill."

"I'm fine." I swallow hard, fighting the rush of adrenaline spiking in my veins. "You want to listen to me about turning around now? No way we make it through that."

"No, not with how fast it's moving." Wes squeezes my thigh one more time, sending little sparks careening through my body before he moves his hand to the gear shift. His fingers tighten around it, knuckles white, and he lets out a long breath before he looks at me. "I'm sorry. You were right. I got caught up in the chase and should have listened earlier. That could have been . . . bad."

"Yeah," I agree. "It could have. Do it again and you're on the first flight back to Colorado, got it?"

My heart pounds in the seconds it takes for him to answer. It's hard to push past the people-pleasing tendencies ingrained so deeply throughout my childhood, but with Wes, I usually don't have that problem. Not that it makes putting my foot down any easier. My thoughts are already scrambling to remind me that he's not entirely at fault—the water *wasn't* visible until we crested the hill.

"That's fair," Wes replies, like I'm being perfectly reasonable. "I thought I saw another road a little ways back. You see it on the map?"

"I don't think that's a road. We'll have to go back the way we came, but the hail should have moved far enough east by now that we could double back and then try this road"—I tap on the iPad screen, then hold it out to him—"that cuts west. Might be the same situation, though, since it runs parallel to this one."

"Damn slow-moving storms," Wes mutters as he begins to turn the car around. "You're probably right. I just hate giving up."

Frustration drips from every word, his knuckles white on the steering wheel. I'm struggling to relax too. I can only hope that he's sincere when he says he hears me. That we're not going to have a repeat the next time he gets too absorbed in the adrenaline of a chase.

We backtrack, try another road, and find that one flooded too. Wes curses under his breath. We're not the only ones in this predicament. The world's worst parade follows us down another road, only for everyone to execute a fifteen-point turn when we hit another flooded area and head back to the state highway yet again.

Tracy and Matt must be stuck somewhere in the line of cars too. I get a text from her after our third attempt to find dry-ish pavement.

No one told me to pack an ark this year!!

I hold my hand out the window as Wes turns us around, again, and take a short video of the temporary river running through the fields. Flooded roads 3, me 0.

Tracy's reply comes back almost instantly. Me? Don't you mean US?? How's it going with Wes? Details!

It's not the first time she's texted me about him, but it's obvious she's not going to stop asking if I keep ignoring her. Rumors are more than likely already spreading thanks to the radar app. I hesitantly type out the truth.

It's fine. He almost drowned us, but we survived.

Good to know I'm not texting with the spirit world. It's okay, though? No detours to the airport?

Give it time.

There's no way for Wes to know what we're texting about, but when Tracy's next message pops up on my screen, I have to fight the urge to throw my phone out the window all the same.

He might surprise you if you give him a chance.

I lock my phone and shove it into my pocket. I don't need Tracy to tell me that Wes doesn't entirely match up with the impression I've been carrying around. I've already realized there's far more to him than I've given him credit for, but he's also still the guy who almost drove us into five feet of water.

While Wes drives, I keep scanning the maps, searching for a road with higher elevation that might have fared better in the torrential rain. "If you take the right up ahead, we'll go south for a few miles, but then it connects into another state highway that runs parallel to this one. If we follow that for another ten or so miles, that should get us where we need to be."

"And away from the crowd because no one wants to go south." Wes's frustration melts away far easier than mine. "Let's go catch ourselves a rainbow."

CHAPTER EIGHT

WES NAVIGATES US AROUND THE STORM, AND WE get lucky a few miles down a mostly dry dirt road. As much as I love rainbows, my attention goes straight to the thick bunches of wild daisies growing on the edge of a farmer's field.

"Gorgeous." I stare up at the sky, scanning the area to mentally line up my shots before reaching for my camera and slapping on a polarizer. Thanks to the angle of the sun and the amount of rain in the air, the twin rainbows are the brightest I've seen in years. We're on the backside of the storm, mammatus clouds hanging down as though the sky is slowly boiling high above us. And with the elevation on top of the caprock escarpment, the clouds are so close it feels like I could reach out and touch them.

Though it's beautiful, I swallow a stab of disappointment. It's too soft for what I want in terms of the contest. Not that *Nature Shots* is the only reason I'm out here, despite it living in my head rent free. I can take a beat to smell the flowers.

Or the scent of rain and mud and the occasional whiff of manure. Same thing, really.

While I beeline for the daisies, Wes sets up in the middle of the road right over the cracked yellow line that leads straight to the rainbows. I'm not sure what story he's going for other than a how-to-get-run-over guide.

I shove the thought aside to focus on my own work—not that I can actually manage to keep my mind on photography for long.

In the heat of the moment, I regretted letting Wes get behind the wheel, but now that things are calmer, I can be more objective. He enjoys needling me, but when it came down to the actual driving, I'm not sure he did anything different than I would have. Sure, I'd have given up on the whole area earlier, but he was right that the water wasn't visible until we crested the hill. And he wasn't driving any faster than the rest of us do out here.

If I ignore the moments in the rain and the small matter of our near drowning, the last forty-eight hours have been kind of nice. Wes is too reckless and it's going to catch up to him one day in ways far worse than a hefty repair bill, but there's a kindness to him that I didn't anticipate.

In all the years I've known him, we've hovered somewhere between professional colleagues and frenemies. I point out his recklessness. He makes cracks about how much I love to ruin a good time. Rinse and repeat.

He's never once looked at me the way he did in my kitchen. Or yesterday morning at the hotel.

Then again, he's never seen me in a semitransparent shirt without a bra either.

The slam of the car door breaks me abruptly out of my wandering thoughts. "Gotta water the ditch," Wes announces.

"Camera is on the back seat. If you decide to strand me here, I'd appreciate it if you at least don't trash my gear."

"Your gear is safe." I roll my eyes. "And thanks for sharing." Turning my attention back to my camera, I squat down low to get the angle I'm looking for. "If you're asking for help, the answer is no."

"Trust me"—footsteps crunch on the gravel shoulder—"there's nothing in my pants I need *help* with." I don't have to look at him to hear the cocky grin.

My red cheeks explode with heat that has nothing to do with the weather. He's baiting me again, and I am *not* falling for it.

I'm also not listening for the telltale sound of his zipper parting or the rustling of his clothes or the—

"Fuck!"

I whip around at the shouted curse, my mind already frantically rummaging through the first aid kit. Did I pack anything to deal with snake bites? Then reality cuts through my panic.

The only thing that's attacked Wes is . . . mud. A great deal of mud. The roadside ditches out here that collect runoff are both steep and several feet deep. With the recent rain, there's about a foot of water—and who knows what else—sitting at the bottom. Wes's entire left side is covered like he's a human pretzel stick that's been dipped in the world's grossest chocolate.

Laughter explodes out of me only to quickly transform into full-fledged cackles. "You fell in," I wheeze, clutching my ribs as a mud-streaked muscle twitches in his jaw. "Oh my god, you really *did* need help."

Still giggling, I lift my camera and press the shutter release, Wes's incredulous expression now committed to the memory card.

"Really?"

"Really." Just to mess with him, I lift the camera again, firing off a couple more shots before lowering it to my side. "Might be my contest entry. They *do* want a story."

A thick *splat* of mud falls to the ground when Wes tightens his hand into a fist. "Yeah, real funny, Sloane. And I'm fine, by the way. Probably going to have a giant bruise, but thanks for asking."

"*Now* you're worried? You could have had glass in your eye less than a week ago and brushed it off like nothing happened. You're fine." I shake my head and gesture toward my car. "But you're absolutely not sitting on my seats like that. I think there's a roll of paper towels in the back."

"You mean to tell me you don't know exactly what you have in that ridiculous tub of supplies?" Wes runs a hand through his hair and then swears again when he smears more mud through it. "Paper towels aren't fixing this. Fuck it."

Between one blink and the next, he rips off his T-shirt, getting even more mud in his hair in the process. He mutters something in a low rumble I don't catch, scrubbing at his face with what was the clean side of the shirt.

But he's not done yet.

Tossing the shirt onto the roof of my car, Wes kicks off his mud-covered boots next, then shoves his jeans over his hips. My mouth goes dry at the sight of so much exposed skin. Shirtless in my kitchen and clean was bad enough. Naked but for some snug boxer briefs, dirtied up, tattoos out? Vicious hunger snaps through me.

What would kissing Wes be like without an audience?

I shake my head to snap myself out of it and open the back hatch where our clean clothes are packed. I've let this dry spell go on for far too long. A few nice moments over the last two days can't override a decade of watching Wes careen from one reckless choice to another. Given his friendship with Matt, and mine with Tracy, giving in to my inconvenient attraction would only lead to awkwardness.

"You take anything else off, and I might actually leave you on the side of the road," I threaten. My own eyes call me a liar, dropping back down to the curve of his ass on such spectacular display. "I'll grab you some wipes. Just . . . stay there."

Wes tosses his arms up, flicking mud everywhere. "Where am I going like this?" He glances down his mud-streaked body, his lips flattening into a thin line. "I think I'll take two showers when we get to the hotel tonight."

"You're going to need them," I agree, fishing out the package of wipes with a grimace. I'm not sure we're getting him clean even using the entire package.

I toss it to him and busy myself with tucking my camera back into its bag. We're losing the light anyway. I assume Wes is done for the day too, and pack up his gear as well before zipping everything shut.

He's barely made a dent in the mud by the time I'm done, a small pile of wipes at his feet. "Don't suppose you've got a hose stashed somewhere?"

"Even if I did, we're short a water source." I sigh and hold my hand out. We're never getting out of here if I leave him to his own devices. "You want help?"

His eyes flash up to mine, sparking with humor and mischief. "Oh, we're back to that again, are we?"

"With the mud, Wes. Help with the mud." I scowl at his smirk, grab a few wipes, and move behind him. "Hold still."

Wes being Wes, he shimmies his hips and twists around to wink at me. "Aren't you a storm chaser? You should be used to a moving target."

I grab hold of his shoulders and turn him firmly away from me. His skin is hot, muscle flexing under my touch—and now my hands are also covered in mud. Grimacing, I use the first wipe to get the worst of it off and start scrubbing the second across his shoulder. "It's like you rolled around in it for fun."

"Definitely not. I do a lot of stupid shit, but this was far from intentional."

We work in silence for a few minutes. It's hard to focus on the task at hand and not get distracted by the ink running down his spine. What emerges from the mud isn't the seemingly random collection of numbers and letters that I originally thought—they're coordinates.

Unbearably curious which places mean enough to Wes to permanently ink them into his skin, I run the tip of my index finger over a swooping thirty-seven. He shivers and his hands still. I swear he's holding his breath, waiting to see what I do next.

Whatever seemed like a good idea at the time, my ass. These aren't random at all. How easily I believed Wes would permanently mark his body on a whim—and how easily he let me.

"Started with Mount Etna," he says, just barely audible over the wind rustling the long grasses. "It was the first photo anyone paid me for." He doesn't volunteer any of the other locations. I don't ask. It's too personal. Too much like asking to see a part of Wes that I not only never thought existed, but have no right to.

And still, I brush my thumb over a stark *N* and can't help asking, "Are you planning to add to it?"

"Maybe," he says. "If there's something worth adding."

It's whisper soft with an undercurrent that turns the conversation intimate despite the wide-open space we're in. With a hasty step back, I crumple the last wipe. "I think that's as good as it's getting. You're probably going to need to wash whatever you're putting on for the drive back too, but it's better than it was. We can look for a place with laundry."

"Sloane?" As I start to move around him, Wes curls his fingers around my wrist in a gentle hold I could easily break but don't. "Thank you," he says quietly, his thumb brushing across my skin with searing gentleness.

"Not like you were getting in my car covered in mud," I say with a forced laugh. With my thoughts already so jumbled, he's being far too serious for me to handle. "Besides, I'm hungry."

Wes doesn't let go. "I know I'm a pain in the ass. You could have left me in Colorado. You probably *should* have."

"You aren't a pain in the ass," I grumble, surprised to find it's not just people-pleaser-Sloane saying it. "Occasionally irritating, sure, but so am I."

"You do love your rules," he agrees, but it's not a criticism. Not when he says it in that warm, affectionate voice, full of humor. "Don't suppose you have a trash bag for all these wipes in your Girl Scout collection of supplies?"

WHEN WE GET back to cell service, a voicemail pops up from my brother. Wes's windows came in, but there's glass stuck in the door mechanism so it's going to be at least a couple more days.

"Not really in a rush at this point." Wes shrugs in the passenger seat, his expression lit by the harsh glare of the parking lot lights as we pull into the hotel. "Unless of course you want to get rid of me. Totally cool if you do."

I frown, something about the way he says it twisting uncomfortably. I'm not thrilled about how close my car—with us inside it—came to going for a swim, but that aside, I like having Wes around more than I expected.

"I don't want to get rid of you," I say firmly. And then, to prevent things from turning too serious, I add, "As long as you don't try to make friends with another mud pit."

He laughs and the moment passes. "Not looking to repeat that anytime soon. You mind telling your brother he can take his time? If you're okay keeping me, that is."

"We'll end up back out that way eventually," I say, ignoring the fact that it's the second time in as many minutes Wes has slipped a self-deprecating comment into the conversation. I'm not sure he even realizes how frequently he implies he's not worth keeping around.

I quickly text Eric that we're not going to be back for at

least another week. My brother replies with a string of question marks. I ignore him. It's chase season. What else would we be doing out here?

"I obviously need a shower in the worst way." Wes slings his camera bag over his shoulder and reaches for his duffel at the same time I go for mine, and there's an awkward pause before he adds, "Give me half an hour and we can grab dinner."

I nod my agreement. I may not have fallen into a ditch, but helping him clean up left me grimy too. I could use a quick shower—and a few minutes to myself.

I let out a long, slow breath once I'm in the quiet dark of my room. Leaning back against the cold of the metal door, I close my eyes and try to clear my mind of thoughts of Wes, anxiety about the contest, worry about what my brothers are or aren't doing for my mom back home, and all the other stresses piling up in the dark corners of my thoughts.

If only counting to ten actually made any of those problems disappear.

At least the shower is hot and clean, with great water pressure. Once I start to relax, it doesn't take long for my thoughts to drift back to all the little digs Wes has made over the last week at his own expense. I've always thought of him as a talented photographer too arrogant for his own good. What if I was wrong? What if it hasn't been arrogance at all?

I emerge in a cloud of steam, scrubbed clean but without any answers. Impulsively, I grab my phone and text Tracy. Matt would probably be the better choice, but he's also more likely to tell Wes.

How well do you actually know Wes?

What do you want to know? I can ask Matt.

I frown, suddenly unsure if I want to talk about my suspicions with her when she's likely to tell Matt about our conversation. If Wes *is* masking his insecurities, he has his reasons. Just something he said.

The typing bubble pops up, disappears, and then pops up again before Tracy finally sends a reply. Seems like it's going well. How long do you think you'll be chasing together?

That's the million-dollar question. I sigh, toying with my phone before I send an answer. Not sure. Just taking it one day at a time. And then, to push the conversation to a safer topic, I add, He fell in a ditch today. Always possible he finally takes himself out and solves the problem for me.

He fell in a ditch and you let him back in your car?!
Also, where are the pictures?

Only after he stripped and used an entire package of wipes to clean off most of it.

Tracy's typing bubble appears and disappears a few times before she sends back, Did you help or just enjoy the view?

The memory of skin and ink and muscle and mud pops into my mind far too easily. It was faster to help.

I bet he appreciated that.

My face burns at the implication. I hastily send back a reply to make it clear that there is absolutely no *appreciation* happening between us. And then have a small panic attack that I sent the text to the wrong person when Wes himself pops up in my notifications.

Thankfully, I *did* send the text to Tracy, but my heart rate doesn't exactly return to normal at the sight of Wes, eyes closed under a spray of water in the shower, a soft smile curving his lips. The photo cuts off halfway down his chest, but I am once again painfully aware that he's sending me naked selfies.

Finally, a Wes-sized shower! My vanquished mud monster thanks you for the hotel selection.

Despite myself, I let out a snort of laughter and set my phone aside to get dressed and absolutely not think about him in the shower. Judging from the parking lot, we're not the only chasers staying here tonight, so I throw on a clean pair of black leggings and a loose T-shirt before twisting my damp hair into a tight braid.

Ignoring the notification from Tracy that looks like nothing more than a string of laughing emojis, I carefully avoid looking at the shower selfie again and text Wes that I'm good whenever he is.

Bring your camera. I want to see those photos you took of me, he texts back. I'll be down in five.

More like he probably wants to delete them, but I already transferred copies to my portable hard drive while I was showering. Grinning to myself, I grab the camera and memory card, and take the stairs down to the lobby.

Wes strolls in a minute later, roadside mud monster replaced by snug dark-wash jeans and a fitted T-shirt that brings out the blue flecks in his eyes. His hair is still damp, and when he sinks down next to me, I'm suddenly surrounded by soap and spice and a hint of citrus. It's far more appealing than it should be.

"Feel better?" I can only hope he doesn't hear the strain in my voice as much as I do.

"You have no idea." He turns toward me with a grimace. "That mud was in places it had no business being."

"Guess you'll have to be more careful next time," I tell him while resisting the mental image of all that bare skin. "You good with just walking to the place across the parking lot? Not like there's many choices."

Wes pushes to his feet and holds a hand out to help me off the small couch. It's not like I need help standing, but I let him tug me up anyway.

The temporary coolness left behind in the wake of the storm has given way to a sultry night. Hot, sticky air presses in around us as we cross to the local steakhouse, which is delightfully air-conditioned.

Inside, it's no surprise that Wes's entrance attracts attention, not only from the female hostess and servers, but also the dozen or so chasers. The more surprising part is that he doesn't seem interested in holding court, offering little more than smiles and a few generically friendly words to anyone who calls out to him as we're led to our table.

It's only when he eases into the booth across from me that I notice how stiffly he's moving. "Hey, you all right?"

His grimace quickly transforms into an easygoing grin I'm beginning to think is his go-to expression to hide behind. "Nothing a margarita won't fix."

"Wes."

There's a long pause where he stares at me, expression unreadable, before the smile slips. "I came down hard when I fell. Nasty bruise, but nothing to be done about it. I'll ice it when I get back to my room." He laughs, though this time I think it's genuine when he raises a brow at me. "Hopefully that's the end of my injuries this season," he says, gesturing to the barely formed scabs on his face.

"It better be."

Wes studies me, his head tipping slightly to the side before the grin is back. "I'm so touched that you care."

"Losing a day of chasing to find an urgent care is not on the agenda." I'm pretty sure he knows I'm lying.

The server interrupts long enough to take our order. When Wes opts for a watermelon margarita, I shrug and order one too. It's not the drink I'd have picked for him, but there's something weirdly attractive about a guy who looks like he could bench press me getting a fruity drink and not giving a shit.

To distract myself, I grab my camera and scroll back to the beginning of the day's shots. "You wanted to see those photos?" I ask with a faux-innocent flutter of my eyelashes.

He snorts out a laugh and curls his long fingers around the camera one-handed. We fall silent, him scrolling through my photos, me checking my email and sending another round of out-of-office reminders.

I look up at his muttered curse. "I knew it was bad," he muses, shaking his head at himself, "but damn. You mind sending me these? My mom will get a kick out of them."

My mom would use a photo like that as a launchpad for a

tirade. It must be nice that he has a good relationship with his, though I can't help noticing that the only times Wes has said anything positive about his family, it's been about his mom. The only mention he made of his father was laced with hurt and anger.

Not that this is the time or place to get into family skeletons.

"Oh, I was going to send them to the group chat later." I widen my eyes with false innocence. "You can download them from there."

I expect him to be annoyed. Wes just laughs before he agrees, "Yeah, that works." Then he turns the camera around, and though I'm expecting it to still be on the mud shots, he's got one of the daisy photos pulled up. It's framed to give the illusion of the flowers sitting at the base of the rainbow where a pot of gold should be. "You have a great eye. This is really beautiful."

I shrug, shutting my camera off and carefully putting it down on the seat next to me before reaching for my drink. "It's not bad, but it's not good enough for the contest."

"Give yourself more credit. I know we talk shit, but you're talented, Sloane."

The dangerously soft tone of his voice has me fidgeting in my seat. "I'm not the one with my stuff already published by *Nature Shots*," I say, hoping to deflect the conversation away from me.

"Not yet," Wes says firmly. His eyes lock on mine and hold me in place with an intense stare. "You could win this cover contest just as easily as I could."

It's nothing I haven't told myself, but coming from him,

the praise sits awkwardly in my stomach. "Or they just invited me, Tracy, and a couple other female photographers so the optics weren't overtly sexist."

A muscle twitches in his jaw, but before Wes can say whatever is about to come out of his mouth, I flash a tight smile. "I'm going to run to the bathroom. Watch my camera?"

"Yeah, of course," he says, the frustration lingering in his voice at odds with the easy words.

A splash of cold water on my face helps. The three guys standing in my way when I head back toward the table, not so much.

"Hey, can I get by?"

They're somewhere around my age, maybe a year or two older. One gives me a not-at-all subtle up and down. "You're the chick with Talbot this season?"

"Wes is chasing with me for now." I'm sure the distinction is lost on him, but it makes me feel a little better. I start to slide around them, but then another one steps into my path.

"I wouldn't let my girl out of the house in leggings like that. Surprised Talbot is okay with it."

I don't bother explaining that Wes has absolutely no say over my wardrobe or that we're not even together in the way this asshole is implying. It won't do any good. There's only one language a guy like this understands.

"Your wife must not like leggings," I say with a shrug.

He scoffs. "I'm not married."

I turn my voice syrupy sweet. "I can't imagine why that is."

He starts to sputter, anger darkening his expression. I've surprised him enough that I manage to dart around the three of them and slide back into the booth. Wes raises one brow and nods toward the group. They look away as soon as they realize he's staring.

"What did they say to you?"

"Nothing important." I take a long sip of my margarita to stall for time. More collected, I manage a smile that must look genuine enough for him to back off. "They're fans of yours. I told them you were in a bad mood tonight so they'd leave us alone."

Doubt etched into the line between his brows, Wes looks at me for a long time without saying a word.

CHAPTER NINE

THE ACTIVE WEATHER PATTERN BLURS ONE DAY INTO the next over the following two weeks. Wake up in Kansas, go to bed in Texas, drive north to Oklahoma, snatch a few hours of sleep, and then a mad dash back south into New Mexico before a long race to Nebraska. Aside from my mother's extremely passive-aggressive texts—You can call me sometime so I know you're not dead in a ditch—I don't hear from my family, which I'm counting as a win.

I'm also much too busy obsessing over the weird shift between me and Wes to linger long on anything else.

Some things are exactly the same as every other year. I'm not exactly surprised when he changes the name of my playlist to "Sloane Michaels and the Horrible, Awful, No-Good Playlist" while I'm inside a gas station—he's complained more than once about the sheer chaos of multiple genres all randomly shoved together without any order—nor is it a shock that he mocks my bad aim when we're killing an hour tossing pebbles at a fence post.

The nightly report on each hotel's shower height, complete with photographic evidence, is decidedly new. And there are the little moments where he keeps surprising me with unexpected kindness. Both toward me—I have been well supplied with coffee—but also to complete strangers.

Yesterday's lunch was yet another foray into the gas station / convenience store / taqueria that has a stranglehold on this part of the country. It's always a gamble ordering tacos from a gas station, but most of the time we luck out. What I *didn't* expect was that when the cashier struggled with her English, Wes effortlessly dropped into Spanish with a kind smile.

As surprised as I am to discover he speaks Spanish, the fact that he likes to mock Mother Nature like a kid slinging playground taunts isn't much of a shock at all.

"What the hell are you doing?" I demand, certain I must not have heard him right.

Wes ignores me and shouts at the sky, "Get it together! My grandma is more impressive!"

"Are you seriously *taunting* the weather?" I glance around, checking for an audience. Some chase days, it's us and our fifty closest friends in a conga line from hell crowding country roads. Today is one of the rare days we've claimed a spot without another soul in sight.

"You call that thunder?" he continues like I haven't said a word, the low rumble echoing in my chest as it rolls across the open fields. "Weak! Do better!"

I have to bite my lip to suppress a smile and double check

that my camera is level while Wes's taunts turn more and more ridiculous as he goes. One minute he's calling it a *witty bitty baby storm* and the next he's telling it to be like Nike and *just do it*.

When I finally lose my composure and let out a laugh, he grins over his shoulder. "I knew fun Sloane had to be in there somewhere."

I shake my head, refusing to participate in this madness. "Whether or not that storm spits out a tornado is a matter of science, not two unhinged storm chasers yelling nonsense at the sky."

"So far I'm the only one doing any yelling." He takes off his sunglasses to give me a pointed look. "Don't knock it until you try it."

"I don't need to try it. You've got it covered."

"Humor me." Wes winks, then turns back to the storm and shouts, "Get your shit together or else Sloane is going to yell at you!"

"Get your shit together or a grown man is going to keep making an ass of himself," I say half-heartedly without bothering to raise my voice. "Satisfied?"

"Not even remotely." He folds his arms across his chest, tugging the thin T-shirt tight against his shoulders. "No one is out here but us. We already know you don't care what I think."

There's that undercurrent to his words again that tightens my chest. I ignore it. Developing feelings for Wes is about as smart as driving a convertible into a hailstorm.

"It's still ridiculous!"

"And?" Wes gestures toward the storm, where the cloud

base is starting to ever so slightly lower. "What's wrong with being ridiculous once in a while?"

"Some of us don't have time for nonsense," I snap, our good-natured bickering taking on a sharper edge that I don't want but can't seem to stop.

Feet planted and arms folded across his chest, Wes doesn't back down. "No one is stopping you right now but yourself."

I open my mouth to protest but nothing comes out. I don't have a good argument for that—because he's right. I'm so used to being the responsible one, the one who at least *appears* to have it together, that the thought of intentionally doing something as silly as taunting a supercell goes against my wiring.

"Here." Wes takes off his Longhorns hat and plunks it onto my head. He takes more time than he probably needs adjusting the fit so it doesn't blow off my smaller head. He's close enough that the scent of his soap surrounds me despite the wind whipping across the fields. When he tucks my hair carefully under the brim, I get the sense he's lingering.

Just before he lets go, his eyes catch mine. Something hungry and dark stares back.

Wes looks away toward the storm, breaking the illusion and replacing his sunglasses. "Pretend you're me," he says simply. "Be an idiot for a few minutes."

My chest tightens at the implied insult to himself. "You're not an idiot."

His playful smirk remains firmly fixed in place. "Have some fun, Sloane."

Now I have to do this, if for no other reason than to prove that I can. Squeezing my eyes shut, I tip my head back and yell, "I could crawl across the interstate faster than you!"

Wes lets out a loud whoop. I pop my eyes open just in time for his sweaty arm to land on my shoulders before he squeezes me into his side. “Yeah, that’s the spirit!”

“I hope you’re happy,” I grumble. I should push him away, but despite the heat of the day, I don’t. Enjoying the temporary feeling of being with someone who wants to have silly, harmless fun with me doesn’t have to mean anything. Even if he has to bully me into it.

“I am.” Wes squeezes my shoulder and pulls me even closer. I glance up, caught off guard by the affectionate note in his words. We’re so close that if I tipped my head back just a little and he leaned in, we’d be kissing.

Which is not something I thought Wes was interested in—but the look on his face is far more than friendly.

At least until he shakes his head and lets go to bring his camera back up and point it at the storm. “It worked!”

The small funnel cloud wobbling out of the storm is a consequence of atmospheric conditions and updrafts, but I’m not about to argue. Not when I’m starting to wonder if that gas station kiss was more than the simple favor Wes claimed.

Especially when I try to give the Longhorns hat back. A hat I’ve seen him wearing for years. That suspicious softness back in his voice, Wes says, “Looks better on you. Brings out the amber in your eyes.”

He slides behind the wheel before I can do more than gape like a fish out of water. A brunette with brown eyes, I rarely get compliments like that. Lifting my hand to touch the brim of the hat, I allow myself a small, pleased smile before hurrying to the car.

The storm collapses without producing a tornado, and then we're on to the next, back in the car and racing down the highway off a tip from one of Wes's friends, who is on the other storm in the area. We also get a couple of texts from Matt, confirming that the reason we had this one all to ourselves is that we picked wrong. Frustrating, but it's all part of the chase.

My mom starts texting again as we're heading for the new storm. I shouldn't even open the message, but since I'm gunning for idiot of the year, I make the mistake of reading it. "For fuck's sake," I mutter as another message comes in before I've even finished the first.

"Everything okay?"

Maybe it's Wes forcing me to relax, or maybe it's wearing his hat on my head, but I answer honestly. "My mom is freaking out over a dead battery."

He takes his eyes off the road long enough to throw me a puzzled glance. "We talking a car battery?"

I let out a humorless laugh and shake my head. "Of course not. That would be worth freaking out over, not that I could do anything about it from six hundred miles away. She's got one of those keypad locks on her front door, but there's a key slot for exactly this reason. She can just use a key for now."

"So why is she texting you?"

"Hell if I know," I mutter, already texting my brothers. Before either of them answers, my mom calls. With only ten minutes before we're in range of the next storm, I don't want to get back in the car to two dozen missed calls, so I begrudgingly answer.

"I already texted Eric and Sam to see if one of them can

stop by to replace the batteries," I say by way of greeting. "And I'm probably going to lose service soon, so I can't talk long."

"Hi, Sloane," my mother replies, sweet as a poisoned berry. "So nice to hear your voice."

"What happened to the reminder I set on your phone to replace the batteries every six months?" I learned a long time ago that trying to soothe her imagined slights only leads to more trouble.

"It was very annoying. I got rid of it."

I tighten my grip on my phone so I don't throw it out the window. "Littering is bad," I mutter under my breath, which gets me a strange look from Wes and an irritated "Speak up, Sloane!" from my mom.

"I'm in Nebraska. I'll send you a link to a YouTube video that walks you through it." Again. "The mini screwdriver is in the top drawer in the kitchen next to the stove unless you moved it after the last time."

"I can see I'm bothering you. I'll just have to call a locksmith."

I pinch the bridge of my nose, fighting for calm. "A locksmith is going to charge you several hundred dollars. This will take less than five minutes. I promise you can handle it."

"I'll invite Henry over for dinner. He'll take care of it."

Henry is the owner of the local hardware store and has been in love with my mother for the last decade. Naturally, since he's a nice man with a steady job and a solid head on his shoulders, Mom wants nothing to do with him. Except when she needs something she can't guilt me into doing. I don't know how he hasn't caught on yet.

"Mom, seriously, you don't need anyone else to do this for you. It's easy." I glance down at the iPad in my lap, refresh the radar, and say firmly, "Look, I've got to go. Eric or Sam will stop by if they can. Use your key until then."

She sniffs a goodbye and hangs up. I let my head fall back into the seat, silently count to ten, and hope my voice is approaching normal when I say, "Storm looks like it's falling apart."

Wes doesn't say anything right away, and when I glance over, his eyes dart from me to the road and back again. "You could try ignoring her," he says. "Works great with my dad."

"Is he also completely helpless?"

"Something like that." There's a beat of silence, heavy with an understanding that passes between us. Wes lifts his hand off the steering wheel like he's going to reach for me, only to replace it a couple of seconds later. "Matt texted again while you were talking to your mom. It's definitely collapsing."

I wonder if he's talking about the storm or me.

OUR AFTERNOON ENDS in disappointment and another long drive to get us in position for the storms the following day. Frustrated and jittery, my thoughts are a tangle of Wes, the cover contest, and the steadily ticking clock on time away from my responsibilities.

The nightly shower report doesn't help. I have to do some light gymnastics to get under the spray in this hotel, which means it hits Wes at roughly nipple level. Bare-chested and wet Wes is not an image I need in my head when I'm about to crawl in bed, his hat not-so-innocently sitting on the nightstand.

I'm asleep for maybe twenty minutes before I jolt awake, the whole building vibrating. It doesn't last long, but in my half-asleep delirium I grab my phone to check if there was just an earthquake in freaking Nebraska.

Instead there's a text from Wes. I think we just found out why this was the only place in town with rooms and it's not the oompa-loompa-sized shower.

Grimacing, I glance toward the shade-covered window. We *are* awfully close to the road, but it's one in the morning. I slip out of bed to peek around the shade, and sure enough, there's a semitruck in the distance. As I watch, another approaches. The vibration of its engine isn't quite earthquake level—thanks half-asleep brain for that one—but it's more than a little noticeable.

Who decided to build a hotel fifty feet from the highway?

I send the text and throw myself back onto the bed with a huff. They can't possibly drive by all night. This is probably just the last couple of drivers finishing up their routes.

That we're nowhere near any kind of logistics hub is a fact I choose to ignore. At least until I'm woken up again forty minutes later. And again twenty minutes after that. And again an hour later.

I finally give up and put on an audiobook, hoping that maybe I'll fall asleep with voices to distract me. It doesn't work. Just after dawn, I text Wes to see if he's awake.

Not sure I ever slept.

Me neither. Want to get out of here and find breakfast?

Fuck yes.

My eyes might be open, but I'm not nearly awake enough to remember my phone has a nasty habit of auto-playing whatever I listened to last when I plug it into the car. Since Wes and I have been together it hasn't been a problem. I've been too tired to do much beyond shower and go directly to sleep once we get to the hotel every night.

Except last night. When I listened to an audiobook.

"When he moans against my pussy, his tongue—"

I whip the power cord out so fast I nearly catch myself in the eye with it. At some point, I'm going to have to look at Wes, but maybe my face will just light the car on fire and take care of that problem.

"Sorry, that was, I was . . . audiobook." I quickly open my playlist and stab the screen before I plug the phone back in. Thankfully all that comes out of the speakers this time is Florence + the Machine.

Wes shifts in his seat. I wait for him to make a joke, but when I finally find my courage somewhere under the floor mats, he's staring at me with curiosity and a gleam of something far more dangerous.

His eyes drop down to my lap, heat boiling in their gray depths. "Don't turn it off on my account." I swear his voice is a full octave lower.

"All good," I squeak before hastily turning over the ignition and throwing the car into reverse. "I'm really hungry. Are you hungry? I'd kill for some coffee. Maybe some waffles. Or pancakes. I never really can choose between the two, but I know how much you like waffles."

Wes's rumbly laugh sounds like sex in the tight confines of my car after my phone's little stunt. "Breathe, Sloane," he murmurs. "Don't worry about it. There's far worse in my browser history."

Great, now I'm too busy wondering what turns Wes on to form a coherent reply. I don't do much better at breakfast, and when I make an excuse about being too tired to function, there's a glint of humor in his eyes when he says, "Me too."

BY THAT AFTERNOON, I've almost convinced myself that anything I thought I heard in Wes's voice following what will forever be thought of as *the audiobook incident* was purely a product of an overactive imagination, too little sleep, and embarrassment.

So when I ask him to get my sweatshirt from my bag while I'm driving, and he produces a bright pink bra in place of my well-worn Rocky Mountain National Park hoodie, I tell myself it's just typical Wes nonsense. I need to stop imagining zebras where there are only horses.

"Put that back!" I all but shout, pointing sharply over my shoulder. "You really are five sometimes, you know that?"

Wes doesn't listen. With my bra dangling off his finger, he waggles his eyebrows and doesn't bother hiding his interest. "I didn't take you for the hot-pink type," he says, completely ignoring my protest. "What other surprises are you hiding?"

"Wouldn't you like to know?" I take advantage of a stretch of straight road to snatch my bra back and stuff it into the driver's door with a scowl.

When Wes reaches into the back seat again, I swear he mutters *You have no idea* under his breath. But that must not be right, because in the next breath he says, "Uh, so, bad news. I think your shampoo or something is leaking." He holds up my sweatshirt, now featuring a giant wet spot in the middle and the overwhelming scent of artificial coconut.

"Shit." I groan, sneaking a glance into the back seat, but I can't take my eyes off the road long enough to figure it out. "Has anything started to fire up or do we have time to stop?"

Wes taps the iPad resting in his lap and shakes his head. "Absolutely nothing. Looking more and more like a bust."

It's not what I want to hear two weeks into my far-too-short chasing window. I've grabbed some good photos, but nothing impressive enough to land me on the cover of *Nature Shots*. If I'm going to pull off what I have in mind, I need big, towering supercells and the right foreground. So far the only storm that gave me that is the one that took out Wes's windows, but I don't love my shots.

At least the less-than-ideal forecast means there's plenty of time to pull over. Sure enough, my shampoo cap came loose, leaving a goopy mess at the bottom of my bag and damp spots on most of my clothes. It should all wash out without staining, which is good, but I don't have another sweatshirt and I'm cold.

I'm also aware that I *shouldn't* be in this heat.

Wes frowns when I shiver. "You're that cold?"

"It's fine," I assure him. Hopefully he doesn't notice the goosebumps on my skin. The inability to regulate my body temperature is a sure sign that a migraine, likely triggered by lack of sleep, is on the way.

But I'm not giving up even a mediocre chase day to hide away in a hotel room. Sometimes the meteorologists get it right. Sometimes a day with an unimpressive forecast spits out picture-perfect storms. For all I know, today is the day I get my contest shot.

If I'm lucky, I'll get it before the slight ache behind my eyes develops into a thousand little daggers stabbing my skull.

"You want me to drive for a bit?" Wes asks a little too casually, still watching me with unwavering focus. "You've driven most of the last couple of days."

Closing my eyes against the bright sunlight might help stave off the worst of the migraine a little longer, so I agree and start to move to the passenger seat. I'm not expecting Wes to drop an enormous sweatshirt on my lap when he slides behind the wheel.

His spiced-citrus scent on the fabric in my lap is almost too strong with my brain going haywire, but I try not to overthink it and pull the hoodie over my head. I'm tall, but he's both taller and broader than me, leaving me swimming in soft cotton. Not that I'm complaining. It's far cozier than mine, even without the shampoo.

I let out a happy little sigh, warmth enveloping me while Wes pulls back onto the road.

"Better?"

The migraine must be getting to me already. I swear there's a rasp in his voice.

"Yeah, thanks." I relax into the seat and hit the button to activate the seat heater. "I'm just going to close my eyes for a little bit."

"You sure you're okay?"

"Of course. Just tired." I fake a yawn and turn my head away from Wes, hoping he doesn't notice that I'm wide-awake the entire time.

CHAPTER TEN

I'M STILL BURROWED IN HIS SWEATSHIRT WHEN WES parks halfway down a dirt road, a small supercell starting to come together a couple miles across the endless stretch of fields to our right. The pain behind my eyes is worse, but on the plus side, if my head explodes, I won't have to decide what to do about my inconveniently growing attraction to him.

"You're awfully pale." He frowns and raises his hand like he's going to touch me before dropping it to his thigh abruptly. "You sure you're up for this?"

"Of course." I summon up a smile and breathe carefully through my nose. We've only got a couple of hours of semi-decent conditions today. I can make it that long. "But if you try to make me yell at the sky again, I reserve the right to leave you here."

My joke doesn't land. Wes doesn't take his attention off me, his frown deepening. "It's eighty degrees. You shouldn't be cold."

“I’m fine,” I insist, reaching for the door handle. And yeah, maybe it takes me a minute to get my feet under me when a little bit of sunshine sends the same signal to my stomach as a roller-coaster drop, but I don’t puke. That’s something.

Wes comes around to my side of the car and stands with his hands braced on either side of my shoulders. It effectively traps me in place. If I wasn’t worried about possibly throwing up on his shoes, his intense focus on me might even be sexy.

“You’re not fine.” There isn’t a shred of doubt in his voice. “Tell me what’s going on with you. You know better than anyone how dangerous it is to be out here if you’re not at one hundred percent.”

“Says the man who takes stupid risks all the time.”

Wes doesn’t budge. “Not with you.”

I squint behind my sunglasses, the brightness of the day not helping the snowballing pain. The cool darkness of a hotel room beckons, but I grit my teeth and try to ignore it. No one knows if *Nature Shots* will host another contest like this, but even if they do, will I be invited back if the image I submit is just okay?

Unlikely.

Pain shortens my temper. “So you’re allowed to take risks but I’m not?” I snap, shifting my weight to duck under his arm.

Wes effortlessly blocks me, his chest almost touching mine. “Not without telling me what has you looking like you’re about to pass out,” he demands, searching my face for an explanation.

“Migraine. Nothing life-threatening. You can stop with this caveman thing now.”

"My mom gets migraines," he says, low and firm. "When she gets the look on her face you've got right now, she stays in bed for two days. You shouldn't be out here, Sloane."

I glare over his shoulder, watching the storm spin almost lazily. I can already tell this particular storm isn't going to do much. The winds are too light for it to be sucking in energy. The forecast was never great. The only other system that might produce anything is way the hell up in South Dakota.

"We're already here. Let's just shoot this storm and then you can lock me up, okay?"

"I'm not trying to lock you up," Wes replies, frustration creeping in. "I'm trying to help."

Sinking my teeth into my bottom lip, I close my eyes and focus on slow, even breaths. I'm already having trouble keeping my eyes fully open, which doesn't bode well for taking any kind of decent photo.

I want to shove Wes away. I want to grab my camera and march out into the field and photograph the shit out of this storm. Not hide in bed because my body decided to have a fit.

But it doesn't really matter what I want when my skull is being held together by red-hot barbed wire.

"Fine." I sag against the car as defeat sours my mood. "You win. But we need to be in Kansas tomorrow, so let's at least do the drive this afternoon."

"That's a six-hour drive."

"Yes, thank you, I can read a map too."

Wes stares down at me like he wants to toss me over his shoulder, frustration hardening his jaw, but all he does is let out a long sigh. "We will *try* to get up to Kansas, but if this gets worse, we're stopping."

"Not a lot of hotels out here."

"There are enough."

We glare at each other, tension ratcheting up. I've worked through countless migraines, and even when I've accepted defeat and slunk into bed to sleep it off, it's always been something I've done alone, even as a kid. I don't need Wes to fuss over me. He didn't come out here to while away the afternoon in a hotel room.

"Why are you being so pushy about this?"

"Why didn't you leave me on the side of the road?" he counters without hesitation.

We're so close we're breathing the same air, the flecks of blue in his gray eyes bright in the sunlight. If either of us so much as shifted our weight, our lips would touch. His gaze drops to my mouth, and for a second I think he's going to kiss me. I *want* him to kiss me. It would be a great distraction from the increasingly sharp pain building behind my eyes.

Wes clears his throat and backs off, scrubbing a palm over his face and staring out at the field with his back to me. "If you really want to stay, I'm not going to force you to do anything," he says, his voice nearly lost on the wind. "But I really think you should take the day off."

"But the contest—"

"Will be there tomorrow." He turns back to me with worry tightening his mouth. "You and I both know that this storm"—he jerks his thumb over his shoulder—"isn't a *Nature Shots* cover in the making."

I swallow hard, a fresh wave of nausea rising as the wind shifts and the acrid scent of manure stings my nose. As much as I don't want him to be, Wes is right. "Okay."

"Okay?"

I nod slowly, closing my eyes and trying to breathe through my mouth. "Yeah. I'd like to try to get at least a couple of hours north, but it's getting worse."

Wes guides me back into the car with gentle hands. "Do you have meds with you?"

"Yeah. Top pouch of my camera bag." They make me tired and loopy, otherwise I would have already taken them, but there's no real point now in pretending I'm going to be getting anything done today.

He grabs the plastic bag with my prescription meds, hands me a fresh bottle of water, and watches with a furrowed brow as I swallow.

We make it two hours before I'm throwing up on the side of the road, just barely holding it in until the car comes to a complete stop. This time, when Wes says we're done, I don't argue.

WES BOOKS US two rooms at the closest hotel he can find while I brush my teeth with bottled water on the side of the road and try not to die of embarrassment. "You can just drop me off and go without me," I croak, my voice hoarse. "This doesn't have to completely ruin your day too."

"My day isn't ruined." He leans around me, opens the passenger door, and nods toward the car. "Hotel is twenty minutes out. Almost there."

The meds aren't exactly working, but they *are* making me

tired. I must fall asleep, because the next thing I know, Wes is extracting me from my seat belt. "I can do it," I protest despite my clumsy fingers. He backs off—at least until I go for my bags.

"I'll come back out for them." He slips an arm around my waist and tugs me into his side. "Let's get you out of the sun."

I want to argue. I have plenty of practice at fighting through migraines when I need to. But his embrace feels good, the heat of him bleeding through our clothes as we walk-shuffle into the cool interior of the lobby.

I sink gratefully onto one of the small couches and close my eyes while he goes to check us in. There must be a pool nearby, the high-pitched shrieking laughter of kids carrying through the lobby and making me wince. I'm still focusing on taking long, deep breaths when Wes returns.

"C'mon, darlin'," he says softly, tucking a room key envelope into his back pocket. "Is there anything I can get you?"

I shake my head and instantly regret it when my vision goes dark around the edges. It takes all my effort to hold it together long enough to get into the elevator, up two floors, and down the hall to my room.

Moaning with relief at the blessed darkness, I stagger toward the bed. I'm dimly aware of Wes tugging off my shoes and putting the room key down on the nightstand. He murmurs something about bags, the car keys jingling in his hand, and then I hear footsteps and the *snick* of the door closing.

What feels like moments later, I blink awake and squint into the semidarkness. A Wes-shaped shadow comes into focus near the window. "Go back to sleep," he says quietly, right before doing something that sounds like ripping tape.

I sit up gingerly and blink in the dim room. The meds must finally be doing something, because I can almost open my eyes fully despite the throbbing pain. "What room are you in?"

"Not ready yet. I'll hang out downstairs for a bit after I finish this."

I frown at the mention of the uncomfortable couch in the lobby. Wes has done so much for me today that it doesn't feel right to banish him to concrete furniture. "If you don't mind the dark you can just stay here." I watch as he rips off another long piece of tape and then presses the curtain to the wall, covering the light gaps to make the room even darker. "Where did you find tape?"

"Hardware store. It's painter's tape, so it will come right off."

I can't blame the migraine for the way my throat goes tight. No one has ever gone out of their way like this for me. Most of the time when I've admitted to having a migraine, the men I've dated have all but rolled their eyes and told me to take some ibuprofen.

Wes finishes taping off the curtains. It's blessedly dark in the room now, just enough ambient light from the various LEDs on electronics and the cracked bathroom door to illuminate the worry creasing his brow. He sits down on the edge of the mattress and sets the tape next to my room key. "You might feel better without the braid."

I start to reach for the elastic, but he bats my hand away with a light touch and unravels my hair before running his fingers through the dusty strands. A sigh escapes when he does it again. "That feels nice," I mumble into the pillow. I don't care that I shouldn't be letting him get this close when I feel too awful to keep him at arm's length. It's too good to stop him.

"You sure you don't want me to let you sleep? They said it could be another hour or two before my room is ready."

I want Wes to stay right where he is, running his fingers through my hair in soothing strokes, but I can't make myself ask for it. Not with words, anyway. When he starts to pull his hand away, I wrap my fingers around his wrist and tug his hand back toward my head.

"Guess I'm staying, then." His soft laugh is laced with what I swear is affection. "Here, this will be more comfortable."

Wes kicks off his shoes and climbs onto the bed next to me before tugging my head onto his lap, my hair fanned out over his thighs. The king-size bed gives us plenty of room for the awkward position, but I forget all about that when he starts to gently knead the rigid muscles along the back of my neck and shoulders.

"Does your neck usually lock up like this?"

"Sometimes. This is a bad one," I whisper into his leg, curling closer. My eyelids are heavy, dragging me down as he delicately works the tension out of my neck. It feels so good that I have to bite back a sigh.

"Anything else I can do?"

"Just keep doing what you're doing." I relax into him despite distant alarm. The voice in the back of my head protests against Wes witnessing me like this—a lump of a human whose own brain launches attacks against her—but I can't bring myself to push him away. Not when he's expertly loosening the muscles in my neck. Not when it feels so good to not have to do every last little thing for myself for once.

Even if I'm all too aware that the next time this happens, when I'm alone again, it will be that much harder.

But I'm still wrapped in Wes's giant hoodie, finally warm, and too tired to do what I should. With the comforting weight of his arm on my shoulders, I let the beckoning blackness have me.

CHAPTER ELEVEN

THE NEXT TIME I WAKE UP, THE FIRST THING I SEE IS A collection of ginger ale, Gatorade, and crackers on the nightstand next to my half-empty bottle of water. Migraine hangovers aren't so different from the normal kind, except you don't get to have any of the fun the night before to earn it.

Groaning as I start to push myself onto my elbow, I'm not expecting the warm touch on my back. "Easy," Wes murmurs, his arm sliding under my shoulders to help me up.

The pain is thankfully almost gone, reduced to a dull ache, but it's too nice to be fussed over to stop him. "What time is it?"

"Almost nine p.m." He brushes a tangled strand of hair back from my face, the touch lingering. "How do you feel?"

"Like I desperately need a shower." I take a tentative sip of ginger ale, and when my stomach doesn't revolt, swallow a bit more. "I haven't looked. Is this one Wes-approved?"

He laughs softly, something like affection lingering in his expression, as if he couldn't be more pleased at the private joke. "Yeah, it's a good one."

I fight the urge to lean into his touch. There aren't many people who know me well enough to share an inside joke. It's probably the meds turning me sentimental, but it's awfully nice to laugh together.

"Have you been here this whole time?" I ask to distract myself from the growing intimacy of the moment.

"Mostly." Wes shrugs and closes his laptop, letting it rest on his legs. "I didn't want to wake you up."

He says it simply, no trace of irritation or annoyance lurking in the words. In fact, if anything, he sounds *pleased*. But he's also plainly left the room at some point, his jeans swapped out for black sweats, and then there's the assortment of drinks on the nightstand that definitely weren't there when I fell asleep.

None of which woke me up, so why did he come back?

"I wasn't sure if you'd be hungry. There's a few more snacks, or I can run out to pick something up if you want to grab that shower. Pretty sure our choices are going to be Subway or pizza, but it beats gas station snacks."

"You don't mind?"

"Not even a little." Wes already has his phone in his hand when he asks, "What's going to be easier on your stomach? Sandwich or pizza?"

"Sandwich."

"Mind texting me what you want? I'll take my time so you don't have to rush your shower."

As much as I tell myself I'm doing just fine on my own, there have been countless times when I've lain on my couch, miserable and alone, wishing that someone would care enough to do exactly what Wes is doing. The nagging thought that I've misjudged him, that his kindness has always been there under the pranks and bravado, is steadily growing louder.

After he heads out to pick up our sandwiches I slowly drag myself out of bed. Getting into the shower takes effort, but once I'm under the spray, the hot water soothes the lingering aches and queasiness. I stand under the water for so long I'm still in there when Wes's muffled *Just letting you know I'm back* comes through the door.

Not giving myself a chance to overthink it, I tug his sweatshirt back on over a clean shirt and shorts after drying off and giving my hair a half-ass blow-dry so it's not dripping.

Wes is propped up against the headboard when I emerge, scrolling on his phone with the bag of sandwiches waiting at his side. I settle in next to him, carefully unwrap the paper to keep crumbs from exploding everywhere, and take a tentative bite to make sure my stomach isn't about to revolt.

"Good?" he asks as he unwraps his own dinner.

"Yeah. I'm hungrier than I thought." I take another bite and chew slowly, a mixture of discomfort and gratitude making it hard to find the right thing to say. It's a good weird to be fussed over this much, but it's still a little strange. "Thank you," I eventually get out. "For taking care of me, I mean. You didn't have to do all this."

"You don't have to thank me for basic decency." It's impossible to miss the undercurrent of irritation in his voice. When I glance up, Wes is peering at me with a mixture of sympathy and frustration I don't follow until he adds, "And I'd really like to have some words with whoever put it in your head that being taken care of when you feel like shit is too much to ask for, but I'm pretty sure I know where this is coming from after the last couple of weeks."

I shrug and try to play it off like there isn't an emotional tsunami slamming into me. "It's fine. I can look after myself."

"Of course you *can*. You just shouldn't have to—and you won't if I'm around."

There's a pretty big *if* in there. One that makes it far less easy to parse my own feelings than it would have once been. And maybe I'll blame it on the post-migraine haze in the morning, but right now, I give in to the impulse to twist toward him and lightly brush my thumb under the healing scrape near his eye. Was it really only two weeks ago that this whole adventure started?

"I can still say thank you," I say quietly, my fingers trailing down his jaw, soft with the neatly trimmed beard he's grown in since the start of my season.

Wes leans into my touch, all but purring as his eyelids grow heavy. "You never answered my question." Slowly he turns his head just a little more, until my fingertips brush the corner of his mouth.

I can't blame the migraine for the shiver that runs through me at the sensation of his breath on my skin. "What question?"

Movement draws my attention down to where Wes has a death grip on his balled-up napkin. "Why didn't you leave me on the side of the road?"

My breath catches and my fingers still, barely resting on his jaw as my eyes snap up to his. The light spilling out of the cracked bathroom door is just enough to make out the vulnerability in his naked stare. "I couldn't." I let out a shaky breath and slide my hand down his neck to rest on the curve of his shoulder. "Why did you kiss me at that gas station?" I whisper, almost certain the answer is in the way he's looking at me. "We could have just left."

One corner of his mouth tips up. "You know why, Sloane."

"I really don't."

Wes moves slowly, first to set his sandwich out of the way, and then to settle one hand on my hip in an unmistakable prelude. "Would it clear things up for you if I do it again?"

Heat rushes through me, anticipation and need tripping over each other. It's such a Wes thing to say, but I've never once heard him use that low rumble of a voice.

I want to hear it again.

"I don't know." I lean closer, my breath catching as his hand slides under the thick hoodie—*his* hoodie—to find a sliver of bare skin above my waistband. "Worth a try, I guess." My eyes flick up to his. "If you want."

Wes runs his fingers through my hair in a light, soothing touch, his expression turning rueful. "Ask me again when you're feeling better."

"I'm asking now."

Banked embers flare into a blaze at my reply. He leans in, but all he does is brush his lips against mine in a feather-light kiss. "That explain it?" he teases, eyes crinkling with laughter despite the firm hold he still has on me.

I shake my head, pressing closer. "Not exactly," I whisper, giddy desire bubbling like champagne in my veins. "Try again?"

With a hum of agreement, Wes tangles his hand in my hair and holds me in place while his mouth caresses mine. Not the insistent demand that exploded out of him at that gas station, but a gentle, beckoning thing that's in no rush. He kisses me like he's savoring a fine wine, the unhurried sweep of his lips and brush of his tongue so gentle in contrast to the way his fingers dig into my hip.

"Clear now?" he breathes against my mouth in a barely audible rasp.

"Maybe." I run my palms up his chest and slide my leg over his thighs so I can press closer. "I think you might need to show me one more time."

Wes drags his hands down my back, lower and lower, until they settle on the fleshy part of my ass. There's something wicked in the curve of his mouth when our gazes lock. "If you insist," he murmurs, accent thickening.

"I do." I shift my weight, our hips not quite touching, and curl my fingers into the soft fabric of his shirt, tugging him closer as anticipation floods my veins.

"Well, then, yes, ma'am." Wes tightens his grip and yanks me the last bit of the way to being pressed together from hip to shoulder, playfulness giving way to raw desire.

His lips demand and soothe with soft nips and tantalizing licks while one hand slides under my clothes to press against my spine, fingers splayed wide. I drink in the pleasured-filled rumble I draw out of him, scratching lightly along the back of his neck and up into his hair. He's breathing hard when he breaks the kiss to nuzzle into me, then sucks in a sharp breath when I lightly scrape my teeth over his throat and kiss a path back to his mouth.

The last bits of himself he was holding back come loose, need tangling with emotion in the sweep of his tongue and the press of his palm on my bare skin. Wes holds me like I'm a prize he's finally won and can't fathom letting go.

A tornado could drop in the hotel parking lot. I wouldn't notice. I've lost myself in the smell of his soap and the taste of his skin, the crisp hair on his chest as I explore under his shirt, the flex of muscle in his abdomen when my touch dances lower.

Lungs burning, I break the kiss and gulp in air, my cheek on his shoulder. Wes's breath is far from steady, his chest rising and falling beneath me as he runs a hand up and down my spine in a soothing stroke. His other hand returns to my hair, sifting through the tangles.

"I hope that clears things up for you."

His voice is wrecked, but the satisfied purr is what sinks into my skin. It's hard not to think of all the little excuses he's found to touch me over the last two weeks, the casual brushes that I'm beginning to think were anything but. I laugh into his throat, press another light kiss to his erratic pulse, and then reluctantly shift my weight back so the tempting ridge of his arousal is no longer against my hip.

"I think I've got it now," I tell him, resting my hands on his shoulders. "Might need a reminder in the morning."

Wes laughs, head thrown back into the pillows, and stretches to kiss the tip of my nose before easing out from under me. "That's a much nicer way to tell me to get out than I expected."

"Hey." I snag his wrist before he gets any farther than standing next to the bed. "You don't have to go right this second. I'd . . . like it if you stayed. At least for a little while. If you want."

Wes gives me a long, indecipherable look. "Are you sure I won't be in your way? I don't want to keep you from resting."

"You're not in my way." Without knowing how long this is

going to last, I'm going to make the most of whatever time we have together. "Migraine isn't gone completely, but I feel a lot better."

His expression turns playful. "Sloane, if you want me to kiss you again, you can just say that."

My instinct to protest dies before the words get out. I *do* want Wes to kiss me again—I want way more than kissing, if I'm honest with myself.

He settles next to me and opens his arms in invitation, waggling his eyebrows in a ridiculous, exaggerated leer. It takes some of the tension out of the room, leaving me laughing as I snuggle into his chest. The soothing brush of his fingers combing through my hair and the steady thud of his heartbeat have me melting into him before long.

"Is there anything other than meds that helps with the pain? Hot washcloth? Ice?" His touch sweeps lower to rest on the back of my neck, massaging the sore muscles that haven't quite unlocked.

"Nah." I sigh into his chest and bury my nose in his T-shirt. "It's not that bad anymore. Should be gone by the time I wake up. This helps," I mumble with a yawn. Clean, fed, and well kissed, sleepiness settles over me. "You make a decent pillow."

With the low rumble of his laugh under my ear, Wes's languid touch lulls me into a light doze. His heartbeat slows into a steady thump, chest rising and falling in deep breaths as he relaxes deeper into the pillows. Contentment washes over me, cocooning us in a dark, warm bubble where I lose all track of time.

It's comfortable and surprisingly easy being with him like

this. But when Wes brushes his lips against my hair in an intimate gesture filled with far more affection than lust, the soft glow of my thoughts turns sharp.

This is too easy. Dangerously easy.

I pick my head up and blink a few times to test the level of pain. An ache lingers behind my eyes, the kind I can ignore if I want to. The kind I can be distracted from.

"There is one thing."

Something in my expression must give a hint of what I'm thinking, because Wes's furrowed brow smooths out into a cheeky grin. "Would this have anything to do with that audiobook?"

I started this, but that doesn't make it any easier to actually ask for what I want. I swallow hard, then shift my weight closer. The hand on my back slides lower, settling on my ass as I lift to bring my mouth close to his ear. "And if it does?"

His chest rises sharply under me with a harshly drawn breath. "Tell me and it's yours," Wes says, all the muscles laid out beneath mine newly tense. "Whatever you want, Sloane."

Heat zips along my skin and settles low in my stomach at the ragged words. I slide back onto his lap, my thighs spread over his, and loop my arms around his neck. His hand finds its way under the hoodie to rest on my back, skin to skin, his thumb brushing over the base of my spine.

Tension coils between us. A faint flush blooms across the top of his cheeks, but Wes doesn't move beyond the light touch at my back. Waiting, despite the half-lidded anticipation he doesn't try to hide.

The moment my mouth touches his, his palm settles on my jaw. I press closer, deepening the kiss and letting out a barely there moan when his grip shifts to my hair. I rock into him, pleasure turning molten at the feel of him hardening beneath me. I do it again, my breathy groan mingling with his choked-off curse before our lips meet.

"Touch me," I murmur against his mouth. "Make me feel good, Wes."

"Yes, ma'am," he says, accent thickening as his control slips. He sucks a kiss against my throat, tongue dancing over my throbbing pulse, and then rolls me beneath him. Another kiss, this one deeper, his weight delicious as he presses me into the mattress.

Wes keeps kissing me as he drops one hand to my bare thigh and slowly drags it up to the waistband of my shorts. I tense with anticipation, forgetting to breathe until he laughs against my lips. His second stroke up my leg ends with his hand sliding under the shorts, cutting off his laughter with a raspy, "No underwear?"

He doesn't give me a chance to reply, not that he needs one. He can feel my bare skin for himself, his fingers slowly moving down along my hip before sinking between my thighs and pressing firmly. I whimper at the pleasure of it, the lingering traces of pain in my head forgotten as he grinds his palm down. My hips jerk involuntarily, a breathless *more* falling off my tongue.

Wes gives me what I need, fingers sinking lower until they slide through slick heat. "I did this to you." His voice is full of satisfaction as he teases me, vowels slipping into each other in an accent as strong as I've ever heard it. "Tell me you're this wet because of me."

I make an incoherent noise, not capable of answering when

Wes slides a finger into me, the touch almost too gentle. Tightening my grip in his hair, I drag his mouth back to mine in a silent plea.

"I got you, darlin'." His touch turns firmer, two fingers sliding in and curling as his thumb goes to work on my clit. We're both still fully dressed, his hand down my pants like we're teenagers in the back seat of a car. I don't care one bit. It feels so good that I don't realize I'm about to come until the orgasm screams through me, leaving my thighs quivering and the rest of me limp.

"Just give me a second." Air saws out of my lungs as I rub my thigh against his hard cock. "That was . . . you're . . . good."

Wes chuckles, easing his hips away from me and stealing another kiss, back to gentle and sweet. "How's the pain?"

I blink, the last bits of it no longer lingering. "Gone."

"Good." He kisses the tip of my nose and pulls back. "You should be able to get back to sleep now."

"But what about . . . You didn't . . ."

Wes rolls off the bed and doesn't make a secret of adjusting the bulge in his pants. "Wasn't about me. We need to get an early start tomorrow if you're up for it. I'll take care of myself tonight." He swoops in for another kiss, this one full of need and promise. "But don't worry, darlin', I'll think of you the whole time."

CHAPTER TWELVE

THANKFULLY, THE COMBO OF EXTRA SLEEP, A HOT shower, and some prescription meds—and okay, definitely Wes too—banish the last traces of the migraine overnight. I'm awake an hour before my alarm, unsurprising with a four-hour nap in the mix.

Instead of getting up right away, I watch the blinking light on the smoke detector above my head. What the hell happens now? Wes kissed me last night. Bought me dinner, *kissed* me, and then gave me probably the best orgasm I've ever had with a guy.

And then he just . . . left.

It's exactly what I'd expect from him. Or it was, before all those kisses that felt far more like a promise than a conquest. He didn't exactly treat me like a hookup last night. He took care of me, was sweeter than any guy I've been with, not to mention the very obvious fact that he got me off without expecting anything. And not in the way that's happened to me before, with promises and assurances they just wanted to give me pleasure, only to sulk when I didn't take it upon myself to return the favor.

And there was that moment, that cozy, intimate moment that felt so good, so right. I was the one who got overwhelmed and turned it into something else. I was the one who asked him to touch me. Wes waited for my cues.

Was it just pity? Another of his games? It felt real. It *sounded* real when he murmured *darlin'* over my skin like a prayer.

The amount of energy I'm putting into this particular thought spiral over his motivations is exactly why I've avoided what happened last night for so long.

Determined to carry on like normal, I yawn my way through getting dressed and, one quick google later, find a local café with decent reviews. I load up on coffee, breakfast sandwiches, and a couple of pastries for the road, and then text Wes for his room number once I'm back in the hotel parking lot.

My mind blanks when he opens the door wearing only a towel and a smirk. "Just got out of the shower," he says unnecessarily, water droplets clinging to his chest and disappearing into the towel clutched at his hip. There's a faint line of ink peeking out just above the towel, another tattoo I haven't seen yet.

"Breakfast." The one-word greeting is all I can manage with a desert in my throat before jerking out the hand holding his coffee.

The sight of Wes, ink shimmering on his wet skin, grinning at me before taking a sip of coffee and letting out a little satisfied groan, should be illegal. Especially after leaving me with the mental image of him *taking care of himself* last night.

I'm a case of arson in the making if the heat in my cheeks is anything to go by.

"Unless you want to be breakfast, I'm goin' to need you to stop lookin' at me like that," he says in a lazy, exaggerated drawl that reminds me far too much of last night.

Only half paying attention, I follow a water droplet as it sinks down, down, down his chest and abdomen. Maybe I wouldn't mind returning last night's favor.

"Sloane." It's more of a growl than my name and far sexier than it has any right to be.

I jerk my eyes up. "You're the one who answered the door like *that*." I slip past the open bathroom door to perch on the edge of the unmade bed. "Could have at least put on some damn pants."

Wes is still laughing when he steps into the bathroom, leaving the door cracked. "How's the morning refresh looking?"

I take a sip of my coffee and double check the forecast on my phone, something in me easing at how normal he's acting. Maybe he really did mean it last night that he wasn't expecting anything in return. "Decent," I call back, willing my body to settle.

Whatever may or may not be happening between us, I can't let it interfere. I've spent far too many years watching my mom drop everything else in her life for the sake of a man. I'll be damned if I turn into her now. In fact, what I should do is tell Wes in no uncertain terms that last night was a mistake.

But then he emerges from the bathroom, unreasonably attractive in a pair of hiking shorts that show off the high curve of his ass and a snug black T-shirt. He props himself up in the doorframe and continues to rub his hair with the towel. "Still thinking Kansas?"

"Somewhere between Dodge City and Wichita is probably our best bet."

"We can grab lunch in Dodge and decide from there. Could get crowded today."

I make a face, but he's right. There's a higher-than-usual chance of tornadoes in the area we're targeting. Combine that with a good road network and fairly flat elevation, and a chaser convergence is all but guaranteed. Navigating around a hundred other chasers is less than ideal and can quickly turn dangerous, but it's also the kind of forecast that might get me something *Nature Shots* worthy.

Wes tosses the towel into the bathroom and prowls over, holding out his hand. He pulls me easily to my feet when I take it and instantly wraps me in his arms. "Forgot to say good morning," he breathes into my ear before lowering his mouth to mine.

Despite the confident way he moves in, there's the slightest hesitation before his lips touch mine. Maybe I'm not the only one with questions, which weirdly helps me relax. I give in to the pleasure of the kiss, melting into him as it deepens into white-hot need. It's as if the years we've spent bickering have been a kind of foreplay building in the background, and now that we've broken the seal, all that pent-up desire is rushing out.

Not that we have time to indulge in it right now.

Squeezing the dip of my waist with a rueful grin, Wes reluctantly lets go. "We should get on the road."

I grab my coffee and nod with an awkward jerk of my head. "We can eat in the car," I say, refusing to look at the bed and all the bad but wonderful ideas it represents.

"Good idea." I'm not the only one a little breathless. Wes shoves his hands in his pockets, almost as if he needs to physically prevent himself from reaching for me.

"Sloane," he calls when I've got my hand on the door, one foot already in the hallway. He waits until I turn to look at him, grins his wicked grin, and gestures to my—his—sweatshirt. "You look good in my clothes."

BY THE TIME we roll into Dodge City, we're far from the only chasers in town. I try to hide my excitement when I spot a few of the research trucks with their distinctive government agency logos and roofs full of equipment parked near the back of the gas station we pull into.

"Always a good sign when those guys are in the area." Wes pumps a fist in the air before grabbing his phone. "Let me see if anyone I know is around."

"How'd you end up making friends with the meteorologists?" I ask curiously. The researchers tend to keep to themselves for the most part.

"Did some work on one of their projects last year."

I blink back my surprise. No one said a word last season. Wild Wes and a methodical research team aren't exactly the type of pairing I'd expect, but then again, he hasn't been nearly as wild as his reputation implies since we've been on the road together.

Or maybe he's just on his best behavior with me.

Unease settles into my thoughts. Kissing Wes was so natural, so *right*, that my doubts faded easily into the background. Now that we've been back in the car for a couple of hours, I can't help wondering what the hell I was thinking. In all the years I've known him, he's never had a girlfriend so much as a series of hookups, flings, and rumors.

But this isn't the time—or place—to have a heart-to-heart. I take a long drink of water, shove my worries aside, and pocket my keys after locking the car.

Jealousy curdles in my stomach when Wes beelines for two attractive women and introduces me. Chloe is wearing a National Weather Service jacket, the deep navy color suiting her dark hair and olive complexion. The rest of her clothes are similar to mine, hair piled in a messy bun and her smile friendly. Haley is a petite and curvy blonde in a faded University of Oklahoma hoodie, a long braid falling over one shoulder.

"Wes has told me so much about you. I've been meaning to get in touch," Chloe says warmly and then holds up her left hand, sunlight sparkling off her engagement ring. "Your work is gorgeous. I'm not sure I can afford you, but any chance you're free to come to Oklahoma in September? We're not planning anything too fancy, just a small thing at a local park."

Finding out that Wes has been shamelessly plugging my wedding work sends the little green monster in my head slinking back into her cave. Especially when he props one elbow on my shoulder, effectively using me as an affectionate armrest.

I glance up at him, relaxing under the warmth of his gaze, and pull up my admittedly busy calendar. My website says I'm fully booked, but there's usually room to squeeze someone in if they can be flexible. "September might be tough, but if you're okay with something other than a Friday or Saturday night, I can probably make it work."

Chloe lets out a squeal of delight, earning a laugh from her friend. Haley gives her a playfully chiding look before turning to me with mock seriousness. "Don't let her monopolize you with wedding talk."

"Oh, I don't mind. Always happy to help another chaser out if I can," I add with a wink.

I've never shot a wedding for another storm chaser, but Chloe doesn't need to know that. Government employees aren't exactly raking in the cash, and all of us out here rely on their forecasting. I can afford to cut her a deal, and besides that, it would be a nice break from the glitz and glam weddings.

"Heard about the new job," Wes says to Haley, offering a friendly smile. "LA is a big step up. Congrats."

She makes a face and exchanges a look with Chloe. "Yeah, it's a huge opportunity, but I doubt I'll be able to get as much time off for chasing. The schedule is crazy."

There's an echo of my own frustration with trying to balance chasing season with my bank account. I offer her a sympathetic smile. "If only tornadoes paid the bills, right?"

"Ain't that the truth." Haley laughs, something melancholy lingering in her smile. "You guys after anything in particular this year?"

Wes launches into an explanation of the *Nature Shots* contest, which eventually leads us into the forecast for the afternoon. Chloe pulls out her phone and hands it over to Wes with a wink. "You tell anyone I let you see the group chat and you're a dead man."

I glance back and forth between them. "What group chat?"

"Meteorologist group chat," Wes explains, though he's distracted. He's quiet for a minute, scrolling through the conversation, and then returns the phone with an enormous grin. "We were heading in that direction anyway, but good to have it confirmed by the pros." He turns toward me, excitement animating his expression. "Ready to go catch a tornado or two?"

"On camera." I narrow my eyes, playfully stabbing a finger into his chest. "*Only* on camera."

TRACY IS WAITING for me as soon as I step out of the bathroom.

"Hey, when did you get here? I was just heading back—"

"Nope, you're not getting away that easily," she cuts in, already tugging me around the side exit, away from where everyone else is gathered outside. "You've been ignoring my texts."

"I texted you twenty minutes ago!"

"Yeah, but you ignored the ten messages before that."

"Most people would take a hint," I grumble, glancing around when she finally lets go. I give her a pointed look. "I don't want to talk about Wes. There's really nothing to talk about."

Tracy's brows shoot up. "You've been alone all this time and *nothing* has happened?"

My blush gives me away before I can come up with a response. Her eyes go wide, a knowing grin taking over her expression. "Something *did* happen!"

"Keep your voice down!" I hiss while scanning again for

anyone who might overhear. "It's not . . . I don't know what it is. Let me figure that out before you interrogate me."

Tracy laughs and then casts a speculative look at me. "So was it a kiss or . . . ?"

Technically we kissed two weeks ago, so it shouldn't be a big deal to admit. I hesitate anyway, checking yet again for anyone coming around the side of the building, before I squeak out a *yes*.

Tracy squeals and holds up her hand for a high five. Sighing, I meet her stare with a silent *Are you really making me do this?* that's immediately met with an unspoken *Obviously yes.* But no sooner do I slap my palm against hers than she's striding around the side of the building shouting, "Matt, you owe me a hundred bucks!"

"You *bet on me*?" I dart after her, not that she bothers to reply with anything but more laughter.

When Wes asks a few minutes later if I'm too hot and want to go sit in the air-conditioned car, I quickly take the out. By the time afternoon rolls around and we're back on the road, I can almost look at him without blushing.

It helps that we're nearly in position with a new storm. Its structure is impressive, defined inflow bands hanging low above the ground as if the storm is crooking a gnarled finger to draw the unsuspecting in.

The slow-moving cell produces a stunning lightning show, but frustration still gnaws at the back of my mind as sunset gives way to twilight and then deepens into inky night. Any other year I'd be thrilled to capture the anvil crawlers racing through the clouds, shading the roiling mass of the storm lavender and deep purple.

This is supposed to be fun, I remind myself as I stare up at the sky, my camera fixed on a tripod with an interval timer going. I need to remember that this is my creative break despite the pressures of the contest.

Easier said than done.

When we finally call it a night, I slide behind the wheel with a yawn, adrenaline fading and allowing exhaustion to creep back in. It hardly helps that it's so dark out here we might as well have fallen off the planet to float through the vastness of space instead of racing down a lonely country road.

By the time I pull into the parking lot of the hotel we booked earlier, we're both dragging. Lightning flickers on the horizon from a far-off storm, the air warm with the lingering scent of hot dust and asphalt.

I can't help a nervous glance at Wes. I don't know what to expect, all the awkwardness of how to end a first date sitting uncomfortably under my skin. Except today wasn't a date. It was just another day of storm chasing, albeit with a very enthusiastic kiss at the start.

Not that Wes seems to share my anxieties. He yawns as he slings his bags over his shoulder and nods toward the diner across the street after I lock the car. Despite the late hour, light spills from its windows and the neon sign by the front door proclaims they're open. Perks of being so close to the interstate.

"I'm going to throw my stuff into my room and grab a bite. Hungry?"

I shoulder my own bags and glance across the road again. My stomach rumbles at the thought of hot, greasy food. We were so focused on chasing we never stopped for dinner. "I could eat."

"What's your diner go-to?"

"Chocolate shake and fries," I answer without thinking about it too much.

Wes lets out a loud bark of laughter, louder still in the deep quiet of the night. "You buy fruit every time we stop for snacks. I was expecting oatmeal."

"Just because I don't want to live off Cheetos and energy drinks for six weeks doesn't mean I'm a health nut," I huff. "And you know damn well that these little diners in the middle of nowhere have the best milkshakes in the country. Or maybe they just taste better after fifteen hours in the car."

One quick stop to check in and throw our things into our respective rooms—three doors down from each other, I can't help noting—we're back in the elevator. This time we're not weighed down by bags, and though Wes stands closer to me than he did pre-kiss, he doesn't touch me otherwise.

I can't decide if I want him to or not.

He does open the diner door for me, sweeping his hand toward the brightly lit interior. "Let's get you that milkshake." He waits for me to walk through the open door and then adds, "We should mention milkshakes to Mae next time we're down her way. I bet she'd make a killing."

The mention of the donut shop owner makes my stomach rumble pitifully, as good a distraction as any. "Great, now I want donuts again."

"I'm sure we'll head back south eventually." The *we* slips out easily, as if it's not a question that we're going to finish out the season together. At least the part I can stay for.

I sink into an empty booth and ignore the growing puzzle that is the man across from me. "That whole saying about diamonds being a girl's best friend? Nah. Give me tornadoes and donuts."

Amusement lights up his gray eyes. Or maybe that's just the reflection of the fluorescent lights buzzing above our heads. "Tornadoes and donuts make terrible jewelry."

"Don't let Mae hear you say that. You know she loves her tornado earrings." I sigh, glancing down at my phone screen and the three hundred unread emails I've been ignoring all day. It's as good a way as any to stop obsessing over Wes. "I need to deal with some things, if you don't mind."

"Your mom again?" he asks, a dark note entering his voice. "Don't take this the wrong way, but your brothers seem pretty useless."

"You don't have brothers, do you?"

A flicker of emotion I can't follow dances across his face, there and gone in an instant. "No," Wes says with lightness that sounds forced. "Only child." His megawatt grin returns as he leans back into the booth. "My parents had me and decided I was it."

The cocky tone to go along with his smirk is trademark Wild Wes, but as the waitress appears to take our order—chocolate shake and fries for me, strawberry shake and fries for Wes—there's that same sense I've gotten anytime he's mentioned his family that something is off.

I brush the thought aside. It's one o'clock in the morning, and neither of us slept more than a few hours last night. Adrenaline and caffeine only keep you going for so long. We're both exhausted. It's not really a surprise we lapse into silence.

The weight of Wes's stare prickles along the back of my neck. I look up to find him watching me, an odd expression on his face. His eyes flick to the server when she drops off our shakes and then snap right back to me.

"What?" I ask, self-consciously running a hand over my ragged braid. "Do I have something in my hair?"

"No." When I lift one of my eyebrows in question, he sighs. "I like you like this. That's all."

A startled laugh bursts out of me. "Exhausted and cranky does it for you?" I tease while silently telling myself not to read too much into the soft way he said *I like you*.

"I've seen you cranky." Wes shrugs, unwraps his straw, and starts to fiddle with the paper wrapper. "In all the years I've known you, you've always been so self-contained. You're different lately. With me."

I'm about to make a quip that kissing is definitely *different* for us, but whether it's the late hour or his intimate tone, I suddenly don't feel like brushing him off with a joke.

"Different how?"

At first I don't think Wes is going to answer. Not with how determinedly he's staring at the straw wrapper as he packs it into a smaller and smaller ball, but finally, so quietly I can barely hear him over the whir of the fans, he says, "Soft."

Soft is an adjective I've actively tried to avoid. Soft is my mother, molding herself into whatever qualities she thinks will benefit her the most. Soft is vulnerable, the last thing a woman alone and fifty miles from anything wants to be.

I don't know what to say, so I dip a couple more fries in my shake and shove them in my mouth. By the time I swallow, I still don't have anything better than a shrug, so I go with honesty. "Soft can be a liability."

Wes's brows shoot up to his hairline. "That's a new one."

"You're a man. It's different."

"Okay, yes, in some ways, it *is* different," he admits. "But it's not *that* different."

My laughter is more of a scoff as I dip another fry. I don't care if I'm getting weird looks from the trucker at the counter. The mix of salty and sweet is just what I'm craving after a long day. "That first day? Those guys whose car you wrote *Honk for dick* on? They called me fresh meat. And I may have fibbed about the guys at the Mexican place—they had *opinions* on my leggings. Both times, they only stopped because *you* were there. There's a bunch of guys out here who think it's perfectly fine to make a woman uncomfortable—until she belongs to another man."

"I'm sorry you have to listen to that shit. Any guy who thinks you don't belong out here has his head up his ass." Heat flashes like distant lightning in Wes's gaze, and his voice turns gruff. "Wasn't aware you belonged to me, though."

I swallow hard, shoving aside the memory of the way he said *mine* before he kissed me that first time. "I don't."

CHAPTER THIRTEEN

WES'S NIGHTLY SHOWER SELFIE ARRIVES NOT LONG after we part ways with another lingering kiss outside my room. The curve of his bare ass peeking out at the bottom of the frame does nothing to help my restlessness. Despite my exhaustion, it's a long time before I'm asleep.

Morning comes far too soon, both of us bleary-eyed and moving slowly. When Wes offers to drive, I wordlessly hand over the keys and drop into the passenger seat.

My sour mood thankfully lifts after a cup of coffee. By the time we stop for gas and a second round of caffeine, Wes is in a better mood too. He slides an arm around my waist while we wait in line to pay and kisses my temple. "Morning, darlin'," he says in a low voice only for me. "You awake now?"

"My eyes are open," I mumble into his shoulder. "Good enough."

He laughs and squeezes me closer. And when we get back in the car, he leans over the center console to slide his hand into my hair and pull my mouth to his. It's another slow kiss, all banked embers instead of raging inferno. When he lets go, his eyes race over my face for a long moment, searching for something.

My phone buzzes in my hand, breaking the spell. "Tracy says she and Matt ran into the research team this morning. They're heading for the same area we are."

She also sent a selfie of herself with a crisp hundred-dollar bill and Matt scowling in the background. He doesn't need to know about that.

Wes flashes me his usual grin, settling back into his seat and starting the car. "Let's go get some killer shots."

MY LINGERING EXHAUSTION melts away as the adrenaline of a good chase kicks in. Wes eventually turns up the volume, "Sloane Michaels and the Horrible, Awful, No-Good Playlist" once again the soundtrack for our drive.

When he starts to sing along, I figure what the hell and join him in the most off-key rendition of my playlist on the planet. He has me giggling before long, belting out Taylor Swift songs right along with the rock bands I figured were more his taste. I'm surprised he knows the lyrics, but when I tease him about it—*especially* after his choice to rename my playlist the way he did—Wes just shrugs. "They're catchy," he says unapologetically before joining in on the chorus.

Let the games begin, indeed.

An hour west of our goal, the severe warnings start to pop

up. "We've got golf balls, ping pongs, and more golf balls," I tell Wes as I skim the details. "Could be some baseballs before the day is done."

He wiggles his eyebrows, his mouth forming a wicked grin. "You're very into ball—"

"Do not finish that sentence." I glare through my laughter. "Maybe they should use fruit instead of sports metaphors in these hail warnings."

"Apple hail doesn't sound nearly as terrifying as baseball hail." Wes grimaces and shoots me a long look. "We'll do the smart thing and steer clear of needing to replace your windows."

"Yes, please." I go back to reading the severe thunderstorm warning details, then check the models again before switching to the most recent radar scans. "Couple of storms are already pushing forty thousand feet." Giddy excitement floods my body as adrenaline kicks in. "I think we're getting something good today."

"Hell yeah we are!" Wes puts his window down, the scent of baked earth and hot asphalt rushing in. A thick blanket of moisture hangs heavily in the air. It's so warm that sweat prickles on the back of my neck after only a few minutes.

We lapse into silence, but unlike the start of the trip, it's an easy quiet, both of us enjoying the freedom of the wide-open road and the promising forecast. Captivated by the way a tiny smile tugs at his lips and his hand sits loosely on the steering wheel, I impulsively grab my camera from the back seat, lean into the door, and snap a photo.

I take another when Wes turns toward me for a few seconds, mischief lighting up his expression. "You want me to pose for you, say the word, darlin'."

My mind leaps straight to Wes tangled in precariously draped sheets. With his dark hair and tattoos and a good smolder, it would be the sort of image I could break social media with—but if I *did* take that kind of photo, it would be for me and me alone.

"I would love to know what you're thinking."

"Yep," I agree, popping the *p* and giving him the same smirk he loves to give me. "You would."

Wes groans a protest and shoots me a red-hot look. "I'll get it out of you later."

"Maybe." I laugh when he grumbles under his breath and point out the windshield. "I think we should take the next exit and target this cell." Holding the iPad where he can see it without taking his eyes off the road completely, I tap on the storm in question. "If I remember right, there's a half-collapsed silo around here somewhere with one of those old-fashioned windmills."

"And some rusty tractors, if we're thinking of the same spot."

I nod, forever amused by the number of storm chasers always prepared to rattle off their favorite farm ruins in five different states. Chasing foreground is as serious a business as chasing tornadoes.

And if I can find a spot with flowers overtaking the ruins, and the storm lines up how I hope, I could get my *Nature Shots* cover today.

Wes exits the highway behind a line of other chasers all thinking the same thing. He takes a random turn down a dirt road, then another, and then another, until we're the only ones kicking up dust. In front of us, the storm looms, distant thunder rolling across the plain.

"We need to find a paved road." I peer nervously out the windshield, the rain column easy to spot against the brighter horizon. "Today is not the day to get stuck in the mud."

Wes points to a distant spot where what looks like a stop sign gleams. "That one should be paved."

Sure enough, the tires smooth out as we hit asphalt. He stomps on the gas, sending us racing closer and closer toward the heart of the storm. The sky is taking on a beautiful if eerie turquoise glow, the colors vibrant above the deep green of the wheat field beneath it. I shamelessly hang out the window snapping photos. Wes is doing the same thing, one hand on the wheel, the other white-knuckle gripping his camera as he takes photos out the driver's side.

"Tornado!" I shout with glee when I spot a swirl of dust kicking up maybe a mile ahead. "Pull over. It's right in front of us!"

Sliding his sunglasses up, Wes peers through the windshield. "I don't think so. Maybe a dust devil."

"Not the way it's moving." I quickly grab my phone and refresh the velocity radar scan, which shows a telltale couplet ahead of us. The distinct delineation of red-shaded winds moving away from the radar and green-shaded winds moving in the opposite direction is a dead giveaway for a tornado. "And not according to this. Pull over or it's going to be on top of us!"

Wes glances at the radar scan, swears quietly, and then quickly whips the car around so we're pointing away from the storm when he pulls onto the shoulder. I hop out and take a few steps into a dandelion-covered field. The bright yellow of the flowers pops against the deep bruise of the sky, and while it's missing the ruins I was hoping for, the whimsical field *does* strike the right note.

And there's a tornado about to drop right over it.

"I was right!" I point at the funnel, sinking down to one knee to fill the frame with as many dandelions as I can.

"Sonofabitch." Wes already has his camera raised to eye level. "We got ourselves a tornado!"

The colors explode in my viewfinder, turquoise sky and cheerful yellow flowers, the deep purple-gray of the cloud base and muddy brown of the tornado growing darker by the second.

"It's going to cross!" Wes shouts over the wind. He gestures toward the road where the stovepipe wobbles closer, shifting from rich brown to menacing black as it sucks up more and more debris. We're still a solid half mile away, which is about as close as I'm willing to get, but if Wes has any awareness of just how fast we may need to bail, he's shoved it aside. Instead, he lies down smack in the middle of the road and waits as the tornado tears a path toward the pavement.

"Wes! Get up!"

I'm not sure he even hears me. We're on a long straightaway, but a car could come through at any moment. I nervously check behind my shoulder over and over, distracted from my own shots. There's a bright flash and boom as the tornado slams into the power lines, and then it's spinning across the road in a furious whirl of shrieking wind.

"Wes!" I shout over the noise, eyeing the tornado as it snaps poles like matchsticks. "We gotta go!" Darting an anxious look over my shoulder for a car, I jog over to him and yank on the back of his shirt. "Now!"

It's another thirty seconds before he scrambles to his feet.

"Shit, sorry, I was just in the zone and . . ." He glances back at the tornado, which is getting bigger. It's either heading our way or turning into the kind of monster we have no business messing with, and it's doing it fast. "Fuck, we gotta go."

His hand is on the small of my back as we sprint for the car, a subtle push to move faster. The eerie whistle-howl of the tornado raises the hairs on the back of my neck. We're way too close. *This* is the reason Wes has the reputation he does. He gets so absorbed in what he's doing, so focused on getting *the* shot, that he forgets how quickly a storm can turn on us.

He's closer to the driver's side. I don't argue as we throw ourselves into the car, slam the doors, and peel out before either of our seat belts are fully clicked into place.

A shower of sparks goes up behind us as another telephone pole crashes into the road, uncomfortably close. "C'mon," Wes mutters, the engine revving as he stomps on the gas. "There was another paved road heading east about a mile south."

"Yeah, but it's three miles after that to the next southbound road." I glance anxiously behind us. The tornado appears smaller, but not by much. We haven't put nearly enough distance between it and ourselves. "Not a lot of room to run if that thing turns."

"I think it's moving north." Wes flashes me a nervous grin, jabbing the button to lower the window before he sticks his head out to look back at the tornado furiously eating up farmland. "We're good!"

He's staring back at the tornado so intently that he doesn't see the power lines stretched across the road until I shout his name.

We skid to a stop inches in front of the sparking wires. "Put your window up," I snap, my heart in my throat as I use the mirror to check the tornado's progress. "We need to get out of here."

"I can get under them if we go onto the shoulder a little." Wes points to an opening that might be big enough for us to squeeze through as another shower of sparks erupts from the tangled wires. "Don't touch anything metal."

"No shit." I take a deep breath as he slowly backs up and angles the car to slip under the lines. He's not entirely calm either, his jaw granite and his knuckles white on the steering wheel, but we manage to clear the debris without incident.

Wes lets out a long sigh as we pick up speed again. "Nothing like a close call to get the heart pumping." My temper flares, but before I can snap back at him that if he'd kept his eyes on the damn road we would have seen it earlier, he reaches for me with a visible tremble in his hand. "You okay?"

I swallow hard, my heart rate not yet back to normal. "That was close. Too close." It's exactly why I didn't want to get sucked into his vortex.

He nods, his hand squeezing around mine. "I know. I'm sorry. I . . . I let myself get distracted. You're right. I should be more careful with you."

With you. I peer at Wes, wondering why it's only my safety that seems to be affecting him at all. But there's no time to wonder with a tornado still devouring dirt behind us.

I refresh the radar, studying the movement on loop and the defined hook that's powering the storm. The road that Wes mentioned is coming up, and while there's no guarantee, running parallel to the tornado is a risk I'm willing to take based on the data. "That left is coming up."

"Yeah?" His eyes flick up to the rearview, checking on the tornado, and then to me. "You sure you're okay with that?"

I settle with the realization he's willing to skip it if I'm uncomfortable. Maybe Wes really does mean it when he says he's sorry for getting distracted. "Let's do it. Just don't lie down in the road again, okay?"

"Got it. No more playing roadkill."

"Wes!"

He flashes me a mischief-filled grin, lifts my hand to his mouth, and presses a kiss to my skin. "Just playin'," he says, though there's a wobble in the words that makes me wonder how much of his blasé attitude is faked. "I'll be careful, promise."

"Better be," I tell him with a sharp look right before he lets my hand go and turns east.

Three seconds later, his window is down again and he's holding his phone out, right hand gripping the steering wheel as he lets out whoops of excitement. I shake my head, fighting a smile. Maybe I should be more concerned, but filming out the window while driving is standard-issue reckless. I can't be mad about something I've done hundreds of times myself.

The lingering unease over everything else that just went down is less easily dismissed.

It's another late night when we finally pull into the hotel parking lot. I'm mid–adrenaline crash, my body so heavy I briefly consider going to sleep in the passenger seat.

Wes isn't doing much better. He lets out a jaw-cracking yawn after shutting the car off, his head lolling back on the seat while we both sit in the sudden silence. "We gotta go inside." He turns toward me and yawns again. "Bed is right there."

"So far." I rub my eyes with a moan and swallow my own yawn. "At least we can sleep in a little. Okay. We can do this."

I sleepwalk my way through check-in, and then we're in another elevator, facing another set of hotel rooms—and another choice about how our evening ends.

"Almost there," Wes says softly, holding his arm in front of the elevator door so I can step out first. We shuffle onto our floor wrapped up in each other, which doesn't make it any easier to navigate the space with our camera bags and duffels. Both of our rooms are toward the end of the hall—I'm in 325 and Wes is across from me in 328.

"It's been a long day," he says at the same moment I blurt out, "I'm so tired I can barely keep my eyes open."

The tension drains out of me as we share a relieved laugh. There's a faint wash of color in his cheeks, his expression soft as he steps into my space and drops his bags at his feet. Cupping my jaw in his palms, Wes leans in and brushes a kiss against my mouth. "We're both exhausted," he says quietly, rubbing his thumb along my cheekbone when he breaks the kiss. "Go get some sleep."

Except he doesn't let go, and I don't make any move to step away. Maybe it's the adrenaline or the day, or maybe it's just that my body has been desperate for the weight of his again, but I'm the one who presses onto my toes and wraps my arms around his neck.

Wes responds instantly, backing me up against the door and kissing me like he's been dying of thirst all day. There's nothing sweet about this kiss, just hunger and need in the plunge of his tongue and the nip of his teeth. I forget we're in the hallway where anyone could see us and roll my hips against his, moaning at the feral sound that rumbles out of him. One hand fists his shirt, dragging him closer, while the other dips under the soft cotton to trace his abdomen, hot, soft skin over rigid muscle.

The ding of the elevator jerks us back to our senses. We break apart, breathing heavily. Wes rests his forehead against mine for a long moment. "Wouldn't be mad if you wanted to invade my dreams tonight," he says in a rough voice before pushing off the door. Eyes still burning with want, he bends to grab his bags. "Good night, Sloane."

The raspy way he says my name sends tingles racing down my spine. I shove my key into the door, but before I go in, I pause long enough to catch his eye over my shoulder and say, "I'll *definitely* be thinking of you when I get in bed."

Ten minutes later, when my hand is between my legs, I shiver at the memory—and promise—of the low groan Wes lets out just before the door shuts.

CHAPTER FOURTEEN

I SLEEP LIKE THE DEAD AND WAKE TO WES POUNDING on my door, already dressed and excitement sparking in his eyes. "Refresh came out twenty minutes ago." He shoves his iPad under my nose, zoomed in to the Storm Prediction Center's tornado forecast for northern Kansas. "Fifteen-hatched. Get dressed."

He slides his hand around the back of my neck, pulls me in for a hard, minty kiss that reignites last night's spark, and then just as quickly lets go with a soft noise of regret. His hand slips down to toy with the thin strap of my tank top. "And now I'm going to get us coffee before the sight of you like this makes me forget what a tornado is."

Not even a fifteen-hatched—a 15 percent chance of tornadoes within twenty-five miles of any given spot in the area, with an even greater chance some of them will be strong—wakes me up enough to process his level of energy. I blink a few times, mumble a semi-coherent reply, and shuffle back into my room to stumble through getting dressed. In a vain attempt to wake up, I splash ice-cold water on my face. I'm not sure that accomplishes much beyond making me shiver.

"Oh thank god," I mutter when Wes is standing outside the elevator in the lobby with a giant cup of coffee. "Gimme."

He laughs, trading me the coffee and taking my heavy camera bag before tucking me into his side. I'm tired enough that I lean into him without thought and take a long sip before I notice our audience. A dozen chasers are spread out across the lobby's seating area with their breakfasts, laptops, and iPads. It's not exactly unexpected given the forecast and how few hotels are out this way—but I wasn't thinking about that in my half-asleep delirium.

I freeze with the coffee cup halfway to my mouth, the not-at-all quiet whispers surrounding us.

Pay up. I told you they were fucking.

She's just trying to get an in with Nature Shots. *Everyone knows Wes is going to win.*

Another chick screwing her way to the top.

Tracy and Matt betting on me was one thing, but strangers discussing my personal life on this level is downright humiliating. I start to slip out from under Wes's arm, but his grip tightens. The way we're pressed together, I feel each of his muscles lock up.

Wes is generally a friendly and easygoing guy. In all the years we've spent snarking back and forth, he's always done it with a grin and a wink. The Wild Wes nickname comes from the questionable risks he takes more than his temperament—the only time I've ever seen him genuinely pissed is when other chasers drive so recklessly they put us all at risk.

And now.

"Hey!" His voice carries easily, shutting everyone up. "Sloane invited me to chase with her, very graciously, after I fucked up my ride. Anything beyond that is none of your goddamned business."

His sharp words shut down the whispers instantly. There's a lot of foot-shuffling and mumbled apologies, all directed at the floor or their laps. I hate that the men gathered in this lobby are having the exact reaction I wanted so badly to avoid, even though Wes defending me without hesitation goes a hell of a long way toward soothing the sting.

We stand there for another long moment in silence before Wes turns us toward the exit without another word. "If anyone says anything to you, I want to know," he says gruffly once we're outside, guiding me toward the car. "You don't deserve any of that shit."

"I know. And I can defend myself, but thank you for what you said."

"You shouldn't have to."

I put my bags in the car and step out of the way so he can do the same. "You realize *Nature Shots* has never featured a female photographer on the cover, right? It's part of why I want to win so badly. It could be a real stepping stone into paid landscape work. And a chance to beat you, of course," I add, bumping his hip with mine to break some of the tension. I'm not sure it works. "But if it's being judged blindly and they still pick me? It's going to be hard for guys like that to bitch that I only won because of some diversity quota. I'd be recognized for my talent."

Finally.

"Never? That can't be right." Wes holds up his palms at my

scowl. "Not saying I don't believe you, just . . . really? Not once?"

"Not once."

"Shit." He fiddles with his hat, taking it off to run his hand through his hair before shoving it back into place. "That's messed up."

"It is." I close the back hatch with a sigh and jingle the keys in my hand. "But the only way I beat them is if I get that shot, so let's go."

THE STORMS DO not disappoint.

We catch a beast of a storm in midafternoon, the open plain showing off the towering cylinder of rotating clouds tightly stacked together. No tornado, but I'm happy when we find a field full of pink and purple wildflowers.

Matt, who's on another storm, sends a snap to the group text of a massive mothership that's been kind enough to loom over a bright red barn and silo. We race south to intercept it, tiny bits of hail pinging off the roof as we skirt the storm before bursting out on the other side. The supercell towers over the farm, just about every chaser we know crowded against the fence line.

Grimacing at the crowd, I pull over on the narrow shoulder and lower my window before hopping out. I glance at Wes, a flicker of unease skating over my skin after what happened this morning, but we're both in work mode when we grab our cameras and hustle across the road to find a clear shot.

Some storms make it easy on us, hovering over the same

area as they lazily spin ever so slowly off to the east. This monster does no such thing, whirling like a top and marching across the plain like an invading army. We barely get five minutes to shoot before hail starts to pelt down, stinging where it makes contact.

It doesn't matter. We're both laughing as we tumble back into the car, quickly slamming the doors shut and raising the windows. I'm shoving my seat belt back into the clip when Wes leans over, sinks his fingers into my braid, and pulls me in for a quick, hard kiss. "Have I told you how much I like chasing with you?"

Blushing, I give him a playful shove back into his seat and shift out of park. "You can butter me up later. Are we staying with this one?"

He nods, once again focused as he taps on his iPad. "It's kicking out a ton of lightning. If we head east and look for a spot, we should get a clear shot."

Sunset isn't far off and the storm shows no sign of slowing. "The low-level jet is going to kick in within a couple of hours." I point through the windshield where the storm is starting to lose some of its organization despite the amount of lightning still pouring off it. "Might get it back together when that happens."

"If it keeps lighting up like this, we could get some great shots of the structure." Wes is quiet for a few minutes, tapping on his phone, and then lets out a triumphant noise. "I'm about to be your favorite person. Take the next left."

"Why?"

"You'll see."

"Wes."

"Sloane."

Shooting him a dark look, I take the left. After several miles and even more turns, I'm starting to lose my patience when we come around a large, swooping bend in the road to reveal a half-collapsed windmill, a lone tree, and a rusted-out tractor with the storm looming behind it all. Beneath the clouds, the horizon has taken on a pale orange glow as the sun sinks lower.

"Well, shit," I breathe out with glee. It's perfect.

"You're welcome," Wes says, smug as can be, and then hurries to grab our tripods from the back. I follow with the cameras. Together we make quick work of setting up our gear and framing our shots. After that, it's just a matter of programming the interval timer and waiting.

Capturing lightning is mostly a matter of luck and patience. I let the first few intervals go by, stop long enough to make sure my frame is in focus and I've got the exposure where I think I need it, and then it's back to waiting.

Wes catches my eye, a slow smirk spreading across his face. "Hey, darlin'," he drawls, lifting his arm in invitation. "You good?"

Butterflies take up residence in my belly when he wraps one arm around my shoulders and another around my waist, my back against his chest, so we can both continue to watch the storm. It's good to be held, even if the intimacy of the way he's holding me makes the questions I've been trying to ignore louder than ever.

"Sloane?"

"Sorry, just watching the storm." It's not entirely a lie, my attention on the sky as lightning splinters the clouds. We're far enough away that thunder rolls across the plain in grumbling rumbles, only the occasional bolt close enough to produce chest-rattling booms.

And yet between me and Wes, it's quiet. Easy. So much easier than I ever thought it could be. Maybe it's that I'm in the eye of his storm. Maybe I've been lulled into a false sense of security and the chaos is soon to return worse than ever.

Or maybe I was just wrong about him.

"I like chasing with you too," I say softly, just loud enough to make sure he hears me over the wind. Tipping my head back to rest on his shoulder, I catch his eyes before he can mask his pleased surprise, the occasional raindrop splattering on my cheek.

His arms tighten when he bends to steal a kiss. It starts sweet and quickly morphs into something else entirely, need pouring off him and pounding in every beat of my pulse.

Until a lightning bolt comes down so close we both jump from the resulting crash of thunder.

"Probably shouldn't get too distracted." Wes lets go with a last lingering kiss before checking on his camera. "Open field. Lightning. All that."

"Is this the part where I call *you* the fun police?"

He flattens his palms over his heart, all exaggerated incredulity. "Sloane Michaels, are you suggesting something *risky*?"

I roll my eyes, but there's no fighting a grin.

"CGs seem to be coming down to the right of the rain." Wes points as another brilliant streak of lightning explodes out of the clouds, illuminating the field and the underside of the storm as it slams into the ground. "I'd kill for a nice big bolt to come down behind that windmill."

"Or a crawler above all of it."

There's a metaphor somewhere in there. Wes preferring the stark, blinding beauty of cloud-to-ground lightning versus my preference for the delicate webbing that races through the clouds like a million electrified fingers.

Almost as if on command, lightning forks above our heads. It's probably out of my frame, but I tip my head back to catch a glimpse. Rain spatters across my cheeks and forehead, a light sprinkle with the occasional fat drop, the heat of the day warring with the cool rain. If someone could capture the scent of hot asphalt with fresh rain in a candle, I'd buy a lifetime supply.

"You know, of all the dangerous stuff out here, none of us really think twice about lightning," Wes says, amusement lacing every word.

"Those are taller than us," I say with a laugh, pointing at a nearby telephone pole.

But he has a point. I may not take it as far as he does, but aren't we all a little reckless out here, chasing lightning and some of the most destructive storms on the planet? A sane person would run in the other direction.

Maybe we're all just different brands of crazy. Maybe Wes and I aren't so different after all.

"What's your lightning unicorn shot?"

"Tornado with a rainbow and lightning." My eyes slide toward him, and I'm thrown by how relaxed he seems. Wes is someone I associate with a nearly frantic sort of energy, an inability to be still. As if he's running from something instead of toward it at all times.

But now, in this field in the middle of nowhere, alone with

me, lightning crackling overhead, he's calm. His posture is easy, his shoulders relaxed, and the faint trace of a smile tugs at his lips.

"What's yours? Your lightning unicorn?" I ask, suddenly curious.

"Lightning with the Milky Way." The sun hasn't set, but I still instinctively glance up as Wes adds, "I've gotten close a few times. I did some work a few years ago for one of the desert outfitters, but the monsoon storms weren't in the right place to make it work."

A trickle of guilt for all my implying that he's just a spoiled trust fund kid returns at the reminder of the various jobs I've known nothing about. "I'd love to see some of the photos if you have any with you. I never have time for monsoon."

Pleasure softens Wes's expression. "Yeah?"

I nod, pressing back into him as his arms tighten around me. "I love your work. I wish I had more time to travel. See glaciers and the northern lights and penguins."

He hums, low and intimate against my skin. "Lightning with the northern lights would be the ultimate goal, but that's even harder to pull off."

"I guess they're called unicorn shots for a reason." I sigh wistfully, a montage of all the hard-to-get shots I've dreamed of flickering by. "The tornado and rainbow was your first time in *Nature Shots*, right?"

I remember seeing the announcement and being jealous as hell of not only the shot Wes got—in June, when I was up to my eyeballs in lace and peonies instead of dust and rain—but that he landed a spot with the magazine at twenty-five.

"Yeah. I sent it in figuring why not. I never thought they'd actually want to license it." He shrugs and adds, "Maybe this is the year you get your unicorn."

I shake my head with a rueful laugh. "I've been trying for that shot for ages. Trust me, I'd love to finally get it this year so I could submit it for the cover, but that would be a miracle. Not to mention everyone else out here would probably get a similar shot if it all lined up."

"There's a ton of people out today, but we're alone here. If a tornado and rainbow were to appear, we would be the only ones who could get a shot with this foreground."

"True." I shrug and turn in his arms, trusting the camera to do its thing while the sky continues to put on a show. I study Wes's expression in the flickering light. "I want to win," I tell him, holding eye contact. "For myself. All joking aside, I just want you to know that. It's not really about beating you. A nice perk," I add with an affectionate squeeze of his shoulder. "But it's not the main reason. The other chasers, they respect you. I want that."

"They respect you."

"You think this morning was a show of respect?" His expression darkens, but Wes doesn't argue. "Outside of our small circle, no one comes up to me and asks for tips. No one asks my opinion on which cells to go after. And you heard what they said this morning. They think that I'm with you as some kind of maneuver for the contest."

"They have no idea what they're talking about."

"You're missing the point." I glance back at our cameras and the storm stretched out across the sky. "I like weddings. Mostly. But I'm tired of the client drama. I want to do more landscape work, and the only way that's happening for me at this point is if I can make a splash somewhere. *Nature Shots* can give me that."

"So let's make it happen," Wes says, like it's that simple. "That's our goal the rest of the season. We'll find you the shot."

I blink, still not entirely used to how generous he is when it comes to supporting me and my goals. Maybe I should be by now, but it's a hard adjustment after years of putting everyone else first. Years where every time someone let me down, my heart just added another brick to the walls steadily built up by disappointment after disappointment.

Wes is starting to make me want to build something else entirely.

"We've got almost a month left," I say quietly. "At some point we'll get close enough to my place to grab your car. You need to get your shots too."

"If you want your space, I get it, but we could finish out the season together. Swap to my car and put the miles on my tires instead of yours whenever we end up out that way." He curls his fingers around my hip and pulls me closer. "Ask the question you really want to ask, Sloane."

"We might be pretty far from Colorado when it's time for me to head home," I hedge. "I wouldn't want you to have to give up chase time to drive me back."

"That's not a question." Wes nuzzles into my hair, his breath warm on my neck. "Ask the real question."

"Practically speaking, it would save a bunch of money to keep chasing together," I say tentatively, my heart beginning to hammer. Logic insists that he's just as into what's happening between us as I am, but I've never been with someone who can draw honesty—and vulnerability—out of me the way that Wes does.

"It would." He laughs quietly, and I instantly regret my words. At least until he says in a low, affection-laced drawl, "Still not a question, darlin'."

I huff and squeeze my eyes shut. "Doyouwanttokeepchasingtogetherfortherestofmyseason?"

Wes curls his fingers around my jaw and tips my chin up, lightning illuminating the gray-blue of his eyes. "I want you to look at me when I say this," he says, so soft it's almost lost on the wind. He waits, patient as ever, until I do as he asks. Only then does his other hand join the first, cupping my cheeks between them. "Have you figured out yet why I kissed you at that gas station?"

The intensity of his unguarded emotions is too much. Focusing on some distant point over his shoulder, I mumble, "Seemed like a good idea at the time?"

"Eyes on me, Sloane." His thumbs gently guide me until our stares lock again. "I kissed you that day because after all these years, once I finally had you in my arms and thought you'd let me, I couldn't stop myself." He swallows, his throat bobbing. "That kiss wasn't a favor. That kiss was a goddamn *reckoning*."

I couldn't take my eyes off him now, even if I wanted to. Not with all the emotion he isn't trying to hide pouring out. The want, the need, but also the vulnerability of the confession. "*Years?*" I repeat, dumbfounded.

Each flash of lightning illuminates his features more starkly, capturing just how serious Wes is when he says, "You're gorgeous." He leans in to press a soft kiss to my cheek. "Talented." He kisses the other cheek. "With a wicked tongue and a sharp sense of humor that I look forward to all year."

Wes pulls back, that intense look still on his face and an unspoken *I want more* floating between us. "Your brother got in touch the other day. Everything's fixed."

"Oh." I swallow my confusion and force my tone to stay light. "You never said anything."

"I didn't. And maybe that was wrong of me, but . . ." He brushes a stray strand of hair off my forehead. "I don't want this to end. I want to finish the season with you."

Maybe I should be annoyed that Wes didn't tell me, but the truth is that we've been chasing together for nearly three weeks now. Even after telling my brother to take his time, some part of me knew that the repairs must be done. I could have texted Eric to ask him myself at any point.

It's only now that I can admit why I didn't—I didn't want to go back to chasing alone either. Even if getting closer to Wes terrifies me. Even if I don't entirely know what any of this means, what will happen in another three weeks when my season ends.

But that's a problem for another time.

"Okay." I trace a path down Wes's broad shoulders and toned biceps to the nip of his waist and the curve of his ass, pressing closer as I push onto my toes. My heart pounds, a staccato rhythm to match the lightning above. "Let's finish my season together."

I tug his mouth down to mine, heedless of the raindrops peppering our skin. Thunder rumbles all around us, flashes flickering against my closed eyelids, but I'm so absorbed in kissing Wes that it's a distant, faraway sound.

At least until our phones start howling.

"Oh shit." I stare down at the emergency message with a twist of unease. "Baseball hail. I didn't think this storm was that strong."

"It's not," Wes says, his voice grim. "But the one coming up behind it is. Time to go."

CHAPTER FIFTEEN

WE AREN'T EVEN BACK TO THE HIGHWAY YET WHEN Tracy calls.

"Hey, Tracy, did you see—"

"Baseballs? Yeah, I saw it. We might have bigger problems." Her grim voice has the hair on the back of my neck standing up before she asks, "You guys anywhere near town? I've got a bad feeling about this."

"No, we're on our way in now. Wes is driving." I hesitate, glancing over at him. His usual easy expression is gone, eyes flicking from the road to me and back again. "You think the town is getting hit?"

Anxiety curdles my stomach. I already know the answer. The possibility of a tornado would only put that tone in her voice for one reason.

"We're a couple miles west. It keeps moving the way it is, if a tornado comes down . . ."

"It'll plow right into them." I squeeze my eyes shut, only opening them when Wes's fingers brush mine. Without thought,

I spread my fingers wide and refuse to overthink the effect something so simple as holding hands has on me.

"It's not looking good."

I glance at Wes. He catches my eye long enough to dip his chin in a nod. "We're heading your way. Just in case."

As soon as I hang up, I juggle finding Tracy's blue dot on the radar app, updating the GPS, and catching Wes up. The hail coming up behind us remains a concern, but when we stop to top off the gas tank, I find a path that avoids it if we're fast.

Wes emerges from the gas station with two cases of water in his arms and a hard set to his shoulders. I hurry to open the car door for him, and when our eyes meet, his are serious. "Just in case," he says softly.

"Let's hope we don't need it."

We make it to Tracy and Matt's location on the side of the road with forty minutes to go until sunset. On the edge of town, two miles south of the seething storm, Wes and I exchange nervous glances as we get out of the car. Light leaks from the horizon and casts the whole scene in an eerie glow.

No one says a word. Wes plants himself next to me, arms crossed and radiating tension. Tracy watches the sky with her hands shoved in her pockets, while Matt paces a short circuit, constantly looking down at the radar app on his phone.

"Funnel." Matt is the first to spot it, one finger pointing upward. His voice is flat, all the usual excitement stripped out by the gravity of what's about to happen.

"Don't do it, you bastard," I mutter under my breath as it wobbles above the town. My stomach knots with dread. "Don't you dare do it."

Wind howls past us, strong enough to send me stumbling. Wes tugs me into his side, his body warm, his scent familiar, and presses a kiss to my temple. Whatever low words of comfort he murmurs are lost on the wind.

We watch in horror as the funnel lowers. Our pleas and curses are entirely ineffective. I'm already dialing the emergency number to call it in when an explosion of dirt transforms the swirling vortex from funnel to tornado. Sirens start to wail less than a minute after I hang up. There's nothing we can do but watch as a stovepipe forms, the column of whirling air quickly turning a blackish brown as it sucks up dirt and debris.

The steel grain silos perched at the edge of town break apart like wet paper as they're sucked into the murk of the storm, quickly followed by a flash of blue-green light and a loud boom as the first transformer blows. The noise turns deafening. The high-pitched train whistle of the tornado, the roar of the wind, thunder, and more exploding transformers tear the evening apart one after the other like apocalyptic dominoes.

When you see a disaster on TV, there's a boundary to it; it can't exist beyond the confines of your screen. On the ground, there's no escaping it. I've never been to a war zone, but I have to think it's not unlike the aftermath of a tornado ripping through a town. It's a level of destruction almost too big for the mind to handle.

Seconds are all it takes. One minute, we're staring at a row of neat houses. The next, trees are ripped out at their roots, roofs are missing, windows are blown out, walls are shredded like tissue, and cars are tossed upside down like toys.

The tornado is still visible, the debris field widening as it roars through the town. With tornado warnings posted fifteen minutes before it touched down, I can only hope residents took it seriously and everyone is safe in a storm shelter.

"Let's go." My voice is hoarse as I turn back toward the car. "We shouldn't drive too far into town in case there's a gas leak. Wes grabbed some extra water earlier. There's probably wires down, and they might be live, so we need to—"

"Sloane." Wes grabs hold of my shoulders in a gentle but firm touch. "We've all done this before." He leans his forehead against mine for a few precious seconds, takes a long breath, and then opens my door for me. The sirens continue to wail behind us. "I'll be right there with you the whole time."

I nod, squeeze his hand one more time, and steel myself for what's coming. It doesn't escape me that Wes never says it will be okay. We both know that while it might be true for us, for the people who live here, it's not.

It only takes a few minutes to reach the edge of the destruction. Uprooted trees tangle in downed power lines. Shingles lay scattered across the road like confetti. Glass crunches under my boots when I get out of the car, the scent of freshly split wood heavy in the air.

We move quickly, emptying our camera bags and leaving our gear tucked under the seats. It's replaced by first aid supplies and bottles of water. I hand Wes the small axe I keep in my emergency kit, stuff another bottle of water in my bag for good measure, and then take a long, slow breath.

His hand grazes my lower back in a comforting touch. "C'mon," he says. "Let's help who we can."

After making sure Tracy and Matt have plenty of water bottles to hand out too, Wes and I head in one direction while they take another. We'll cover more ground in separate pairs.

The first couple of houses aren't damaged too badly, families emerging unscathed from their storm shelters. But as we move deeper into town, the damage quickly grows worse. I peer into cars parked on the side of the road with their windows smashed out, relieved when I find them empty.

I try very hard not to think about the image of Wes's car in a similar state and how badly that could have ended. Our eyes catch when I reach out to squeeze his hand. I'm pretty sure I'm not the only one thinking about that moment right now by the way his throat bobs before he looks pointedly away.

We start knocking on what's left of front doors, ears straining for cries for help in the near-deafening silence that falls once the tornado sirens abruptly cut out. No one answers, but at the muffled bark of a dog, Wes glances back at me before shoving his shoulder into the door we just knocked on. Hard.

"Anyone inside?" he shouts, ducking under the branch that's sticking through one of the front windows. "Call out if you need help!"

The house groans when he pushes his way inside. "Careful!" I hiss, reaching for the back of his T-shirt and grabbing a fistful of fabric. "You don't need to get trapped in there too."

This time, the barking is accompanied by the faint sound of a man's voice, too quiet to make out words. Wes hesitates, takes another step into the house, and waits to see if anything else shifts. "I'll be okay," he says over his shoulder, but that doesn't stop him from pointing toward the debris-littered yard. "Wait out here while I see what we're dealing with."

Apprehension tightens my throat. "If it's not safe for me, then—"

"Sloane. Please. I know you're capable, but I can't handle you being in here with me, all right?"

The strangeness in his voice clicks into place. Fear. Wes is afraid for me—and we don't have time to argue about it. I nod, take a step back, and wait the longest two minutes of my life for him to come back out with an elderly man's arm slung over his shoulders. A black lab follows so closely that Wes nearly trips on his way past the door barely hanging on to one hinge.

"Damn dresser tipped over," the man says as we help him out to his driveway where, by some miracle, his car sits undamaged. "Couldn't get out of the closet."

We linger long enough to make sure he's able to sit down, hand him a bottle of water, and then we're on to the next house.

Before long, the town is swarming with first responders. We help where we can and get out of the way where we can't. Someone hands Wes a chainsaw, and he goes to work taking apart tree limbs blocking access to roads while carefully avoiding the downed power lines strewn everywhere.

I lose track of time, squinting against the low angle of the sun as I work, heat and humidity rebuilding rapidly in the wake of the storm. It's one of the cruelest things—not twenty minutes after ruining lives, the sky is painted with one of the most stunning sunsets I've ever seen. I swear it's hotter now than it was before the storm, sweat dripping from every inch of me as I hand out water bottles next to one of the EMTs.

Night creeps in a little at a time and then all at once, the darkness broken by an army of flashing blue and red lights, the endless buzz of chainsaws filling the air.

I meet the eyes of strangers over and over, offering what little comfort I can. My thoughts stagger between guilt and grief. This would have happened whether we were here or not, but it's hard not to feel like the worst kind of vulture. This town will bear the scar of today for years to come. I'm going to climb into a clean, dry vehicle and drive away from the carnage. It's hard to reconcile that something I love, the season I look forward to all year as an escape, can quickly turn into someone else's private hell.

I nearly jump out of my skin when a hand lands on my shoulder. "Sloane," Wes rasps, sawdust and dirt streaked across his face. His shirt is soaked in sweat, dotted with mud and what looks like blood. I hope it's not his. "You're bleeding," he says, holding my wrist with exquisite gentleness so he can study the long scratch on my forearm that I didn't notice.

I think one of the tree branches got me when I helped Wes pull someone out through what used to be their living room window, but it's impossible to know. "I'll clean it later."

The EMT next to us glances at my arm, seemingly noticing the long scrape for the first time. "Not much left for y'all to do," she says, not unkindly. "We appreciate the help, but might as well get on out of here."

My first impulse is to argue, but she's right. There's a fine line between helping and getting in the way. The last thing we need to do is tip over into the latter. Wes slings his arm around my shoulders, and despite the sweat and dirt and exhaustion, I press into his side just to feel how very alive he is against me.

We catch up to Tracy and Matt on our way back to the car. Their expressions match ours, mud-streaked, weary, and just a little haunted. Tracy's attention drifts toward Wes's arm around me. "You know where you're staying tonight?"

His fingers flex on my shoulder, his grip tightening and relaxing so quickly I suspect it's unintentional.

"Not yet." He glances down at me. "Should probably figure that out, though. Anything around here is going to be full with families and first responders. Might need to drive for a bit."

"We found a place just over the Nebraska border that had rooms. I'll text you a link." Matt's jaw cracks open with a wide yawn. He barely stops himself from wiping at his eyes, grimacing at the grime covering his hands. "We can all do the drive together. Everyone is tired. Roads are going to be dark."

"Thanks." I slip out of Wes's hold to throw my arms around Tracy. It's not the first time we've witnessed this kind of destruction, and it's unlikely to be the last, but it doesn't get much easier. Her arms tighten, holding on just a fraction longer than she usually would, before she starts yawning too, and we all agree it's best to get on the road before anyone falls asleep.

"I'll drive," I tell Wes, nudging him toward the passenger seat. "You did the heavy lifting."

The fact that he doesn't argue tells me just how exhausted he is. Wes drops into his seat with a groan, then fishes around in the back seat for a bottle of water. "Let me see your arm before we go anywhere."

"I'll deal with it at the hotel."

"You'll deal with it now." It's gently said, but he isn't backing down. I sigh and give him my arm after he slathers sanitizer over his hands, trying not to wince as he dabs at the crusted blood with some napkins from the glove box. Antibiotic ointment goes on next, followed by a large bandage from the bottom of his bag.

As soon as he's done fussing over me, I pull out behind Tracy and Matt. "Does that place Matt booked still have rooms?"

"Checking now." Wes frowns, his expression illuminated in the pale blue light of his phone screen. "Says they've got two left."

I chew on my lip and stare at the red glow of Tracy's taillights as we make our way back toward the highway. I'm about to reply with a flip comment. Another joke to hide that this thing between us *is* something I want—just like I've done for most of my life.

Maybe it's the long stretch of darkness pressing in all around us. Maybe it's that I just watched Wes spend hours putting himself at risk to help strangers. Maybe it's the conversation we had in that field full of lightning.

Maybe I'm just too tired to keep pretending I don't want this as much as I do.

I tighten my grip on the steering wheel and sneak a quick glance at him before I slowly ask, "You think we should leave one open if someone else needs it?"

"Would be the responsible thing to do," Wes says, exhaustion and emotion drawing out his accent. His hand slides across the dark interior of the car and settles on my thigh in a loose hold. "If that's what you want."

Warmth floods my veins. I drop my hand on top of his and give him a light squeeze. "I don't want to be alone tonight."

Wes squeezes back. "Neither do I."

IT'S NEARLY MIDNIGHT by the time we all drag ourselves into the lobby of the hotel, four exhausted and bedraggled storm chasers weighed down by duffels and camera bags.

Naturally, the guy at the front desk moves like he's trapped in glue as he checks Tracy and Matt in first. He's going for friendly, rambling on about the pool—which closed two hours ago—despite the late hour and how visibly drained we all are.

When it's finally mine and Wes's turn, I give Tracy's shoulder a sympathetic squeeze. "Don't wait for us. Go sleep."

She leans closer, her voice barely audible when she says, "Sharing rooms now?"

"We didn't want to take both in case someone else needed it," I hiss back, thankful that Wes is dealing with the chatty desk clerk and isn't paying attention to our conversation.

"Mmmhmm." Tracy gives me one of her infamous you-are-full-of-shit-and-we-both-know-it looks. Matt thankfully chooses that moment to clear his throat and save me from more questions. At least for tonight.

One long-winded attempt by the desk clerk to make the continental breakfast as appealing as a ten-course tasting menu in Paris later, Wes hands me a key and barely manages to stifle a yawn. "C'mon, darlin'." He settles his hand on my hip as we shuffle toward the elevator. "Let's go fall down."

"Shower," I mutter into his shoulder. Tracy's teasing aside, I'm glad I won't be alone tonight. Under the sweat, the familiar scent of Wes is a balm on my jagged edges. "We both really need to shower first."

He hums his agreement, but it's not until he pushes open the door to our room and my eyes drift to the large bed in the middle of the space that it really sinks in. We're alone, in a hotel room, and this time it's far from medicinal.

"There's a twenty-four-hour diner across the street. Why don't I grab us some takeout while you get cleaned up?" Wes sets his camera bag down gently on the floor and then drops his duffel next to it before stretching his arms above his head and yawning.

My stomach rumbles a reminder that our stop for lunch was over ten hours ago. "Grilled cheese and a giant pile of fries sounds great."

"Yeah it does." He flashes me a tired smile and bends to grab his wallet from his camera bag. "Go get clean. It'll help."

I can't help a laugh when I step into the bathroom and glance over at the shower. I'll have to stoop to fit. Wes is going to have to practically bend himself in half.

Shoving aside the thought that a naked, wet Wes is shortly to occupy the same space I'm standing in, I hurry through the shower, wincing and hissing as the hot water finds every last nick and scrape I've collected over the course of the evening. At least when I pull the bandage off my arm, the scrape isn't nearly as bad as it originally looked.

By the time Wes is back, I'm perched on the edge of the bed in a clean pair of sleep shorts and a tank top, towel-drying my hair as best I can in the chilly air-conditioning. He frowns when I shiver, pausing with his outstretched hand only halfway within reach.

"I got you a chocolate shake too," he says hesitantly, giving the cup in his hand a light jostle. "But if you're cold . . ."

"Don't care. Today absolutely calls for chocolate." I push to my feet so I can take the drink from him, sucking down a gulp that makes my teeth sting. "This is amazing. You're the best," I say before brushing a kiss against his cheek, more touched than I want to admit that he remembered my weakness for chocolate milkshakes.

Wes's eyes are soft and full of affection when he gazes down at me. "You are remarkably easy to please sometimes."

I shrug. "I'm a simple girl."

He laughs and reaches into his bag for the giant hoodie I reluctantly returned after my migraine episode. "You are one of the most complicated women I've ever met, Sloane." He holds out the hoodie, satisfaction softening his expression when I take it. "And before you get in your head, I *like* complicated." Leaning closer, he brushes his lips against my hair before turning back to his bag and grabbing his shower kit. "Put that on so you stop shivering."

With a mock salute, I yank the soft cotton over my head and press my face into the fabric. His scent fills my nose, but it's the tiny, satisfied smile I catch on his face as he heads for the bathroom that warms me the most.

A few seconds after he shuts the bathroom door, his groan is loud enough to be heard through the flimsy wood. I giggle to myself and continue to happily devour french fries. He's barely in the shower for five minutes before the water shuts off and he emerges, still dripping, with a towel clutched at his waist.

"That shower"—Wes jabs a finger back toward the bathroom—"is designed for children. I nearly took my head off getting in."

My laughter fades as I take him in. "You look just fine to me."

It's not the lighthearted quip I intend, but in my defense, a nearly naked Wes with water droplets sliding down his chest, highlighting delicious curves of muscle, is no small thing to ignore. His skin shimmers in the low lamplight, the birds scattered across his chest rippling with each movement as he takes a few steps closer.

"Fine, huh?"

Perched on the edge of the bed as I am, I have to tip my head back when he comes to a stop. "Yep. Perfectly fine." One of my hands gets a mind of its own, rising to follow a water droplet down his chest and abdomen before disappearing into the towel.

Goosebumps erupt over his skin. Wes takes a step back with a choked cough, knuckles white where he's clutching the towel. With a final smoldering look, he heads back into the bathroom. This time when he emerges, he's dry and wearing black sweatpants.

Gray would have been better. No shirt, though. Not complaining.

Wes sinks down on the bed next to me, but rather than reaching for his food, he lets out a long sigh and tips his head over to lean on my shoulder. His hair is still damp and tickles my neck, his breath warm where it fans across my collarbones. "I wish we could do more to help," he says quietly, his words nearly lost in my skin.

My heart squeezes. "Me too," I reply, just as quietly. I lift one hand and gently drag my nails over his scalp. He presses closer, leaning into me, and of all the moods I've found him in, I don't think I've ever seen Wes let his guard down like this. "It's not like any of us want these storms to hit houses instead of fields, and I know it's better for us to help than to just outrun it, but . . ."

"Still feels like we're intruding," he says softly, the words half lost in my hair. Wes slips one arm around my waist and tugs me just a little closer when I let out a quiet "Yeah."

We stay like that for a few more minutes before he pushes himself upright and grabs his own grilled cheese. I pull up the forecast while he eats, and we fall into the more familiar rhythm of evaluating our options for tomorrow.

There's nothing familiar about the way my heart races when we finally get into bed together.

After everything today—our conversation in the field, his confession, the abrupt shift to disaster and destruction—my emotions are raw and close to the surface. Cracking my heart open even more and letting Wes have a closer look is far scarier than anything we faced today.

Sex will shift our relationship in a way there's no coming back from. Unless of course he's terrible—which I sincerely doubt—but the truth is, I have no idea what he's like in bed.

But I sure could give a cat a run for its money with my current level of curiosity.

Clicking off the lamp only makes it worse. In the dark, every little sound is amplified. The rasp of starched sheets over skin. Every breath Wes takes. My own heartbeat pounding in my ears. The distant rumble of thunder. I turn onto my side, but then I can't get comfortable, so I turn onto my other side. It doesn't help.

Wes sighs, mutters something under his breath I don't catch, and rolls toward me. I'm in his arms a breath later, his chest warm against my back and his arm a solid weight across my waist. "Sleep, Sloane," he murmurs, nuzzling into my hair. "I've got you."

His warmth sinks into me, and it's been such a long day I should be asleep in seconds. Instead I become aware of every inch of his body touching mine. Freshly showered, the scent of his soap is strong, only adding to the sensation of being surrounded by him. His thighs are pressed to mine, the bare skin of his forearm resting on my stomach where my shirt has ridden up.

"Sloane . . ." My name emerges as a garbled plea when I shift my weight again. Wes slides his hand to my hip and tightens his hold. "You okay?"

My thoughts are racing, a tangle of guilt and grief over today's destruction, and even more guilt over the fact that I'm quickly becoming consumed with something else. Something I don't entirely know how to verbalize, but when I press my ass back into Wes, he gets the message.

And I get hard evidence his thoughts aren't far from mine.

"You trying to start something, darlin'?" Wes rubs his palm down the outside of my thigh and back up in a slow stroke. When I stay quiet, he dips his mouth to my shoulder and presses an open-mouthed kiss to my skin in what feels like invitation.

Guilt momentarily wins. "No," I whisper. He goes utterly still, his grip loosening and his body easing away from mine. I grab his hand before he can pull it off my thigh and hold tight. "Wait. Maybe. I don't know."

I do know. I want to lose myself with Wes for a little while. I want him to kiss me and tease me and play with me. I want to close my eyes and see the vibrant life in his instead of a tornado swallowing houses.

But I also don't want to open a door that I'll never be able to shut. I'm not a casual sex sort of person. Sometimes I wish I was. This all would be so much easier if I could just enjoy myself and let the chips fall where they may.

I'm already in dangerously deep. I want to believe Wes meant it when he said he's wanted to kiss me for years. I want to trust him that he chose not to tell me his windows were fixed because he wants more time with me.

The thread of panic that's been building since we got in bed has other ideas. "I don't do casual," I blurt, immediately followed by a curse under my breath. That was supposed to be an inside-my-head thought. "Sorry, I—"

"Don't you dare apologize." There's a beat of silence before Wes lets out a long sigh. "I knew we should have had this conversation yesterday."

My heart sinks. I concentrate on keeping my breath even. "Got it," I mumble, easing away. "You don't have to explain."

Wes tugs gently on my shoulder, nudges me onto my back, and leans over me. My vision has adjusted to the darkness, all the little LED lights and the glow of the parking lot leaking around the edges of the curtains enough for me to take in his expression. A slight groove between his brows, lips just barely parted, he stares down at me as though he might be able to read my mind if he looks hard enough.

He might actually manage it.

"What part of *years* was unclear to you, darlin'?" His eyes glint in the dark. "I get why you might think that that's all I want here, based off my history. You're wrong. My reasons for staying single have had a lot more to do with the amount I travel and how hard that can be for someone at home. I tried, in the beginning, but a lot of women don't get why I can't just take the corporate job my dad keeps trying to push on me and keep photography as a hobby."

I barely manage to contain a snort of laughter. Wes belongs in an office the way a wild mustang belongs in a zoo enclosure.

"Let me be clear," he continues. "I want you. I *have* wanted you. When I said 'years' earlier, it wasn't an exaggeration."

Desire and embarrassment rush into my cheeks. I've been so wrapped up in my own crap that I've invented my own reasons for his behavior and ignored the simplest explanation—Tracy and Matt, the two people who know us best, have been right all along.

"Sloane?"

"Yeah?" I ask, still too dazed to form a full sentence.

"I'd really like to kiss you now."

As soon as a breathless *yes, please* leaves my mouth, Wes slams his lips into mine, one hand on the back of my neck in a possessive hold I like far too much. The kiss doesn't last long, but his mouth might as well be a brand.

"You and me? It was never going to be casual," Wes says in a quiet, intense murmur when he breaks the kiss. Our breaths saw in and out like we've both just outrun a storm. "We good?"

I stare up at him, searching for some hint that he's just telling me what he thinks I want to hear. That he might not mean it. All I find is patience and warmth. "Yeah," I whisper into the dark, so quiet it's a miracle he can hear me over the hum of the air-conditioning. "We're good."

Reaching up, I curl my fingers into his hair and tug lightly, drawing his mouth down to mine in a languid kiss. Our lips and tongues tease, slowly reigniting the fire in my belly that never quite goes out when Wes is around.

"If you need me to say it," I murmur against his skin, "this is me, starting something."

"That so?" Wes's rough voice scrapes over me. His laughter fades quickly, replaced by pure need when he curves his fingers around my jaw to keep me in place for a kiss that holds nothing back. His other hand skims down over my body, then under my shirt, his thumb caressing the dip of my waist and then higher. I groan into his mouth when he reaches my nipple, my nails digging into his shoulder in an attempt to bring him closer.

"I haven't stopped thinking about your hands on me," I confess in a breathless rush, arching into his touch when he palms my breast.

"Just my hands?" A wicked laugh sends heat pooling low in my belly. "Because," Wes begins, lowering his mouth to my shoulder and trailing kisses down to my chest, "I've been thinkin' an awful lot about getting my mouth on you." His tongue dips under the neckline of my tank top in a filthy tease. "I've been thinkin' about how good you'll taste coming on my tongue." He lifts his head and stares down at me, dragging the neckline of my tank top a little lower and staring like he wants to take a bite out of me. "How's that sound?"

"Great," I squeak, right before swallowing a moan when he lowers his mouth to my breast.

It's late, and we should both be too exhausted for this, but he takes his time anyway, mapping my breasts and hips with light touches that transform into punishing pleasure, only to soften into a tease. He peels my tank top off slowly, satisfaction gleaming in his eyes at the sight of my bare skin. We kiss and touch, my lips tracing his tattoos like I've wanted to since that morning in my kitchen. His hands roam the entire time as though he can't bear to stop touching me.

I'm gasping for air by the time he hooks his thumbs into the waistband of my shorts. Wes isn't in any better shape, his chest rising and falling with each harsh breath.

Wordlessly, I lift off the bed to help him. My shorts land somewhere on the floor, but my attention is fixed on the rapt expression I can just barely make out on his face. His hands drop to my hips and hold me in place as he takes in my nakedness.

Self-consciousness stirs, but it's quickly swept away by the way Wes bites his bottom lip and reaches into his pants to stroke himself. "Your hips drive me wild. I have a real love-hate relationship with those damn leggings."

I've always thought my hips were wider than they should be. But under his rapt gaze, the thought melts away. I can't argue with him when he's looking at me like that.

"You going to stare or you going to do something about it?" I tease when I try to sit up, only for him to gently push me back down. "Or do I just . . ." Sliding one hand down my stomach, I lift one brow and give him a taunting smirk. ". . . take care of myself?"

I don't get far before Wes snatches my wrist and pins it down to the bed, his weight finally lowering onto me. "That's my job tonight," he growls, then takes my mouth in a devastating kiss.

My mind blanks under the onslaught, fingers tangling into his hair as he works his way down my body. The heat of his mouth is electric against my air-conditioner-cooled skin.

By the time Wes plunges his tongue into me, I'm so worked up I arch off the bed in a desperate attempt to get him deeper. He only laughs, pure male satisfaction that vibrates against my clit and nearly makes me come on the spot.

Two fingers slide into me before I can choke out a reply. I manage to gasp his name, my fingers clenched tight in his hair as he lowers his mouth back to my body. I nearly scream with frustration at the teasing lick of his tongue, but then he curls his fingers, strokes deep, and sucks hard on my clit.

And then he stops.

"That's it, darlin'," Wes murmurs, twisting to lightly bite my inner thigh while I writhe under his hold. "You ready to come for me?"

The sounds I manage are little more than breathless pleas and curses. He leaves me precariously teetering on the edge for a few seconds longer, his eyes hooded and intense as he takes in the state of mindless lust he's reduced me to, before Wes finally, *finally* lowers his mouth again.

My hand plunges into his hair and holds tight, desperate for relief. He groans against me, pleasure and need mingling, his tongue lashing my clit while his fingers rub a spot inside me that makes me detonate.

I might black out for a few seconds.

When my brain finally unscrambles, Wes is stretched out next to me, his arm around my waist and my cheek resting on his chest. The rest of me is half sprawled on top of him, limbs loose and boneless, shivers of lingering pleasure twitching through me.

I slide my hand down his chest and under his waistband, still struggling to catch my breath, and circle my fingers around his straining cock. "Your turn," I murmur into his skin, treating him to the same slow start he used to torture me.

"Sloane . . ." His fingers curl around my hip, flexing with each stroke as though he's fighting to hold himself in check. Then his free hand comes down on my jaw, tilting my mouth up for a kiss while I continue to use my hand on him. It isn't long before his breaths turn to ragged pants, the kiss turning desperate right before I break it to put my mouth to better use.

"Fuck," Wes groans when I lower my lips over him, swirling my tongue to collect his salty taste. I glance up to find he's pushed onto his elbows, watching as I take him deeper. "Shit, Sloane, your mouth . . ." He takes a shuddering breath, never taking his eyes off me as I set a rhythm of licking and sucking, my free hand wrapped around the base of his cock. "This is going to end far too fast."

I should torture him, pay him back for the way he kept me on edge, but I want to see Wes come undone too badly to wait. My hum of pleasure has him cursing, and that's before my hand travels lower to gently fondle his balls, already pulled tight to his body. He swears again, groaning my name with a hint of warning I choose to ignore. I flick my eyes up to his, catch his gaze, and hold it while sucking hard.

Wes comes with a hoarse cry, hips jerking and abs clenching. He's still breathing hard when he drags me up his body, kissing me deeply despite tasting himself on my lips. I'm so worked up again from watching him that I start to lower my hand between my legs for some relief. He instantly growls, "My job," and plunges his fingers back inside me, his thumb deliciously rough on my clit.

The second orgasm is fast, a rising tide of pleasure that sneaks up with little warning. We collapse into a sweaty tangle, the sound of the rain outside filtering back into my awareness while I struggle to catch my breath.

After everything that came before, the intimacy of what we just did is the final blow. My feelings for Wes aren't something I can ignore, even if they do terrify me in their strength. But as he drags me back into his arms, as his kisses turn slow and languid, I let myself believe that maybe, just maybe, I could be the one to tame some of his wildness.

CHAPTER SIXTEEN

NEITHER OF US IS IN ANY MOOD TO GET UP WHEN our alarms go off.

Wes groans into my hair and nuzzles closer. "Don't wanna," he grumbles, adorably sleepy. His hand slides down my thigh and back up to press low on my stomach to keep me in place. "Let's just stay in bed today."

"Don't tempt me." I yawn, fumbling for my phone and blearily silencing the alarm before automatically refreshing the forecast model I already have up. In the seconds it takes to load, I valiantly ignore that it's morning and I'm going to have to deal with the consequences of my choices last night.

Eventually.

Wordlessly, I pass the phone over my shoulder to Wes. I can't decide if I'm relieved or disappointed that our target area is far enough away that lingering here isn't an option. My body definitely wants to stay tangled up with him and find out just how good the hard cock nestled against my ass would feel inside me. Emotionally, I'm a bigger mess than a rural gas station after a hundred chasers blow through.

"Guess we've got places to be." He nips my shoulder before reluctantly pulling away. "Shower to wake up?"

Unabashedly naked Wes is a sight to behold. He preens at my perusal, stretching his arms high above his head and letting me look my fill before stalking over to my side of the bed. Bracing one hand on the mattress, he uses the other to hook a finger into the sheets and drag them down to my waist. "One of these days," he says, his voice still hoarse from sleep and deliciously rough as he takes in my naked breasts, "I would love to photograph you like this. Just for me."

Despite the bolt of desire his words bring on, I can't help a laugh, dragging myself up to rest against the pillows. "Remember one of those times you wanted to know what I was thinking about? Exactly that. You, naked, on the other end of my lens."

His lips curve into a pleased grin while his eyes burn. "Guess it's meant to be."

My stomach flips. Something tells me Wes isn't just talking about a naughty photo shoot. Or maybe I'm just imagining more behind the wicked tilt of his smile than there is.

"Whenever you want to take those photos, I'm all yours," Wes adds, thankfully oblivious to the direction of my thoughts.

"After storm season." I groan at the reminder of what's waiting for me in just over three weeks. "And June weddings."

Running a one-woman business takes so much time and energy there isn't always much left over for anyone else, especially by the time my family is done with me. June is my busiest month, but my calendar is never really quiet outside of the weeks I spend on the plains.

It's a huge part of why I've barely dated. The few times I tried for anything serious, the guys were always understanding—at first. That quickly morphed into almost constant complaints that I didn't make them a priority. With Wes on the road through the end of June and then jumping right into monsoon season for the summer, our time for each other is going to be limited.

Not that he seems concerned about it.

"We'll figure it out. Am I showering alone?"

"Yes. We need to get going," I remind him with a playful shove. There's nothing to be done about my worries right now. I'm just going to have to wait to see what happens when summer camp is over.

"An unfortunately valid point." Wes saunters off to the bathroom, giving me a delicious view of his muscled ass and the tattoos running down his spine. "Don't worry, darlin'. I'll still send you your daily shower porn."

"I think you need to work on your definition of porn!" I call after him with a shake of my head. He's still laughing when the bathroom door closes.

Forcing myself out of bed, I grab a shirt from the top of his bag and pull it over my head before checking emails and messages. Of course there are at least ten from my mother, and four more from Eric.

Deciding my brother is the lesser evil, I tap his name first.

I don't have room to store Wes's car at the garage forever. Put it in your driveway. Keys on the counter.

You're welcome.

Fix your second step. Almost broke my damn leg trying to get in your house.

Stay safe out there, okay? I don't want to have to be the one to tell Mom if anything happens to you.

I'm glad Wes isn't present to witness the riot of emotions that have me sucking in a breath. When he told me that Eric finished the repairs days ago, I wanted to believe his motivations were good. That he meant it last night when he said he isn't interested in casual with me.

Under his antics, Wes possesses a sweet streak I never expected. He makes me feel cared for, cherished, in a way very few people ever have. He's generous with his affection, and he's *definitely* not bad in bed.

But he also loves photography with a single-minded obsession that can easily turn toward recklessness. I've witnessed it time and time again over the years. Dented bumpers. Shredded tires.

This season hasn't been any different. That dangerous and pointless hook punch. His windows. The time he nearly drove us into that flooded road. Lying down in the middle of the road with a tornado barreling right at us, so distracted by his need to get his shot that we nearly got clotheslined by downed wires.

Wes goes after what he wants. It's a quality that's made him a successful photographer, but what would it mean for us long term? I already have a family that puts their goals, their wants, ahead of mine at every turn.

All of my mother's relationships start out with sunny skies. I've seen her showered with gifts and affection time and time again. For a month. Maybe two. And then I've watched her smiles turn brittle over and over again, watched her exhaust herself trying harder and harder and harder to be what those men wanted in the end.

Never once has she bothered to look for the inevitable storm lurking just over the horizon. What might come after the honeymoon phase.

When it comes down to it, I still don't know if Wes will make me a priority when it takes effort. When I'm not in the same car, or even the same state.

Last night might have been a mistake. Not because I didn't want or enjoy what happened between us—I did—but that might be the problem. The deeper I let him carve himself into my heart, the more likely it will destroy me if—when—he makes impulsive and reckless decisions at the expense of our relationship.

I shove the thought aside. The emotional minefield of contemplating my future with Wes will have to wait. We're together now, and with three more weeks until I need to return to Colorado, I don't need to figure it all out right now with the scent of his skin still on mine.

I do need to deal with my mother.

More than half of the messages are the usual overly dramatic guilt trips. No one ever mowed the damn lawn. She's been fined by the HOA. Again. She wants me to *deal with that uppity witch*—the HOA president, Sharon Campbell—and somehow magically solve her problems from five hundred miles away.

I'm still fuming when my phone lights up with another text from Eric. Call Mom. She's freaking out. Sam and I tried to calm her down but you know how she is. She doesn't listen to us.

I almost throw my phone.

Wes finds me glaring at it, my temper running so hot that not even the sight of him in a towel distracts me. "Um, Sloane? What happened in the last ten minutes?"

"My mother." I don't look up, continuing my furious texting. "I've never met a woman so determined to be so helpless."

"Did both of your brothers go out of town?"

"Nope." I pop the *p* with sarcastic pep. "They just made it my problem."

Wes reaches out and gently pries the phone out of my hands. "They can wait. Go shower, eat some breakfast, and then call your brothers and tell them to deal with it."

I shake my head and hold my hand out for my phone. "It's not worth the fight. They're just going to make excuses."

"They make excuses because they know they can," Wes says, not unkindly.

I start to protest, to insist that's not true, but plainly it is. Every year it's gotten to me more and more that my brothers can't ever seem to hold up their end after agreeing to deal with Mom while I'm gone. I've wondered so many times what would happen if I just blocked their numbers for the whole six weeks. I've never been able to bring myself to do it—and deep down I know why.

"Mom was eighteen when she had me. Sometimes I'm not

sure who raised who." I force a brittle smile and wrap my arms around myself before going on. "When my brothers came along, things were good for a few years, but their dad wasn't very interested in a stepdaughter. He had even less patience for my mom's crap and took off when I was eight."

Wes lays his hand on my thigh, palm up. I stare at it for a long moment, the sensation on my skin weirdly disconnected from the words coming out of my mouth. It takes more effort than it should to take his hand.

"And then the only one left to take care of everyone was you," he says quietly, his fingers tight on mine.

"Yeah. There were so many times . . ." I shake my head and blow out a breath, as if that could rid me of the memories. "I didn't want them to know how often she didn't show up for them. I knew what it was like to be forgotten, so I made sure they weren't. They were my responsibility. I guess some part of me hasn't fully let go of that."

"But they *weren't* your responsibility. They were your mom's, and *you* were her responsibility too." Wes glances down at my phone in his other hand with a frown. "I get why you wanted to protect them as kids. You shouldn't have had to—but I get it. They're adults now, Sloane. They're never going to change if you keep taking care of everything."

Wes takes a deep breath and then adds, "I love my mom, but I spent a long time fighting her battles with my dad just for her to pretend like whatever god-awful shit he said to her never happened. Like he doesn't flaunt his affairs right in front of her. It's gotten to a point where I can't do it anymore. He's been trying to use her as a weapon against me almost my entire life. The only way it ends now is if *she* decides she's had enough. I know it's not easy, but at some point, we have to stop trying to fix it all."

"I know." I clear my throat, hoping to also clear the itchy feeling brought on by Wes seeing far more of the pain my family has caused me than I'd like. It doesn't work. "Everything you're saying makes a lot of sense, but I just . . . how?"

He gives me a rueful smile and presses a kiss to my temple. "Time," he says quietly. "Time and a decent therapist."

My discomfort eases slightly. I'm still embarrassed by my family situation, but it helps to know Wes has been there. And maybe it gives me a little courage too.

I hold out my hand. "I'm going to need my phone back."

Wes perches on the edge of the mattress next to me while I dial Eric. As soon as he answers, I bark, "Hold on," and then add Sam to the call.

"What the fuck, Sloane?" he grumbles. "I was asleep. Like a normal person at seven in the morning."

"Too bad." I glance at Wes and then throw myself into the deep end. "I need you to take care of this lawn thing with Mom. Her yard is barely bigger than a postage stamp. One of you must have an hour in your day to go over there and handle it."

"The garage is busy!"

"I have plans with Cassie!"

Their protests fall on top of each other, just like I knew they would. "And I'm five hundred miles away. You can't possibly tell me there hasn't been any time at all in the last three weeks where either of you could mow the lawn."

"You could have just done it when you were here," Eric says sullenly. "Maybe I'd have had time if I wasn't working on your boyfriend's fuckup. Do you have any idea how long it took me to pick out all that glass?"

"Wait, Sloane has a boyfriend?"

"Yeah," Eric confirms. "You remember that guy she got drunk and bitched about?"

"Oh, I looked him up. Good job, Sloane."

"First, it's been like three weeks since I was home. Even if I *had* mowed the grass, it would need to be done again by now." I press my palm to my forehead, struggling not to let my frustration show. "Second, I don't have time for this crap. Someone needs to mow the damn lawn and keep Mom from getting into it with Sharon Campbell again. Which one of you is going over there and when?"

"I don't have time."

"I told you, I'm busy."

"And I'm in fucking Nebraska!" I all but shout, my hand so tight around the phone it's a wonder it doesn't break. I squeeze my eyes shut, take a long breath, and reach deep for some semblance of calm.

The back of my eyelids have no answer, but when I open my eyes, Wes says in a voice too low to be overheard, "You've been making yourself crazy trying to deal with this. *Tell* them that."

I hesitate, my brothers' protests in the background barely registering. I've heard this song so many times it's practically white noise, but I've never really let them see the toll it takes on me. Maybe it's time to stop protecting them from that too.

"I don't care," I cut into the middle of Sam's long-winded whining about how he won't be able to get his workout in today. "This is my time *away*. All I've done is deal with this bullshit. You two need to grow up and stop expecting me to fix everything. You're not kids anymore."

Wes gives me an encouraging smile and squeezes my hand. I suck in a breath, waiting for the next volley of excuses. Instead, the line is so silent I swear I can hear the sound of my own pulse hammering away.

"You're better at dealing with Mom," Sam says eventually, though for once it's contrite. "She doesn't listen to me."

"Because she knows we'll just let Sloane deal with it," Eric says with a sigh. "A buddy of mine works for his dad's landscaping business. I can probably get him to go mow the lawn for a six-pack, but I'm not dealing with the HOA lady."

"Thank you." I take another breath, glance at Wes, and then add, "Sam, you're going to be a lawyer soon. Talking to Sharon will be great negotiation practice."

"Fine," he says sullenly. "I can try, but no promises."

I blink, stunned. My brothers might be mad about it, but unless they're completely full of shit—not their usual style—Wes's suggestion may actually work.

"Please text me updates. I'm not sure what kind of service I'll have today."

"Yeah, yeah. Be careful," Eric grumbles before adding a begrudging "Love you."

"Don't end up in Oz or whatever," Sam adds, still sulky, but with his own "Love you."

"Love you too. Tell Mom I'm fine."

I hang up with a relieved sigh and let myself sink against Wes. "I can't believe that worked," I mumble into his chest, suddenly exhausted by the conversation. "I just hope they actually do what they say they will."

Wes kisses my temple and squeezes me a little closer. “Watching you stand up for yourself was kinda hot.”

Pushing myself upright, I shake my head and shove his shoulder. “Please do not mention *hot* and my brothers so close together. Gross,” I say with a fake gag, but I get what he’s doing and appreciate it.

“Fair enough.” He ducks down again so his lips are close to my ear. “I want to hear more about you talking to your brothers about me anyway.”

“*Bitching*,” I correct, suppressing a shiver at his low words. “Leave it to you to take that as a compliment.”

Neither one of us mentions that Sam called Wes my boyfriend.

“You were thinking about me,” Wes says with smug satisfaction before smacking a loud kiss against my cheek. “Go get your sweet ass in the shower while I work on finding breakfast.”

CHAPTER SEVENTEEN

THERE'S A LOT OF WAITING AROUND THAT COMES with storm chasing. Most of the time, it works out that we can while away the hours at a truck stop or gas station. Having access to running water is a definite preference, but sometimes the forecast has other plans.

Halfway down a dirt road, I kill the engine after lowering all four windows and let out a content sigh. We're surrounded by lush green fields, not another soul in sight for miles. That will change if the storm follows the path we think it will, but for now, it's just the rustle of the wind in the wheat and the scent of baked earth.

I grab my phone for a quick radar check and then swipe into my text notifications. To my amazement, Eric sent a photo of Mom's freshly mowed lawn about an hour ago. Sam must have also dealt with the HOA fine, because the only other texts from my mom are a series of complaints about how nice it is that *some* of her children care about her.

I roll my eyes and don't bother replying.

"Your brothers take care of the lawn?"

Locking my phone, I drop it into a cupholder and turn to Wes with a nod. "Shockingly, yeah, they did." I lean back into the seat and let my eyes fall shut as the breeze tickles my skin through the open window. "Frisbee before I fall asleep?" I ask with a yawn.

"I have a better idea." He waggles his brows before releasing his seat belt and reaching for mine. "When's the last time you made out in a car?"

"Other than the last couple of weeks?" I laugh, unable to help a roll of my eyes as he brings my palm to his mouth and presses an open-mouthed kiss there. "Probably when I was fifteen."

"A couple of kisses do not a make-out make." Wes sinks his teeth into the fleshy bit of my palm, not hard enough to hurt, but the pressure shivers through me. "Just say the word, darlin', and I'll show you exactly what I mean."

"You can't be serious."

He lowers my hand and gives me a stare so full of heat he might singe the surrounding fields. "Come over here and find out."

My breath stutters. Anyone could see us if they drove by, but what are the chances of that happening? The road we're on doesn't even have all that great of a vantage point as far as photos go. It's just a spot that happens to have decent cell reception so we can check the radar as the storms initiate over the next hour or two.

Before I can second guess myself, I grab on to Wes's shoulders and slide from the driver's seat over to the passenger side—and by slide, I mean topple into his lap with the grace of a sack of potatoes.

He helps me right myself with a chuckle, one hand splayed low on my back. The tips of his fingers slide under the waistband of my shorts, teasing the slightly sweaty skin as his other hand cups my jaw. "I love it when you give me that look," he sighs, stroking my bottom lip with his thumb.

"What look?" I grumble as I attempt to settle into a more comfortable position. Wes is a big guy, and while my car isn't tiny, there's not a ton of room when you add my long legs to the mix.

"The look you get when you know I'm going to talk you into doing something you want to do but think you shouldn't," he says with a wink.

I quickly forget all about finding a place for my knees when Wes tugs me more firmly into him, my thighs spread wide over his hips. His hand on my back dips further into my shorts, kneading the curve of my ass as his tongue plunges deep. He kisses me like he's been suffocating for days and I'm his only hope of a breath of air.

"Convinced yet?" he rumbles against my ear, nipping the lobe lightly.

"Mmm, I don't think so," I whisper back, his playful mood contagious. He was right. I do want this. Badly. "What else you got?"

Wes growls. Honest to god growls, the sound rushing straight between my thighs. But that's nothing compared to when he reaches for my tank top, yanks the neckline and my bra down in one rough motion, and treats my nipple to the wet, hot slide of his tongue.

"Fuck, that's good," I gasp. Playfulness evaporates as lust roars through me. Every drag of his tongue, every light nip of his teeth, spears me with a bolt of fresh desire. I don't even realize I'm rocking my hips in a fruitless search for friction until his hand clamps down to keep me in place.

"Need a minute." With a flush high in his cheeks that has nothing to do with the hot breeze blowing through the windows, Wes flicks his eyes up to mine while dragging in a ragged breath, indecision racing across his features.

Then, with a last lingering look steeped in regret, he gently tugs my bra and shirt back into place. "I don't want the first time I'm inside you to be on the side of the road."

I swallow hard, pushing my hand through his dark hair while struggling to contain my own lust. Between the rasp in his voice and the sheer *want* in his eyes, I'm not sure I've ever felt so desired before. Definitely not with all my clothes on, parked on the side of the road.

Wes leans into my touch like a great big cat eager to be pet and watches me through narrow slits. "Sorry," he says with a rueful chuckle. "I know I started it."

"Nothing to apologize for." I press a light kiss to his mouth and start to ease my way back to the driver's side, but he only tightens his arms around my waist.

"I like holding you," he says softly, leaning further back into the seat and pulling me with him. It's almost too hot for it, even with the breeze. I rest my cheek against his shoulder anyway, savoring the closeness.

I drag my finger over the top of his shoulder, skimming one of the bird tattoos. He's in a muscle tank today that exposes the curve of his biceps and the smattering of birds I now know extend from his chest.

"I got them when I was eighteen. My parents fought a lot when I was a kid. I mean, they still do."

Wes strokes a hand down my back, a soothing touch I suspect is for himself as much as it is for me. There's too much of an echo of the way I talk about my own childhood in his voice, an undercurrent of old pain that won't be dulled by words. I brush my lips over one of his tattoos and am rewarded with a soft sigh.

"When I was little, I used to hide in my closet when their fights got bad, dreaming of a way to escape," he continues. "Things never got violent, but the things my dad would say. To her, about her, about *me* . . . I used to wish I could just fly away. I made the appointment mostly as a way to piss him off. He *hates* tattoos. Some horseshit about real men not needing to disfigure themselves. But then I saw the birds and thought that if I was going to give the old man a big middle finger, I should do it in a way that meant something to me."

"What did he say when he saw?"

Wes laughs bitterly, his chest vibrating under me. "That I was turning out to be the disgrace he always knew I would be."

I jerk my head up. Anyone who grew up with loving parents would be baffled by the calm arrangement of Wes's features despite sharing the painful memory, but it's a look I know well—a look that says it's not worth being upset about when it was just one of a thousand cuts from the people who were supposed to protect us.

I don't say *I'm sorry*. It feels too meaningless. Instead, I tell him I understand the only way I know how.

"I was nine the first time Mom forgot Eric's birthday. She was out on one of her dates, and it was so late that the only thing open was the gas station, but I couldn't let him go to school without cupcakes on his birthday. So when he asked me if she was still going to make them, I lied, sent him to bed, and used some of the money a neighbor gave me for shoveling her driveway to buy a box mix." I shake my head at the memory with a humorless laugh. "Those poor kids were probably picking eggshells out of their teeth for days, but Eric had cupcakes."

"He had a sister who gave a shit," Wes says quietly, toying with the end of my braid. "Worth some crunchy cupcakes."

We spend the next hour swapping childhood war stories. I tell Wes about helping my brothers with their homework and forging my mom's signature on permission slips she forgot to sign. Driving her home from bars long before I got my license. Getting a job at fifteen that paid cash under the table since I wasn't really old enough and using that money to buy my first camera.

I giggle when he tells me about the times his mom would bring him down into the kitchen and try to teach him to cook when his father was away on business, but my heart breaks when he talks about cold, formal holidays. I made the best of the holidays with my brothers the years my mom was too wrapped up in her own life to remember she had kids who still believed in Santa. Though I wouldn't call it *merry*, it was better than the icy silence Wes describes.

After a while, we fall quiet. We're both sweaty, the breeze

doing little to cool us under the heat of the sun, but it's a long time before I climb back into my own seat.

And when Wes reaches for my hand that night at a tiny bar crammed full of our friends, I think maybe we could find the things we never had in each other.

AFTER A COUPLE of cocktails and one not-so-subtle kiss at the bar the night before, confirmation that Wes and I are together quickly spreads beyond our inner circle. The looks and whispers of *Finally* and *It's about time* aren't exactly quiet when we show up at the gas station du jour to wait for storms to form.

While Wes heads inside to refresh our water supply, I cross the parking lot to where Tracy is sprawled across a picnic table bench sunning herself. Matt is with her, tapping away at his phone with a frown.

Tracy flips her sunglasses up, squints for a couple of long seconds, and then offers a sly grin. "You look awfully relaxed, Sloane. I wonder why that could be."

"Don't start," I warn her. "Not one word from either of you."

Matt holds up his hands and shakes his head with exaggerated dismay. "I'm just saying, if you could have waited until the end of the season, I wouldn't be out a hundred bucks."

Tracy grins and waggles her fingers at her fiancé. "Don't be a sore loser."

Matt shakes his head. "You know we share a bank account, right?" Then he turns to me and adds, "Seriously, watching the two of you circle each other the last couple of years has been painful. I'm glad you figured your shit out."

I blink. "*Circle* each other?"

"Like two hot lions," Tracy confirms, nudging her shoulder into mine. "That man has been looking at you like you're a tasty snack forever. You seriously didn't notice? Because you look back."

"Everyone looks at Wes." I glance back over my shoulder by habit, easily picking him out where he's joined some chasers I don't know well, his head tipped back and his shoulders shaking with laughter. Our eyes catch and hold for a few seconds, his expression shifting to molten heat before someone taps his shoulder and he reluctantly turns away.

"Not like *that*." Tracy snorts. "Just be sure to invite us to the wedding."

"We aren't . . . We haven't . . . It's only been like two weeks!" I squeak, throwing up my hands. "I don't even know what's going to happen when I go back to Colorado. The whole thing could fall apart."

"Nah. Hot phone sex," Tracy says without hesitation at the same time our friend Andrea wanders over with her sister Ashley in tow. They're more Tracy's friends than mine, but I give them a friendly wave.

"Who's having phone sex?" Ashley asks with a little too much interest in her grin. "Hey, Sloane. Haven't seen you much this season." Her attention slides across the parking lot to where Wes is holding court. "Saw you were chasing with Talbot. How'd that happen?"

"Um, long story."

"Heard it was more than chasing," Andrea says with obvious curiosity as her attention flicks between me and Wes. "Everyone knows he's been half in love with you for years."

Everyone has to be a stretch. I gulp and laugh off the comment. Lust, sure. Wes cares about me, but calling it love is a step too far.

Not in the mood to contemplate that any further, I leave my friends to gossip among themselves and join Wes. He slides an arm around my shoulder almost as if he's not aware he's doing it and pulls me into his side. The teasing starts immediately, and though my stomach lurches uncomfortably at my personal life being a topic of discussion *again*, Wes endures it with little more than a sheepish grin. He ignores the heckling to plant a kiss on my temple, the sweetness of the gesture at war with the bubbling discomfort I'm trying so hard to ignore.

The more public this is, the more questions I may have to answer next year if it all falls apart.

"You okay?" Wes asks quietly, his lips hovering over the shell of my ear.

I nod. We probably both know I'm not exactly telling the truth, but the steady weight of his arm around me *does* help. We're in this together.

Thankfully the conversation turns when Tracy, Matt, and her friends head our way. I didn't notice when she was lying down that her engagement ring is back in place on her left hand, the diamond sparkling in the sunlight.

Ashley must not have noticed until now either. She lets out an excited squeal and grabs Tracy's hand. "Oh, it's even prettier in person!"

Andrea elbows her sister out of the way, cooing over the ring. "I don't think I've heard the engagement story."

Tracy beams at Matt. "We were hiking. He stopped and said he had to tie his shoe. Then he whips this *gorgeous* ring out of nowhere."

"Not nowhere. My pocket." Matt laughs, his hand on her back. "My *zippered* pocket. You know how terrified I was that I was going to drop it on the trail?"

"When's the wedding?" Andrea asks.

Tracy's expression falls, her comment from weeks ago echoing in my head when she manages a tight smile. "No date yet."

Her parents don't exactly hate Matt, but they're less than thrilled that he's not the good church boy they envisioned for their daughter. She's told me a little bit about their opinions, but the look on her face says there's a lot more she's been keeping to herself.

"My parents are pushing hard for the whole church, white dress, three-hundred-guests-I-barely-know routine, which is the last thing either of us wants," she explains for the rest of the group's benefit. "We really should just go to Vegas. Weddings are such endless stress and a giant waste of money." Tracy gasps, her hands flying to her mouth as she looks at me with horror. "I don't mean that *you're* a waste of money!"

I wave her off, not the least bit offended. "I see how the wedding sausage gets made. I get it. If I ever get married, I don't want the fuss. Just my friends and some sunshine." I force a grin past my guilt and add, "Oh, and a decent photographer."

I pretend not to notice the way Wes tenses when I say *if* I ever get married.

Matt's expression turns speculative while the group laughs. "You know," he starts slowly, his arm settling around Tracy's waist. "We have most of our friends here. My parents are only a couple hours away. We *could* just get married in a field." His eyes settle on me, wide with hope. "We might even be able to talk Sloane into taking photos."

"A storm chaser wedding!" Tracy lights up, genuine excitement bubbling out of her for the first time since the conversation turned to her engagement. "Wait, are you serious? I would *love* that."

Suddenly everyone's attention shifts to me. I hesitate, momentarily thrown by the weight of expectation, but Wes's solid presence steadies me—and the photos would be epic.

"I'd love to!" I smile sheepishly and add, "I don't know anything about how to make it legally binding, but I do know how to photograph storms *and* weddings."

"Oh my god, thank you!" Tracy squeals and darts forward to throw her arms around me. "I was going to ask you for recommendations in LA if we ever set a date, but I like this option so much better!"

"You are going to have the best damn wedding photos I can give you," I promise, hugging her back.

Matt happily slides his arm back around his fiancée once she lets me go. "You sure you don't mind, Sloane? We will absolutely pay your normal rate."

"Just tell me when and where." I'll argue with them about payment later. Tracy is the closest thing I have to a best friend. No way am I charging her more than a nice dinner out.

Besides, I'm burnt out on shooting big, elaborately staged weddings with demanding brides and even more demanding mothers. Tracy and Matt aren't that couple. They're two photography nerds who love storms and just want to get married without all the fuss. There won't be a mother-in-law who shows up wearing white that I need to painstakingly edit to another color in each frame; there won't be a family of twenty to wrangle into one shot and tedious head-swapping edits to make everyone look decent.

This is exactly the kind of wedding I'd *love* to shoot.

We chat a little longer and form a tentative plan to have the wedding in about a week to give Tracy and Matt time to get their side of things in order. Not that they're on their own—offers to help with a cake or flowers get tossed around pretty quickly. Someone even volunteers to drive down to Mae's for a couple dozen donuts.

Distracted by all the potential ways to shoot the wedding, I almost miss the sound of my name. Wes shakes his head with a fond smile as if he knows exactly what had my focus. Once he has my attention, he gestures to a guy I think I've met once before who's standing a few feet away.

"Adam needs a jump. You've got cables in your emergency kit, right?"

"Oh, yeah, sure." I hold out my hand to Wes for the car keys. Since his shorts have actual pockets and not the sad suggestion of them that come with women's clothing, he's turned into the keeper of the keys. "Where are you parked?"

"I don't want to bother you. Wes can do it."

I narrow my eyes. Now I remember why Adam is vaguely familiar. He's the same guy who saw me driving last week and made a snide comment about Wes *letting* me drive. I didn't bother mentioning it to Wes. It wasn't worth the trouble.

But I'm certain that not wanting to "bother" me has nothing to do with Adam's insistence that Wes handle it.

Wes shrugs. "Sloane's car, Sloane's cables." He's still being his usual friendly self, but I know him too well now. There's an edge to his voice.

"C'mon, man, she doesn't know how to—"

"We're leaving anyway," I interrupt. It's not exactly true. We were going to leave in ten minutes, once Tracy and Matt were done buying snacks, but they'll understand.

I turn to walk toward the car. Wes doesn't say a word, but the arm he keeps around my shoulders is a show of silent support I'm grateful for. I lean into him, close enough to catch the muttered *Jackass* under his breath.

"Wait, no, c'mon, man!" Adam protests behind us. "It was just a joke—"

Wes stops, breathes in sharply through his nose, and glances back over his shoulder. "Explain it, then," he says calmly. "Jokes are meant to be funny, right?"

"You're going to leave me stranded because your girl can't take a joke?"

"No." Wes looks down at me, and there's a flash of something hard on his face before he directs his attention back to Adam. "You did this to yourself, *man*. Might want to work on those jokes."

We both ignore his next protest. I don't say a word until we're a quarter mile down the road, and even then, all I manage through my anger is a barely audible "Thank you."

"Don't thank me." Disgust curls around the edge of Wes's words, emotion thickening his accent. "I didn't see it before, but I'm starting to think you deal with way too much of that shit."

"It's why I want the cover so badly," I say quietly. "I would really love to shut all of those assholes up." I force myself to loosen my fingers on the steering wheel before they start to go numb and let out the sigh I've been holding in. "I'd much rather focus on Tracy and Matt's wedding, though. You up for playing assistant?"

Wes stares out the window, a muscle twitching in his jaw, his breaths slow and measured as though it's taking effort to calm down. I reach across the front seat and wrap my fingers around his. I appreciate how much he cares, but I also don't want to waste another minute on yet another asshole with shitty opinions.

"I've never shot a wedding," Wes says eventually with a sigh. He gives my fingers a light squeeze and kisses the back of my hand. "But of course I'll help you, darlin'. Whatever you need."

"I'll give you some pointers," I promise. "You'll do great."

"What equipment do you usually use? I've got a few different lenses with me. No flash or reflectors, though."

"Me neither," I admit with a rueful laugh. "Should be able to make it work, though. My good portrait lens is at home, but it's not like Tracy and Matt want formal portraits."

"We're not that far from Colorado. We could run back to your place and grab your usual gear."

We've talked about finishing the season together. Wes hasn't faltered since that conversation—but he also hasn't had much of a choice, has he? Not without having to rely on me to bring him back to his car. This is the closest we've been to Colorado in weeks.

"I don't think we would miss much," Wes goes on, his attention on his iPad. "Tomorrow's a car wash, but the day after is looking pretty good up north. We could detour to your place and spend the night there instead of a hotel. Grab your extra gear, maybe a little extra sleep with how hard we've been going. If you agree, that's my vote."

I let go of his hand and reach for my water to give myself time to think past a twist of unease. What he's saying makes sense. I *am* exhausted, and while I could make do with the gear I have, I'd prefer the lens I left at home.

We would also have almost the entire night to ourselves. In the privacy of my house, away from paper-thin hotel walls.

As for the lingering fear that Wes could change his mind once his keys are in his pocket, well, if that's how it's going to end, at least I'll know. Before I get myself in any deeper.

"Colorado it is."

CHAPTER EIGHTEEN

DAYLIGHT IS LITTLE MORE THAN A PINK SPLASH ACROSS the peaks when we pull into my driveway. Wes's SUV, new windows gleaming in the fading light, is right where Eric said it would be.

There's a weird ache in my chest at the sight. In the five years since I bought the house, there's never been anyone but my family waiting for me when I get home—and those unannounced visits never end well. What would it be like to come home to someone?

What would it be like to come home to *Wes*?

The sudden longing brought on by the thought surprises me with its strength. I kill the ignition and lean back into the driver's seat without looking at him before he can catch the *want* that's probably painted all over my face. It's too big. Too dangerous when I still don't entirely trust that he's in this as much as he says he is. No matter how badly I'd like it to be true, if I learned anything from my mother's parade of men, some of life's biggest disappointments come packaged in pretty words.

Wes reaches for the door handle. "I guess we better go inside."

"A break from the car would be great," I reply with a laugh that hopefully doesn't sound as forced as it feels. With his arm slung around me, we grab our bags and start for the door.

"If there's time before we leave tomorrow, I'm fixing that death trap stair," Wes grumbles when he steps over the rotting step. "It won't take long, and I'll feel better knowing you're not going to hurt yourself." He yawns, waiting at my side while I fiddle with the lock and pretend I'm not having feelings about how casually he insists he's going to fix something I've been meaning to do for a year. "I'm thinking we order a pizza and crash early. You in?"

Like we're a couple who just got home and are about to spend a night curled up together on the couch. It's a fleeting glimpse of the life I just imagined—and I like it far too much.

"As long as we can get something green with that pizza," I tell Wes as we shuffle into the house. "And I don't care what sort of insane delivery fee they want to charge. We are *not* getting back in the car tonight."

"What do you want? I'll take care of it."

I blink. "You mean that, don't you?"

He gives me an odd look and mutters something about a low bar and people with shovels. "It's just pizza, darlin'."

"I know. I just . . ." I flush. "It's really nice, that's all. I get tired of deciding all the things. You don't make me do that."

It isn't until that moment I realize how true it is. In the last three and a half weeks on the road together, I can't remember Wes once turning to me at the end of the day and demanding to know what the plan was for dinner. Most of the time he'd already looked at the options and gave me two or three to pick from. It made the decisions so effortless that I hardly realized I was deciding at all.

"I like looking after you." Wes presses a kiss to my temple. "Go relax. You mind if I throw laundry in while we're here?"

"If I ask you to throw mine in too am I going to end up with all my clothes three sizes too small?" I ask. I'm only half teasing.

He shakes his head with a low noise. "Sloane, darlin', I know you've got your reasons, but one of these days, I'm going to need you to stop assuming that I'm as useless as your brothers."

"That wasn't what . . ." Guilt stains my cheeks instantly despite his gentle tone. "Sorry. I just—"

"You don't need to apologize." Wes cups my jaw in his palm and drops a light kiss on my forehead before pointing at the door that leads to the basement. "Laundry down there?"

I nod, watching him go before grabbing my camera bag and heading for my office while my emotions engage in a mental melee. I don't bother flipping on any lights, just drop the bag on my chair and then duck into my bedroom to change into something more comfortable. Except when I open my closet, I skip right over the sweats and grab a long maxi dress that's both soft against my skin and features a plunging neckline. The fabric is thin enough that it might actually be a nightgown, but since I only ever wear it around the house, that's never been a problem.

I doubt Wes is going to mind.

I'm still finger-combing out the remnants of my braid when I yawn my way back into the living room at the same moment he emerges from the basement. He's changed too, now in loose gray sweatpants and yet another black T-shirt. He freezes with his hand still on the doorknob, hunger replacing weariness. "I like that one."

"And I like those sweatpants." I let my stare dip lower. "Though I really hope you wear underwear in public."

It startles a laugh out of him. Wes glances down, as if he wasn't already aware that his pants leave *nothing* to the imagination. Maybe we had similar thoughts. "We're not in public, though, are we?" he teases with a smug grin.

I let out a pleased squeak when he sweeps me into his arms, deposits us both on the couch, and kisses me like it's been ten months instead of ten hours, before reluctantly pulling away. "Got a place you like or should I pick?"

I pluck his phone out of his hand and pull up my favorite pizza shop in town. We bicker over toppings for a few minutes—pepperoni and pineapple *absolutely* go together and Wes is just wrong about olives—but once the order is placed, he tosses his phone onto the ottoman and waggles his eyebrows at me, heat and mischief building in his eyes. "They said thirty to forty minutes. What do you think we should do with ourselves until then?"

His playfulness is contagious. I tap my chin like this is a difficult question and widen my eyes innocently. "The grocery store is only ten minutes away. You need anything before we head back out? I think I could grab some water, maybe a few apple—"

My giggles die when Wes rolls me under him on the couch, his hands skimming over my body. "There's something about you in a dress that makes me a little feral," he admits in a low rasp. "You don't actually want to go to the grocery store, right?"

I shake my head, reaching up to drape my arms around his neck and pull him closer. We kiss slowly at first, his weight pinning me to the couch, his scent surrounding me. Neither of us rushes it. The kisses gradually deepen from sensual to something hotter, soft caresses that grow into my nails digging into his shoulder and his fingers dancing down my thigh.

"I bet I can make you come before the pizza gets here," Wes says in a low rumble while gathering fistfuls of my dress with one hand. "Wanna find out?"

My breath catches. The unsatisfied ache between my legs screams *Yes, please!* but I'm not in the mood to get interrupted by a delivery driver. "They could be here soon," I hedge, glancing at my watch. It's already been twenty minutes.

"I better be fast, then." Wes kisses me again, though his hand doesn't move until I mutter *Fuck it* under my breath and pull him down by the back of his neck.

It could be that I've been dying to get his hands on me again, or it could simply be that he's that good, but he winds me up with near expert precision. Less than ten minutes later, he shoves me off a cliff, my chest heaving and pleasure rolling through me in wave after wave.

Breathing hard, I almost miss the sound of a phone buzzing on the ottoman. Wes licks his fingers clean with a wicked grin, radiating smug satisfaction. I'm about to yank him back down when his phone buzzes again.

He glances at the screen with a huffed laugh. "That'll be the pizza," he says, oh-so-pleased and a little breathless as he helps me pull my dress down and sit up. "Told you I could do it."

"You'll notice I didn't contradict you." I point down the hall to the bathroom with shaky fingers. "You answer the door. I'm going to clean up the mess you made."

And pretend my legs aren't wobbly with little spasms of pleasure still making my muscles twitch.

"You liked it." Wes glances down and smirks at the very obvious erection straining his sweats. "But, uh, about the door? Slight problem."

I give him a firm stroke over his pants. "I'm not seeing any problems."

He presses against my hand despite his choked laughter. "You want me to scar the driver?"

"Good thing we ordered contactless," I remind him before removing my hand and taking a step toward the bathroom. "Maybe after we eat we can see what other sorts of bets you want to make."

"I don't need to win bets when I have you," Wes says with the sort of sincerity that tightens my throat in a heartbeat. Then he grins. "Even if you are an uncivilized menace who doesn't understand the majesty of olives on pizza."

AFTER WE FINISH eating, Wes heads into the basement to throw laundry into the dryer while I clean up from dinner. Anticipation turns my hands clumsy. By unspoken agreement, neither of us tried to move things any further than fooling around, despite sharing a hotel room most nights. Not when we were both so exhausted we could barely keep our eyes open.

Tonight we have all the time in the world. The quick and dirty orgasm Wes gave me on the couch did nothing to cool my lust; if anything, it was an appetizer.

The fact that he's been at half-mast ever since doesn't help either.

My eyes dart down the dim hallway toward my bedroom. There's still so much we haven't talked about. *After* looms larger and larger the closer we get to the end of my chase season, an enormous question mark looming on the horizon. Physical intimacy with Wes is already intense. I already care too much. It's *already* going to wreck me if this was all a game to him. Is it really smart to tie another knot in our emotional threads right now?

I still haven't asked him about the cars again, now that we're here. Now that the choice isn't one he's making at the risk of being stranded hundreds of miles from home.

Wes finds me in the kitchen nursing a glass of water, my free hand braced on the counter. Nervous energy tightens my grip on the glass. It'll be fine. I want this. I want *him*. He wants me.

I'm still terrified of taking down this last wall between us.

Wes stops in front of me, a slight furrow between his brows. He reaches out to gently tuck a strand of loose hair behind my ear. "What's going on in that beautiful mind of yours, darlin'?"

"It's nothing." I summon a smile, toss back the last of my water, and set the glass in the sink. He hasn't done anything to deserve my doubts. I've been in and out of therapy enough to understand that I trust the familiarity of chaos in a way I don't trust peace. I was fine when we were on the couch earlier. There's no need to ruin the evening with my anxieties. "Ready for bed?"

"Not until you tell me what's got you all twisted up," he says from behind me. He's close enough that I can practically feel the heat of him, but he doesn't touch me. As though I'm a feral cat he doesn't want to spook.

Even lost in the spinning vortex of my doubts, I know Wes deserves better than being hissed at. He's been nothing but honest with me. Far more patient than I deserve. Coming here thinking I'd be testing him, testing *us*—it's the sort of thing my mother would do. Keeping my worries to myself, pretending they're not real to keep the peace, is something I learned from her.

And Wes sees right through it.

I stare at him helplessly, struggling to push past the instinct to hide. His expression remains open, posture relaxed. Patient. Wes is so damn patient with me. Even now, he could easily accept my brush off.

I've been trying so hard to avoid turning into my mother. To not pick the kind of men who leave wreckage in their wake. But she's never been entirely blameless in those relationships either, keeping secrets, playing pretend. If I keep going down this path, it will eventually poison this fragile thing that's been growing between me and Wes for weeks.

"I told you I don't do casual," I finally say, my voice barely above a whisper.

"I remember." Wes slowly runs one hand through his hair and peers at me, concern morphing into something sharper before he takes a long breath. "I told you . . . has this *felt* casual to you?"

I don't know how to explain the paradox of my thoughts. How to communicate that the reason I'm crashing out is that it *hasn't* seemed casual. That ever since he said anything between us was *never* going to be casual, I've wanted—badly—to believe him. That deep in the most hidden corners of my bruised heart, it terrifies me that I've started to want so much more than I ever thought possible.

"No," I say quietly. "It doesn't feel casual."

"Good, because my feelings for you aren't casual, Sloane. But you brought this up for a reason." Each syllable is carefully controlled, but I know Wes well enough to see the frustration beneath the calm he's trying to project. "Talk to me, darlin'."

"Wes, I . . ." Forcing air into my lungs, I lean back against the counter and curl my palms around its edge in an effort to ground myself. "You don't think this is all happening really fast? There's a lot we haven't talked about. Life stuff. Big stuff."

"Then let's talk about it." He takes a step back, then another, until he's leaning against the opposite counter. "Fast isn't always a bad thing," he says softly. "Not for me. Sometimes when you know, you *know*."

My breath catches at the implication, but I'm not ready to ask if he means it the way I think he does. I stare down at the floor, tracing the cracks in the tile I keep meaning to fix, and reach for the truth.

"My mom jumps from relationship to relationship. She throws herself in headfirst from the start. She's done it my whole life. Every single time, she says she *knows*. Not one of those relationships has ended well, including three marriages."

"You are not your mother." Wes pushes off the counter, takes a step toward me, and then stops with his arms folded across his chest. "I don't have many dealbreakers. Not when it comes to you. You already know I travel a lot. Is that going to be a problem in the future?"

I bite my lip, hating the flicker of hurt that crosses his face at my hesitation. "It won't be easy," I admit. "But it's not a dealbreaker for me, no. I travel for weddings more and more myself."

"That's one down. I'm not particularly attached to Houston. Do you want to stay here, close to your family?"

"Not so much my family." I shrug, some of my tension starting to uncoil at his matter-of-fact approach. "But I like being near the mountains."

"Okay." Wes breathes out a sigh. "Now a big one. Kids?"

I shake my head, internally bracing for his answer. "Considering I pretty much raised my brothers . . . no, not for me."

"Me neither." He unfolds his arms and comes to stand at my side, adopting a similar pose with his hands braced on the counter at his back. "Is marriage on the table? Not now," he adds, probably because my eyes almost fall out of my head. "But one day."

"I think so, yeah," I whisper. My heart pounds at the enormity of the thought. "One day."

His lips curve with familiar mischief. "Dogs?"

"With the amount we both travel?"

Wes shrugs. "Dogs travel."

"I've never had a pet," I admit, something soft and warm taking root in my chest. "Always wanted a cat."

"Noted." The humor fades as his eyes latch on mine, dead serious. "Any other dealbreakers for you?"

I resist the urge to shake my head. I've never had a conversation like this. No one yelling or crying or carrying on over big, emotional topics. Just a calm exchange of information. It's a welcome change to realize that Wes isn't going to lose his shit if I tell him the truth.

"You scare me sometimes," I say after a beat. "You call it impulsive. I call it reckless. I can't . . . I need to know I'm not going to get a call one day because you went off half-cocked and got yourself hurt. Or worse."

Wes lets out a sharp breath and then nods. "The thing with my windows was a bit of a wake-up call. You were right that day. It could have been a lot worse. I got lucky."

He pauses, shifts his weight from foot to foot, and then adds, "I've told you enough about him that it probably isn't a surprise my dad can't take a joke. Any kind of criticism, he loses it. Been that way since I was a kid. I decided a long time ago that I didn't want to be a thing like him. That I wouldn't take myself too seriously and end up bitter and angry about everything. I think what happened is that I tend to not take *anything* seriously, but there are some things that are worth being serious about. *You* are worth being serious about, Sloane."

I swallow hard. "No more stupid risks?"

"No more stupid risks," Wes confirms. "But you know chasing is dangerous. I can't promise there won't be a close call or two in the future."

"I know. I get that part. I just want to know that you're not going to do anything to make it *more* dangerous."

"I won't. Besides, if I get my way, I'll have you with me next season to keep me in line." Wes slides his hand along the counter, tentatively resting his fingers on mine. "Anything else?"

I take a deep breath and push off the counter, moving to stand in front of him. He just admitted he wants us to be together a *year* from now. It should be enough to banish any lingering doubt, but just to make sure, I force myself to ask the question that's been on my mind since we decided to come back to Colorado. "Do you want your car, now that we're here?"

"My car?" Confusion wrinkles his brow. "I was going to say we could swap out for a bit, put the miles on my tires, but if you don't want to, I'm good with sticking with yours."

The last bit of my hesitation vanishes at his genuine bafflement. There's a small part of me that feels enormously stupid for doubting Wes, but we needed to have this conversation. *I* needed it, not just for his words—though I'll be holding some of those close for a long time to come—but for the undeniable proof that he's exactly who he's shown himself to be in our time chasing together.

Physical distance isn't going to make or break our relationship if we talk to each other, a lesson Wes has just deftly taught me. It won't always be easy to make this work, but he's proven at every step he's willing to try. The least I can do is meet him halfway.

I close the last remaining bit of distance between us and let my palms rest lightly on his chest. "You sure you're not sick of me and my horrible, awful, no-good taste in music?"

Wes lights up, a grin full of mischief curving his lips. "Darlin', you and your ridiculously unorganized playlist make my life interesting," he says, settling a loose arm around my waist.

Neither one of us is in a hurry to move. We stand together in my kitchen, my cheek on his shoulder, one of his hands idly toying with my hair, and breathe each other in. I trace idle patterns on his chest and listen to the steadiness of his breath, the catch in it when I accidentally graze one of his nipples with my nail. The muscles in his abdomen tighten when I drag my fingertips lower, and I swear he stops breathing when I rest my hand on his waistband, all of the anticipation and want from earlier flooding back in with my doubts quieted.

But there's one more thing I need to say before we leave this kitchen.

"Wes?"

"Hmm?"

"Thank you," I say softly. "For calling me on my shit. For making me talk about it."

"I'm not letting you go that easily," he says, quiet but intensely serious. "I get you're used to doing everything on your own. I can handle an independent woman. Just don't shut me out, all right?"

"I'll do my best." I glance down the hallway toward my bedroom and lift a teasing brow. "Still want to take me to bed?"

"Always." But despite the flare of heat in his eyes, Wes doesn't move. "Earlier, when you said you're tired of giving instructions . . . you got me thinking."

Nervous anticipation floods my veins. "Oh?"

"Nothing kinky. Not tonight anyway." Burying his free hand in my hair, he lightly massages my scalp. I might not have a migraine this time, but it feels just as good. "I need your promise you'll tell me if you don't like anything."

"I think we both know that I have no problem telling you when I don't like something."

Wes grins and drops a light kiss on the top of my nose. "In that case," he murmurs, bending to lift me in one smooth motion, "legs around my waist." I never did put panties back on after I cleaned up earlier, so when my dress bunches around my hips, the only thing between me and his semi-hard cock is the thin layer of his sweatpants.

He grunts softly at the contact, his breath hissing through his teeth when I grind against him.

It's a slow walk to my bedroom, each step producing delicious friction. Wes pauses halfway down the hall to press me into the wall and claim another searing kiss, but once we're next to the bed, he doesn't toss me down like I expect. He lowers me slowly to my feet, my body dragging against his, and then reaches behind his head to grasp his shirt one-handed. It comes off with a yank, and then he rasps, "Take off my pants."

I slip my hands under his waistband and lightly scratch my nails low on his stomach on either side of his cock, making sure not to touch it. His eyes slip closed when I do it again, my name a plea on his lips when I finally work his waistband down over his hips. Gravity does the rest.

"Naughty." Wes groans when I give him a firm squeeze. "I like it."

He kicks free of his pants and sinks down onto the edge of the mattress naked, then holds out a hand to me. I take it eagerly, settling on his lap with my knees on either side of his hips. Muscles deep within me clench at the sight of all that bare skin, and that's before he gets my dress off, leaving me in nothing but long strands of dark hair spilling over my shoulders.

"I love your hair." Wes leans closer and draws in a deep breath. "I especially love that I get to see it like this," he adds, gathering the heavy mass of waves over one shoulder to give him access to my throat. Lightly massaging the nape of my neck, his thumb digs into a knot formed by long hours behind the wheel.

I don't bother biting back my moan. Pressing my face into his skin, I kiss the curve of his shoulder and start to work my way up. "That feels good."

His hum of satisfaction vibrates in his chest as he strokes down my thighs. He leans back ever so slightly, creating space for his hands to glide up and down, his thumbs dipping in between my legs but not touching where I really want him before he starts to drag them back down again.

"Eyes on me, Sloane."

The last time Wes said those words, it was an emotional plea. His voice is rougher now, accent thicker, but under the sensual command, he's asking the same thing.

Look at me. See me. Be present with me.

It's all there in the depths of his gray eyes, the color darker in the dim light of my bedroom. Or maybe that's just the intensity of his stare.

My breath stutters when Wes sweeps his thumbs higher, so close to where I want him, I swear I feel the ghost of his touch. He holds me captive with a wicked grin and strokes down again. It's delicious torture, this teasing, but as soon as my lashes start to lower, his hands still.

"Sloane."

My eyes flutter open, my mind blank but for the way he's looking at me like I'm his entire world. It's almost too intimate, but I force myself to keep my attention on his face. Wes rewards me by finally, finally pressing his thumbs into me.

And then he stops, sliding his hands back to my hips.

"I was thinking we could play a game." His grip tightens when I try to move, the desperate need for friction growing. "Do you want to know the rules?"

I stare at him, laughter bubbling out despite how much I want him to touch me. "Really? *You* want to talk about rules? *Now?*"

That earns me a grin, wild and playful, but Wes doesn't relent when I press against his hold again, craving, *needing*, his body on mine. "The rules are simple. I ask you a question and give you two possible answers. You pick one. Easy choices."

"What sort of questions?"

He resumes the slow, firm circles of his thumb. "This?" I curse him when he stops after a few seconds, but it's only for a moment. Then his thumb is replaced by the heel of his palm, roughly grinding against me. "Or that?"

"First one." Erotic delight heats my blood as I realize what he's up to.

Wes gentles his touch immediately, his thumb returning as he leans in to kiss me. "Want to keep playing?" he murmurs against my mouth, his tongue darting out to tease my bottom lip.

The combination of teasing and erotic command turns my body molten. "God yes."

He chuckles, then maneuvers us so that I'm sprawled out

beneath him, my hair splayed across a pillow. "Stay with me, darlin'," he says in a rough whisper, resting his weight on one elbow while his other hand dances over my ribs. "This?" He curves his fingers around my breast and gently kneads. "Or that?" His touch turns sharper, pinching my nipple between his finger and thumb.

"Second." I gasp when he does it again and squeeze my thighs around his hips, grinding against him as much as I can.

Wes keeps going, his voice growing increasingly ragged with each *this* or *that* that slips past his lips. I'm so turned on that it's a small miracle I don't combust on the spot, every muscle taut as I wait for the next couplet of touches as he maps my body.

"You're killing me." At least that's what I mean to say. What comes out is more moan than words as he swirls his tongue just under my belly button, more torment than relief.

He lifts his head, lips kiss-bitten and cheeks flushed. "It'll be a good death," he rasps, then goes right back to tormenting me.

It's unlike anything I've ever experienced, the push and pull of this sensual game. If me in a dress makes Wes feral, this is doing the same for me—and not just because of the way he's touching me, like he's already discovered every spot on my body that craves him.

Wes sees me. Sees what I need—and gives it to me without hesitation. This game of his is a turn on all by itself, but more than that, he's learning what I like without putting it on me to explain it to him.

It's one of the hottest things I've ever experienced.

I'll get him back for this, already fantasizing about all the ways I might be able to reduce him to a desperate puddle of a human, but for tonight I'm more than happy to float in the haze of need he's spun around me.

Wes shifts his weight until the hard ridge of his cock is lined up just right and then grinds his hips into mine. It's a tease, almost, but not quite where I want him. The pressure on my clit feels amazing, but I'm growing desperate to have him inside of me. I lift off the bed to rub against him, and his whole body shudders with his groan. His kisses take on a desperate edge in the first obvious sign that this is getting to him as much as it is me.

He pushes up onto his knees and gazes down at me, his grip on my thighs keeping me spread out in front of him like a feast. His chest rises with each rapid breath, the muscles in his abdomen taut with strain.

"Wes, please, I—" And then I can't form words at all because his mouth is between my legs, that wicked tongue pure magic. I'm so worked up that he doesn't even get to *this or that*. With his fingers curled inside me and his tongue lashing over my clit, I snap like a rubber band and fly over the edge.

Thighs trembling, I'm still fighting to catch my breath when Wes gives me a smug smile from between my thighs. "Sensitive." He drops a feather-light kiss to my inner thigh, then another low on my belly before pushing onto his knees. "Rookie move, but I left the condoms in my bag. Don't you go anywhere, darlin'."

I don't want him to leave, even to step into the next room. I catch his hand before he can leave the bed. "I have an IUD, and I haven't been with anyone since my last test. You?"

His flicker of surprise melts into white-hot arousal. He

makes a noise deep in his throat and stares down at me with naked longing. "Same, but are you sure?"

"If you're more comfortable—"

"I would love nothing more than to feel you bare around me," Wes cuts in before I can finish my thought. He cups my jaw in his palms, his stare intense. "The fact that you trust me enough to offer? Yeah, I'm into that."

My face heats at the emotion in his voice, the feelings I've been trying to guard for weeks bursting at their carefully sewn seams. Not knowing what to say, I kiss him, pouring all my wants and desires into it.

Wes drags me into another deep, luscious kiss, letting me push him onto his back and curl into his side. His chest heaves under my touch, his fingers tangling in my hair as I kiss and lick my way over his tattoos. Especially the one I've only seen a few times but haven't had the leisure to explore, a forked lightning bolt low on his hip.

His groan lowers into a grunt when I slide my hand between us to wrap around his straining cock. "Fuck, Sloane, do that again," he begs when my thumb finds a particularly sensitive spot. I repeat the caress, my own desire ramping back up at his obvious pleasure in my touch.

He doesn't let me play long. A faint sheen of sweat covers us both when he loops his arms under mine and tugs me back up his body for a wild, breathless kiss that breaks only when I'm beneath him again. He reaches between us, teasing me with a rub of his cock against my clit. His eyes flick up to mine, burning in the darkness. "You're sure?"

"Extremely." I wrap my fingers around his and guide him lower. He hisses out a curse as he sinks in the barest amount, my slick body more than ready for him. But it's not until I gasp out a frantic *Yes, Wes, please* that he slides in with a deep groan of satisfaction.

Heat and pressure and pure pleasure are all I know. Wes flexes his hips in slow, deliberate strokes, taking his time despite the way every muscle stands out in his arms and shoulders. One of his hands finds mine, palm to palm, our fingers tangling as our kisses turn sloppy.

"You feel amazing." Another snap of his hips, the angle hitting something so exquisite I forget to breathe. My inner muscles contract on the bolt of pleasure, and his rhythm stutters as he groans through another curse.

"Please don't stop," I beg, meeting each thrust with a lift of my hips, clenching around him as he winds me higher and higher.

Wes squeezes my fingers, still twined with his where he's pressing my hand down into the mattress, and buries his face in my throat. "Never."

The raspy promise is enough to tip me over into a second orgasm. It only takes half a dozen hard, deep strokes until he follows with a hoarse cry into my neck.

We lay together, our breaths ragged pants, our hands still clutched together as the ripples of pleasure fade. There's a faint tremble in his bicep when Wes lifts his weight off me, eyes soft and a lazy, satisfied grin curving his mouth. He steals another slow kiss before rolling us so I'm tucked into his side.

I know with absolute certainty that what we just did was far more than fucking. My feelings for Wes have grown deep roots, pieces of him so thoroughly entwined with pieces of me that I may not ever be able to dig him out.

For the first time, the thought doesn't outright terrify me.

I need to clean up before I fall asleep, but I let myself sink into the afterglow. Wes has one arm around my back in a loose hold, while his other slowly works to untangle my hair. "I am never going to get enough of you," he murmurs, pressing a kiss against my temple.

The tenderness cracks my heart wide open. "Asking you to come chasing with me was one of my better ideas," I mumble into his skin.

"Sex was that good?" he asks with a chuckle.

"It was," I agree. But that self-deprecating tone is lurking in his voice, so I kiss his shoulder and add, "*You* are that good. No one has ever . . ." Grappling with the tightness of my throat, I search for the right words before settling on "I've never felt so . . . safe with someone."

Emotion flashes across his face as soon as I say it, and I wonder if it hits Wes as hard as it hits me that after years of calling him reckless, *safe* is the word I landed on. He tightens his arms around me, stretching to meet me halfway in a kiss so gentle and intimate my throat tightens. One kiss turns to another, slow and content building into need and heat until we're lost to each other all over again.

CHAPTER NINETEEN

MY SMALL HOUSE IS MY SANCTUARY. THE ONE PLACE I can really be myself and not worry about what anyone else thinks. Having Wes here, waking up with him, is even better than I could have imagined.

"Morning, beautiful." He flexes his hand where it rests on my stomach and pulls me tight into his chest. One of his thighs is between mine, crisp hairs tickling my soft skin.

"What time is it?" I ask with a yawn, flexing my hips in a slow, teasing roll. There's a pleasant soreness between my legs along with a faint burn on the inside of my thighs from Wes's facial hair—a delicious reminder of exactly what we got up to last night. And again at some vague early hour, half asleep and languid as we moved together.

Wes maneuvers me under him when I start to reach for my phone, his expression sleep-hazed and delightfully rumpled. "We have time." He rocks his hips, his half-hard cock rapidly rising to the occasion. "Want to find out how many orgasms are too many?"

My laughter gets swallowed up by a moan as he lavishes attention on one of the many spots he found last night that drive me wild. "I'm not sure we have time for *that*," I say breathlessly, sliding my hand around the back of his neck and scratching lightly.

"No, probably not." His hand skims over my ribs, then my hip, and down my thigh. With a firm grip, he pushes my leg out and up, making room for himself. "I'll settle for two."

Despite the fact that we need to get up, Wes takes his time. His kisses build, slow and sleepy at first, growing into tender passion. He breathes out my name in gasps and groans, holding on to me like he doesn't ever want to let go. Unlike last night's filthy whispers and playful moments, in the soft light of morning, neither of us says much.

That's new too. I don't have to fill the silence with Wes. I don't need words to hide behind, not when he easily offers me his own naked vulnerability. Not when every kiss is a promise, and every touch is a question I want to answer with *Yes, yes, yes.*

This time, after he's kept his word and turned me all but boneless, he doesn't gasp his pleasure into my throat. Even with his arms trembling from the effort of holding himself up, he looks down into my eyes and lets me see every flicker of emotion. And then, our bodies still connected, his breaths still ragged, he leans down to press a tender kiss to my temple.

I wrap my arms around his shoulders and squeeze tight until his weight crushes me into the mattress. I don't care. Who needs to breathe when their heart is overflowing with too many emotions to count?

Wes is the first to move, reluctantly pushing back up on his elbows. He brushes his thumb lightly under my eye and smiles, sated and so content I wouldn't be shocked if he started purring.

"We should get up," he says reluctantly. "I checked the forecast while you were sleeping. Going to be a long drive today if we want to be in South Dakota tomorrow."

I stretch my neck up to steal one last kiss and then playfully shove his shoulder. "You're the one trapping me here."

"Sloane?"

"Mmm?"

"I'm really glad it was you who found me that day on the side of the road."

"Me too."

Wes leans in to brush one last soft kiss against my mouth and then gets out of bed with a groan. "If you want to grab a shower first, I'll get started on breakfast."

BREAKFAST IS WAITING when I get out of the shower. Wes puts a plate into my hand, gives my legging-covered butt a hearty squeeze, and throws a wink over his shoulder on the way to the bathroom for his own shower.

"Keep that up and we're going to miss the storms tomorrow!" I call after him.

He pauses at the bathroom door long enough to prop his hip against the frame and raise one smoldering brow. "Darlin', don't tempt me."

"Go!" I gesture sharply toward the shower with a slice of crispy bacon, laughter spilling over.

I finish my breakfast quickly before ducking into my office to grab the extra camera gear for Tracy and Matt's wedding. Then I impulsively head back into my bedroom, my mind on the dress shoved to the back I've been looking for an excuse to wear for ages.

I bought it almost two years ago, so the first question is going to be if it even fits. With a deep breath, I toss my clothes onto the bed, pull out the garment bag, unzip the shimmering pink silk, and step into it.

The bodice is fairly modest. A sweetheart neckline curves up into wide straps while the multilayered skirts flare out. The back is where the real drama comes in, cut so low there's a mere inch of fabric between where the dress stops and my ass starts.

Sucking in my breath, I carefully do up the side zip and gather the skirts to check the mirror on the other side of my bedroom. It still fits—in fact, I'm pretty sure it looks better now than it did two years ago.

"That dress was made for you."

I turn to find Wes staring at me from the doorway with his hip propped against the frame. He's pulled on a pair of shorts, but hasn't gotten to a shirt yet, one hand lazily rubbing a towel against his damp hair.

"You like it?" I do a little twirl, the silk fanning out around my legs.

Wes steps into my bedroom and tosses the towel on the bed. He doesn't stop until he's close enough to drag his fingertips along the neckline. A riot of goosebumps erupts in his wake. "I want to ask why you're wearing this, but I'm not sure I care."

Lust and something else, something far deeper, stare back at me. "I know I don't deserve you, but damn if I'm not going to try to keep you anyway."

The free fall from flirty to emotional is so fast I don't have time to swallow the lump in my throat. "Promise?"

Wes slides his hand into my hair and leans his forehead against mine. His breathing is rough, emotion turning his voice hoarse when he says, "Yeah, Sloane. I promise."

IT'S A LITTLE weird to be in Wes's car, and not just because it's loaded with features I can't afford. The interior has a lingering new car scent, but mostly it smells like him, spice with a hint of citrus.

Wes is driving, one hand on top of the steering wheel, the rest of his large frame relaxed into the leather seat. His other hand rests on the gear shift. I impulsively lay mine on top of his, relaxing even further when he spreads his fingers. After a few minutes, he lifts our hands to his mouth and presses light kisses to the back of my hand without ever taking his eyes off the road.

He wears a faint smile when he lowers our hands to rest on the center console, utterly at ease but for his attention to the road. Like he's just as content as I am in this moment, not talking, not really doing much of anything except breathing the same air.

The long hours in the car turn into some of my favorite moments as we fall back into the rhythm of racing after storms from one end of the plains to the other. Sometimes we sing along to my ridiculous playlist. Sometimes we let the music play and sink into comfortable silence, content to exist together. And sometimes, often late at night when the darkness presses in around us, we talk, our conversations taking on a new intimacy that no longer scares me quite so much.

Wes entertains me with stories of his travels, everything from the stunning beauty of the midnight sun in Norway, the frigid cold of an Antarctic polar plunge, and the blazing heat of a Namibia desert. But in between the glory days, he slips in the quieter moments. He talks a lot about his mom, who bought him his first camera and spent childhood summers with him on a ranch somewhere south of Amarillo while his dad often traveled for work.

"I think that's what got me into storms," he says late one night as we head for our hotel, the wind farm surrounding us blinking red and eerie in the darkness, like we've been dropped into the middle of an alien world. "Mom used to yell for me from the porch when I'd be out there trying to take photos of lightning long before I had any idea how to actually get it in focus or exposed correctly."

"It was lightning on the mountains for me," I reply in the same hushed voice. "There was this park close enough to ride my bike to that had a killer view of the mountains. I used to watch the sky in the summer, waiting for thunderheads to billow up. Then I'd just sit there for hours."

Wes doesn't say anything. He doesn't need to—the exquisitely gentle brush of his lips against my knuckles communicates plenty. Some people have churches. Wes and I have storms.

CHAPTER TWENTY

TRACY'S TEXT COMES A FULL WEEK AFTER WE LEAVE my house, confirming they're ready whenever the weather wants to cooperate. Her parents refuse to attend on the grounds the wedding won't be in a church, but Matt's parents love the idea. His dad even got ordained to serve as justice of the peace.

Ten days before my chase season comes to a close, fifteen of us gather at the edge of a field halfway down a dirt road. Getting everyone here was a feat of coordination, and we need to keep an eye on the storm spinning to our northwest, but we're intentionally farther away than any of us would usually be.

Neither Matt nor Tracy opts for formal wear. He's in a pair of dark-wash jeans with a tailored vest over a deep green button-down rolled to his elbows. Tracy's sundress is blush pink, the full skirt whipping around her legs in the wind. She's curled her hair, leaving it wild and free, with only the barest amount of makeup on her face.

Not wanting to upstage her, I leave my dress in my bag, much to Wes's disappointment. His eyes light up with interest when I promise to put it on for him some other time when we're alone.

Joy and excitement swirl on the wind currents. Despite the absolute mayhem it took to pull this off, now that everyone is here, the only tension is anticipatory—with the exception of Matt's parents, who keep eyeing the dark clouds and frequent lightning erupting behind the group with concern.

"Ready?" I murmur to Wes when he moves beside me, his arm resting easily around my hips.

He holds up his camera with his free hand. "Been looking forward to you bossing me around." Leaning closer, his lips brush my ear as he adds, "You can boss me around anytime you like." His hand slides down to squeeze my ass, not even the slightest bit repentant when I elbow him in the ribs.

"Stop that," I chide, though it's not very effective when I'm grinning like a fool. I've grown to crave the affectionate way he touches me every chance he gets, even when we have an audience. "I'm working. You wait your turn."

"I remember when you said that at Cora and Shawn's wedding." Wes straightens with a chuckle. "Highlight of my night."

I roll my eyes and bump my hip into his. "Please. The ten minutes you spent with me was hardly the highlight of that night."

"Darlin', the only reason I showed up to that wedding was you."

"What?" My whole body whips toward his. "How did

you even know I'd be there? You asked me what I was doing there!"

"No, I said you were far from home. Which was true." Wes laughs at my glare. "I grew up with Shawn. Cora knows I'm a photographer and sent me a message asking if you were as good as her friend claimed. I said she wouldn't find better." He shrugs, his eyes straying to the storm and darkening. "My dad told me I had better be at the wedding. I was planning to skip it just to spite him, but you were going to be there. It was worth giving up the chase days to have you play with me for those ten minutes."

"I scowled at you the entire time."

"Mostly," Wes says, good-natured humor returning to his voice and his shoulders relaxing. "But, for the record, the only one I wanted to spend any time in a corner with that night was you."

I tip my head back and stroke my fingertip down the line of his jaw. "You do an awfully good job of hiding how sweet you are."

"Our secret." Wes gives me a quick, hard kiss and then holds up the camera. "Where do you want me?"

With one final check of the various radar scans and someone assigned to keep an eye on the storm, the wedding gets underway.

It's the least-formal and lowest-budget wedding that I've shot since I got my start doing backyard weddings for some friends from high school—but infinitely more fun.

Matt's dad conducts the ceremony like he's at an open-mic night, keeping everyone laughing while Wes and I dart around taking photos. Tracy's pink dress pops against the green of the grass and the deep blackish-gray of the sky, and the way that Matt beams at her is as perfect as a wedding that took two years to plan.

And when they kiss after reciting their vows, I decide not to tell them that there's a lucky lightning bolt in the background. That can be a happy surprise when I give them the final edits.

Tracy gives us all a big grin, her cheeks flushed and her eyes sparkling. "So . . . we're chasing this thing, right?"

WHEN TRACY SAYS she plans to chase in her dress—"Best reception idea ever!"—Wes and I offer to stick with her and Matt for the rest of the afternoon and grab a few more shots of them with the storm. It's easy enough to take my own shots in between, but more than that, an idea is starting to form.

I thought florals in the foreground would work to juxtapose beauty versus the destructive nature of a storm, but despite producing some pretty images, something remains missing from every frame I've taken so far. Tracy silhouetted in her wedding dress against the dark sky is a light bulb moment. I'm not getting the emotion I want from the flowers, but the deep, vibrant pink silk of my dress ruffling in the wind might just do it.

But not today. Today I'm here for Tracy and Matt.

Almost as if Mother Nature wants to give the couple a wedding gift, the storm decides to show off. From a distance, the structure is almost textbook, striations in the clouds clearly visible. As it gains power, everyone watches the velocity radar scans with building excitement as a strong couplet emerges and a funnel cloud starts to form high above us.

But the real gift is when the storm *does* finally drop a tornado—miles and miles from any town—the angle of the sun is low enough to generate a stunning rainbow behind it. I snap a handful of frames of Tracy and Matt, only to have them wave me off and point at the scene in front of us.

"Get your shots too, Sloane!" Tracy yells over the wind. She pauses long enough to sling an arm around my shoulder in a quick hug. "I love you, and I'm so buying all your drinks tonight whenever we find a bar, but go do your thing!"

It's sheer impulse that has me grabbing my tripod. I position it low to the ground and quickly set up intervals. It's worth the extra seconds of setup time. The steadiness of the tripod allows for a slightly longer exposure to pop the colors of the rainbow, and if I'm very lucky, ensure any lightning bolts are crisp.

Wes decides to stay freehand, though he takes up a position a few feet away from me after double checking he's not in my shot and points his camera at the sky. "You going for that unicorn?"

"I'm feeling far too superstitious to answer that question." The storm *is* still kicking out a decent amount of lightning, though with how much daylight remains, it's going to be tough to get it to show up on camera. "Ask me once we're back in the car."

The tornado doesn't last long. I get just over five minutes before it ropes out, which means there are close to a thousand frames for me to choose from—and hopefully one of them has a lightning bolt. There was one in particular that came down in an almost perfect position I'm praying my shutter was open for.

Giddy at the possibility that I may have grabbed a contest-worthy shot, I start scrolling through the frames once we're in the car. I still want to try the dress idea forming in my mind, but if I just got the shot I think I may have, there's no question that I'm going with the unicorn. It's too rare not to.

I pointedly ignore the fact that there are at least twenty other photographers out here who could have gotten the same shot. Not all of them were invited to participate in the contest—but Wes was. And he was standing right next to me.

"You want to keep with it or head for town?" he asks as we pull back on to the road. "I'm good either way."

"You sure? I'd love to be able to get Tracy and Matt a few photos tonight if you don't mind heading back now." The decision was already made that we'd all stay in Amarillo. It's only two hours from where we currently are, and the storms tomorrow are forecast to initiate along the border with New Mexico.

"You're telling me you want to go back to town, check into our room, and ignore me to edit photos?" Wes flashes a teasing grin. "That's true romance right there."

"HOLY SHIT, I got it!" I tip my laptop toward Wes where he's propped up next to me against the headboard working on his own photos. "I can't believe it."

"I can." He takes my laptop after pushing his own out of

the way to study the image. The tornado is in the foreground, the angle of the sun turning it mostly white with a brown swirl of dust at the base. The rainbow arcs behind it with a tack-sharp lightning bolt in the distance just to the left of the tornado. "This is incredible. The slightly longer exposure caught the light just right, and that low angle comp was such a smart choice. Are you going to submit it?"

"I think so." I hesitate, and then ask, "Did you get it too?"

"Nope. Maybe if I'd been smart like you and grabbed the tripod I would have." Wes leans closer to brush a kiss against my cheek. "Proud of you."

Warmth floods my veins. "Stop it," I grumble. "You keep looking at me like that and we're not making it out of this room tonight."

Wes dances his fingers up my thigh, stopping short before he gets to anything fun. "And that would be a bad thing?"

"No." I sigh, grabbing his hand and pressing a kiss to his open palm. "Yes. We *did* tell Tracy and Matt we'd join them at the bar tonight."

"Right. That." Wes opens his laptop and spins it to show me the image he's been working on. I asked him to focus on Matt during the ceremony so I could stick with Tracy. While wedding photography might not be Wes's preference, his talent with a camera isn't limited to landscapes. He's captured Matt's dreamy expression perfectly.

"You want to help me shoot weddings more often? That's great."

"Not the weddings you usually do, but . . ." A thoughtful crease forms between his brows. "This could be your thing. The nontraditional weddings, I mean."

I can't help a laugh, shaking my head. "There are not enough people who want to get married in the middle of a thunderstorm to pay my mortgage."

"No, but there *are* a lot of couples who don't want to deal with a big elaborate ceremony. I have some friends in Moab that shoot weddings out in the backcountry. Super small. You'd be great at something like that."

It sounds too good to be true. The magic of weddings but without all the pomp and circumstance that's starting to burn me out. "You really think that's a viable way to make a living?"

"I think there are far fewer photographers willing to get up at two in the morning to hike to the top of a mountain for sunrise with a forty-pound bag of gear than there are couples who want that kind of wedding. Especially in our generation. Most of us can't afford to drop thirty grand on a party." His lips twist into a rueful smile. "Hell, I *can* afford it, but the idea of being stuffed into a suit and under a microscope for an entire night sounds awful."

"Something to think about, I guess," I say slowly. The idea has merit, but with only an hour and a half until we're due to meet Tracy and Matt at the bar she dropped in the group chat, there isn't time to dig into it. "Thank you for the suggestion. I'll look into it," I tell Wes, stretching to press a kiss to his cheek. "*After* I get these done. Stop distracting me," I add with a playful shove.

"Yes, ma'am."

I shiver at the memory of the last time those words left his lips and point sharply at his laptop. "Focus!"

Wes holds up his palms in a show of innocence that is immediately overruled by the wicked curve of his mouth.

"It will be faster if we shower together," he says when I finally declare I'm done editing.

"Lies." I shake my head and pull off my shirt, tossing it into his face. He catches it one-handed and doesn't try to hide how he presses the fabric to his nose, inhaling my scent. I make it all the way to the bathroom door before I twist back to ask, "You coming?"

His face lights up like he's won the lottery. With four long strides, he lifts me by my thighs and carries me the two steps into the bathroom. "Not before you do."

CHAPTER TWENTY-ONE

WHEN I EXPLAIN THE COMPOSITION I'M CONSIDERing featuring my dress to Wes the next morning, he lights up. "Put you out in a field with some lightning and you'd pass for a Valkyrie." His gaze roams hungrily over me. "That would make a great contest entry to go with the shot you got yesterday. Let's do it."

"A Valkyrie, huh?" I slash my arm like I'm wielding an imaginary sword and stop just short of pretend-slicing off his head before I relax with a laugh. "Not far from what I'm envisioning, though. I just need to find the right spot. I only have"—I glance at the date on my watch—"nine days left to get this right."

"Let's focus on that today, then. If it doesn't work, we'll try again tomorrow."

"You need to figure out your shot for the contest too," I remind him.

"And I will," Wes assures me with a light kiss on the tip of my nose. "But I've got another month of chasing ahead of me.

We can focus on you and make sure you get what you need before you have to go home."

It shouldn't be a big deal, but the dirty secret of being chronically single is that the only person who makes you a priority is, well, you. To everyone else, there's always someone more important.

It's damn good to be Wes's priority.

The weather sends us northwest in pursuit of a lazily spinning supercell spitting out lightning every couple of seconds. We stop a few times to photograph the storm's structure from a distance before pushing on in search of the right setup for the shot I have in mind.

I know we've found it the second I get out of the car twenty minutes later. A long stretch of pale gravel road runs straight to the horizon, the storm looming over rich green fields to my left, while off to the right, blue sky peeks out from behind soft white clouds. The road neatly bisects the wrath of the storm with nature's more gentle side, allowing me to stand smack in the middle.

I've always loved storms in part because no one tells Mother Nature to swallow her rage. There's a paradoxical beauty in supercells, in the swirl of the clouds and the turquoises of a powerful storm, in the pinks and oranges and reds that sunset splashes across the towering mass of destruction. Storms are probably one of the reasons we think of weather in feminine terms—beautiful, yes, but deadly under the surface.

Barefoot in the middle of a country road, wearing an unapologetically vibrant pink dress as a storm rages in the atmosphere high above, I let that same power wash over me. Sure, it's just a dress, but it's the kind of dress my mother has always wielded as a weapon, all romantic lines and yards of fabric flowing out of the bodice to swirl around my legs. And it's a color I've avoided out here for years, a deliberate attempt to remove anything that might tempt the good ol' boys club to treat me like anything other than a fellow photographer.

This shot is more than a photo. It's a reckoning. With my mother. With the photographers who've told me to go back to weddings.

And maybe, most of all, with myself.

"Ready?" Wes gently adjusts a strap across my shoulder so that it lies flat and rakes his gaze over me. My resulting shiver has nothing to do with the wind.

I take a deep breath and reach for the end of my braid, remove the elastic, and hand it to Wes to shove in his pocket. He moves behind me, sifting his fingers through the tangles, taking his time. When he's done, he slides his hands down to my bare shoulders and digs his thumbs into the tired muscles until he's coaxed me into relaxing against him.

"Nervous?"

"Not exactly." I tip my head back to rest on his shoulder. "It's just weird, being on this side of the camera."

Wes brushes loose hair back from my eyes, his expression soft. "You're amazing, Sloane."

I raise one brow in a tease. "Me or the dress?"

"The dress is nice, but you could be doing this in muddy leggings and it would still work. You're so talented. Talented and determined. You've made space for yourself out here, even when the idiots didn't want to let you. It doesn't matter if you're telling someone else's love story with their wedding portraits, or if you're out here telling *your* story. This is your gift.

"I may not have always known how to tell you in a way you'd hear me, but I've always been so impressed by you," Wes continues. "Today included. This is going to turn out amazing." He squeezes my shoulders one last time and then straightens. "Where do you want me?"

I gather up the long skirt in one hand before I turn, pausing to rub my thumb along his jaw. From under the rim of his baseball hat, his gaze is reverent. It's almost overwhelming, having someone believe in me the way Wes does after a lifetime of the opposite.

"Thank you," I murmur, pressing my lips to his in a light kiss before squaring my shoulders. "Stand here to start so I can test the framing and light."

I dart over to where I've left my camera on the tripod, a heavy weight attached to the bottom to make sure it doesn't go anywhere in the wind. Peering through the viewfinder, I let out a little squeal of excitement.

The very tip of the inflow band practically points its crooked finger at the spot where the road disappears over the horizon, while to the left a vibrant green field of winter wheat glows under the menacing clouds. Behind the low-hanging cloud, rain darkens the sky further, turquoise ominously filling the entire left side of the frame, while to the right, blue sky and a hint of sunlight bathe the scene.

"A little to the left," I call to Wes, watching him move closer to the middle of the road to mark the spot for me. My goal is to use perspective to block the rest of the road from view with my shoulders, to create the illusion that I'm the only thing standing between the viewer and the storm. Wes is taller, so I may need to adjust where I stand a little more, but having him as a placeholder is a good start.

I take a test shot of Wes with his legs planted wide, shoulders back. He's in dark jeans today with his usual black T-shirt, and let's just say the view from the back is almost as good as the one from the front.

I move to stand directly in front of him, making sure to center myself between his feet so I'm in the same spot I've tested. We have plenty of time—this part of the storm looks dramatic, but if a tornado drops, we're miles away from the potential danger zone.

"Okay." I breathe out and twist around to give Wes the all clear. "I'm going to take a test shot, and then can you stand here again while I go check it?"

This would be so much easier if I could mark the spot with tape like they do on film sets, but tape and a dirt road don't exactly work together. Lucky for me, Wes makes a great assistant.

He moves out of the frame and waits for me to trigger the shot using the remote in my palm, and then slides right back into position while I jog back to the camera to review the image. My position is good, but the exposure is a little too bright for the pink. I make a few small adjustments, and we repeat the whole process until I'm satisfied.

I set up the interval timer, the shutter clicking away while I return to my spot, anticipation crackling in my veins. Wes presses a kiss to my cheek before he backs away, his own camera hanging loosely from one hand. "I'm going to take some shots too. Just for me," he's quick to add with a smoldering look.

Beneath the dress, I press my thighs together and hope he chalks up the flush in my cheeks to the heat of the day as I make a shooing motion. "Let's get the shot. *Then* you can have your wicked way with me."

A familiar playful gleam enters his eyes. "You wearing anything under that dress?" He brushes his hand over my hip and sucks in a sharp breath when he doesn't feel anything but smooth silk. "Fuck, you're not, are you?"

I shrug, enjoying myself far too much. "Didn't want to ruin the lines."

"And you call me a menace," Wes grumbles, dropping his hand and moving back out of the frame. "Now turn around so you can make your masterpiece."

Swallowing my laugh, I face the storm, take a deep breath, and relax my shoulders. As if on cue, the wind rises, tossing my hair back over my shoulder and ruffling the full skirt. I'm careful not to move, but when Wes lets out a low whistle, curiosity gets the better of me.

"Good?" I call over my shoulder, careful not to move my feet.

"From the preview that popped up, I think you're going to be very happy." He pulls his phone out of his pocket, fiddles with it and the camera for a few seconds, and then jogs over to me. "Take a look. I can hold the spot for you again if you want to change anything, but I think you got it."

My breath catches when I realize he's used the camera's Bluetooth to drop the raw image onto his phone so I can see it without disturbing the setup. And he's right—the shot is perfect. Exactly what I envisioned when the idea first formed yesterday. A woman in a delicate pink dress, facing down some of the most powerful weather on the planet.

"This is going to get you that cover," Wes says, affection and pride coating every word. "It's a compelling image."

I glance up, his confidence in me a warm glow deep in my chest. "Come here," I murmur, and using the remote still tucked into my palm, I restart the intervals right before drawing Wes down into a kiss.

We spend another ten minutes in the same spot, hop back in the car, and repeat the process a couple more times. I'm not sure I like any of the other compositions more than the first setup, but it's good to have options.

I shimmy into a pair of leggings and Houdini my way back into a bra and tank top on the side of another dirt road, the car and Wes acting as a privacy screen, before carefully replacing the dress in its garment bag. "That's going to need a hell of a dry cleaning." I wince at the dust and blades of grass clinging to the hem.

"Sloane, darlin', the last thing I'm thinking about right now is your dry cleaning." Wes backs me up against the car once the door falls shut, caging me in with his hands planted on either side of my shoulders just like the afternoon the migraine took me out. Except this time, his eyes burn with need. "And if it's all right with you, I'd really like to post one of those shots of us together on my social media. Because not only do you look incredible, but I can't think of a better way to make it clear that I'm all yours."

I don't think twice about grabbing a fistful of his T-shirt and yanking him into me.

THE LAST WEEK of my chase season passes in a blur. We cover just over three thousand miles, the storms keeping us on our toes as we race first north, and then south before rushing east, just to hurtle west the following morning. My days are a frenzy of radar scans and forecast models, craning my neck toward the sky, and snarking at Wes—who snarks right back, mischief behind every playful twist of words.

As for our nights, well, those are a different kind of frenzy altogether.

It's not a surprise when Tracy and Matt's wedding photos make the rounds among the broader network of our chaser friends and acquaintances. What I don't expect is that suddenly, it's not only Wes who gets stopped for a chat. When we pop by an informal picnic being held in the back of a truck stop on Memorial Day, no fewer than ten different people want to talk to me. Not only about how much they love Tracy and Matt's photos, but also could I do the same for them?

Not everyone wants to get married in a random farmer's field, of course. But just like Wes predicted, there are a lot more couples looking for ceremonies in alpine meadows and on backcountry cliffs than I ever thought. What starts as a promise to draw up a quote for a wedding someone wants to have on the sand dunes of a nearby national park next year grows into a list of potential clients a dozen deep.

Wes, to his credit, refrains from saying *I told you so*—but he does get a smug look about him every time someone else comes up to me for the rest of the trip.

And then, just like that, it's over.

We squeeze every last minute we can out of my final day,

lingering to photograph a spectacular sunset that lights up a picture-perfect barber pole supercell. I couldn't ask for a better farewell from Mother Nature, but the atmosphere in the car is decidedly melancholy when we pull into my driveway an hour before dawn. Wes cuts the engine, lets his head drop back into the seat, and turns toward me with a tight smile. "Home sweet home," he whispers, every minute of the ten-hour drive in his weary voice.

Our little bubble is about to burst. Even if he lingers with me another night, I have three weddings and an engagement shoot over the next four days to prepare for, a mountain of emails to deal with, and all the other assorted chores that need to be done after being gone for so long.

I blame the sudden urge to cry on lack of sleep and drag myself into the house, Wes at my side. Within fifteen minutes we've collapsed into bed, and though I should be exhausted enough to fall asleep immediately, my eyes stubbornly refuse to shut. His heartbeat is steady under my ear, his skin warm against my cheek. He's got to be tired too, but when I glance up at his face, he's watching me, eyes gleaming in the faint light leaking around the edges of the curtains.

"Two weeks," Wes says gruffly, running a knuckle down my cheek. "That's my limit."

Despite the sadness threatening to choke me, I push myself up onto an elbow with a teasing smile. "Going to need a little more information there."

I expect his usual humor. His serious expression doesn't budge. "I refuse to go more than two weeks without you. I don't care how many hours I have to drive, or what kind of flights I have to deal with. Two weeks, Sloane. No more."

A little thrill goes up my spine at his pronouncement. "Okay," I agree, cupping his jaw and leaning down for a kiss. "Two weeks. We can look at our schedules in the morning." I glance wryly at the pale light seeping around the edge of the curtains. "The later morning."

Wes hums his agreement, wrapping his arms around me and shifting my weight so I'm sprawled across him. These kisses are comfort and relief and care, soothing the anxious tension that's been humming along in the background since we woke up knowing it was our last day of chasing together.

This time, when I settle with my head tucked under his chin, sleep is waiting.

WES IS AS reluctant to leave as I am to let him go. We stay in bed an hour longer than we should and then linger over breakfast, sipping coffee on my porch in the warm morning air. My attention snags over and over again on the repaired step, an indelible sign that he was here.

It's only when I recognize I'm getting emotional over a stair tread that it sinks in just how much it's going to suck to watch Wes drive away, even with plans to see each other in two weeks. He'll still be out chasing, but we block out a few non-wedding weekdays for him to either hop on a quick flight or drive back, depending on where the storms take him. We add a plane ticket to Houston for me at the end of June, when Wes will return home for a week or two before heading for monsoon season in Arizona.

Once plans are made, showers are taken, dishes are washed, and his car is repacked, we're out of excuses. I have errands and emails waiting for me, none of which will go any faster distracted by six-plus feet of sexy charm in my house.

"Going to be weird being in the car alone again," Wes says gruffly when I walk him out to the driveway. He leans back against the driver's door and pulls my hips flush to his. "All I want to do right now is kidnap you."

With my palms flat on his chest, I lean my forehead onto his shoulder and laugh into his T-shirt. And maybe sneak one more big breath of his intoxicating scent. "Kidnapping probably wouldn't be a satisfactory excuse for my clients if I don't show up for their weddings."

His arms tighten around me, hard enough that my breath catches, but I don't ask him to loosen his hold. The pressure feels good. Proof that he's going to miss me as much as I'm going to miss him.

"I'll call you when I get to wherever I stay tonight," Wes promises, nuzzling his cheek against my hair. "How late will you be up?"

"Call even if it's late." I tip my head back so I can catch his heavy gaze under the shadow of his hat. "I don't have to leave until ten tomorrow. I can sleep in a bit."

"Okay. One more kiss for the road." Wes bends, and though I'm expecting a quick kiss, he doesn't care that we're in full view of my neighbors. Tongues and teeth and need explode between us like it might be years before we see each other instead of eleven days. Not that I have much room to talk when I'm clinging to him like a barnacle the whole time.

When Wes finally loosens his hold, I take a step back and fold my arms around myself to keep from reaching for him again. "You should go or you'll miss the storms."

"I gotta tell you, Sloane, in this moment?" He doesn't take his eyes off me for a second. "I don't really give a damn about storms."

There's so much emotion packed into the quiet words that I almost ask him not to go. The way he's looking at me, longing and tenderness and something *more* in the line of his lips, I think he'd stay if I asked him to. Blow off chasing and spend every minute we can together in between my client work. Linger with me in the happy bubble I never thought I'd find, just a little longer.

"I had the time of my life chasing with you this season, Wes, but we both know you need to go," I say gently. "This only works between us if we can go back to our normal lives without everything falling apart."

"I know. And you're right. I just . . ." Wes sighs, one hand on the door handle. "I'm going to miss you like hell, Sloane."

"I'm going to miss you too." I take a shaky breath. "Now go away." I make a shooing motion with my hand, smile to soften my words, and try not to cry when he finally backs out of the driveway. I have far too much to do to lose time to a little breakdown, and besides, there's no reason for it. Wes will be back in less than two weeks. I'll be too busy to even notice.

"Get it together, Sloane," I tell myself as I head back in the house, purposely stepping on the repaired stair. I have a mountain of things to do to distract me. He'll be back before I know it.

CHAPTER TWENTY-TWO

TIME PASSES IN FITS AND STARTS.

As I dodge ice sculptures and five-foot-high centerpieces, I can't help comparing the lavish weddings I'm photographing to Matt and Tracy's low-key ceremony. These six-figure weddings are visually stunning, but I miss the creativity of a less traditional ceremony as I work through yet another shot list obviously helped along by Pinterest.

I need to get serious about looking into what it will take to shift my business. It's a risk—a change in strategy is always going to be a risk. But if I somehow manage to win the *Nature Shots* contest, the cash prize could give me the cushion I'd need to be comfortable losing out on some bigger contracts while I get the new venture established.

Nevertheless, wedding weekends go by in a blink. It's the nights alone in my bed, or the long stretches of editing in my office, where time slows to a crawl. I'm not sure if burrowing into the sweatshirt Wes left behind—quite purposefully since

I found it folded under my pillow—helps or makes me ache for him even more.

He resumes the tradition of the daily shower selfies, though, and as much as it makes me miss him more, I look forward to the sometimes silly, sometimes steamy nightly reminder that he's thinking of me.

In the summer heat, it's not unusual for me to opt for dresses when I'm not working. But the selfies I snap in them and send Wes? Those are all for him.

Missing him is just as hard as I thought it would be. It's easier too, the little reminders that we're on each other's minds soothing the sting of separation. At least until I make a rookie mistake and wear his hoodie to my mom's.

"I know a man's clothing when I see it," she sniffs as soon as I walk in the door.

"Hi, Mom. Nice to see you too." I don't bother to choke down the sarcasm. This is the last place I want to be, but Eric and Sam have been good about following the rotation we agreed on when I got home. Today it's my turn.

"Honestly, Sloane, he might like seeing you in that shapeless thing in your bedroom—cavemen, all of them—but you dress like you're still a child. Never mind wasting months of your life on that reckless hobby."

I barely manage to swallow the *Are you fucking kidding me* and brush past her, heading for the kitchen where she claims to need help changing a light bulb. As much as I want to give her a piece of my mind, I want to get out of here without a fight more. Wes will be here tomorrow. I'd much rather focus on that.

"I assume it belongs to tall, dark, and handsome that you

refused to introduce me to?" Mom presses, teetering after me into the kitchen. Why she's got four-inch heels on in her own house, I'll never understand. "You need to make an effort with a man like that."

My tenuous hold on my temper falters. "Yes, the sweatshirt belongs to Wes. And you know where I met him, Mom?" I mimic her snide tone. "My *reckless hobby*."

"Well, now you've caught him, you'll need to work to keep him. When was the last time you had a wax?" Mom barrels on. "I'll make you an appointment with my girl. Your hair is so dark. Highlights at minimum, but really, a nice honey blonde could work with your skin." She pauses in her litany of my shortcomings long enough to tip her head to the side and scowl at my face. "I'll call Dr. Barre too. A little filler will fix that line you're getting."

Amazing the phone calls my mother is capable of when she wants to be. Can't call a damn lawn service on her own for two months, but the plastic surgeon's office is probably saved to her favorites for easy access. Typical.

"Mom," I grind out, the hold on my emotions that's held for thirty years threatening to finally collapse, "Wes likes me just the way I am. He likes *this* version of me. Maybe you could try that."

I might as well be having a conversation with the wall. She purses her lips, hands on her hips, and shakes her head like I'm the one who can't seem to keep her life together without someone else constantly picking up the pieces. "You're not getting any younger, Sloane. You need to get that man to marry you before he gets tired of waiting for you to settle down. Getting pregnant wouldn't hurt. You don't want to be alone like me when you're old. And don't sign any prenups. I looked up his family. Even divorced, you'll be set for life. Stop wasting time with this silly photography nonsense and focus on the things that matter."

I've spent nearly all my life holding my emotions back behind a dam when it comes to my mother. And every single brick of that dam has had a steep price, demanding piece after piece of me.

This time, I refuse to reach for another brick. This time, I'm not bracing the dam. I'm blowing it up.

"Because that worked out so well for you, didn't it?" I snap, pushing to my feet. "Like I've told you a million times, I don't want kids. I did my time raising Eric and Sam because *you* were too busy with your boyfriends. Stay the hell out of my relationship, Mom. Go to therapy, figure out your shit, and change your own fucking light bulbs."

My heart is beating so fast it's a miracle I don't spoil my dramatic exit by passing out. I ignore my mom's crocodile tears and insistence that she's a good mother, that she was there for us when it mattered—laughable—and I keep right on ignoring her when she moves on to the insult portion of the standard performance that comes with not getting her way.

It's been a couple of years since I last talked to a therapist, but for the duration of my drive home I repeat what the last one told me like a silent mantra. It's not my fault my mother is emotionally immature. It's not my job to change her. I can love her and not be her emotional punching bag.

I'm so worked up that when there's a knock on my door two hours later, I almost don't answer. At least until I catch a glimpse of Wes's SUV through the window. Then I can't get there fast enough, flinging the door open so hard it bounces off the wall. Thankfully it doesn't hit me. I'm too busy throwing myself at Wes.

"Hi, darlin'," he murmurs into my hair, his arms bone-crushingly tight around me. "Goddamn did I miss you. I know I'm a day early but I wanted to sur—"

"Early is good," I interrupt, tipping my head back for a kiss. "I'm so glad you're here."

His mouth comes down on mine. Wes tastes like coffee and the candy he's obsessed with. It's so achingly familiar that I can't help deepening the kiss until we're both panting and possibly in danger of someone calling the cops for lewdness.

It's only once Wes lets go of me to pick up his bags and come into the house that his eyes narrow. "You've been crying."

"Got into it with my mom." I can't help rubbing at my eyes self-consciously despite knowing it will only make the swelling and redness worse. "Usual stuff. Just lost my temper today."

Wes pulls me back into his arms and kisses my forehead. "I'm sorry she doesn't see the woman I do," he says softly. "You're amazing, Sloane."

I take a deep breath, inhaling the familiar scent of dust and sweat and Wes all rolled up into one, then tip my head back to meet his tired gaze. "I missed you."

"I missed you too. Let's try to forget about our parents for a few days, yeah?"

"Yes, please."

"Good." A devilish glint in his eyes, he lowers himself enough to toss me over his shoulder with a playful smack on my ass. My surprised shriek quickly morphs into giddy laughter when he marches us toward my bathroom. "I desperately need a shower. And you."

I WAKE TO sunlight pouring into my bedroom and Wes propped up on his side next to me. There's a steaming cup of coffee on my nightstand, a sure sign he's been up for a while, but I'm in no rush to leave my bed.

If the last two weeks were our first test, having him here again feels like passing with flying colors. It wasn't easy. Some nights, alone in my bed, I missed him desperately. But now that he's here, there's no awkwardness finding our way back to each other.

We just . . . fit.

"You watching me sleep?" I tease, poking the relaxed muscle in his chest and turning on my side.

"Maybe." Wes smooths his palm over my shoulder and down my bare arm. "The light in here is great in the morning."

"Leave it to you to be thinking about photography while naked in bed."

His laughter is a low, seductive rumble. "I've been thinking about you in that dress on the other side of my lens for the last hour."

Heat pools low in my belly, sleepiness fading. "You were serious about that?"

"Mmmhmm." He drags his fingertip along the sheet where it just barely covers my breasts and tugs, his eyes rapt on my skin. "Only if you're up for it."

I've always preferred being behind the camera to being in front of it. I've never really thought about what it might be like to be *under* it.

Twenty minutes later, Wes has me on my back in the middle of the bed while he stands over me, barefoot and wearing only a pair of unbuttoned jeans. He's hard, cock straining against his zipper. My teeth sink into my bottom lip as I stare and press my thighs together.

I've done boudoir sessions for brides in the past, and there's usually not much about it that I find sexy. My mind is too wrapped up in angles and lighting and the various requests the bride made before the shoot started.

Taking these kinds of photos with Wes in the privacy of my bedroom is something else entirely. The only thing that stops me from pouncing on him is that I want my turn behind the camera.

He groans and drops his arm to the side with his camera dangling from his fingers before sinking to his knees. He's still hovering over me, thighs spread over mine, the pressure on his zipper dragging it down an inch. "Bite your lip again. And let me just . . ."

Wes reaches out and gently tugs on the dress's neckline and straps until the fabric barely covers my nipples. The silk is already hopelessly wrinkled—consequences of me dropping the dress to the floor not that long ago so that he could take a few shots of me from behind, standing in the puddle of silk—but it's nothing a good steam won't fix.

A small furrow of concentration forms between his brows, and then Wes sets the camera down before he leans over me to take hold of my wrists. Dragging my arms over my head, he crosses one wrist over the other in an illusion of restraint and then rocks back onto his heels, hands on his thighs as he studies the scene he's created.

"Keep your arms like that," he rasps before picking up the camera again. His breath catches as he stares through the viewfinder, takes a handful of shots, and then lowers it again. "I'm going to spend far too much time looking at these when we're apart."

I arch my back a little more and give him a sultry smile. "Glad I can keep you company in all those lonely hotel rooms."

Wes shakes his head slowly and reaches out to brush a loose strand of hair off my face. "Oh, I'll be thinking of you when I get in bed every night," he says, low and rough. "But if you think that's the only time I'll be missing you, you're very, very wrong, Sloane."

I forget how to breathe. His stare is unwavering, and as intense as the moment is, there's new vulnerability in his eyes. Overwhelmed by the sheer *want* and maybe some other four-letter word, I curve my hand around the back of his neck and pull him down.

I've learned that Wes communicates his feelings with touch. There have been a lot of kisses between us since that first one, but there's never been one quite like this. This kiss sinks beneath my skin, wraps me up in the intimacy of the morning, and refuses to let go.

It's the kind of kiss that can brand a person on your soul.

Gently pushing him away, I take a shaky breath and try to recapture the teasing, light mood of the morning. "If you think you can make me forget I haven't had my turn, *you* are very, very wrong."

Chuckling under his breath, Wes lifts the camera again with a murmured "Don't you dare move yet." It's only after he's taken a few more shots that he swings his leg over my thighs and slides off the bed to set his gear back in his bag. "Fair is fair." His gaze devours me while he holds out my camera. "Where do you want me?"

I point to the bed. "Let me just change real quick. I don't want to damage the dress."

"Need help?"

"Oh no you don't." I dart out of his reach, grinning at his playful huff. "No touching. Yet."

His stare rests heavy and hot on my back while I strip off the dress and hang it in my closet. Naked, I saunter over to where Wes tossed his T-shirt earlier and yank it over my head, inhaling deeply and ignoring the throb of arousal between my thighs that only intensifies under his hungry attention.

I'm not sure if I can call it payback when we both enjoy it so much.

Wes is a collection of beautiful lines on the other end of my lens. Hard lines that form his jaw, the breadth of his shoulders, the slant of his brows, but softer ones too. The curve of his lips stretched into his familiar wicked grin, the dip of his waist, and the hills and valleys of soft skin draped over taut muscle.

But what's really doing it for me is the look in his eyes and the coiled tension of holding himself back from what he really wants—what we both want.

"Hold this for a second." I hand him the camera and kneel between his spread thighs where he's sitting on the edge of the bed. I carefully drag his zipper down the rest of the way, pull the denim apart, and push on his knees to widen his legs. The strain on his underwear is borderline obscene.

Wes sucks in a sharp breath and stares at me with volcanic intensity. "Sloane . . ." He breathes out my name with a hint of warning.

"You had your turn," I remind him with a wink before I pop up, tell him to lean back on his elbows, and snap a few shots while he smolders at me like he's about to burn the bedroom down. Between his heavy-lidded stare, dark tousled hair, neatly trimmed beard, and the ink splashed across his body, he's every woman's bad-boy fantasy come to life.

But he's all mine.

"No one is ever going to see these photos but us." We talked about it briefly before Wes took the first shot, but I want the reminder fresh before I make my next request.

He nods. "Just me and you, darlin'. I don't want to share you."

"I don't want to share you either." I intend it to come out flirty. Instead my words are thick, the mood shifting between us from hot and heavy back to intimate. Especially when I let out a long breath and say softly, "Touch yourself, Wes. Slowly."

His eyebrows fly up, but his hand obediently slides down his stomach to palm his cock under his boxer briefs with a strangled groan. He tips his head back to expose the column of his throat, his eyes going heavy-lidded with pleasure. The muscles in his abdomen bunch and flex as he strokes himself, chest heaving with each breath.

Wes watches me through slitted eyes when I make an adjustment to his position. "You have no idea how much I want to throw you onto this bed right now."

Laughing softly, I hold my camera off to the side and lean

in for a kiss. I still have every intention of taking more shots, but Wes has other ideas. His arms come around me before he carefully takes the camera and sets it out of the way.

"I'm a selfish bastard, I know." His hands travel to my hips, caressing bare skin under the hem of his stolen T-shirt before pulling me flush against him. "I need you, Sloane."

I pull the shirt over my head before wrapping my arms around his neck and pressing my bare chest to his. "Then have me," I whisper, dragging my nails lightly over his shoulder. "And don't be gentle."

ϟ

THE THREE DAYS we spend together are far too short. I'm distracted, juggling client emails and calls and texts with edits during the day. I offer Wes so many apologetic smiles that I begin to wonder if my mom was right and my face *will* freeze that way. The nights at least are still entirely ours, and whether we're on the couch editing our personal photos or bingeing some ridiculous TV show, we're together.

Wes brings up the contest our last night. There won't be any lingering in the morning—I have a long drive to Telluride for the first of several weddings this weekend—so we're up later than we should be, stealing every last second together.

"Have you decided what you're going to submit?" He trails his fingertip down my arm and then flips my hand over to draw idle patterns on my palm.

"I think so. Maybe." I hum my contentment, enjoying the light touch he's tracing over my skin, and snuggle closer. "The unicorn is such a hard shot to get, and I didn't see anyone else posting a version with lightning like I got on social media. I think it's probably my best bet." I sigh. "But I love the dress photo too. It's different. Maybe too different."

"Or maybe just the right amount of different. You really think it would hurt to throw it in as a contender? It's telling a great story."

I shrug. The photo with the dress *does* have more to say. It *is* powerful. It *is* unique—but I don't think the contest is interested in those things when they come wrapped in a pretty pink dress. "Maybe, but it could also affect the scoring if anyone recognizes me. We both posted that shot of us together with me in the same dress. Given their history, it's not a chance I want to take."

I toy with the hem of his shirt, twisting the soft cotton through my fingers. "It's risky, Wes. I wish it wasn't, but this is too important." I push myself fully upright, leaning into the couch cushions and ignoring the movie we've been half watching. "If I win, it would give me the seed money to try out the adventure wedding thing, plus the extra bump in exposure and publicity would really help sell me to prospective clients. I can't afford it otherwise."

"If it's about the money, I can always loan you—"

"No," I say firmly. "I don't want your money. That's not why I'm with you."

Wes pulls out his phone and quickly scrolls to the image he transferred off my camera before tapping the screen. "*This* is creative talent, Sloane. I'm not saying your shot with the tornado and lightning and rainbow isn't good. It's fantastic. But that shot is half luck. Nature is doing a lot of the work for you. The dress composition you came up with isn't a matter of just executing when conditions are right. It's got something to say. Something powerful and unique to you."

He's not entirely wrong. There are plenty of photographers who could have gotten the trifecta shot, if they were in the right place at the right time. I still made my own choices about how to frame it, how to edit it, but it's an image where nature is the whole story.

But that doesn't change that I only have one shot at this.

Struggling to keep my frustration in check, I blow out a breath. "This isn't up to you."

"You could always submit both."

"You know I can't do that!" I snap with growing irritation. Even if he's found some loophole for multiple submissions, I'm not interested. I want to win honestly. "Wes, I love that you want to support me, but I said no."

The word *love* hangs in the air between us. His eyes drop to my mouth, and when his lips part, for a second I think he's going to say it. It's right there in the way he's looking at me, need and desire and pride and maybe just a tiny bit of frustration too.

"Okay, darlin'," Wes says instead, drawing me into his arms. "No more shop talk tonight. Just you and me. Sound good?"

I breathe out a sigh of relief, not quite managing to shove aside the thought of how long the days are going to become again once he leaves in the morning. I may already have a ticket to Houston in a couple of weeks, but I'm dreading the separation again.

I can decide which photo to submit later. Tonight, all I want is Wes.

CHAPTER TWENTY-THREE

I'M NOT SURE I HANDLE BEING SEPARATED FROM WES particularly *well*, but at least my clients are thrilled with the much-faster-than-expected turnaround for their edits. Also, my house has never been so clean. I even find time to call Tracy and talk about nothing when she's sitting around waiting for storms as she and Matt finish out the season.

I load my lightning-tornado-rainbow photo to the *Nature Shots* contest page a week before the deadline, glass of wine in hand. Taking an extra-large gulp of wine, I hesitate with my finger hovering over the *submit* button. On my other monitor, the dress shot is still open from my last-minute waffling on which photo to go with.

Wes thinks I look like a mythical creature in that dress. With the storm raging in front of me, complete with a distant though distinct lightning bolt, I can't say I disagree. It's a modern take, sure, without the armor or sword or shield—or mythical wings—but the image does invoke a sense of power and defiance. It's telling a story, but I'm still not convinced it's the right story for *Nature Shots* to choose me.

Maybe things would be different if I had the option to send both shots, if I could take the chance while still having a "safe" photo in the running, but the rules are clear. Only one photo per photographer. Only one chance to get it right. And whether I wish it were different or not, the less overtly feminine option is the obvious choice.

Decision reaffirmed, I click *submit*, finish my wine, and put myself to bed after sending Wes a Can't wait to see you text.

Humming to myself two endless days later, mood buoyed by the promise of Wes waiting on the other end of the short flight to Houston, I throw on the same maxi dress I wore the first time he stayed with me. I can chalk up the flush in my cheeks to the heat of the hair dryer, but the sparkle in my eyes is all anticipation. Especially when I remember our text exchange last night.

I have a surprise for you when you get here.

I hate surprises.

I think you're going to like this one . . .

Shivering at the promise, I grab my phone to order an Uber to the airport. Habit has me tapping on my email for a last-minute check for anything urgent from clients. Thankfully, there's nothing I need to deal with, but there *is* an email from *Nature Shots*.

Curious what they would be emailing about so soon, I open the email—only for my stomach to drop through the floor.

> Dear Ms. Michaels . . . regret to inform you . . . violation of contest rules . . . previously submitted . . . disqualified.

Convinced there must be some mistake, I blink a few times and try to read the message again. I've been disqualified for violating the rules against submitting more than one image per photographer, except that's impossible. I triple-checked my submission. There was only one file with one image attached.

Which is when I notice the file attachments at the very bottom of the email. One is the file I submitted. The other is labeled Valkyrie.jpeg.

"No," I whisper, my thumb shaking as I tap to download the attachment. "Wes wouldn't . . ."

Except he must have, because there I am, pink dress billowing in the wind, lightning in the distance.

Wes is the only one I sent a copy of the finished photo to. For his *personal* collection. How did they even get it when we can only submit one photo each?

Except as soon as the thought passes, I remember how basic the submission form was. There were only a handful of fields: name of photographer, email address of the photographer, name of image, and date the image was taken. Nowhere did it ask for the name of the person submitting the file. Anyone with the link could, theoretically, upload whatever they wanted.

Uber forgotten, I dial with shaking fingers. Betrayal burns hot as I listen to the phone ring once, twice, and then there's Wes and his oh-so-casual "Hey, darlin', everything all right with your flight?" like he hasn't been sneaking around behind my back.

"How could you?" Tears I don't bother trying to wipe away spill down my cheeks. "I told you when you were here that I was going with the other shot. I *told* you it wasn't your decision to make!"

There's a long beat of silence followed by his sigh. "I know that. And I'm sorry that I didn't listen to you. All of your photos are stunning, Sloane, but I wanted to give the judges the chance to pick between them. I thought it would be a nice surprise if it was chosen, and if not, well, it wouldn't hurt anything."

"Wouldn't *hurt* anything?" The bitter noise that comes out of my throat isn't precisely a laugh. "You deliberately violated the contest rules."

"I didn't—" Wes cuts himself off. There's a rustle of fabric, the sound of footsteps cutting through the sudden silence. "I don't know what you're talking about," he finally says, his accent thickening in an emotional tell I wish I didn't recognize.

There's only one reason he would say those words in that tone of voice. It's so typically Wes that it all makes a horrible kind of sense.

"I know you sure as shit weren't listening on the call when Carter went over them, but I—quite foolishly it seems—assumed that for something this important, you would, I don't know, go back and *read the fucking rules*," I seethe.

Wes sucks in a breath. "I'm sorry. I obviously missed—"

"Did you read the fucking rules, Wes?" I cut in. I don't need to hear excuses while my heart slowly fractures piece by piece. "Or did you just go off half-cocked and do what *you* wanted to do without any thought to how it might impact *me*?" I don't give him a chance to reply before spitting out, "I've been *disqualified*. For duplicate entries. Because the rules very clearly stated one entry per photographer."

"Shit. I . . . I'm so sorry, Sloane. There's never been a limit before and I . . . well, that doesn't matter. This is obviously my fuckup. Let me call them. I'll explain, and by the time you get here, it will all be straightened out."

I shake my head and scowl when I catch a glimpse of my reflection in the mirror. Hair styled, makeup perfect, a dress that shows off my curves and the nip of my waist. I wasted my entire morning trying to look extra nice for a man who couldn't even read a goddamn email.

I haven't spoken to my mother since the day I lost my temper on her, but somehow, it's still her snide voice in my head screaming *I told you this would happen*.

"I don't think it's a good idea for me to come to Houston right now."

"Sloane, please." Wes's voice cracks, raw emotion pouring over the line. "The last thing I was trying to do was screw things up for you. I can fix this."

"It's not just the rules." I shake my head, wiping tears away with sharp, jerky motions. "I *told* you this wasn't your decision. I *told* you why I didn't want to submit the photo. I *trusted* you."

"I know. It's just . . ." He takes a long breath. "Not reading the rules is my bad, and I'm going to call them and explain that. But that photo is stunning. The concept, the composition, the technical pieces. It belongs on that cover. *You* belong on that cover. I get why you're pissed at me, and I deserve that, but I was trying to help," he insists, something desperate creeping into his voice. "Please, Sloane."

Unbelievable. Even now, when I've been *disqualified* because of him, Wes is still trying to tell me he knows best. I don't know why I'm surprised. I'm the idiot who started sleeping with him and let lust alter my perception. Underneath it all, he's the same guy he's always been.

"Yeah, well." I let out a harsh, bitter laugh, the soundtrack of a dream crumbling. "That's not happening now, is it? One photo per photographer. They were very clear." I pause and then, through clenched teeth, ask the question I already know the answer to. "How many photos did you submit for yourself, Wes? More than one?"

"I haven't sent mine in yet. I have a few narrowed down and was going to ask you to help me decide tonight when you got in." He hesitates, and then in a whisper-soft voice pleads, "Please get on the plane. We can talk about this when you get here."

I don't care that he's practically begging, desperation tightening his words. It's too little, and it's way too late. "You're out of your mind if you think that's happening after what you just cost me."

"I can fix it," Wes repeats. "I'll call Carter Walsh right now and tell him it's entirely my fault. Just . . . please don't shut me out."

I almost cave, the way his voice cracks a battering ram against my freshly re-guarded heart. Then I think about the parade of men and endless tears pouring down my mom's face every time one of them left for good. It was never the first time they made her cry.

This is the first time I've cried over Wes, and I'll be damned if it's not the last.

"That's just it." I strip all the emotion out of my voice. Tears might still be pouring down my cheeks, but I learned a long time ago how to fall apart behind closed doors only after doing what needs to be done. "There's nothing else to say. You think you're above the rules. You've *always* thought you were above them. Wild Wes strikes again. I refuse to get caught in the crossfire of your shitty choices."

"If you're not getting on that plane, I'll come to you." Keys jingle softly in the background, a sound far too merry for the way each word scrapes out of him like broken glass. "Whatever it takes to make this right, I'll do it. You're too important to me. Making this right is too important to me."

"You knew how much this contest meant to me. You *knew* how badly I wanted to win entirely on my own merit. I didn't want your help. I didn't need your help." I let out a shuddering breath and add, "I don't need *you*."

Wes's breath catches like I've hit him. "I'm not saying I didn't fuck up. I did. But we can work through this. What we have, it's worth fighting for."

It's the right thing to say, but really, they're just words. Through the haze of tears, I stare down at the dress I was so excited for him to see me in. Now it's just a reminder that this whole thing started because Wes was somewhere he shouldn't have been, doing things he shouldn't have done.

He's always been Wild Wes. I'm the fool for believing he could be anything else.

"This is never going to work. You clearly don't respect me—"

"That's not true," he cuts in, sharp with frustration. "I respect the hell out of you."

I shake my head, exhaustion starting to override the hard edge of anger. I've always known it would come to this. "Then why did you go behind my back?"

The line is silent for so long that I don't think Wes is going to answer before he finally says in a tight, carefully controlled voice, "I'd really like to have this conversation face-to-face. If you don't want to come to Houston, say the word, and I'm on the next flight to Colorado."

"I can't do this," I whisper, which isn't an answer, but it might as well be. "I have too much going on with my family and my business to be with someone I can't trust."

"I see." The flat words dig the knife in deeper. I've never heard Wes so devoid of emotion before. "You might not trust me, but I'm a man of my word. I'll call Carter. I *will* fix this."

"It's too late." It's a miracle my voice doesn't break, because my heart is splintering. "What do you think Carter is going to do, even if you manage to talk to him? The rules are the rules. You can't fix this." Silent tears stream unchecked down my face. "Just . . . leave me alone. That's what I want."

"I'll give you your space. I owe you that much and more, but, Sloane, I'm not willing to give up this easily. I have calls to make." Wes's voice drops into a ragged whisper, grief and regret choking every word. "When you're ready to talk, I'll be here."

I hang up before the sob I've been holding back tears me apart.

I LET MYSELF fall apart until my living room fades from day into night. Then I get off the floor, wash my face, strip off the dress, and dump it in the trash. Maybe it's shock, or maybe I've just torn through too many emotions to have anything left as I go through the process of opening drawers and putting away the rest of the things from my suitcase.

Wes and I didn't even last three months together. I will not completely disregard every other aspect of my life just because he turned out to be exactly who I thought he was from the start. I will *not* be my mother and go to pieces for weeks over a breakup.

Calmer, I open my email and reread the full message from *Nature Shots* again. Without blind rage and betrayal clouding my thoughts, I realize that I'm not disqualified from the contest entirely. Only the second entry is.

Wes wasn't entirely wrong. The situation *is* fixable—at least when it comes to the contest.

They're *my* images. I should be able to simply swap out the one he sent first on my behalf—without my permission—for the one I intended to use all along. I can't imagine *Nature Shots* would want to go forward with an entry I knew nothing about.

The email is signed by Amelia Romero. Her name is vaguely familiar, but her signature doesn't include a title, just a phone number. It's too late to call now, but in the morning, I'll straighten this out. Myself. I don't care what Wes says about calling Carter. I'm not trusting him to fix this for me.

I'm not trusting him ever again.

After several long hours of tossing and turning, I sleepwalk my way through making coffee and toast, then sit on my couch and force myself to eat every bite even though it tastes like sawdust. I don't think about the time I've spent in this exact spot wrapped up in Wes. I don't think about how happy and content and safe I felt with him. I just stare resolutely at the clock and do the mental math on time zones.

With LA an hour behind, it's too early to call Amelia, so I take my coffee into my office and work on client photos until the timer I set buzzes right at ten.

"Hi, this is Sloane Michaels," I say when she answers, hoping the scratchiness in my voice isn't nearly as obvious to her as it is to me. "You emailed me yesterday, and I—"

"Sloane!" Amelia sounds downright thrilled. I'm so stunned after the perfunctory email yesterday that I almost don't hear her when she says, "You were on my list for this morning as soon as I finished my coffee. You've saved me a call!"

"I have?"

She laughs, as if this whole thing is a grand joke. My temper stirs to life, only to be doused in a bucket of ice water at her next words.

"I have no idea how Wes Talbot got Carter's personal cell phone number, but he straightened out the mix-up with your photos. The good news is that the deadline isn't until tomorrow, so if you can just let us know which one you'd like to use before then, you'll be all set."

Wes is a lot of things, but he's never been a liar. He did what he said he would. The protective ice I've wrapped myself in cracks, longing and hurt and betrayal just waiting to spill out. I take a deep breath and ruthlessly slap mental duct tape over the crack.

"That's a relief. He definitely did not have my permission to submit that photo." I can't bring myself to say his name. Not now, with all the emotions in my head too tangled up to make sense.

"I'm so sorry for what you must have felt when you got my email, but I have to tell you, it's a fantastic image. Gave me shivers when I saw it. That sky and the dress and the pose. Lord knows this place could use some good old-fashioned female rage."

As Carter's assistant, Amelia doesn't have anything to do with judging the contest. Even Carter doesn't get to cast a vote, leaving it up to the impartial panel *Nature Shots* selected—but I hear what she's saying loud and clear.

I swallow hard, no longer so certain about my choice. I love the dress photo. I picked a different option not because I thought it was objectively better, but to fit the magazine's mold.

Maybe *some good old-fashioned female rage* is the right call. It might cost me the contest, but at least it won't cost me a piece of my soul. I can always get a small-business loan and launch the adventure weddings that way. I don't *have* to play by someone else's rules.

Maybe if Wes reminded me of that, tried to talk to me about it one more time instead of going behind my back, this all could have turned out differently.

"Thank you," I say to Amelia. "That's exactly what I was going for when I created the image."

"You nailed it." She pauses, the *click-clack* of her keyboard audible before she gently adds, "Would you like some time to think about it? Like I said, we just need to know by end of day tomorrow. You can email me when you decide."

Since I'm still sitting at my desk, I click over into my personal folder and give the photo of me in the dress a long, critical look. The day it was shot, I felt powerful *and* feminine. Like some part of me could stare down the storms of life without flinching. Like I'd finally found a way to embrace the side of me that likes pretty dresses and pink silk without feeling like I was caving to my mother's criticisms. Like just this once, I didn't have to try to be one of the guys to avoid being objectified by other storm chasers.

But then when it was time to submit, I flinched. I went with the safe option. The one that met what I thought the magazine wanted. What other photographers would expect of a woman. It wasn't my mother, or Wes, or even the magazine—*I* put myself in a box.

Wes ignored my express wishes and lost my trust in the process. But that isn't a good enough reason to turn down this opportunity to decide if I want to stay in that box, or if I want to be the woman in the photo.

The woman in the photo would be brave.

"That's okay," I tell Amelia, certainty settling in my bones. "I'll leave it. The dress photo, I mean."

"Are you sure? You won't be able to change your mind."

"I understand."

"Okay, Sloane. I'll let Carter know. And for what it's worth, I think you're making the right decision. I'll be rooting for you when they announce the winners in three weeks. Good luck."

CHAPTER TWENTY-FOUR

WES CALLS ABOUT AN HOUR AFTER I HANG UP WITH Amelia. I don't answer. I send four more calls to voicemail before the day is over.

It's another three days before he calls again. I ignore that too. Hours later, long after midnight, with occasional fireworks still going off from the July Fourth holiday, I'm still at my desk. I'm already ahead on my workload, but editing another set of client photos is a tidy way to avoid arguing with myself over listening to the last voicemail Wes left—but I'm not distracted enough to not notice when my phone lights up with a text.

I'll back off for now, but I'm not giving up on us.

One tiny sob escapes before I ruthlessly swallow the rest and delete the voicemail without listening to it. I'm not strong enough to face that underneath the anger, underneath the hurt, I *miss* Wes.

Some part of me wants to forgive him. Late at night, when I'm alone in my bed, a little voice inside me whispers that maybe he deserves a second chance. He made things right with *Nature Shots*, just like he said he would.

But I've always known that everything between us was little more than a house of cards ready to collapse at the first stiff breeze. I *knew* getting too close to him would turn me into collateral damage. That when it all came down, *I* would be the one scraping myself up off the floor yet again. That Wes would do what he always does and somehow skate by without a single consequence.

And for the ten days after our disastrous phone call, it sure as hell looks like that's exactly what happens. At least until I finally text Tracy for permission to use some of her wedding photos to promote my hopeful pivot to adventure weddings.

Oh good. You ARE alive.

I deserve that. I've been avoiding Tracy—and everyone else—to throw myself into work. It's not unusual for June, when she's still out chasing, and I'm up to my eyeballs in brides, but I won't pretend I haven't been leaning hard into the excuse this year.

Sorry! June is always nuts.

Less than twenty seconds after I send my reply, Tracy calls. My thumb hovers over the screen as I debate sending her to voicemail. There's no way she's calling right this second just to talk about a handful of photos on my website.

Matt must have told her about the breakup by now. Of course she wants to know what happened. The worst part is, I can't even blame her. Any normal person would have called and unloaded the whole sad story, but her husband is the closest thing Wes has to a best friend. Putting Tracy in the middle isn't fair either.

But I just asked her for a favor. And I can't avoid everyone forever, so I swallow past the lump in my throat, squeeze my eyes shut at the tears that seem to lurk just beneath the surface these days, and answer the call.

"Of course you can use the photos," Tracy says by way of greeting.

"Great! I'll—"

"We ran into Wes this afternoon," she cuts in. "He looks awful. Like he hasn't slept in a week."

Does he feel like a part of him died too?

"You know Wes," I say with forced cheer. "He doesn't know when to stop chasing."

Tracy doesn't laugh at my pitiful attempt at humor. "He hasn't talked to Matt in weeks beyond trading intel. He's been keeping to himself. We both thought he was moping about you going home, but then earlier today . . . I'm worried, Sloane. I think he's lost weight. He just pumped gas, went inside to grab some energy drinks, and left without so much as a wave. Is everything okay between you two?"

I blink, surprised. "He didn't tell Matt?"

"Tell Matt *what*?"

It's a struggle not to choke on the sudden knot in my

throat. A wounded noise escapes despite my best effort to keep it in, and Tracy's tone goes from frustrated to concerned in a blink. "Sloane? Hey, you okay?"

"I . . . We . . . It's over." I stumble over my words, but at least my voice only shakes a little. "You've known Wes a long time too. He's not relationship material."

Saying it aloud hurts more than it should.

"Once you two finally got together, Matt told me how much Wes has always talked about you," Tracy says slowly. "He kept it to himself to avoid putting me in a weird spot with you—knowing I'd want to tell you—since he'd promised Wes he wouldn't let it get back to you."

"No," I insist, shaking my head. "That can't be true."

"Do you remember the twin tornadoes in Wyoming last year? How we all went to the bar that night?"

"Yeah, but—"

"Everyone was in such a good mood. *You* were in such a good mood that you hugged Wes. He brought that hug up for months. I don't know what happened, but I saw you together. The way you look at each other . . . that doesn't come around all that often." She pauses, and then more gently than I deserve, she asks, "When did it end?"

"A little over a week ago," I mumble, like I don't know that it was June 30th at 1:57 p.m. when everything fell apart.

There's a beat of silence. "And you've kept this to yourself this whole time? You could have called me, Sloane."

I deserve the reproach in her voice. I open my mouth to explain that I didn't want to put her in the middle of it. The words die on my tongue. It's what I've been telling myself, but the truth is, I'm used to handling my problems on my own.

I'm *used* to not having help, to having to rely only on me, myself, and I at all times.

It's part of why this all hurts so much. Wes dangled the possibility of something better in front of me for weeks—and then snatched it all away.

"It's just been a lot," I say. "I was going to tell you. I . . . needed to get my head on straight about it first."

"What the hell happened?"

Tracy groans when I finish telling her the whole ugly story. "Goddammit, Wes." She mutters something else under her breath too low for me to hear, and then I catch a muffled *They broke up* followed by the faint sound of Matt's swearing. "Did you tell *Nature Shots* what happened?" Tracy asks, her voice clear again. "I can't believe he did that to you. I'm so sorry."

"He called them. They were gracious about it, but . . ." I blink away the fresh burn of tears that I don't have the energy for. "I can't get past it. That he went behind my back like that."

"What did he say when you talked to him?"

That photo is stunning. The concept, the composition, the technical pieces. It belongs on that cover. You *belong on that cover. I was trying to help.*

When Wes first said those things to me, they sounded like nothing but excuses. Even his apologies sounded like excuses.

Except rather than using those words as an opening salvo in the manipulation Olympics, he quietly backed off. No lavish gifts designed to blind me to his crimes. No endless phone calls and texts to wear me down. No overblown promises. No volatile flip-flopping from nasty name-calling to begging.

In short, none of the standard behavior I've come to associate with the words *I'm sorry.*

"He said he was trying to help," I tell Tracy. "It's all just words."

"That sounds very . . . final."

"It doesn't really matter anymore. I'm going to put my energy into this adventure wedding thing and try not to think about it," I say firmly.

Tracy's silence is loud as the seconds tick by, but eventually she must decide not to push me. She tells me about her shot, and eventually, our conversation turns toward our usual topics without any further discussion of the Wes-shaped elephant lurking on the line with us.

THE FIRST HALF of July melts away in a frenzy of weddings and arranging bookings for my new business model. As exhausting as it can be, I'm grateful to fall into bed too tired to do much more than pass out.

My social media does respectable numbers most days—everyone loves a glamorous wedding—but when I put up a shot of Tracy and Matt, along with details on my pivot to smaller, more intimate ceremonies in nontraditional locations, my DMs and inbox explode. Wes was right. There's an enormous market for this sort of thing.

Except I'm not thinking about Wes anymore. A two-week pity party is more than enough.

If only my heart would listen.

The morning in late July when the winners are set to be announced via a live-stream presentation, I take out my frustration and anxiety on some poor, hapless chicken breasts, pounding them into thin cutlets and then tossing them into a homemade marinade. My brothers are coming over for dinner tonight. It may not be the best move with the contest announcement, but things have gotten better between us.

The very long talk we had after I finally lost it on Mom helped. She's not speaking to any of us at the moment, which is just as well. I think we all need the break. I'm not sure I'll ever stop feeling somewhat parental toward Eric and Sam, but we're trying to figure it out.

Besides, Sam always brings the strong microbrews he likes. I can drown my disappointment in expensive beer.

Still, I can't help wondering if I even have a real shot at winning. Amelia's words have dogged my steps for the last three weeks, rattling around in my thoughts on late-night drives back from venues.

I want to win. Badly. Not just for the money. Not just to prove myself to the chasing community. Not even for the bragging rights of being the first woman on the *Nature Shots* cover.

I want to win for *me*. To prove to myself that I'm the woman in the photo. Brave. Capable. A force of nature.

Unable to sit still, I pace my office like a caged beast while Carter Walsh starts the video call and runs through the preliminaries. Just to torture everyone a little more, the sponsors take turns expressing their appreciation for our art and the unique challenges that go into photographing storms, blah, blah, blah.

I'm about to crawl out of my skin when they finally get to

the part we're all here for. Tracy takes third place with her rainbow and tornado shot. I grab my phone and quickly send her an all-caps text that's mostly exclamation points.

My breath stutters when I hear Wes's name next. He's come in second with a shot I recognize from our time together. If I wasn't standing next to him when he took it, it would be hard to believe he didn't photoshop the lightning bolt crashing down, perfectly centered between the ruins of old farm equipment.

Some part of me expected him to win the whole thing. The fact that he came in second is so much of a surprise I'm barely paying attention to the rest of the announcement—until I hear my own name.

". . . Sloane Michaels, with a stunning image aptly titled *Valkyrie*, to be revealed at the awards gala. Congratulations to the winners and to everyone who submitted. You are all supremely talented and didn't make this easy for the judges. Details on the ceremony to be held next month in Los Angeles will be emailed out in the next forty-eight hours. Thanks for joining us!"

My phone starts ringing and doesn't stop. I'm too stunned to answer, frozen in the middle of my office and staring at what is now a blank window where the live stream once was.

I won.

I'm going to be on the cover of *Nature Shots*. This time, when the numbness cracks, there's no stopping the tears that flood down my cheeks.

Wes is the person whose voice I want to hear most right now. He's the one I want to celebrate this moment with. He's the one I want to hear whisper in that low bedroom voice *I'm so proud of you, darlin'*.

But Wes isn't here.

My phone continues to light up with a flood of incoming texts. I didn't realize how invested the overall chasing community was in this contest—every chaser I know in possession of my phone number sends well wishes and joking complaints that I've been hiding a stunning image.

I'm in too much of a daze to wonder why my brothers are bothering to knock when I hear someone at my front door, never mind why they're two hours early for dinner. I pull the door open and blink at the sight that awaits me. Then I blink again, certain I've hallucinated the enormous bouquet of flowers dwarfing the delivery guy.

He peers out from behind the blooms, juggling a clipboard. "Sloane Michaels?"

"Yes?"

"I'm going to need you to sign for these." A glass vase is thrust into my hands. "Careful, it's heavy."

I eye the bouquet, a mix of roses and peonies and calla lilies all in deep shades of pink that too closely match the dress in my cover photo—*my cover photo!*—to be coincidence. It must have cost a small fortune to get them to my doorstep within an hour of the announcement.

Either *Nature Shots* has a hell of a publicist working overtime, or . . .

"Who are they from?" I croak.

The delivery guy shrugs. "Not my department. Mind signing? Got a few more deliveries to make."

"Right, yes, of course." I barely manage to scribble my name on the electronic pad without dropping anything. Then it's just me and the emotional landmine of a bouquet.

I bring the vase into the kitchen and set it on the counter before eyeing it with trepidation. There's a card tucked into the middle of the blooms, the small envelope a pale pink taunt as my kitchen fills with a delicious floral scent.

"Don't be ridiculous," I scold myself after a few minutes of silent standoff with the flowers. I pluck the card out and quickly rip it open, determined to get this over with.

I'm so proud of you. I miss you.

I slap my palm over my mouth to stifle the sob that breaks free. It's what I wanted to hear, but the impersonal serif font just emphasizes the current chasm between us.

I trace my fingertip over the slant of the *W* beneath the short message and struggle to keep breathing as longing slams into me. Burying my face in the flowers, I take a deep breath of their sweet scent. My emotions are all over the place. Anything I decide now will be a knee-jerk reaction. I debate sending Tracy a photo of the bouquet for advice, but she just won too. Better to let her celebrate in peace without my relationship drama.

Wes and I will both be in Los Angeles in a couple of weeks for the gala. If I'm going to let him back into my life, into my heart, I need to be certain it's the right choice, not an emotional reaction in an emotional moment.

Today, I start small. First by digging the pink dress out of my closet and promptly dropping it off at the dry cleaner. And then, once I'm home and have changed my mind so many times I'm sick of thinking about it, I send a simple text.

Thank you for the flowers.

It's a pretty half-assed olive branch. Wes replies in less than a minute anyway.

I'm glad you like them. And then, barely thirty seconds later, I'm sorry, Sloane. You were right about all of it. I didn't stop to think about my actions or how they would make you feel. I won't make excuses. I should have listened and respected your decision.

And then, a few seconds after that, I miss you so fucking much.

I give myself a minute to consider my response. I miss Wes, but I'm not ready to open that door. Not when I'm expecting my brothers in half an hour. Not with the high of my win still racing through my veins. But for the first time since I opened that email, I'm no longer as certain as I once was that what Wes did is truly unforgivable.

I take a deep, shaky breath and reply, Let's talk when we're both in LA. Congrats on your shot too.

The typing bubble appears and disappears too many times to count. I chew my lip while I watch, knowing I should put my phone down and do something else before the guilt and want and anxiety win. Instead I stay right where I am until Wes finally sends back, I'm not trying to make excuses, but there are things I should have told you earlier. I can wait until we're in LA, but I would like the chance to explain.

I don't overthink my reply, but once it's written and my thumb is hovering over the screen, I chicken out. I stare at it for far too long, second-guessing if honesty really is the best policy when it comes to Wes. If I'm giving him too much power, too much room to hurt me all over again.

I don't send the text. I also don't delete it. I just lock my phone and let it clatter onto the counter before turning my focus to the dinner I promised my brothers.

"WHAT'S WITH THE flowers?" Sam plunks a six-pack on my counter and stares at the pink blooms like they're crime scene evidence.

Eric grabs one of Sam's beers, ignores our brother's protest, and uses the bottle opener on his keys to pop the top before declaring them *fuckup flowers*.

"Definitely fuckup flowers," Sam agrees. Both of them turn to me with expectant faces.

"Who fucked up?" Eric drops his keys on the counter and pokes at the flowers, probably looking for the card I already hid in my office. "You broke up with that Wes guy, right? Kind of a shame. He seemed solid."

"*Solid?*" I gape at my brother, who hasn't liked a single man I've dated. "Since when are you a fan of Wes?"

Eric and Sam exchange a long look. "What did he do?" Sam grabs a beer of his own and then ducks around me to inhale the spicy scent wafting from the meat sizzling on the stove. "Can you show Cassie how to make your recipe?"

I shove him away and flip the chicken over. "If you don't

like the way she does it, you can always make them yourself. Just be grateful she's willing to cook for your sorry ass."

"She loves my ass." Sam smacks his own butt with nauseating pride. "Squats, baby."

Making a retching noise, I take the beer Eric offers and down several long gulps. "I do *not* want to hear about your ass, Sam."

"That's fine," Eric says, a little too cheerful for how his eyes are narrowed on the bouquet. "You can tell us about what Wes did that he's sending you flowers weeks after you dumped *his* ass."

Time to steer the conversation away from my disastrous love life. "If you're done talking about asses, I was going to tell you that I won the cover contest."

"Wait, really?" Eric asks at the same time Sam says, "Are you serious? That's awesome!"

"Yeah. Found out a few hours ago."

"Well, congrats! You going to show us the photo that won?" Eric leans against the counter while he sips his beer and throws a look of exaggerated hurt at Sam. "She tells us nothing. Her own brothers, and we're the last to know."

"Give me that," Sam demands, taking the tongs out of my hand. "Go get your laptop. We want to see the photo. And then I want to know why you look so miserable if you won this contest. Also, why did I not know that you broke up with that guy?"

"Because you've had your head so far up Cassie's pus—"

"You're just jealous. Maybe if you took a shower once in a—"

"I own my own business, fuckface. You're the one working yourself to death for some guy in a suit. You think—"

"I think you're both idiots," I interrupt, snatching back the tongs before launching into a brief recap of my fight and subsequent breakup with Wes. When I'm done, they both stare at me, Sam's expression thoughtful, while Eric is looking at me like I'm the idiot.

"They *are* fuckup flowers," Sam says slowly. He cocks his head to the side, glancing between me and Eric. "But dude put some effort into it."

I grab the chicken out of the pan and drop it onto a waiting cutting board before reaching for my knife. "What is this, some sort of birds-of-a-feather-fuck-up-together nonsense? Been to the florist recently yourself?"

"Of course he has," Eric says before Sam can defend himself. "So, look, I'm going to say a thing, and you're probably going to hate it, but if you kick me out, I'm taking tacos with me." He pauses, glances at the knife I'm now using to chop up the chicken, and takes two steps back while Sam snickers. "Wes fucked up. Complete fumble on his part. But he also told you he was going to fix it, and from what you said, that's exactly what he did. No one is perfect. I think it says a lot about the guy that he took responsibility. And he plainly still cares about you or he wouldn't be sending serious-effort flowers. Those didn't come from a grocery store."

"Really? You too?"

Eric holds up his palms and takes another step back. "You think you can put the knife down? You're kind of scary right now."

Rolling my eyes, I finish chopping the last two pieces of chicken and set the knife aside. And then I finally put words to the one fear I haven't been able to get past.

"How many times have Mom's losers screwed up and tried

to make up for it with flowers or some other over-the-top gift? How do I know this isn't just the start of a pattern I want nothing to do with?"

"You don't." Sam sets down his beer. He comes closer, his palms gentle on my biceps. "But you're not Mom, Sloane."

"And Wes isn't some barfly loser like the guys she always picks," Eric adds. "None of those wastes of life have ever stood up for her outside of an excuse to throw hands, never mind taken care of her when she's been sick. It's not the same."

Confused, I blink at Eric. "How do you know Wes took care of me? I never told you that."

"You were asleep. I called to check if you were coming back anytime soon to pick up his car. He was practically whispering. When I told him to speak up, he said you had one of your migraines and had fallen asleep on him, so he wasn't doing anything to wake you up. He didn't mention it?"

"No." But now that I think about it, Wes only told me he'd heard from Eric days after it happened. I glance between my brothers, but my attention inevitably drifts right back to the flowers. "I just don't want to turn into Mom."

"The fact that you're worried about it means that you won't," Eric says simply. "Hear the guy out. If he screws up again, leave him. But if you ask me, he made a mistake, he's genuinely sorry, and he's already said there's stuff you don't know. You're going to this awards dinner anyway, right?"

"It's my first cover. I'm definitely going."

"What have you got to lose by seeing what he says?" Sam takes another sip of his beer and shrugs. "Maybe it works out. Maybe it doesn't. You're never going to know if you don't talk to him."

"When did you get so wise?" I mutter before grabbing the chopped chicken and sliding it into a bowl next to everything else laid out on the counter. "Eat before it gets cold."

Eric grabs a taco shell and starts shoveling more meat into it than will ever fit, but he pauses and looks me in the eye. "We're assholes and don't say it enough, but we get how much you did for us as kids. How much of Mom's crap you hid from us. You wouldn't have done any of that if you were like her. Maybe Wes is a good guy. Maybe he's not. But I don't think this one thing is enough to give up on someone who makes you happy."

My sniffle is exaggerated, but the tightness in my throat is real. "You're annoying when you're right."

It's only later, after my brothers have left and I'm just a little tipsy from the beer, that I find myself delving into my closet. When I finally pull Wes's sweatshirt out from behind the stack of boxes where I shoved it after our fight, I press it to my nose and draw in the ever-so-faint trace of his scent left in the fabric.

Yanking the sweatshirt over my head, I grab my phone and finally hit *send* on the text I typed out earlier.

> We can talk in LA. I love the flowers. I'd be lying if I said I didn't miss you. Just give me some time.

A notification pops up a few seconds later. I'll wait as long as you need me to.

CHAPTER TWENTY-FIVE

AFTER TWO WEEKS OF ASKING MYSELF HARD QUESTIONS, I spend every minute of the flight to Los Angeles, and the subsequent ride to the hotel where the gala is being held, quietly losing my shit.

With five minutes to spare, I nervously smooth down the silk dress and give myself a critical once over in the hotel room mirror. Maybe it's too on the nose to wear the dress from the cover shot, but it's not like I packed another one.

The fact that all I can think about in the elevator is the look on Wes's face the first time he saw me in it, well, that's a problem I'm just going to have to ignore. Easier said than done when his ravenous gaze locks on me seconds after I step into the ballroom.

Maybe it was a mistake to wait until tonight to talk to him. Maybe we should have done this over the phone, or FaceTime, or bought a cheap plane ticket. Because I know the second his eyes land on me that if I had let him, Wes would have been on a plane to Colorado weeks ago.

The sight of him in formalwear has the same jarring *otherness* it did months ago at his friend's wedding, but his suit is a little loose now. Tracy was right. He *has* lost weight. But it's not just that. His usual easy confidence has gone brittle, shadows under his eyes and his lips not quite forming a smile as we stare at each other.

Wes moves before I do. His first step is tentative. Then he's weaving through the tables and other guests with single-minded determination, using the advantage of his long legs to cut through the crowd with ease. I should move, step into the hallway, meet him halfway, *something*. I remain frozen, my heart pounding with nervous anticipation as I watch him approach.

When he stops in front of me, he sucks in a breath before he says anything. His eyes race over my face, searching and just a little desperate.

The sound of my name in his all-too-familiar husky murmur triggers an avalanche of memories so strong I can't suppress a shiver. We're in the middle of a crowded room, and yet everything else, every*one* else, falls away.

The ache in my chest turns sharp when I catch a whiff of his spicy citrus scent. The seconds tick away between us, and I need to say something, anything, but all I can do is clasp my hands together to keep from reaching for him.

Wes lifts one hand from his side like he's going to touch me, but it lands on the back of his neck instead as he says, "I'm so glad you're here." His accent bleeds through despite the low tone, thick as honey.

"Me too." I clear my throat and tighten my fingers around my clutch in the hope they'll stop shaking. "Wes, I—"

"Sloane! I was wondering where you were," Tracy says as

she rushes up and throws her arms around me. "You look *hot*!" She steps back, an amused grin curving her lips upward as she glances between me and Wes, and then adds a little too pointedly, "Doesn't she?"

"Tracy!" I hiss at the same time Wes says, "She always does." His eyes snap to mine, not quite so frantic now, but no less intense. "Though I'm rather fond of that particular dress."

My mouth goes dry at the cascade of memories. The yards of pink silk suddenly feel like so much more than a dress as flashes of Wes twirling me on a dirt road, head thrown back in laughter, mingle with the blazing heat of his dark stare in my bedroom, all that silk pooled at my feet.

Tracy's giggle breaks the intensity of the moment. "Okay, you two, awards first, hot make-up sex later."

Heat erupts in my cheeks as I sputter, but then Wes laughs. Not his usual laugh—a hoarse, rusty echo of it, as if he hasn't worked those particular muscles in a long time. And then our eyes meet again, and his laughter fades. He crooks his arm toward me, an invitation and an offer. I don't let myself overthink it as I slip my arm into his.

"I have so many things I need to say to you," Wes murmurs as we wind our way toward our assigned table, too soft for Tracy to hear over the hum of voices filling the room. The way his accent weaves in and out reminds me far too much of late nights on long stretches of open road and whispers in the dark. "Right now, I'm just glad you're here, Sloane. Really fucking glad."

He pulls out my chair, his warm palm ghosting over my bare back. I lean in just before I sit, my lips close to his ear to make sure he hears me. "Me too."

Carter Walsh chooses that moment to appear. There's a flurry of introductions, and though I'm half holding my breath when he turns to Wes with a wry expression, I don't miss the way his eyes dart toward me just before he says, "Wes, always good to see you. At least when you're not interrupting dinner with my wife."

"Won't happen again." Wes lets his arm rest on the back of my chair as he relaxes into his own. The very tips of his fingers graze between my shoulder blades as he drops his arm, the contact so brief I'm not sure it was intentional. "I promise," he adds without taking his eyes off mine.

Carter's low chuckle reminds me that we're far from alone. I reach for my water and take a long sip while Tracy smirks across the table. *Unhelpful*, I mouth. Her smirk only grows wider.

The lights dim when Carter moves toward the stage to begin the opening remarks. I barely hear a word he says, not when I'm hyperaware of Wes next to me.

Despite the lingering tension lurking under the surface, it's no small thing to find that, even with our edges a bit jagged, the part of me that's always been drawn to Wes is still there. That when he tugs at his collar and catches my eye, a small, private smile passes easily between us at the shared memory of that Houston wedding months ago. The night that, looking back, marked the first subtle shift in our atmosphere.

Tracy takes the stage first. Her short speech flies by, and then she's sinking back into her chair and reaching for her champagne while shooting me a *Thank god that's over* look across the table. I mouth back *Proud of you* with a beaming grin.

Her eyes light up. She points at Wes and then tips her

champagne flute toward me with a raised brow I choose to ignore.

And then Wes gets to his feet with one last lingering look in my direction.

"Thank you," he says, all charm when he grips the edge of the podium and faces the audience. He gestures to his photo, blown up and resting on an easel beside Tracy's. Mine is there too, covered with champagne velvet in preparation for the upcoming grand reveal. "I know I'm supposed to get up here and tell you about my image, but tonight isn't about me. It's about Sloane Michaels."

The silence that fills the room is more curious than anything, everyone holding their breath right along with me as Wes scans the crowd. He's not known for his modesty.

"Sloane is as talented as she is driven, with a singular ability to turn images into an allegory for human emotion. You'll see for yourself in a minute when I shut up."

He pauses, laughter rippling through the crowd.

This time, when his eyes catch mine, the mask is gone, replaced by the naked vulnerability of regret. Then he turns back to the audience and flashes one of those charming Wild Wes grins. I might be the only one in the room who notices it's a shadow of the real thing.

"Don't let the pink dress fool you into thinking she's anything other than a force of nature. Sloane, get up here and take your well-deserved victory lap."

I stand automatically and move toward the stage in a daze while applause fills the ballroom. Wes waits for me by the short flight of stairs, his hand extended like the perfect gentleman. There's no way he doesn't notice how sweaty my palm is when he helps me onto the stage. Especially when he holds on a few seconds longer than strictly necessary.

My hammering heart drowns out whatever nice things Carter says about my photograph before he pulls the velvet off the print. "Nice dress," he deadpans into the microphone, offering the audience a wink before stepping back to make room for me.

Far too aware of Wes only feet away, I glance down at my notes. They're a little smudged from my sweaty palms. Good thing I practiced this speech so much that once I start, muscle memory should take over.

"When I came up with this concept, I was interested in the juxtaposition of beauty and destruction. That's one of the things that drew me to storm chasing early on. These storms are as stunning as they are deadly. The best image of my career"—I gesture to the blown-up photograph behind me—"could also be the worst day of someone else's life."

I swallow hard, unprepared for the memory of Wes, sweaty and exhausted and hefting a chainsaw to help tornado victims. The audience is silent, all those eyes staring up at me. This isn't the moment to fall into my own head, and yet I can't help glancing back at him for just a second. Eyes shining with emotion, he dips his chin in the tiniest acknowledgment.

"I wanted to capture that dichotomy," I continue, "and I wanted to do it in a way that evoked both the wildness of the storm and the careful box of femininity. So many women hide their ferocity behind gowns and smiles, but storm chasing is meant to be a little wild. When we're out there, we're *all* part of that storm." My eyes flick back to Wes. "The beauty *and* the destruction."

I take another breath and turn my attention to the audience before the desperate ache in my chest steals my voice. I thank Carter and the magazine for the opportunity before posing for photos with one of those enormous cardboard checks and the various judges and sponsors.

When it's time for a shot with all the winners, Wes stands awkwardly at my side. He shifts his weight when his arm brushes mine and mutters an apology before looking away—but not before I catch the flash of pain in his eyes.

It's not the first time either. I've seen it every time he's stopped himself from reaching for me almost half a dozen times tonight.

On my other side, Tracy slings an arm around my shoulders and plants a smacking kiss on my cheek. "You okay?" she whispers with a tiny, barely perceivable nod toward Wes.

"I think so." I slide one arm around her waist, and without letting myself think about it too much, rest my other lightly on Wes's back. His whole body shudders with the contact, and then his arm settles low behind me, the expensive fabric of his jacket soft on my bare skin and warm with the heat of him. Something tentative and full of hope blooms in his eyes when I glance up.

"Thank you," I say quietly, momentarily forgetting there's a photographer waiting who isn't interested in watching us stare at each other. "For what you said up there."

"Every word was the truth."

"I know, but—"

"If everyone could just look into the camera, we'll get you folks off to the party as quickly as we can," the photographer interrupts in a familiar pleasant-but-about-to-not-be tone.

“After we’re done here, can we talk?” Wes says in a low voice, his lips barely moving to appease the photographer. “Alone, without interruptions.”

The camera clicks as the shutter releases in a staccato burst. I hold my smile fixed in place, but when the photographer finally declares we’re done, I meet Wes’s eyes. Beneath his mask of affability, there’s a wild edge, as though he’s terrified that I’ll vanish if he so much as looks away.

“We can’t just disappear, but later,” I say quietly. “I promise.”

His fingers tighten at my hip. “I’m holding you to that.”

My smile is tiny but it’s genuine. “Good.”

PROFESSIONAL OBLIGATIONS KEEP us networking for another hour. Wes’s stare is heavy on me the entire time, and the few moments I stare back, I’m always the first to look away. By the time the gala is winding down, my feet hurt, and there’s the start of a headache forming behind my eyes. I’m beyond ready to change out of this dress—and I’m as ready as I’m going to be for my conversation with Wes.

Tracy glances at her watch, tips back the last of her champagne, and gestures toward the door with her empty glass. “You going to be okay if I head out?” Her attention drifts toward the bar where Wes is laughing with Carter. “Matt’s out front, but I can tell him to come back.”

I wiggle my toes with a wince. “Go home to Matt. I’m going to head up to change, I think.”

Tracy kicks off her shoes and stoops to grab them before leaning in for a hug. With a kiss on my cheek, she wiggles her fingers and darts for the exit, heels dangling from one hand. "It's okay to forgive him. Love is a good thing, Sloane," she tosses back over her shoulder before disappearing into the night.

Love. I've been afraid to call it that, afraid that saying it aloud would make everything that's happened hurt so much more, but now that we're here, now that repairing things between us doesn't seem so impossible after all, I can't call it anything else.

I'm in love with Wes Talbot—and I'm almost positive he's in love with me.

I scan the crowd again, but he's no longer by the bar where I last saw him. Shifting my weight, I give the dwindling crowd one more quick look before glaring down at my own gorgeous but painful heels. I'm not brave enough to whip them off right here like Tracy.

Deciding I'll text Wes after I change—the conversation we need to have is definitely a private one—I head for the elevator. These shoes have got to go.

Stabbing the button for the elevator harder than necessary, I stare at the unmoving floor numbers. "Come on," I mutter impatiently. "I need out of this dress."

"I'd be happy to help with that," Wes drawls from behind me right as the elevator doors open with a *ding*. It's such a *Wes* thing to say, so typically *us* that I let out a startled laugh. For a few seconds, it's like the last six weeks never happened.

And then reality comes crashing back. The faint amusement on his face falls, tightening into the pained expression I've caught him trying to mask over and over again tonight.

"Sorry," he says gruffly, dropping his gaze to the floor. "That was out of line." He shoves his hands in his pockets, and then immediately pulls one back out to rake his fingers through his already-disheveled hair. "I can grab the next one."

The flirty comment was one sort of reminder. This is another.

Wes is still the man who sees what I need and gives it to me, who takes care of me when I need it, without expecting the same in return.

The man who made a mistake—and did everything in his power to fix it. Even when he knew there was no guarantee I would forgive him. Even when he was on a stage in front of the people who can make or break our careers, he put me first.

I step into the elevator, hold down the button to keep the doors open, and gesture with my free hand to the empty space. "We can share."

Emotions dance across his expression too fast to follow, but there's no mistaking the tentative hope. "You're sure?"

I swallow past my nerves and ignore the growing impulse to step into his arms and just skip the part where we have the hard conversation—but *not* talking is how we got here. "Yeah, Wes. I'm sure."

It's only once the doors close that I realize he absolutely *reeks* of alcohol. I back away as much as I can in such a confined space and hold on to my clutch so hard my fingers ache. "We can talk tomorrow," I say quickly, my gaze fixed on the steadily climbing numbers. I'm too emotionally drained to confront the stab of disappointment knifing through me. I thought this conversation was just as important to him as it is to me, that it was worth being sober for. "Maybe in the morning—"

"I'm not drunk." Wes takes a step closer, his eyes clear

when they meet mine. He moves slowly, giving me plenty of time to avoid the careful fingers that curl around my wrist and guide my hand to his chest. His very wet chest. "Server tripped. It's white wine. I was going up to my room to change before I found you."

"Oh." I let my hand drop awkwardly and force my eyes back to his. "Well, don't let me stop you. That can't be comfortable."

"You think I give a shit about that right now?" His throat bobs with the force of his swallow, his voice stripped bare. He lifts one hand as if to reach for me again, only to quickly shove it in his pocket. "All I want is to make things right between us."

The charm act from our chase season is gone. What's left behind is raw vulnerability and fragile hope. Aching need. And yet Wes isn't pleading. He isn't pressuring me. Even now, when it's obvious by his rigid posture and tight expression that it's taking everything in him to hold back, he's going at my pace.

It's terrifying to need someone the way I need Wes Talbot, terrifying to put my trust in him again, but we're storm chasers. Our lives are all about calculated risks.

If we can put our lives on the line for tornadoes, surely it's worth risking my heart for love.

I'm holding on to my clutch so hard the zipper bites into my skin. A ragged whisper is all I can manage as emotion threatens to choke me. "I miss you."

"I'm so sorry, Sloane. I'm so fucking sorry," Wes rasps. "I have been fucking miserable without you."

"I forgive you." I speak slowly, making sure he knows I

mean it. "You have things you want to say, and there are things I should say too, but I want to start there. I forgive you. I . . . I want to try to figure the rest out."

A tremor goes through him, his big body all but collapsing into mine. I let myself sink into him. Sink into the comfort and safety of being held so securely, the familiar scent of his skin, and the bone-deep certainty that beneath all the bullshit, this man sees me in a way no one ever has. Sees all my scars, all my baggage, and wants me just the way I am.

The elevator doors open with a loud *ding.* We barely manage to break apart and get out before they close again, the air charged with emotion.

"You wanted to change out of that," Wes starts gruffly. He reaches into his pocket and extracts a room key. "I should rinse off too. Come to my room when you're done. Ten-thirteen."

I almost tell him that I don't care, but what we're doing here, it's not something to be rushed. It's like Wes said to me months ago—some things are worth being serious about.

He might stop breathing when I wrap my fingers around his and press up onto my toes to brush a barely there kiss against his jaw. "I won't be long."

The weight of his stare follows me until the hallway curves out of sight. I quicken my pace, hurrying through stripping out of the dress and shoes. When I rush out of the room barely ten minutes later, I'm once again wearing Wes's hoodie.

With my lips still tingling from the warmth of his skin, something about pulling the soft cotton over my head clicks the last pieces into place. It's not just that I've forgiven Wes for the stunt he pulled with the photos—I've finally accepted that despite my fears, despite my knee-jerk instinct to lock him out the second he screwed up, I don't have to repeat my mom's mistakes.

My pulse is thunder in my ears when I knock. Déjà vu hits hard when Wes opens the door, black sweatpants low on his hips and water droplets clinging to his bare chest while he rubs his hair with a towel. "Hi, darlin'," he says with an almost shy smile as he starts to swing the door wider. "Come in—" His throat bobs with the force of his swallow, his eyes wide when they drop to my chest. "You kept it."

Three simple words, and yet there's so much hope packed into them that my knees nearly buckle. I should say something, tell him *of course* I kept it, cozying up to some version of him even in my hurt. But I don't have the capacity for words. Not when Wes is looking at me like I'm the answer to every wish he's ever had.

I launch myself at him, clinging to his shoulders and choking on a gasp when his arms come around me in an instant to crush me closer. His skin is hot from the shower, heartbeat steady if a little fast under my cheek. It's so damn good my eyes burn.

Neither one of us says a word. The door falls shut behind me, cocooning us in the quiet of the hotel room. It's a long time before I finally straighten. "Sorry," I mumble, scrubbing a hand over my face and probably smearing mascara everywhere. "I—"

"Don't." Wes cups my jaw and gives me one of his intense stares, his entire focus centered on me. "Don't ever apologize for needing to be held. I needed that too." He swallows, his eyes dropping to my mouth before he adds softly, "You ready for that talk?"

After putting this off for so long, the direct question should stir up my anxieties. Instead it reminds me of the last serious talk we had. *When you know, you know.*

"I'm ready," I whisper. I'm not just talking about the conversation, and I think by the way his eyes warm, Wes knows it too.

"I've made a lot of mistakes, Sloane. Especially with you." He settles his palm on my cheek and then continues, "There's something I should have told you a while ago. I need you to know that I wasn't full of shit. That when I said you were worth taking seriously, I meant that more than I've meant anything in my life. It's been killing me that I might have lost you. That I'd have no one to blame for that but myself."

Tipping my face up to his, I shake my head. "That's not entirely true," I say softly.

"I'm not perfect. I don't expect you to be either." Wes leans his forehead into mine. "We're a lot alike sometimes. I should have told you this earlier. I just didn't want to admit that, despite having learned a long time ago who my dad really is, he can still get to me. So I didn't tell you that the day Carter went over the rules, we were arguing when the call started. The same horseshit about photography not being a real career, but he didn't hang up on me like he usually does when he gets tired of yelling."

Wes lets out a bitter, pained laugh as he straightens. "He cut me off. I've avoided taking money from my parents for years, so that part isn't a big deal. He can't do anything about the trust my grandfather set up, but he said that if I ever wanted to set foot on his property again, I'd better be prepared to man up."

The need to make sure Wes knows that his father's narrow views are bullshit, that he's loved just how he is, almost has the words spilling out—*I love you I love you I love you*—but he isn't finished.

"Mom is planning her big sixtieth birthday party out at the ranch," he continues, his fingers toying idly with my hair. "He knows exactly how much it would kill her for me to miss it. I told him I would be there no matter what. He said he'd report me for trespassing. Reminded me how close he is to the sheriff out that way."

My heart aches at the realization that the entire time Wes was helping me work through my own problems with my mom, he was dealing with this. Alone. We really are awfully alike sometimes.

"I wish you'd told me it was that bad." I reach up to gently run my fingers through his damp hair. "I get you were trying to help with the photo. I love"—my voice wobbles—"I love that you want to take care of me, but strength isn't hiding your pain from me, Wes. I'm sorry that I didn't see what you were going through, and I'm sorry it took me so long to give you the chance to explain."

I press my palms to his chest, needing to feel the heat of him. Beneath my fingers, his heart is racing. "I've been so afraid that if I forgave you, I'd be no better than my mother. But I'm not her. And you're not your father."

The soft, tender expression on Wes's face mirrors the gentle sweep of his thumb over my bottom lip. "Sloane, I—"

He's cut off by the shrill sound of his phone. Pink stains his cheeks as he twists away to grab it off the dresser, quickly stabbing the screen. I drink in the familiar sight of his tattoos—

only to realize there's a new set of numbers running down his spine. I've spent enough time punching coordinates into photography planning apps to know that 37° north and 100° west mark a spot somewhere in Tornado Alley.

"Sorry, I wasn't sure how long you would be, so I set an alarm in case I fell—"

"You added one." I blink hard against the burning behind my eyes. "Where?"

Wes goes utterly still before slowly turning around. "I did." He rubs absently at a spot on his arm before adding, "I had it done when I was in Houston at the end of June."

I have a surprise for you when you get here.

I hate surprises.

I think you're going to like this one . . .

I gulp in air as the pieces begin to fit together. "Where?"

"I don't want to pressure you into—"

"Wes. Where."

"The place, the moment, I knew you were it for me." He takes a shuddering breath and summons up a tentative smile. "Where I let myself hope, for the first time, that I could be the same for you."

"Where?" I repeat, my voice cracking as emotion finally wins and a tear slips down my cheek. I move, not stopping until I'm close enough to tangle our fingers together and breathe in the familiar scent of his skin. "Tell me where."

Wes gently brushes the tear aside. "The side of the road in Kansas where you put me back together."

The enormity of it knocks the breath from my lungs. "But that was . . . We weren't . . ."

"The thing I can't stop thinking about," he says, the words choked, "the thing I keep coming back to, that I should have told you months ago, is that my dad trying to take the ranch from me? All it did was prove that *home* isn't there, or even my condo. It's not a place at all. Not for me."

Wes leans in to brush an achingly sweet kiss across my forehead. "You're my home, Sloane. I love you." His voice breaks, eyes shimmering in the low light when he pulls back, cupping my jaw in his palms. "I love you so much it's hard to breathe without you."

Tears slip down my cheeks. Wes is there to catch them, gently wiping away each salty drop. I let out a choked laugh, my heart brimming as I say the words we both need so desperately to hear. "I love you too."

His mouth crashes into mine before I even finish my sentence. It's more emotion than finesse, the kiss desperate, his hands tight on my back, crushing me close. I cling to his shoulders, just as frantic for the taste of him, the heat of his body against mine, the way we fit together. Our lips chase each other's, too needy to be parted. Some dim part of me is aware of my back colliding with the wall, the ragged sound I make when Wes presses his weight into me, solid and so very *real*.

I relearn his textures in greedy touches. The smooth silk of his skin where his shoulder meets his throat. The flex of muscle beneath my fingertips. The delicate softness of the hair at the back of his neck, and the delicious sound he makes when I tug on his bottom lip oh so gently with my teeth.

If I'm greedy, Wes is a man at worship. The initial frenzy between us settles into slow touches, his fingers a delicious drag down my ribs and along the outside of my thigh. I'm left gasping as he drops kisses on my cheeks, my eyelids, my jaw, anywhere he can reach.

His chest heaves against mine when he reaches for my hands and laces our fingers together. "I was so terrified I'd lost you for good."

"I've never felt this way about anyone else." I cup his jaw and brush my thumbs under exhausted eyes that shine with relief and love. I swallow back rising tears and brush my fingers through his hair. "I'm not sure exactly when I fell in love with you. It might have been in a field under a sky full of lightning, or it might have been when you bullied me into resting when I had that migraine." I swallow hard. "It scared me, how hard I fell for you. I'm sorry I let the fear win."

When Wes kisses me this time, murmuring my name into each press of his lips, it's softer, slower. "Just don't run from me again, darlin'. Tell me if you get scared. Get mad when you need to. But don't run. Please."

"I promise to try. I'm not perfect either, but, Wes? If I do run . . ." I smile up at him through my damp lashes. "Chase me."

EPILOGUE

A YEAR AFTER TRADING CHURCH BELLS—BUT NOT chasing lightning—for the whisper of the wind through evergreens and wedding marches for birdsong, I have no regrets. I'm not certain I can say the same for my friends.

"You know what, I take it back. There is absolutely nothing wrong with a big wedding in a nice, comfortable, air-conditioned venue," Tracy huffs.

At my side, Wes laughs, his headlamp bobbing in the pale blue light of the hour just before dawn. He's barely winded.

"We're almost there," he says with the same good-natured cheer that made me want to turn him into bear breakfast the first ten times we did this hike.

"You said that a mile ago," Matt protests.

"Hey, you're not the one carrying this damn dress," Tracy grumbles from behind me. "Jesus, Sloane, is this thing made of bricks?"

"Silk chiffon." I glance back, wincing when I blind both her and Matt with my psychotically bright headlamp. It was a gift from Wes to celebrate the first time I did this hike with a client, so it seemed fitting to wear today. Even if I have blinded our friends half a dozen times. "A good twenty yards of it."

There's a rustle of plastic as Tracy adjusts the bag. "You're paying for however many massages it takes to un-fuck my body from this ordeal."

"What do *we* get?" Eric complains. I don't have to glance behind me to see the look he's exchanging with Sam. "I don't drag myself out of bed at one in the morning to hike a goddamn mountain in the dark for nothing."

"You do for your sister," I remind him, letting Tracy and Matt pass so that I can join my brothers. "And you get the satisfaction of knowing you were there when she got married."

"If I don't die of oxygen deprivation before we make it to the top." Sam shoves me up the trail. "Keep going. If we miss sunrise and you try to make me do this again, I make no promises you'll survive the hike down."

Tracy and Matt's laughter floats back down the trail. I'm glad they're still having something of a good time. While we could have hired photographers who specialize in weddings, in the end, Wes and I decided that we wanted to be surrounded by the people who care about us the most.

The *thwack thwack thwack* of helicopter blades in the distance fills the air before long. I don't want to know what it cost, but since Wes rarely throws around his money, I didn't argue when he chartered a flight for his mom—and mine—to be flown to the top of the mountain.

Everyone else, my whining brothers included, was given the option of hiking or flying. It's their own fault they're not on the chopper, though in hindsight, I probably should have sent the dress up that way. I was too paranoid to let it out of my sight.

My relationship with my mom is still rocky, but things are getting better. It helps that Wes relocated to Colorado and we live together now. My brothers and I still help her when she really needs it, but we're not at her constant beck and call. Mostly, though, I think it's the therapist she's been going to. We'll get there one day.

I'm not sure the same can be said of Wes's father. They're still not speaking. In the end, it was his father who got banished from the ranch, not us. The fact that his mom filed for divorce when she found out about his dad's threats didn't help matters, but she seems a lot happier, and that makes Wes happy.

We crest the summit just as the eastern sky takes on a warmer glow. It's cool up here, which is going to make changing into my dress unpleasant, but at least the breeze dries the sweat off my skin quickly. A pack of wet wipes does the rest. By sheer coincidence, they're the same brand I had in my car the day Wes fell in the mud.

Or maybe not, if the smirk he throws my way is any indication.

With Tracy wrestling a sheet into a privacy screen, I strip out of my hiking clothes and carefully get into the dress. It's the one extravagance I allowed myself, a bespoke creation from one of Tracy's LA designer friends modeled after the pink dress I wore in my *Nature Shots* cover. This version is the palest blush and more elaborate, with a long train and tiny crystals sewn into the bust that start thick along the sweetheart neckline before trailing down the skirt like scattered stars.

Then, almost as carefully as I handled the silk chiffon, I

remove my watch and peel away the gauze hidden beneath the band. I told Wes a tiny white lie that I burned myself baking cookies, but I think he'll forgive me when he sees the delicate numbers and letters inked into my wrist. We've hiked this summit enough times now that he'll recognize the coordinates as soon as I rotate my wrist after he slides the ring on in a few minutes.

I'm just pulling my hair out of the heatless curlers I put in at the start of the hike when the helicopter touches down on the far side of the summit. Tracy stretches her arms wide, holding the sheet in front of me and protecting the dress from the dust the blades kick up until they slow and eventually stop. My mom's voice carries in the sudden silence as she declares Wes to be her favorite son-in-law.

"He's the only one you're getting!" I yell from behind my sheet, sharing a laugh with Tracy right before she shouts for Wes to look away.

Maybe it's silly after we just spent the last couple of hours hiking a mountain together, but we decided that once we were in our wedding clothes we'd try not to see each other until the moment Tracy and Matt were ready. I almost tell her not to worry about it when she hands the sheet over to Eric and picks up her camera, but the look on Wes's face when he sees me a few minutes later? That deserves to live on in pixels and print for the rest of our lives.

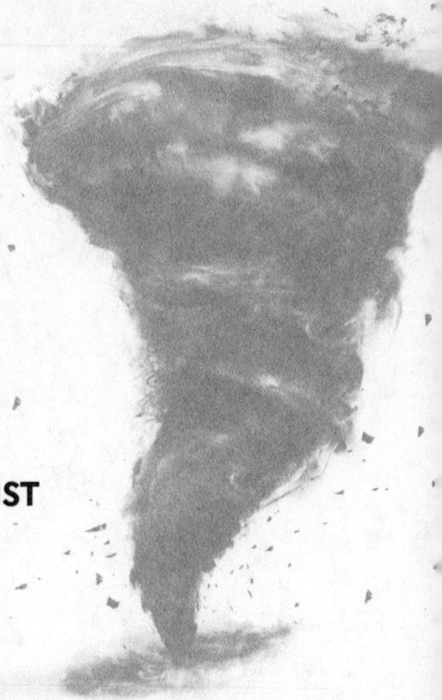

SLOANE MICHAELS AND THE HORRIBLE, AWFUL, NO-GOOD PLAYLIST

". . . Ready for It?"—Taylor Swift
"Hurricane"—Luke Combs
"Set Fire to the Rain"—Adele
"My Church"—Maren Morris
"Have You Ever Seen the Rain?"—Creedence Clearwater Revival
"Raining on Sunday"—Keith Urban
"Hurricane Drunk"—Florence + the Machine
"After the Storm"—Mumford & Sons

SHHH, WE'RE HUNTING TORNADOES

"Thunderstruck"—AC/DC
"The Thunder Rolls"—Garth Brooks
"Ride the Lightning"—Metallica
"Hurricane"—Panic! At the Disco
"Thunder"—Imagine Dragons
"Calm Before the Storm"—Fall Out Boy
"Ain't No Love in Oklahoma"—Luke Combs
"Tornado"—Little Big Town

ACKNOWLEDGMENTS

Writing is a deeply personal thing. Maybe that's why the stereotype of a writer is so often one of solitude, but I think most writers will tell you that it's a team sport. And I am so lucky to have an amazing team surrounding me. I'm going to attempt to thank everyone (and preemptively ask the forgiveness of anyone I miss).

Christina Miller, I couldn't ask for a better advocate, and I'm so very happy we took a chance on each other. Thank you for always being just a text away, for your patience, and for your willingness to always go along with my chaos with a smile. May there be many more pink blazer days in our future!

Mary Baker, you saw the heart of these characters and this story so clearly. Thank you for your invaluable suggestions, eye for detail, and expert GIF usage. I'd also like to thank the rest of the PRH team—Anika Bates, Kristin Cipolla, Katie Ferraro, Christine Legon, Megan Elmore, Katie Anderson, and Ashley Tucker. Finally, an enormous thank-you to Julia JM for illustrating such a gorgeous cover!

Hannah and Celia, thank you for all the late-night conversations, brainstorming sessions, and the very enthusiastic ABSOLUTELY YES when I first floated the idea of a storm-chasing romance.

To my friends and family outside of publishing, especially those of you who've listened to me ramble on about writing for decades, I remain incredibly grateful for your support. Dan, my brother, my accomplice, and my very favorite road-trip copilot, I'd say I'm sorry about the pieces of you in this book, but we both know that's a lie (love you). The Friends Without Benefits, for celebrating all of my wins as if they're your own and being so excited for this book (we're still never discussing the spicy scenes). My parents, for the endless reams of paper and legal pads I wrote my very earliest "books" on that are undoubtedly stashed away in some (hopefully deep) corner of a closet even to this day. Rachel, for nerding out and loving me and my writing so fiercely (but also finish the thing). Elissa, for teaching me the strength that exists in softness (and always being willing to look at my "underpainting" draft). Cassandra, for pushing me to reach higher (and lying to me about that first manuscript—we can both admit now it was bad!).

To the Berkletes and other authors I've met over the course of this wild ride, thank you for being the very best "coworkers" and welcoming me with such open arms. There are far too many authors to name individually, but an extra special thank-you goes out to Allie, Amanda, Emily, Megan, Molly, and Rachel for being such excellent cheerleaders, "how does this work, actually" consultants, and sounding boards. I am in awe of all of you, and sometimes I really can't believe I get to hang with such talented, funny, encouraging, and lovely humans.

Mike, thank you for everything you've taught me about storm chasing, photography, the best gas station snacks, and how to remain chill when making questionable safety choices.

I remain forever grateful for all the work Jen Walton and Girls Who Chase are doing for women in storm chasing and meteorology. Thank you for being constant advocates and educators. I firmly believe the community you've built is a big part of why more and more women are allowing themselves to chase storms *and* their dreams.

And finally, to you, reader, for taking a chance on a debut author.

Keep reading for a preview of

BLOW ME AWAY

the next romance from Heather Frances!

TYLER

I USED TO LIKE RUNNING. THEN A REDHEADED DEmon named Lana came into my life.

"Don't you dare." I'm proud of myself that it's more words than gasps, but there's only so much I can do after nearly forty minutes on a treadmill with sweat dripping off every inch of me. Seriously. There's a dark streak on the treadmill belt from it.

Lana smirks and presses a button to increase the incline of the running belt. Twice. "Anyone can do anything for a minute," she chirps with her special brand of malice and positivity.

"Your minute was up—*shit*." She presses the damn button again. I grit my teeth and force my legs to move, muscles burning, and think of the sweet, sweet relief of throwing myself in the pool when I'm done with today's workout.

I should get ten whole minutes to myself before I have to get ready for my first meeting. But only if I can satisfy my trainer and get her out of my house on time.

It's not the life I expected when I was cast as a meteorologist on the latest prestige drama to come out of the streamer-of-the-moment—my job consists of about 70 percent taking off my clothes (the reason the studio hired Lana to torture me) and 30 percent talking about the (fake) weather. It's not the most mentally stimulating, but given what they pay me for five months of filming, I'm not about to complain. At least not outside the privacy of my own head.

"I hate you," I tell Lana between gasps when she finally puts an end to today's torture session. It only took another ten minutes on the treadmill and fifteen minutes of the kind of core exercises that will make even breathing hurt tomorrow.

Lana only laughs and tosses a towel at me. "Tyler, if I had a brick for every client who says that, I'd be building myself a mansion twice the size of this place."

"That's not saying much." I mop sweat off my face and jerk my head toward the rest of the house. It's up in the Hollywood Hills, which is admittedly sweet real estate. It also means that the house is crammed into a narrow warren of a neighborhood and comes with an eye-watering price per square foot for what would be a normal house just about anywhere else in the country.

Can't beat the view, though.

"Yeah, yeah. For a bunch of tough guys, y'all whine a lot." Lana laughs at my predictable scowl and bends to grab a water bottle from the mini fridge tucked into a corner of the tiny gym. "Serena never complains like you boys."

I let out a snort of laughter but gladly take the water. "Serena has turned complaining into an art, so I'm calling bullshit on that one."

Then again, if the rumors are to be believed, Lana and my costar aren't keeping things *entirely* professional.

"Yeah, maybe," Lana says. The hint of pink rising into her cheeks is rather suspect given I keep the temperature in here as low as the air-conditioning will go. "I left one of those protein shakes you like in your fridge. Make sure you get at least—"

"Lana." I shake my head, then cover my annoyance with an easy grin. "We've been at this for two years. I know the routine."

She holds up her palms with an apologetic smile. "Okay, okay. Just doing my job." Her eyes sweep over me clinically, an artist evaluating her work. "Tomorrow is biceps and back. Drink plenty of water!" she calls back over her shoulder as she heads for the door.

I let out a loud groan as soon as it shuts and force my heavy legs to move. A couple of slow, easy laps in the cold pool will help to stretch the muscles. I just need to drag myself to it.

Scrolling notifications as I move through the house, I flip by most of them. Reminders about meetings, three different questions from my publicist, a handful of texts from the assistant I begrudgingly hired last year, and a link to a social media post from one of my friends with the text **Isn't this that weather girl you pissed off?**

Pretty sure that's just her natural state, I text back before clicking the link. I'd prefer to forget the whole interaction with Haley Morgan, but Gabe finds the situation hilarious in the way only someone who's known you your entire life can. Despite the whole thing going down two years ago when my casting in *On Air* was first announced, he's determined not to let me forget about my awkward run-in with the woman and periodically sends me posts about her. Last time it was a compilation of various poses from a promo shoot with her wearing a hot pink skirt and looking like a smoke show. The time before that was a video of her very patiently explaining an atmosphere (atmospheric?) river, not that I remember much beyond it making sense at the time.

I told Gabe he was welcome to try shooting his shot and see if he fared any better.

The post he sent today is several slides long. Rumors swirl over abrupt departure of *Good Morning LA* meteorologist reads the first slide, a screenshot of an article from a local news site. The next is a video that starts playing automatically. Haley's face fills the square, her expression tight and far more like the woman who berated me than the usual perky show she puts on every morning. By the time I get my volume turned up, all I catch is "I quit."

"Whoa," I mutter under my breath before restarting the video. Quitting on a live show is ballsy, but when I play the whole thing back, the cold fury in her voice can't be missed. I want to roll my eyes at her declaration that she's no one's weather girl—she took major offense to being called a weather girl when we met too—but there's that emphasis on *no one's* that stops me. Haley Morgan is an ice queen, sure, but she's never struck me as stupid. I talked to her for less than five minutes. It was clear from that limited interaction that she's likely one of the smartest women in this town.

Quitting your job live on the air, while under contract, isn't something anyone does over nothing. Especially not in an industry where everyone knows everyone and pissing off the wrong network can mean never working again.

Wild, I text back to Gabe. Wonder what set her off.

I'm fishing. Gabe and I grew up together in San Diego. When his career took off, he gave me a job running his social media accounts. Not the usual path to acting, but thanks to good ol'-fashioned Hollywood nepotism, his agent convinced a colleague to take me on. All these years later, both of our careers are thriving—but Gabe remains more plugged into whisper networks than I'll ever be. Probably because he actually likes the networking and socializing that comes with making a living as an artist.

I wait another minute, sipping deliciously cold water in the shade of the house, but Gabe doesn't reply. Considering he's supposed to be getting ready for his show in London tonight, that's probably for the best. I'll get whatever I can out of him later.

Stripping off my shirt, I toss it onto a lounge chair and drop my phone on top of it. I only make it two steps closer to the pool before the screen lights up again with a call. I frown at the name, not sure why my assistant is calling when none of her texts were urgent, but these are the only ten minutes I have to myself today. Shrugging off Emma's call, I dive into the pool.

I ALLOW MYSELF to linger in the pool for an extra five minutes and then race through a shower. Somehow in the combined twenty minutes, my phone notifications accumulate faster than the paparazzi answering a tip call—and those assholes are *fast*.

I don't have time to call Emma back before my first appointment, a strategy session with my manager. That runs long, which means I don't get to her until after the podcast interview taping.

"Finally," she says with all the talent of a woman capable of turning a single word into a lecture. In the hierarchy of Hollywood, I vastly outrank my own damn assistant, but Emma is the studio head's granddaughter, and therefore untouchable. "I've been trying to get ahold of you for *hours*."

"I've been on calls. What's up?"

If she's offended by my brusqueness, she at least manages to hide that. "I found a replacement for Dr. Hunt. You'll need to go meet her tonight to sign off on it, but she—"

"What replacement?" I stop halfway between my home office and kitchen and resist the urge to add *what the fuck*. Dr. Hunt is the scientist I handpicked to teach me about storm chasing for my character's arc next season. I had to fight like hell with the studio to get it approved, between the month out of LA and the insurance liability—the fact that Dr. Hunt is considered one of the foremost experts on tornadoes and the storms that make them happen was a big part of how I got it all green-lit. In fact, it was heavily implied that the *only* reason it got green-lit was due to Dr. Hunt's involvement.

I've been looking forward to this for months for more reasons than I'm ever going to get into with Emma. My stomach roils at the thought of the whole thing getting called off, but more than that, I'm irritated to only be finding out now that Dr. Hunt is being replaced.

It's not the first time I've been the last to know about something that directly impacts me.

"Oh, no one filled you in? Her kid broke her leg. But one of her previous students is available. I already cleared it with everyone," Emma says smoothly, a good reminder for my less-than-charitable thoughts. She's a nepo baby through and through, but she's also great at what she does. "Anyway, she said if she could have picked anyone, this is who she'd send in her place."

"High praise." I run a hand through my hair before yanking open the fridge to grab the protein shake Lana left. "Who is it?"

"I want you to keep an open mind," Emma says, which isn't an answer. "She'll be at Cuppa at eight tonight. We need a decision fast if we need to keep looking."

"If you tell me who—"

"Cuppa. Eight. Gotta go," Emma trills into the phone before unceremoniously hanging up.

Scowling at my now-dark phone screen, I don't bother trying to call her back. I don't have nearly the power you'd think I would despite being number two on the call sheet for a megahit show—even over my own assistant. If Emma wants me to walk into this meeting cold, that's what's going to happen.

So despite not particularly wanting to drag myself out of the house after a long day, I make the short drive down to the coffee shop I've frequented since moving into the Hills. It's far enough out of the way of the usual tourist spots that anyone who recognizes me is likely someone else in the industry. The locals and the staff are used to me by now.

Given my friendship with paparazzi-bait Gabe, it's little surprise that people like to run their mouths about my big party lifestyle. The truth is that I barely manage to stifle a yawn as I step into the cafe just before eight. The sun hasn't even been down a full hour, twilight lingering in shades of blue above, but I could easily crash now.

After ordering myself an iced tea and a couple of cookies as a consolation prize for a long-ass day, I slip into a booth tucked into the back and check my phone. There's another text from Emma wanting to know if I've made it here.

Yes, I type back. Now will you tell me who I'm meeting?

Blonde, early 30s. You can't miss her.

I scowl at the screen. I can begrudgingly admit that despite being cornered into hiring Emma, she's usually pretty helpful. And yet tonight, for reasons of her own, she's decided to screw with me.

I'd bail on the whole thing if it wasn't for the fact that without a meteorologist, the trip doesn't happen. The insurance company won't let me try to chase a tornado on my own, and even if they did, I don't know what I'm doing. People gossip about Gabe and I barely having two brain cells between us, but contrary to public opinion, I *do* know the difference between satisfying my curiosity and getting myself killed.

Emma, on the other hand, might have lost her mind. She's right—I can't miss the blonde woman who walks through the door a few minutes later, her brows slanting down and her mouth pressed into a thin line. She's dressed more casually than I've ever seen her, dark jeans that show off her ass and a loose sweater that dips in the front. She's shorter than I remember, but she's also in sandals instead of the deadly heels she had on the last time I saw her.

My thumbs fly over my phone. You can't be serious.

She's got the qualifications, Emma replies instantly. If you really can't work with her, we can try to find someone else.

Try. I shove my phone in my pocket and get to my feet. With barely two weeks until this whole thing is supposed to happen, I don't need Emma to spell it out for me. I'm lucky she found *one* potential replacement. There might not be another.

"Haley Morgan, my very favorite weather girl." I pitch my voice low to keep it from carrying over the whir of espresso machines and milk steamers. It's a gamble to use that phrase when she's already told me she hates it, but I figure it will get her attention.

It might work a little too well. Haley whips around, eyes narrowed and spitting fire. It's a look I remember.

Despite my better judgment, I haven't entirely forgotten how that first meeting started. The way that time seemed to slow for just a moment when she crashed into me and tipped her face up to mine. I blinked. She blinked. I tried to form words, half wondering if I'd gotten something in one of my contacts—and then she opened her mouth.

Turns out the weird sensation in my gut was nothing more than the consequences of some questionable leftovers the night before.

This time, I blame my stomach flip on dread. I'm about to try to charm a woman determined not to be charmed. A woman who definitely isn't happy to see me by the way her features contort into an almighty scowl. The feeling is somewhat mutual—Haley Morgan isn't the person I'd pick to spend a month in close quarters with—but we're both here for a reason. I know mine—and I have to think hers has something to do with quitting her job on the spot this morning.

"What are *you* doing here?" Haley's eyes dip down to my chest and then dart back up. "I see you've finally found a shirt at least."

I can't help a grin. She's prickly and cold as a glacier, but that day when she ran into me—quite literally—her hands were soft and warm on my bare skin. It wasn't my idea to take my shirt off as part of the morning show interview, but two years ago I was dumb enough to go along with it.

Haley looked then, and she's looking now. At least all those hours on that damn treadmill are doing something.

"What's wrong, princess?" I ask with innocently wide eyes. Maybe matching her energy isn't my best tactic, but I'm not in the mood to let her dictate this conversation. "Past your bedtime?"

"My name is *Haley*. Not *weather girl*. Not *princess*. Haley."

I open my mouth to fire back, but then it registers. She sounds exhausted. Of course she does. Whatever pushed her into quitting her job, it happened *this morning*. And I know enough about morning news programs to know that it probably *is* past her bedtime.

"Sorry." I scrub my palm over my face and try again. This time I remind myself that I might need her to say yes far more than she needs me to want her on this trip. "I grabbed a table in the back where we can talk."

Haley gives me a weird look. "And why would I do that?"

Emma didn't tell her either. Great. I lean closer to make sure I'm not overheard. "To talk about the . . . training. In Oklahoma."

Haley's face contorts into some interesting expressions. The sort of expressions that usually come just before telling a guy to fuck right off, but all she says is, "Is that what you're calling it?"

I glance pointedly around the cafe. "You signed an NDA before you came here, yeah?"

Her mouth pinches with irritation. "Fine. After you."

Neither of us speaks until we're settled in the corner. I slide one of the cookies I grabbed earlier across the table on a napkin as a peace offering. Lana will flip out if it gets back to her that I ate two cookies only days before a magazine cover shoot. But beyond the demands of my tyrannical trainer, I haven't forgotten Emma's implied warning. Sugar is as good a peace offering as any.

I need this. I've been looking forward to it for too long. A chance to learn something, a chance to actually *think* and not just stand around with my shirt off. And if I play my cards right, maybe a chance for a lot more than that.

"What's this?" Haley pokes the cookie like I've offered up a poisoned apple.

"Well, when some flour, sugar, and butter love each other very much—"

"I know how cookies are made." She snaps off a piece and pops it into her mouth, chewing slowly. "Cookie for dinner seems appropriate for the day, though, so."

I don't respond right away. It's a trick I've learned over the years, letting other people fill the silence with their preconceived notions of who I am and laughing it off. I brace for more of the same insults Haley hurled at me two years ago, more insinuations that there's nothing but protein powder and dumbbells between my ears.

She breaks off another piece of the cookie and watches me while she chews before she eventually asks in a surprisingly even voice, "Why am I here, Tyler?"

"To talk about Okl—"

"You really want to spend a month in a car with me? They're long days." She fidgets with one corner of the napkin and then quickly folds her hands in her lap. "Eight to ten hours is normal, but twelve to sixteen isn't that unusual."

"Right." I draw out the *i* and eye her over the rim of my cup before taking a sip and setting it down. "You know those are pretty standard set hours, right? I'll be just fine sitting in an air-conditioned car. Practically a vacation. Maybe I should be asking *you* if you can handle the long days?"

Haley's mouth tightens into a thin line, but she can't argue with my logic. She shifts in her seat, the motion pushing her sweater entirely off one shoulder. She doesn't seem to notice, and I definitely *shouldn't* notice the smoothness of her skin. "I'm just saying, if the reason I'm here is for you to see if we'll get along, we figured that out two years ago."

A decade of media training is the only thing that stops me from scoffing. "Seriously? It was *two years* ago. Also, that was a big misunderstanding."

Her eyes narrow to dangerous slits. "So you weren't parading around the studio with your shirt off?"

"That wasn't my—"

"And you didn't ignore me saying how much I hate being called a weather girl and continue to—"

"Oh, c'mon, I was joking around—"

"And you didn't top all of that by accusing me of sexually harassing you for tripping over *your*—"

"Okay," I cut in as my patience rapidly evaporates. "I absolutely did not do that. What I said was—"

"This! This is exactly what I mean!" Haley gestures between us with a rapid back and forth of her hand. "This conversation isn't any different than the one we had two years ago. You really want to spend an entire month doing this?"

Not even remotely, but no matter how prickly she's being, I don't think Haley's shitty attitude is who she really is. Maybe I would if I hadn't already trolled through her social media videos, but this is the same woman who takes the time to break down complex science for the masses in her free time on her personal page. A woman who is obviously brilliant, and yet just quit her job on live TV this morning.

And then there's the *no one's weather girl* part. It didn't occur to me until this moment with her sitting across from me in the casual sort of outfit her on-camera persona would *never* wear, but maybe we have more in common than I originally thought.

I can't help suddenly wondering if Haley knows something about being valued more for her looks than the thoughts that exist behind her pretty eyes too.

"Of course not. I just figured once you stopped taking out your bad day on me, you'd turn out to be reasonable," I tell her, hoping my hunch proves true. "Look, I'm serious about learning as much as I can about storm— the topic. If you're serious about teaching me, and you have the background to keep me in one piece, I'm good. When Emma talked to Dr. Hunt, she said you'd be her first pick as a replacement. So, we're back to, is this going to be a problem or not?"

Something I've said throws her. The carefully neutral expression she's been clinging to since we sat down flickers, her features softening in something that might be gratitude. But then she clears her throat and steely resolve takes over. "It won't be a problem."

"Great," I agree instantly. "Emma will add you to the flight—"

"That's it?" Haley's eyes pop wide. "You're not going to ask anything else before you put your life in my hands? Really?"

I fight the urge to roll my eyes. We're getting along—sort of. Maintaining the peace needs to be the priority right now. "If one of the leading researchers in the field says you're good, you're good."

A faint hint of pink washes into her cheeks, but Haley is all business. "I guess we're done here, then." Popping the last of the cookie in her mouth, she grabs her drink and gets to her feet, finally adjusting the distracting sweater sleeve. "Have Emma send me the flight details. Pack light."

Photo by Daniel André Champagne

Heather Frances is a writer, photographer, lifelong weather nerd, and occasional storm chaser cleverly disguised as an adult with a day job in finance (though she really prefers writing kissing books). When not at home in New England drinking far too much coffee, you'll find her somewhere with questionable cell phone service, camera in hand.

VISIT HEATHER FRANCES ONLINE

HeatherFrances.com

HeatherFrancesAuthor